THE EXTRA DAY

ALGERNON BLACKWOOD

1st WORLD
LIBRARY
Literary Society

The Extra Day

Algernon Blackwood

© 1st World Library, 2006
PO Box 2211
Fairfield, IA 52556
www.1stworldlibrary.com
First Edition

LCCN: 2006936161

Softcover ISBN: 978-1-4218-3018-6
Hardcover ISBN: 978-1-4218-2918-0
eBook ISBN: 978-1-4218-3118-3

Purchase *"The Extra Day"*
as a traditional bound book at:
www.1stWorldLibrary.com/purchase.asp?ISBN=978-1-4218-3018-6

1st World Library is a literary, educational organization
dedicated to:

- Creating a free internet library of downloadable ebooks

- Hosting writing competitions and offering book
  publishing scholarships.

1ˢᵗ World Library Literary Society

Giving Back to the World

"If you want to work on the core problem, it's early school literacy."

- James Barksdale, former CEO of Netscape

"No skill is more crucial to the future of a child, or to a democratic and prosperous society, than literacy."

- Los Angeles Times

Literacy... means far more than learning how to read and write... The aim is to transmit... knowledge and promote social participation."

- UNESCO

"Literacy is not a luxury, it is a right and a responsibility. If our world is to meet the challenges of the twenty-first century we must harness the energy and creativity of all our citizens."

- President Bill Clinton

"Parents should be encouraged to read to their children, and teachers should be equipped with all available techniques for teaching literacy, so the varying needs and capacities of individual kids can be taken into account."

- Hugh Mackay

CONTENTS

CHAPTER I

THE MATERIAL

Judy, Tim, and Maria were just little children. It was impossible to say exactly what their ages were, except that they were just the usual age, that Judy was the eldest, Maria the youngest, and that Tim, accordingly, came in between the two.

Their father did his best for them; so did their mother; so did Aunt Emily, the latter's sister. It is impossible to say very much about these three either, except that they were just Father, Mother, and Aunt Emily. They were the Authorities-in-Chief, and they knew respectively everything there was to be known about such remote and difficult subjects as London and Money; Food, Health and Clothing; Conduct, Behaviour and Regulations, both general and particular. Into these three departments of activity the children, without realising that they did so, classed them neatly. Aunt Emily, besides the special duties assigned to her, was a living embodiment of No. While Father allowed and permitted, while Mother wobbled and hesitated, Aunt Emily shook her head with decision, and said distinctly No. She was too full of warnings, advice, and admonitions to get about much. She wore gold glasses, and had an elastic, pointed nose. From the children's point of view she must be classed as invalid. Somewhere, deep down inside them, they felt pity.

The trio loved them according to their just deserts; they

grasped that the Authorities did their best for them. This "best," moreover, was done in different ways. Father did it with love and tenderness, that is, he spoilt them; Mother with tenderness and love, that is, she felt them part of herself and did not like to hurt herself; Aunt Emily with affectionate and worthy desire to see them improve, that is, she trained them. Therefore they adored their father, loved their mother, and thought highly—from a distance preferably—of their aunt.

This was the outward and visible household that an ordinary person, say, a visitor who came to lunch on Sunday after church, would have noticed. It was the upper layer; but there was an under layer too. There was Thompson, the old pompous family butler; they trusted him because he was silent and rarely smiled, winked at their mischief, pretended not to see them when he caught them in his pantry, and never once betrayed them. There was Mrs. Horton, the fat and hot-tempered family cook; they regarded her with excitement including dread, because she left juicy cakes (still wet) upon the dresser, yet denied them the entry into her kitchen. Her first name being Bridget, there was evidently an Irish strain in her, but there was probably a dash of French as well, for she was an excellent cook and *recipe* was her master-word—she pronounced it "recipee." There was Jackman, the nurse, a mixture of Mother and Aunt Emily; and there was Weeden, the Head Gardener, an evasive and mysterious personality, who knew so much about flowers and vegetables and weather that he was half animal, half bird, and scarcely a human being at all—vaguely magnificent in a sombre way. His power in his own department was unquestioned. He said little, but it "meant an awful lot"—most of which, perhaps, was not intended.

These four constituted the under layer of the household, concealed from visitors, and living their own lives apart behind the scenes. They were the Lesser Authorities.

There were others too, of course, neighbours, friends, and visitors, who dwelt outside the big iron gates in the Open

World, and who entered their lives from various angles, some to linger, some merely to show themselves and vanish into mist again. Occasionally they reappeared at intervals, occasionally they didn't. Among the former were Colonel William Stumper, C.B., a retired Indian soldier who lived in the Manor House beyond the church and had written a book on Scouting; a nameless Station-Master, whom they saw rarely when they accompanied Daddy to the London train; a Policeman, who walked endlessly up and down the muddy or dusty lanes, and came to the front door with a dirty little book in his big hands at Christmas-time; and a Tramp, who slept in barns and haystacks, and haunted the great London Road ever since they had once handed him a piece of Mrs. Horton's sticky cake in paper over the old grey fence. Him they regarded with a special awe and admiration, not unmixed with tenderness. He had smiled so nicely when he said "Thank you" that Judy, wondering if there was any one to mend his clothes, had always longed to know him better. It seemed so wonderful. How could he live without furniture, house, regular meals—without possessions, in a word? It made him so real. It was "real life," in fact, to live that way; and upon Judy especially the impression was a deep one.

In addition to these occasional intruders, there was another person, an Authority, but the most wonderful Authority of all, who came into their lives a little later with a gradual and overwhelming effect, but who cannot be mentioned more definitely just now because he has not yet arrived. The world, in any case, speaking generally, was enormous; it was endless; it was always dropping things and people upon them without warning, as from a clear and cloudless sky. But this particular individual was still climbing the great curve below their horizon, and had not yet poked his amazing head above the edge.

Yet, strange to say, they had always believed that some such person would arrive. A wonderful stranger was already on the way. They rarely spoke of it—it was just a great, passionate expectancy tucked away in the deepest corner of their hearts.

Children possess this sense of anticipation all the world over; grown-ups have it too in the form of an unquenchable, though fading hope: the feeling that some day or other a Wonderful Stranger will come up the pathway, knock at the door, and enter their lives, making life worth living, full of wonder, beauty, and delight, because he will make all things new.

This wonderful stranger, Judy had a vague idea, would be—be like at least—the Tramp; Tim, following another instinct, was of the opinion he would be a "soldier-explorer-hunter kind of man"; Maria, if she thought anything at all about him, kept her decision securely hidden in her tight, round body. But Judy qualified her choice by the hopeful assertion that he would "come from the air"; and Tim had a secret notion that he would emerge from a big, deep hole—pop out like a badger or a rabbit, as it were—and suddenly declare himself; while Maria, by her non-committal, universal attitude, perhaps believed that, if he came at all, he would "just come from everywhere at once." She believed everything, always, everywhere. But to assert that belief was to betray the existence of a doubt concerning it. She just lived it.

For the three children belonged to three distinct classes, without knowing that they did so. Tim loved anything to do with the ground, with earth and soil, that is, things that made holes and lived in them, or that did not actually make holes but just grubbed about; mysterious, secret things, such as rabbits, badgers, hedgehogs, mice, rats, hares, and weasels. In all his games the "earth" was home.

Judy, on the other hand, was indubitably an air person—birds amazed her, filling her hungry heart with high aspirations, longings, and desires. She looked, with her bright, eager face and spidery legs, distinctly bird-like. She flitted, darted, perched. She had what Tim called a "tweaky" nose, though whether he meant that it was beak-like or merely twitched, he never stated; it was just "tweaky," and Judy took it as a compliment. One could easily imagine her shining little face peeping over the edge of a nest, the rest of her sitting warmly

Algernon Blackwood

upon half a dozen smooth, pink eggs. Her legs certainly seemed stuck into her like pencils, as with a robin or a seagull. She adored everything that had wings and flew; she was of the air; it was her element.

Maria's passions were unknown. Though suspected of being universal, since she manifested no deliberate likes or dislikes, approving all things with a kind of majestic and indifferent omnipotence, they remained quiescent and undeclared. She probably just loved the universe. She felt at home in it. To Maria the entire universe belonged, because she sat still and with absolute conviction—claimed it.

CHAPTER II

FANCY—SEED OF WONDER

The country house, so ancient that it seemed part of the landscape, settled down secretively into the wintry darkness and watched the night with eyes of yellow flame. The thick December gloom hid it securely from attack. Nothing could find it out. Though crumbling in places, the mass of it was solid as a fortress, for the old oak beams had resisted Time so long that the tired years had resigned themselves to siege instead of assault, and the protective hills and woods rendered it impregnable against the centuries. The beleaguered inhabitants felt safe. It was a delightful, cosy feeling, yet excitement and surprise were in it too. Anything *might* happen, and at any moment.

This, at any rate, was how Judy and Tim felt the personality of the old Mill House, calling it Daddy's Castle. Maria expressed no opinion. She felt and knew too much to say a word. She was habitually non-committal. She shared the being of the ancient building, as the building shared the landscape out of which it grew so naturally. Having been born last, her inheritance of coming Time exceeded that of Tim and Judy, and she lived as though thoroughly aware of her prerogative. In quiet silence she claimed everything as her very own.

The Mill House, like Maria, never moved; it existed comfortably; it seemed independent of busy, hurrying Time. So thickly covered was it with ivy and various creepers that the

Algernon Blackwood

trees on the lawn wondered why it did not grow bigger like themselves. They remembered the time when they looked up to it, whereas now they looked over it easily, and even their lower branches stroked the stone tiles on the roof, patched with moss and lichen like their own great trunks. They had come to regard it as an elderly animal asleep, for its chimneys looked like horns, it possessed a capacious mouth that both swallowed and disgorged, and its eyes were as numerous as those of the forest to which they themselves properly belonged. And so they accepted the old Mill House as a thing of drowsy but persistent life; they protected and caressed it; they liked it exactly where it was; and if it moved they would have known an undeniable shock.

They watched it now, this dark December evening, as one by one its gleaming eyes shone bright and yellow through the mist, then one by one let down their dark green lids. "It's going to sleep," they thought. "It's going to dream. Its life, like ours, is all inside. It sleeps the winter through as we do. All is well. Good-night, old house of grey! We'll also go to sleep."

Unable to see into the brain of the sleepy monster, the trees resigned themselves to dream again, tucking the earth closely against their roots and withdrawing into the cloak of misty darkness. Like most other things in winter they also stayed indoors, leading an interior life of dim magnificence behind their warm, thick bark. Presently, when they were ready, something would happen, something they were preparing at their leisure, something so exquisite that all who saw it would dance and sing for gladness. They also believed in a Wonderful Stranger who was coming into their slow, steady lives. They fell to dreaming of the surprising pageant they would blazon forth upon the world a little later. And while they dreamed, the wind of night passed moaning through their leafless branches, and Time flew noiselessly above the turning Earth.

Meanwhile, inside the old Mill House, the servants lit the lamps and drew the blinds and curtains. Behind the closing eyelids, however, like dream-chambers within a busy skull, there were rooms of various shapes and kinds, and in one of these on the ground-floor, called Daddy's Study, the three children stood, expectant and a little shy, waiting for something desirable to happen. In common with all other living things, they shared this enticing feeling—that Something Wonderful was going to happen. To be without this feeling, of course, is to be not alive; but, once alive, it cannot be escaped. At death it asserts itself most strongly of all—Something Too Wonderful is going to happen. For to die is quite different from being not alive. This feeling is the proof of eternal life—once alive, alive for ever. To live is to feel this yearning, huge expectancy.

Daddy had taught them this, though, of course, they knew it instinctively already. And any moment now the door would open and his figure, familiar, yet each time more wonderful, would cross the threshold, close the door behind him, and ... something desirable would happen.

"I wish he'd hurry," said Tim impatiently. "There won't be any time left." And he glanced at the cruel clock that stopped all their pleasure but never stopped itself. "The motor got here hours ago. He can't STILL be having tea." Judy, her brown hair in disorder, her belt sagging where it was of little actual use, sighed deeply. But there was patience and understanding in her big, dark eyes. "He's in with Mother doing finances," she said with resignation. "It's Saturday. Let's sit down and wait." Then, seeing that Maria already occupied the big armchair, and sat staring comfortably into the fire, she did not move. Maria was making a purring, grunting sound of great contentment; she felt no anxiety of any kind apparently.

But Tim was less particular.

"Alright," he said, squashing himself down beside Maria, whose podgy form accommodated itself to the intrusion like a cat, "as long as Aunt Emily doesn't catch him on the way and begin explaining."

"She's in bed with a headache," mentioned Judy. "She's safe enough." For it was an established grievance against their mother's sister that she was always explaining things. She was a terrible explainer. She couldn't move without explaining. She explained everything in the world. She was a good soul, they knew, but she had to explain that she was a good soul. They rather dreaded her. Explanations took time for one thing, and for another they took away all wonder. In bed with a headache, she was safely accounted for, explained.

"She thinks we miss her," reflected Tim. He did not say it; it just flashed through his mind, with a satisfaction that added vaguely to his pleasurable anticipation of what was coming. And this satisfaction increased his energy. "Shove over a bit," he added aloud to Maria, and though Maria did not move of her own volition, she was nevertheless shoved over. The pair of them settled down into the depths of the chair, but while Maria remained quite satisfied with her new position, her brother fussed and fidgeted with impatience born of repressed excitement. "Run out and knock at the door," he proposed to Judy. "He'll never get away from Mother unless we let him KNOW we're waiting."

Judy, kneeling on a chair and trying to make it sea-saw, pulled up her belt, sprang down, then hesitated. "They'll only think it's Thompson and say come in," she decided. "That's no good."

Tim jumped up, using Maria as a support to raise himself. "I know what!" he cried. "Go and bang the gong. He'll think it's dressing-time." The idea was magnificent. "I'll go if you funk it," he added, and had already slithered half way over the back of the chair when Judy forestalled him and had her hand upon the door-knob. He encouraged her with various instructions about the proper way to beat the gong, and was just beginning a scuffle with the inanimate Maria, who now managed to occupy the entire chair, when he was aware of a new phenomenon that made him stop abruptly. He saw Judy's face hanging in mid-air, six feet above the level of the floor. Her face was flushed and smiling; her hair hung over her eyes; and from somewhere behind or underneath her a gruff voice said sternly:

"What are you doing in my Study at this time of night? Who asked you in?"

The expected figure had entered, catching Judy in the act of opening the door. He was carrying her in his arms. She landed with a flop upon the carpet. The desired and desirable thing was about to happen. "Get out, you lump, it's Daddy." But Maria, accustomed to her brother's exaggerated language, and knowing it was only right and manly, merely raised her eyes and waited for him to help her out. Tim did help her out; half dragging and half lifting, he deposited her in a solid heap upon the floor, then ran to the figure that now dominated the dim, fire-lit room, and hugged it with all his force, making sounds in his throat like an excited animal: "Ugh! ugh! ugh!...!"

The hug was returned with equal vigour, but without the curious sounds; Maria was hugged as well and set upon her feet; while Judy, having already been sufficiently hugged, pushed the arm-chair closer up to the fire and waited patiently for the proper business of the evening to begin.

The figure, meanwhile, disentangled itself. It was tall and thin, with a mild, resigned expression upon a kindly face that years and care had lined before its time: old-fashioned rather, with soft, grey whiskers belonging to an earlier day. A black tail-coat adorned it, and the neck-tie was crooked in the turned-down collar. The watch-chain went from the waist-coat button to one pocket only, instead of right across, and one finger wore a heavy signet-ring that bore the family crest. It was obviously the figure of an overworked official in the Civil Service who had returned from its daily routine in London to the evening routine of its family in the country, the atmosphere of Government and the Underground still hanging round it. For sundry whiffs of the mysterious city reached the children's nostrils, bringing thrills of some strange, remote reality they

Algernon Blackwood

had never known at first-hand. They busied themselves at once. While Tim unbuttoned the severe black coat and pulled it off, Judy brought a jacket of dingy tweed from behind a curtain in the corner, and stood on a chair to help the figure put it on. All knew their duties; the performance went like clockwork. And Maria sat and watched in helpful silence. There was a certain air about her as though she did it all.

"How they do spoil me, to be sure," the figure murmured to itself; "yet Mother's always saying that *I* spoil them. I wonder...!"

"Now you look decent at last," said Judy. "You smell like a nice rabbit."

"It's my shooting-coat." The figure cleared its throat, apparently on the defensive a little.

Tim and Judy sniffed it. "Rabbits and squirrels and earth and things," thought Tim.

"And flowers and burning leaves," said Judy. "It's his old garden-coat as well." She sniffed very audibly. "Oh, I love that smoky smell."

"It's the good old English smell," said the figure contentedly, while they put his neck-tie straight and arranged the pocket flaps for him. "It's English country—England."

"Don't other countries smell, then?" inquired Tim. "I mean, could any one tell you were English by your smell?" He sniffed again, with satisfaction. "Weeden's the same," he went on, without waiting for an answer, "only much stronger, and so's the potting shed."

"But yours is sweeter *much*," said Judy quickly. To share odours with an Authority like the Head Gardener was distinctly a compliment, but Daddy must come first, whatever happened. "How funny," she added, half to herself, "that

England should have such a jolly smell. I wonder what it comes from?"

"Where *does* England come from?" asked Tim, pausing a moment to stare into the figure's face. "It's an island, of course—England—but—"

"A piece of land surrounded by water," began the figure, but was not allowed to finish. A chorus of voices interrupted:

"Make a story of it, please. There's just time. There's half an hour. It's nice and dark. Ugh! Something very awful or very silly, please...."

There followed a general scuffle for seats, with bitter complaints that he only had two pointed knees. Maria was treated with scant respect. There was also criticism of life—that he had no lap, "no proper lap," that it was too dark to see his face, that everybody in turn had got "the best place," but, chiefly, that there was "very little time." Time was a nuisance always: it either was time to go, or time to stop, or else there was not time enough. But at length quiet was established; the big arm-chair resembled a clot of bees upon a honeycomb; the fire burned dully, and the ceiling was thick with monstrous fluttering shadows, vaguely shaped.

"Now, please. We've been ready for ages."

A deep hush fell upon the room, and only a sound of confused breathing was audible. The figure heaved a long, deep sigh as though it suffered pain, paused, cleared its throat, then sighed again more heavily than before. For the moment of creation was at hand, and creation is not accomplished without much travail.

But the children loved the pause, the sigh, the effort. Not realising with what difficulty the stories were ground out, nor that it was an effort against time—to make a story last till help came from outside —they believed that something immense

　　　　　Algernon Blackwood

and wonderful was on the way, and held their breath with beating hearts. Daddy's stories were always marvellous; this one would be no exception.

Marvellous up to a point, that is: something in them failed. "He's trying," was their opinion of them; and it was the trying that they watched and listened to so eagerly. The results were unsatisfying, the effect incomplete; the climax of sensation they expected never came. Daddy, though they could not put this into words, possessed fancy only; imagination was not his. Fancy, however, is the seed of imagination, as imagination is the blossom of wonder. His stories prepared the soil in them at any rate. They felt him digging all round them.

He began forthwith:

"Once, very long ago—"

"How long?"

"So long ago that the chalk cliffs of England still lay beneath the sea—"

"Was Aunt Emily alive then?"

"Or Weeden?"

"Oh, much longer ago than that," he comforted them; "so long, in fact, that neither your Aunt Emily nor Weeden were even thought of—there lived a man who—"

"Where? What country, please?"

"There lived a man in England—"

"But you said England was beneath the sea with the chalk cliffs."

"There lived a man in a very small, queer little island called

Ingland, spelt 'Ing,' not 'Eng,' who—"

"It wasn't *our* England, then?"

"On a tiny little island called Ingland, who was very lonely because he was the only human being on it—"

"Weren't there animals and things too?"

"And the only animals who lived on it with him were a squirrel who lived in the only tree, a rabbit who lived in the only hole, and a small grey mouse who made its nest in the pocket of his other coat."

"Were they friendly? Did he love them awfully?"

"At first he was very polite to them only, because he was a civil servant of his Government; but after a bit they became so friendly that he loved them even better than himself, and went to tea with the rabbit in its hole, and climbed the tree to share a nut-breakfast with the squirrel, and—and—"

"He doesn't know what to do with the mouse," a loud whisper, meant to be inaudible, broke in upon the fatal hesitation.

"And went out for walks with the mouse when the ground was damp and the mouse complained of chilly feet. In the pocket of his coat, all snug and warm, it stood on its hind legs and peered out upon the world with its pointed nose just above the pocket flap—"

"Then he liked the mouse best?"

"What sort of coat was it? An overcoat or just an ordinary one that smelt? Was that the only pocket in it?"

"It was made of the best leaves from the squirrel's tree, and from the rabbit's last year's fur, and the mouse had fastened

Algernon Blackwood

the edges together neatly with the sharpest of its own discarded whiskers. And so they walked about the tiny island and enjoyed the view together—"

"The mouse couldn't have seen much!"

"Until, one day, the mouse declared the ground was ALWAYS wet and was getting wetter and wetter. And the man got frightened."

"Ugh! It's going to get awful in a minute!" And the children nestled closer. The voice sank lower. It became mysterious.

"And the wetter it got the more the man got frightened; for the island was dreadfully tiny and—"

"Why, please, did it get wetter and wetter?"

"THAT," continued the man who earned his living in His Majesty's Stationery Office by day, and by night justified his existence offering the raw material of epics unto little children, "that was the extraordinary part of it. For no one could discover. The man stroked his beard and looked about him, the squirrel shook its bushy tail, the rabbit lifted its upper lip and thrust its teeth out, and the mouse jerked its head from side to side until its whiskers grew longer and sharper than ever—but none of them could discover why the island got wetter and wetter and wetter—"

"Perhaps it just rained like here."

"For the sky was always blue, it never rained, and there was so little dew at night that no one even mentioned it. Yet the tiny island got wetter every day, till it finally got so wet that the very floor of the man's hut turned spongy and splashed every time the man went to look out of the window at the view. And at last he got so frightened that he stayed indoors altogether, put on both his coats at once, and told stories to the mouse and squirrel about a country that was always dry—"

"Didn't the rabbit know anything?"

"For all this time the rabbit was too terrified to come out of its hole at all. The increasing size of its front teeth added to its uneasiness, for they thrust out so far that they hid the view and made the island seem even smaller than it was—"

"I like rabbits, though."

"Till one fine day—"

"They were all fine, you said."

"One finer day than usual the rabbit made a horrible discovery. The way it made the discovery was curious—may seem curious to us, at least—but the fact is, it suddenly noticed that the size of its front teeth had grown out of all proportion to the size of the island. Looking over its shoulder this fine day, it realised how absurdly small the island was in comparison with its teeth—and grasped the horrid truth. In a flash it understood what was happening. The island was getting wetter because it was also getting—*smaller*!"

"Ugh! How beastly!"

"Did it tell the others?"

"It retired half-way down its hole and shouted out the news to the others in the hut."

"Did they hear it?"

"It warned them solemnly. But its teeth obstructed the sound, and the windings of its hole made it difficult to hear. The man, besides, was busy telling a story to the mouse, and the mouse, anyhow, was sound asleep at the bottom of his pocket, with the result that the only one who caught the words of warning was—the squirrel. For a squirrel's ears are so sharp that it can even hear the grub whistling to itself inside a rotten

Algernon Blackwood

nut; and it instantly took action."

"Ah! IT saved them, then?"

"The squirrel flew from the man's shoulder where it was perched, balanced for a second on the top of his head, then clung to the ceiling and darted out of the window without a moment's delay. It crossed the island in a single leap, scuttled to the top of the tree, peered about over the diminishing landscape, and—"

"Didn't it see the rabbit?"

"And returned as quickly as it went. It bustled back into the hut, hopping nervously, and jerking its head with excitement. In a moment it was perched again on the man's shoulder. It carefully kept its bushy tail out of the way of his nose and eyes. And then it whispered what it had seen into his left ear."

"Why into his left ear?"

"Because it was the right one, and the other had cotton wool in it."

"Like Aunt Emily!"

"What did it whisper?"

"The squirrel had made a discovery, too," continued the teller, solemnly.

"Goodness! That's two discoveries!"

"But what *did* it whisper?"

In the hush that followed, a coal was heard falling softly into the grate; the night-wind moaned against the outside walls; Judy scraped her stockinged foot slowly along the iron fender, making a faint twanging sound. Breathing was distinctly audible. For several moments the room was still as death. The figure, smothered beneath the clotted mass of children, heaved a sigh. But no one broke the pause. It was too precious and wonderful to break at once. All waited breathlessly, like birds poised in mid-air before they strike ... until a new sound stole faintly upon the listening silence, a faint and very distant sound, barely audible as yet, but of unmistakable character. It was far away in the upper reaches of the building, overhead, remote, a little stealthy. Like the ominous murmur of a muffled drum, it had approach in it. It was coming nearer and nearer. It was significant and threatening.

For the first time that evening the ticking of the clock was also audible. But the new sound, though somewhat in league with the ticking, and equally remorseless, did not come from the clock. It was a human sound, the most awful known to childhood. It was footsteps on the stairs!

Both the children and the story-teller heard it, but with different results. The latter stirred and looked about him, as though new hope and strength had come to him. The former, led by Tim and Judy, broke simultaneously into anxious speech. Maria, having slept profoundly since the first mention of the mouse in its cosy pocket, gave no sign at all.

"Oh, quick! quick! What did the squirrel whisper in his good right ear? What was it? DO hurry, please!"

"It whispered two simple words, each of one syllable," continued the reanimated figure, his voice lowered and impressive. "It said—*the sea*!"

The announcement made by the squirrel was so entirely unexpected that the surprise of it buried all memory of the disagreeable sound. The children sat up and stared into the figure's face questioningly. Surely he had made a slight mistake. How could the sea have anything to do with it? But no word was spoken, no actual question asked. This overwhelming introduction of the sea left him poised far

Algernon Blackwood

beyond their reach. His stories were invariably marvellous. He would somehow justify himself.

"The Sea!" whispered Tim to Judy, and there was intense admiration in his voice and eyes.

"From the top of its tree," resumed the figure triumphantly, "the squirrel had seen what was happening, and made its great discovery. It realised why the ground was wetter and wetter every day, and also why the island was small and growing smaller. For it understood the awful fact that—the sea was rising! A little longer and the entire island would be under water, and everybody on it would be drowned!" "Couldn't none of them swim or anything?" asked Judy with keen anxiety.

"Hush!" put in Tim. "It's what did they *do?* And who thought of it first?"

The question last but one was chosen for solution.

"The rabbit," announced the figure recklessly. "The rabbit saved them; and in saving them it saved the Island too. It founded Ingland, this very Ingland on which we live to-day. In fact, it started the British Empire by its action. The rabbit did it."

"How? How?"

"It heard the squirrel's whisper half-way down its hole. It forgot about its front teeth, and the moment it forgot them they, of course, stopped growing. It recovered all its courage. A grand idea had come to it. It came bustling out of its hiding-place, stood on its hind legs, poked its bright eyes over the window-ledge, and told them how to escape. It said, 'I'll dig my hole deeper and we'll empty the sea into it as it rises. We'll pour the water down my hole!'"

The figure paused and fixed his eyes upon each listener in turn, challenging disapproval, yet eager for sympathy at the same time. In place of criticism, however, he met only silence and breathless admiration. Also—he heard that distant sound *they* had forgotten, and realised it had come much nearer. It had reached the second floor. He made swift and desperate calculations. He decided that it was *just* possible ... with ordinary good luck ...

"So they all went out and began to deepen the rabbit's hole. They dug and dug and dug. The man took off both his coats; the rabbit scraped with its four paws, using its tail as well—it had a nice long tail in those days; the mouse crept out of his pocket and made channels with its little pointed toes; and the squirrel brushed and swept the water in with its bushy, mop-like tail. The rising sea poured down the ever-deepening hole. They worked with a will together; there was no complaining, though the rabbit wore its tail down till it was nothing but a stump, and the mouse stood ankle-deep in water, and the squirrel's fluffy tail looked like a stable broom. They worked like heroes without stopping even to talk, and as the water went pouring down the hole, the level of the sea, of course, sank lower and lower and lower, the shores of the tiny island stretched farther and farther and farther, till there were reaches of golden sand like Margate at low tide, and as the level sank still lower there rose into view great white cliffs of chalk where before there had been only water—until, at last, the squirrel, scampering down from the tree where it had gone to see what had been accomplished, reported in a voice that chattered with stammering delight, 'We're saved! The sea's gone down! The land's come up!'"

The steps were audible in the passage. A gentle knock was heard. But no one answered, for it seemed that no one was aware of it. The figure paused a moment to recover breath.

"And then, and then? What happened next? Did they thank the rabbit?"

"They all thanked each other then. The man thanked the

Algernon Blackwood

rabbit, and the rabbit thanked the squirrel, and the mouse woke up, and—"

No one noticed the slip, which proved that their attention was already painfully divided. For another knock, much louder than before, had interrupted the continuation of the story. The figure turned its head to listen. "It's nothing," said Tim quickly. "It's only a sound," said Judy. "What did the mouse do? Please tell us quickly."

"I thought I heard a knock," the figure murmured. "Perhaps I was mistaken. The mouse—er—the mouse woke up—"

"You told us that."

The figure continued, speaking with greater rapidity even than before:

"And looked about it, and found the view so lovely that it said it would never live in a pocket again, but would divide its time in future between the fields and houses. So it pricked its whiskers up, and the squirrel curled its tail over its back to avoid any places that still were damp, and the rabbit polished its big front teeth on the grass and said it was quite pleased to have a stump instead of a tail as a memento of a memorable occasion when they had all been nearly drowned together, and—they all skipped up to the top of the high chalk cliffs as dry as a bone and as happy as—"

He broke off in the middle of the enormous sentence to say a most ridiculous and unnecessary thing. "Come in," he said, just as though there was some one knocking at the door. But no single head was turned. If there was an entry it was utterly ignored.

"Happy as what?"

"As you," the figure went on faster than ever. "And that's why England to-day is an island of quite a respectable size, and why everybody pretends it's dry and comfortable and cosy, and why people never leave it except to go away for holidays that cannot possibly be avoided."

"I beg your pardon, sir," began an awful voice behind the chair.

"And why to this day," he continued as though he had not heard, "a squirrel always curls its tail above its back, why a rabbit wears a stump like a pen wiper, and why a mouse lives sometimes in a house and sometimes in a field, and—"

"I beg your pardon, sir," clanged the slow, awful voice in a tone that was meant to be heard distinctly, "but it's long gone 'arf-past six, and—"

"Time for bed," added the figure with a sound that was like the falling of an executioner's axe. And, as if to emphasise the arrival of the remorseless moment, the clock just then struck loudly on the mantelpiece—seven times.

But for several minutes no one stirred. Hope, even at such moments, was stronger than machinery of clocks and nurses. There was a general belief that somehow or other the moment that they dreaded, the moment that was always coming to block their happiness, could be evaded and shoved aside. Nothing mechanical like that was wholly true. Daddy had often used queer phrases that hinted at it: "Some day—A day is coming—A day will come"; and so forth. Their belief in a special Day when no one would say "Time" haunted them already. Yet, evidently this evening was not the momentous occasion; for when Tim mentioned that the clock was fast, the figure behind the chair replied that she was half an hour overdue already, and her tone was like Thompson's when he said, "Dinner's served." There was no escape this time.

Accordingly the children slowly disentangled themselves; they rose and stretched like animals; though all still ignored the figure behind the chair. A ball of stuff unrolled and became

Algernon Blackwood

Maria. "Thank you, Daddy," she said. "It was just lovely," said Judy. "But it's only the beginning, isn't it?" Tim asked. "It'll go on to-morrow night?" And the figure, having escaped failure by the skin of its teeth, kissed each in turn and said, "Another time—yes, I'll go on with it." Whereupon the children deigned to notice the person behind the chair. "We're coming up to bed now, Jackman," they mentioned casually, and disappeared slowly from the room in a disappointed body, robbed, unsatisfied, but very sleepy. The clock had cheated them of something that properly was endless. Maria alone made no remark, for she was already asleep in Jackman's comfortable arms. Maria was always carried.

"Time's up," Tim reflected when he lay in bed; "time's always up. I do wish we could stop it somehow," and fell asleep somewhat gratified because he had deliberately not wound up his alarum-clock. He had the delicious feeling—a touch of spite in it—that this would bother Time and muddle it.

Yet Time, as a monster, chased him through a hundred dreams and thus revenged itself. It pursued him to the very edge of the daylight, then mocked him with a cold bath, lessons, and a windy sleet against the windows. It was "time to get up" again.

Yet, meanwhile, Time helped and pleased the children by showing them its pleasanter side as well. It pushed them, gently but swiftly, up the long hill of months and landed them with growing excitement into the open country of another year. Since the rabbit, mouse, and squirrel first woke in their hearts the wonder of common things, they had all grown slightly bigger. Time tucked away another twelve months behind their backs: each of them was a year older; and that in itself was full of a curious and growing wonder.

For the birth of wonder is a marvellous, sweet thing, but the recognition of it is sweeter and more marvellous still. Its growth, perhaps, shall measure the growth and increase of the soul to whom it is as eyes and hands and feet, searching the world for signs of hiding Reality. But its persistence—through the heavier years that would obliterate it—this persistence shall offer hints of something coming that is more than marvellous. The beginning of wisdom is surely—Wonder.

Algernon Blackwood

CHAPTER III

DEATH OF A MERE FACT

There was a man named Jinks. In him was neither fancy, imagination, nor a sign of wonder, and so he—died.

But, though he appears in this chapter, he disappears again so quickly that his being mentioned in a sentence all by himself should not lead any one astray. Jinks made a false entry, as it were. The children crossed him out at once. He became illegible. For the trio had their likes and dislikes; they resented liberties being taken with them. Also, when there was no one to tell them stories, they were quite able to amuse themselves. It was the inactive yet omnipotent Maria who brought about indirectly the obliteration of Mr. Jinks.

And it came about as follows:

Maria was a podgy child of marked individuality. It was said that she was seven years old, but *she* declared that eight was the figure, because some uncle or other had explained, "you're in your eighth year." Wandering uncles are troublesome in this kind of way. Every time her age was mentioned she corrected the informant. She had a trick of moving her eyes without moving her head, as though the round face was difficult to turn; but her big blue eyes slipped round without the least trouble, as though oiled. The performance gave her the sly and knowing aspect of a goblin, but she had no objection to that, for it saved her trouble, and to save herself trouble—according to nurses, Authorities, and the like—was her sole object in existence.

Yet this seemed a mistaken view of the child. It was not so much that she did not move unnecessarily as that it was not necessary for her to move at all, since she invariably found herself in the middle of whatever was going on. While life bustled anxiously about her, hurrying to accomplish various ends, she remained calm and contented at the centre, completely satisfied, mistress of it all. And her face was symbolic of her entire being; whereas so many faces seem unfinished, hers was complete—globular like the heavenly bodies, circular like the sun, arms and legs unnecessary. The best of everything came to her *because* she did not run after it. There was no hurry. Time did not worry her. Circular and self-sustaining, she already seemed to dwell in Eternity.

"And this little person," one of these inquisitive, interfering visitors would ask, smiling fatuously; "how old is she, I wonder?"

"Seven," was the answer of the Authority in charge.

Maria's eyes rolled sideways, and a little upwards. She looked at the foolish questioner; the Authority who had answered was not worth a glance.

"No," she said flatly, with sublime defiance, "I'm more. I'm in my eighth year, you see."

And the visitor, smiling that pleasant smile that makes children distrust, even dislike them, and probably venturing to pinch her cheek or pat her on the shoulder into the bargain, accepted the situation with another type of smile—the Smile-that-children-expect. As a matter of fact, children hate it. They see through its artificial humbug easily. They prefer a solemn and unsmiling face invariably. It's the latter that produces chocolates and sudden presents; it's the stern-faced sort that play hide-and-seek or stand on their heads. The Smilers are bored at heart. They mean to escape at the first opportunity. And the children never catch their sleeves or coattails to prevent them going.

"So you're in your eighth year, are you?" this Smiler chuckled with a foolish grin. He patted her cheek kindly. "Why, you're almost a grown-up person. You'll be going to dinner-parties soon." And he smiled again. Maria stood motionless and patient. Her eyes gazed straight before her. Her podgy face remained expressionless as dough.

"Answer the kind gentleman," said the Authority reprovingly.

Maria did not budge. A finger and thumb, both dirty, rolled a portion of her pinafore into a pointed thing like a string, distinctly black. She waited for the visitor to withdraw. But this particular visitor did not withdraw.

"*I* knew a little girl—" he began, with a condescending grin that meant that her rejection of his advances had offended him, "a little girl of about your age, who—"

But the remainder of the rebuke-concealed-in-a-story was heard only by the Authority. For Maria, relentless and unhumbugged, merely walked away. In the hall she discovered Tim, discreetly hiding. "What's *he* come for?" the brother inquired promptly, jerking his thumb towards the hall.

Maria's eyes just looked at him.

"To see Mother, I suppose," he answered himself, accustomed to his sister's goblin manners, "and talk about missions and subshkiptions, and all that. Did he give you anything?"

"No, nothing."

"Did he call us bonny little ones?" His face mentioned that he could kill if necessary, or if his sister's honour required it.

"He didn't *say* it."

"Lucky for him," exclaimed Tim gallantly, rubbing his nose with the palm of his hand and snorting loudly. "What *did* he say, then—the old Smiler?"

"He said," replied Maria, moving her head as well as her eyes, "that I wasn't really old, and that he knew another little girl who was nicer than me, and always told the truth, and—"

"Oh, come on," cried Tim, impatiently interrupting. "My trains are going in the schoolroom, and I want a driver for an accident. We'll put the Smiler in the luggage van, and he'll get smashed in the collision, and *all* the wheels will go over his head. Then he'll find out how old you really are. We'll fairly smash him."

They disappeared. Judy, who was reading a book on the Apocalypse, in a corner of the room, looked up a moment as they entered.

"What's up?" she asked, her mind a little dazed by the change of focus from stars, scarlet women, white horses, and mysterious "Voices," to dull practical details of everyday existence. "What's on?" she repeated.

"Trains," replied Tim. "We're going to have an accident and kill a man dead."

"What's he done?" she inquired.

"Humbugged Maria with a lot of stuff—and gave her nothing—and didn't believe a single word she told him."

Judy glanced without much interest at the railway laid out upon the floor, murmured "Oh, I see," and resumed her reading of the wonderful book she had purloined from the top shelf of a neglected bookcase outside the gun-room. It absorbed her. She loved the tremendous words, the

Algernon Blackwood

atmosphere of marvel and disaster, and especially the constant suggestion that the end of the world was near. Antichrist she simply adored. No other hero in any book she knew came near him.

"Come and help," urged Tim, picking up an engine that lay upon its side. "Come on."

"No, thanks. I've got an Apocalypse. It's simply frightfully exciting."

"Shall we break *both* legs?" asked Maria blandly, "or just his neck?"

"Neck," said Tim briefly. "Only they must find the heart beneath the rubbish of the luggage van."

Judy looked up in spite of herself. "Who is it?" she inquired, with an air of weighing conflicting interests.

"Mr. Jinks." It was Maria who supplied the information.

"But he's Daddy's offiss-partner man," Judy objected, though without much vim or heat.

Maria did not answer. Her eyes were glued upon the other engine.

"All black and burnt and—full of the very horridest diseases," put in Tim, referring to the heart of the destroyed Mr. Jinks beneath the engine.

He glanced up enticingly at his elder sister, whom he longed to draw into the vindictive holocaust.

"He said things to Maria," he explained persuasively, "and it's not the first time either. Last Sunday he called me 'his little man,' and he's never given me a single thing since ever I can remember, years and years ago."

Then Judy remembered that he invariably kissed her on both cheeks as though she was a silly little child.

"Oh, *that* man!" she exclaimed, realising fully now the enormities he had committed. She appeared to hesitate a moment. Then she flung down her Apocalypse suddenly. "Put him on a scarlet horse," she cried, "pretend he's the Beast, and I'll come."

Maria's blue eyes wheeled half a circle towards Tim. She did not move her head. It signified agreement. Tim knew. Only her consent, as the insulted party, was necessary before he could approve.

"All right," he cried to Judy. "We'll put him in a special carriage with his horse, and I'll make out a label for the window, so that every one will know." He went over to the table and wrote "BEAST" in capital letters on a half-sheet of paper. The cumbersome quill pen made two spongy blots.

"It's the end of the world *really* at the same time," decided Judy, to a chorus of general approval, "not only the end of Mr. Jinks." She liked her horrors on a proper scale.

And the railway line was quickly laid across the room from the window to the wall. The lamps of oil on both engines were lit. The trains faced one another. Mr. Jinks and his scarlet horse thought themselves quite safe in their special carriage, unaware that it was labelled "Beast" with a label that overlapped the roof and hid all view of the landscape through the windows on one side. Apparently they slept in opposite corners, with full consciousness of complete security. Mr. Jinks was tucked up with woolly rugs, and a newspaper lay across his knee. The scarlet horse had its head in a bag of oats, and its bridle was fastened to the luggage rack above. Both were supplied with iron foot-warmers. There was a *fearful* fog; and the train was going at a *TREMENDOUS* pace.

So was the other train. They approached, they banged, they

smashed to atoms. It was the most appalling collision that had ever been heard of, and the Guard and Engine-Driver, as well as the Ticket-Collectors and Directors of the Company, were all executed by the Government the very next day from gallows that an angry London built in half an hour on the top of St. Paul's Cathedral dome.

It took place between the footstool and the fireplace in the thickest fog that England had ever known. And the horrid black heart of Mr. Jinks was discovered beneath the wreckage of a special carriage next to the luggage van. It was simply black as coal and very nasty indeed. The little boy who found it was a porter's son, whose mother was so poor that she took in washing for members of Parliament, who paid their bills irregularly because they were very busy governing Ireland. He knew it was a cinder, but did not discover it was a heart until he showed it to his mother, and his mother said it was far too black to wash.

The accident to Mr. Jinks, therefore, was a complete success. The butler helped with the mending of the engine, and Maria informed at least one Authority, "We do not know Mr. Jinks. We have other friends."

"But, remember," said Judy, "we mustn't mention it to Daddy, because Mr. Jinks is his partner-in-the-offiss."

"*Was*," said Tim. The remains they decided to send to what they called the "Hospital for Parilysed Ineebrits with Incurable Afflictions of the Heart."

CHAPTER IV

FACT—EDGED WITH FANCY

But the children were not always so vindictive and blood-thirsty. All three could be very tender sometimes. Even Maria was not wholly implacable and merciless, she had a pretty side as well. Their neighbour at the Manor House, Colonel William Stumper, C.B., experienced this gentler quality in the trio. He was Mother's cousin, too.

They were inclined to like this Colonel Stumper, C.B. For one thing he limped, and that meant, they decided, that he had a wooden leg. They never called it such, of course, but indicated obliquely that the injured limb was made of oak or walnut, by referring to the other as "his living leg," "his good leg," and so forth. For another thing, he did not smile at them; and for a third, he did not ask foolish questions in an up-and-down voice (assumed for the moment), as though they were invalids, idiots, or tailless puppies who could not answer. He frowned at them. He said furiously, "How are you, creatures?" And—he gave usually at least a shilling to each.

"That makes three shillings altogether," as Tim cleverly explained.

"But not three shillings for each of us," Maria qualified the praise. "*I* only got one." She took it out of her mouth and showed it by way of proof.

Algernon Blackwood

"You'll swallow it," warned Judy, "and then you won't have none at all."

If received early in the week, they reported their good fortune to the Authorities; but if Sunday was too near, they waited. Daddy had a queer idea of teasing sometimes. "Just in time for to-morrow's collection," he would be apt to say; and though he did not really mean it perhaps, there was a hint of threat in the suggestion that quenched high spirits at the moment.

"You see, he takes the plate round," Judy told them, "and so feels ashamed." She did not explain the feeling ashamed. It was just that her father, who always did things thoroughly, had to say something, and so picked on that. "Monday or Tuesday's safest," was her judgment.

Maria rolled her eyes round like a gigantic German doll.

"Never's best," she gave as her opinion.

But that was sly. The others reproved her quickly.

"Daddy likes to know," they told her. "Monday or Tuesday's all right." They agreed just to mention the matter only. There was no need to "say a lot."

So they liked this Colonel Stumper, C.B. They liked his "title," declaring that the letters stood for "Come Back," and referring to their owner as "Come Back Stumper." Some day, when he was gone for good, he was to be promoted to K.C.B., meaning "Kan't-Come-Back." But they preferred him as he was, plain C.B., because they did not want to lose him. They declared that "Companion to the Bath" was just nonsense invented by a Radical Government. For in politics, of course, they followed their father's lead, and their father had *distinctly* stated more than once that "the policy of a Radical Government was some-funny-word-or-other nonsense," which statement helped them enormously in forming their own opinions on several other topics as well. In personal disagreements, for instance—they never "squabbled"—the final insult was to say, "My dear, you're as silly as a something-or-other Radical Govunment," for there was no answer to this anywhere in the world.

Come-Back Stumper, therefore, though casual outsiders might never have guessed it, was a valuable ally. He was what Mother called "a character" as well, and if the children used this statement in praise of him, while adopting in their carelessness a revised version, "he has no character," this was not Come-Back Stumper's fault. He was also an "extinguished soldger," and had seen much service in foreign parts. India with its tigers, elephants, and jungles, was in his heated atmosphere deliciously, and his yellow tint, as of an unripe orange, was due to something they had learned from hearsay to describe as "curried liver trouble." All this, and especially his dead or wooden leg, was distinctly in his favour. Come-Back Stumper was real. Also, he was hard and angular in appearance, short, brisk in manner, square-shouldered, and talked like a General who was bothered about something in a battle. His opinions were most decided. His conversation consisted of negatives, refusals and blank denials. If Come-Back Stumper agreed with what was said, it meant that he was feeling unwell with an attack of curried-liver-trouble. The children understood him. He understood the children, too.

"It's a jolly morning, William," from Daddy would be met with "Might be worse" and a snort like the sneeze of the nursery cat, but a direct invitation of any sort was simply declined point blank. "Care to see The Times, William?" ensured the answer, "Oh, *no*, thanks; there's never anything worth reading in it." This was as regular as breakfast when Cousin William was staying in the house. It was, in fact, Daddy's formula when he settled into his armchair for a quiet half-hour's read. Daddy's question was the mere politeness of a host. It was sham, but Cousin William's answer was as real as breakfast. The formula was a mechanical certainty, as certain as that pressing a button in the wall produced Thompson in the room.

Algernon Blackwood

Accordingly, when Mother said, "Now, don't bother your Cousin William, children; he doesn't want you," this individual would instantly shoulder arms and state the exact contrary with fiery emphasis.

"If you've no objection," came the testy answer, "and if it's all the same to you, Cecilia"—a shade sarcastically, this—"it's precisely what I *do* want."

And he would look at the children in a way that suggested the most intimate of secret understanding between himself and them. More, he would rise and leave the room with the impetus of a soldier going out to fight, and would play with Judy, Tim, and Maria in a fashion that upset the household routine and made the trio unmanageable for the Authorities for hours afterwards.

"He's an honourable gentleman like the gentlemen in Parliament," declared Judy, "and that's my opinion of why I think him nice."

"And when I'm grown-up," was Tim's verdict, "I'll be a soldger just exactly the same, only not yellow, and taller, and not so thick in the middle, and much, much richer, and with C.B. in front of my name as well as at the end."

Maria, not being present at the time, said nothing audible. But she liked him, too, unquestionably. Otherwise she would have announced the fact without delay. "He *is* a lump rather," she had been heard to remark, referring to his actual bulk and slowness of movement when in play. But it was nicely, very nicely meant.

"I am sure your Cousin William would rather be left alone to read quietly," said Mother, seeing the trio approach that individual stealthily after tea in the library one evening. He was deep in a big armchair, and deep in a book as well. The children were allowed downstairs after their schoolroom tea for an hour when nothing particular was on. "Wouldn't you,

William?" she added. She went on knitting a sort of muffler thing she held up close to the lamp. She expected no reply, apparently.

Cousin William made none. But he raised the level of his book so that it hid his face. A moment before, the eyes had been looking over the top at the advancing trio, watching their movements narrowly.

The children did not answer either. They separated. They scouted. They executed a flank attack in open order. Three minutes later Colonel Stumper was surrounded. And no word was spoken; the scouts just perched and watched him. He was not actually reading, for he had not turned a page for about ten minutes, and it was *not* a picture book. The difficulty was, however, to get him started. If only Mother would help them! Then Mother, unwittingly, did so. For she dropped her ball of wool, and finding no one at hand to recover it, she looked vaguely round the room—and saw them. And she shook her head at them.

"Don't bother him just now," she whispered again, "he's got a cold. Here, Maria, pick up my wool, darling, will you?" But while Tim (for Maria only moved her eyes) picked up the wool obediently, Cousin William picked up himself with difficulty, tossed his book into the deep arm-chair, and stalked without a single word towards the door. Mother watched him with one eye, but the children did not stir a muscle.

"William, you're not going to bed, are you?" she asked kindly, "or would you like to, perhaps? And have your dinner in your room, and a warm drink just before going to sleep? That's the best thing for a cold, I always think."

He turned at the door and faced her. "Thank you very much," he said with savage emphasis, "but I am *not* ill, and I am *not* going to bed." The negatives sounded like pistol shots. "My cold is nothing to speak of." And he was gone, leaving a trail of fire in the air.

The children, cunning in their generation, did not move. There were moments in life, and this was one of them, when "stir a finger and you're a dead man" was really true. No finger stirred, no muscle twitched; one pair of eyelids fluttered, nothing more. And Mother, happy with her recovered ball of wool, was presently lost in the muffler thing she knitted, forgetful of their presence, if not of their very existence. Signals meanwhile were made and answered by means of some secret code that birds and animals understand. The plan was matured in silence.

"Good-night, Mother," said Judy innocently, a few moments later, stepping up and kissing her.

"Good-night," said Tim gravely, doing likewise.

Maria kissed, but said no word at all. They did not linger, as their custom was, to cuddle in or hear a fairy story. To-night they were good and businesslike.

"Good-night, duckies," said Mother, glancing at the clock on the mantelpiece. "It's not *quite* bed-time yet, but it's been a long day, and you're tired out. I shall be up presently to hear your prayers and tuck you up. And, Judy, you might tell Jackman—"

But the room was empty, the children vanished. The door banged softly, cutting off the sentence in its middle, and Mother resumed her knitting, smiling quietly to herself. And in the hall outside Come-Back Stumper was discovered, warming his Army back before the open fire of blazing logs. He looked like a cart-horse, the shadows made him spread so. Maria pushed him to one side. She pushed, at least, but he did not move exactly. Yet somehow, by a kind of sidling process, he took up a new position in regard to the fire and themselves, the result of which was that they occupied the best places, while he stood at one corner in an attitude which resisted attack and yet invited it.

"Good-evening," remarked Maria; "are you warm?"

"Oh, no," exclaimed Tim, "that's not it at all. The thing is, shall we play hide-and-seek, or would you really rather go to bed, as Mother said, and have dinner and hot drinks?"

"Nonsense," cried Judy with authority. "He's got an awful cold, and he's got to go to bed at once. He's shivering all over. It's Nindian fever."

"No, really, really—" began Stumper, but was not allowed to finish.

"Thin captain biscuits soaked in hot milk with ginger, nutmeg, lemon, and whisky," announced Judy, "would be best." And she shot towards the door, her hair untied and flying.

"But, my dear, I assure you—"

"Or Bath Olivers," she interrupted, "because they soak better. *You* know nothing," she added motheringly; "no man ever does." There was contempt in her voice as well as pity.

"*Why* do you know nothing?" inquired Maria, with a blaze of staring eyes, as the door slammed upon her vanishing sister.

"*I* think you know everything," said Tim with pride, decidedly, "only you've forgotten it in India. I think it's silly."

"The milk and stuff?" agreed the soldier. "Yes, so do I. And I hate biscuits, and ginger makes me hot and ill—"

"Iller than you are already?" asked Maria, "because that means bed."

"Maria," he snapped angrily, "I'm not ill at all. If you go on saying I'm ill, of course I shall get ill. I never felt better in my life."

Tim turned round like a top. "Then let's play hide-and-seek," he cried. "Let's hide before Judy gets back, and she can come and never find us!"

Cousin William suggested they were not enough to play that game, and was of opinion that Aunt Emily might be invited too.

"Oh, no," Tim gave his decided verdict, "not women. They can't hide properly. They bulge."

And at that moment Judy appeared in the doorway across the hall.

"It's coming," she cried. "I've ordered everything—hot milk and Bath Olivers and preserved ginger and—"

Cousin William took the matter into his own hands then, for the situation was growing desperate. "Look here," he suggested gravely, yet without enthusiasm, "I'll take the milk and stuff upstairs when I've got into bed, and meanwhile we'll do something else. I'm—that is, my cold is too bad to play a game, but I'll tell you a story about—er—about a tiger—if you like?" The last three words were added as a question. An answer, however, was not immediately forthcoming. For the moment was a grave one. It was admitted that Come-Back Stumper could play a game with credit and success, even an active game like hide-and-seek; but it was not known yet that he could tell a story. The fate of the evening, therefore, hung upon the decision.

"A tiger!" said Tim, doubtfully, weighing probabilities. "A tiger you shot, was it, or just—a tiger?" A sign, half shadow and half pout, was in his face. Maria and Judy waited upon their brother's decision with absolute confidence, meanwhile.

Colonel Stumper moved artfully backwards towards a big horsehair sofa, beneath the deer heads and assegais from Zululand. He did it on tiptoe, aware that this mysterious and suggestive way of walking has a marked effect on children in the dark. "I did not shoot it," he said, "because I lived with it. It was the most extraordinary tiger that was ever known—"

"In India?"

"In the world. And I ought to know, because, as I say, I lived with it for days—"

"Inside it?"

"Nearly, but not quite. I lived in its cave with the cubs and other things, half-eaten deer and cows and the bones of Hindus—"

"Were the bones black? However did you escape? Why didn't the tiger eat you?"

He drew the children closely round him on the sofa. "I'll tell you," he said, "for this is an inaugural occasion, and I've never told the story before to any one in the world. The experience was incredible, and no one would believe it. But the proof that it really happened is that the tiger has left its mark upon me till I die—"

"But you haven't died—yet, I mean," Maria observed.

"He means teeth, silly," Tim squelched her.

"Died in another sense than the one you mean," the great soldier and former administrator of a province continued, "dyed yellow—"

"Oh-h-h! Is that why—?"

"That is why," he replied pathetically. "For living with that tiger family so long, I almost turned into one myself. The tiger nature got into me. I snarl and growl, I use my teeth ferociously when hungry, I walk stealthily on tiptoe, I let my

Algernon Blackwood

whiskers grow, and my colour has the tint of Indian tigers' skins."

"Have you got a tail, too?"

He glared into the blue eyes of Maria, sternly. "It's growing," he whispered horribly, "it's growing."

There was a pause in which credulity shook hands with faith. Belief was in the air. If doubt did whisper, "Let me see, please," it was too low to be quite audible. Come-Back Stumper was surrounded by an atmosphere of black-edged glory suddenly; he wore a halo; his feet were dipped in mystery.

"Then what's an orgully occasion?" somebody asked.

"This!" replied Stumper. But he uttered it so savagely that no one cared to press for further details. Clearly it was a secret and confidential moment, and "inaugural occasion" had something to do with the glory of wearing an incipient tail. Glory and mystery clothed Stumper from that moment with Indian splendour. At least, *he* thought so....

"And the tiger?" came the whispering question.

"Ugh-h-h-h!" he shuddered; "I'll tell you. But I must think a moment quietly first."

"His tail hurts," Maria told Tim beneath her breath, while they waited for the story to begin.

"So would yours," was the answer, "if you had a cold at the same time, too. A girl would simply cry." And he looked contempt at her, but unutterable respect at his soldier friend.

"This tiger," began the traveller, in a heavy voice, "was a—a very unusual tiger. I met it, that is to say, most unexpectedly. It was in a tropical jungle, where the foliage was so thick that the sunlight hardly penetrated at all. It was dark as night even in the daytime. There were monkeys overhead and snakes beneath, and bananas were so plentiful that every time my elephant knocked against a tree a shower of fruit fell down like hail and tickled its skin."

"You were on an elephant, then?"

"We were all on elephants. On my particular elephant there was a man to load for me and a man to guide the beast. We moved slowly and cautiously. It was dark, as I said, but the showers of falling bananas made yellow streaks against the black that the elephant constantly mistook for tigers flying through the air as they leaped in silent fury against the howdah in which we crouched upon his back. The howdah, you know, is the saddle."

"Was the elephant friendly?"

"*Very* friendly indeed; but he found it difficult to see, and all of a sudden he would give a hop and a jump that nearly flung me off his shoulders. For a long time—"

"That was the bananas tickling him, I suppose?"

"This continued without anything dangerous happening, but all at once he gave a tremendous leap into the air, lifted his trunk, trumpeted like an Army bugle, and then set off at full speed through the tangled jungle. He had stupidly stepped upon a cobra! And the cobra, before it was squashed to pulp, had stung him between the big and little toe."

"On purpose?" Judy asked.

"In an Indian jungle everything's done on purpose. My elephant raced away, trumpeting in agony, at twenty miles an hour. The driver lost his balance and fell off; the other man, scrambling along to take his place and steer the monster, fell off after him, taking both my guns with him as he went; and I myself, crouching in the swaying howdah, and holding on for

48   Algernon Blackwood

grim death, continued to tear through the jungle on top of my terrified and angry elephant. Then, suddenly, the branch of a tree caught the howdah in the middle and swept it clear. The elephant rushed on. The howdah, with myself inside it, swung in mid-air like a caught balloon. But I saw it could not hold on long. There was just time to scramble out of it into safety upon the branch when there came a sound of ripping, and the thing fell smash upon the ground some twenty feet below, leaving me alone in an Indian jungle—up a tree."

And he paused a moment to produce the right effect and reap the inevitable glory of applause.

Out of the breathless silence sprang a voice at once: "Was the elephant badly hurt?" And then another: "I thought elephants were too big to feel a bite like that." Followed by a third—Maria's: "It wasn't fair to step on it and expect it to do nothing."

But no single word about his own predicament—its horror, danger, loneliness, and risk. No single syllable. Even the Hindus, the driver, and the man who carried the guns, were left unmentioned. Bananas were equally ignored. The tiger itself had passed into oblivion.

"Thanks most awfully," said Tim, politely, after an interval. "It must have been awful for you." It was said as spokesman for the other listeners. All were kind and grateful, but actual interest there was none. They took the pause to mean that the story was at an end; but they had not cared about it because they—did not believe it.

"Simply awful," the boy added, as though, perhaps, he had not made it quite clear that he wished to thank yet could not honestly praise. "Wasn't it, Judy?" And he jerked his head round towards his elder sister.

"Oh, *awful*—yes," agreed that lady.

But neither of them risked inviting the opinion of Maria. Her uncompromising nature was too well known for that. Nevertheless, unasked, she offered her criticism too: "Awful," she said, her podgy face unmoved, her blue eyes fixed upon the ceiling. And the whole room seemed to give a long, deep sigh.

Now, for the hero, this was decidedly an awkward moment; he had done his best and miserably failed. He was no story-teller, and they had found him out. None the less, however, he was a real hero. He faced the situation as a brave man should:

> For his tale was mediocre,
> And his face of yellow ochre
> Took a tinge of saffron sorrow in his fright;
> Yet he rose to the occasion,
> Without anger or evasion,
> And did his best to put the matter right.

"Tell me how you knew," he asked at length, facing the situation. "What made you guess?"

"Because, in the first place, you're not an atom *like* a tiger, anyhow," explained Judy.

"And you made the jungle so very dark," said Tim, "that you simply couldn't have seen the bananas falling."

"And we *know* you haven't got a tail at all," Maria added, clinchingly.

"Of course," he agreed; "your discernment does you credit, very great credit indeed. Few of the officials under me in India had as much."

Judy looked soothingly at him and stroked his sleeve. Somehow or other she divined, it seemed, he felt mortified and ashamed. He was a dear old thing, whatever happened.

"Never mind," she whispered, "it really doesn't matter. It was

Algernon Blackwood

very nice to hear about your tiger. Besides—it must hurt awfully, having a cold like this."

"I knew," put in Tim sympathetically, "the moment you began about the bananas falling. But I didn't say anything, because I knew it couldn't last—anything that began like that."

"But it got wonderful towards the end," insisted Judy.

"Till he was in the tree," objected her brother. "He never could really have got along a branch like that."

"No," agreed Judy, thoughtfully, "that *was* rather silly."

They continued discussing the story for some time as though its creator was elsewhere. He kept very still. Maria already slept in a soft and podgy ball on his lap....

"I am a lonely old thing," he said suddenly, with a long sigh, for in reality he was deeply disappointed at his failure, and had aspired to be their story-teller as well as playmate. Ordinary life bored him dreadfully. He had melancholy yearnings after youth and laughter. "Let's do something else now. What do you say to a turn of hide-and-seek? Eh?"

The miraculous Maria woke at this, yawned like a cat, and nearly rolled off on to the floor. "I dreamed of a real tiger," she informed every one. But no one was listening. Judy and Tim were prancing wildly.

"If your cold isn't *too* bad," cried Judy, "it would be lovely." No grown-up could have been more thoughtful of his welfare than she was.

"I'll hide," he said, "and in five minutes you come and find me." He went towards the door into the passage.

"Choose a warm place, and keep out of draughts," she cried after him. And he was gone. He nearly collided with a servant carrying a tray, but the servant, hearing his secret instructions, vanished again instantly in the direction of the kitchen. Five minutes later—an alleged five minutes—the children began their search. But they never found him. They hunted high and low, from attic to cellar, in gun-room, scullery, and pantry, even climbing up the ladder from the box-room to the roof, but without result. Colonel Stumper had disappeared. He was K.C.B.

"D'you think he's offended?" suggested Judy, as they met at length in the hall to consider the situation.

"Of course not," said Tim emphatically, "a man like that! He's written a book on Scouting!"

"I've finished," Maria mentioned briefly, and sat down.

On Judy's puzzled face there appeared an anxious expression then. His cold, she remembered, was very heavy. "I looked under every sofa and into every cupboard," she said, as though she feared he might have choked or suffocated. They stood in front of the fireplace and began to talk about other things. Their interest in the game was gone, they were tired of looking; but at the back of their minds was a secret annoyance, though at the same time a sense of great respect for the man who could conceal himself so utterly from sight. A touch of the marvellous was in it somehow.

"There's no good hiding like *that*," they felt indignantly. Still it was rather wonderful, after all. A man "like that" could do anything. He might even be up a chimney somewhere. He might be anywhere! They felt a little creepy....

"P'raps he *is* a sort of tiger thing," whispered some one ... and they were rather relieved when the drawing-room door opened and Mother appeared, knitting her scarlet muffler as she walked. The scene of scolding, explanation, and excuses that followed—for it was half an hour after bed-time—was cut short by Maria informing the company that she was "awfully tired," with a sigh that meant she would like to be carried up to bed. She was carried. The procession moved slowly, Tim and Judy bringing up the rear. But while Tim talked about a water-rat he meant to kill next day with an air-gun, Judy used her eyes assiduously, still hoping to discover Cousin William crumpled up in some incredible hiding-place. They told their mother nothing. The matter was private. It was between themselves and him. It would have to be cleared up on the morrow—if they remembered. On the upper landing, however, there was a curious sound. Maria, half asleep in the maternal arms, did not hear it, apparently, but the other two children exchanged sudden, recriminating glances. A door stood ajar, and light came through it from the room within. This curious sound came with it. It was a sneeze—a regular Nindian sneeze.

"We never thought of looking *there*," they said reproachfully. Come-Back Stumper had simply gone to bed.

CHAPTER V

THE BIRTH OF WONDER

Meanwhile their father alone grew neither older nor larger. His appearance did not change. They could not imagine that he would ever change. He still went up to London in the morning, he still came down again, he still continued to grind out stories which they thought wonderful, and he still, on occasions, said mysteriously, "A day will come," or its variants, "Some day," and "A day is coming." Yet, though he had Fancy, he had not Imagination. He did not satisfy them. For while Fancy may attend the birth of Wonder, Imagination alone accompanies her growth. Daddy was too full of stationery and sealing-wax in his daily work to have got very far.

Aunt Emily also still was there, explaining everything and saying No, shaking her head at them, or holding up a warning finger. Their outward life, indeed, showed little change, but it included one important novelty that affected all their present and all their subsequent existence, too. They made a new friend—their father's brother.

When first his visit was announced, they had their doubts about him—"your Uncle Felix" had a very questionable sound indeed, but the fact that he lived in Paris and was a writer of sea-stories and historical novels counterbalanced the handicap of the unpleasant "Felix." For to their ears Felix was not a proper sort of name at all; it was all right for a horse or a dog or even for a town, but for a man who was also a relation it was a positive disaster. It would not shorten for one thing, and for another it reminded them of "a king, or some one in a history book," and thus did not predispose them in his favour. It was simply what Tim called a "beastly name." Aunt Emily, however, was responsible for their biggest prejudice against him: "You must remember not to bother him, children; you must never disturb him when he's working." And as Uncle Felix was coming to stay for several weeks in the Mill House, they regarded him in advance as some kind of horrible excitement they must put up with.

However, as most things in life go by contraries, this Uncle Felix person turned out just the opposite. Within an hour of his arrival he was firmly established as friend and ally, yet so quickly and easily was this adjustment brought about that no one could say exactly how it happened. They themselves said nothing—just stood and stared at him; Daddy and Mother said the expected things, and Aunt Emily, critical and explanatory as usual, found it necessary to add: "You'll find it such a quiet house to work in, Felix, and the children will never interfere or get in your way." She was evidently proud of her relative and his famous books. "They'll be as good as gold—won't you, Judy?" by which name she referred to the trio as a whole.

Whereupon Judy smiled and nodded shyly, Tim bent down and scratched his stocking, and Maria, her face expressionless, merely stared at her aunt as though she—Emily, that is—were a piece of inanimate furniture.

"I see," said Uncle Felix carelessly, and glanced down at the trio.

That was all he said. But it was the way he said it that instantly explained his position. He looked at them and said, "I see"; no more than that—and it was done. They knew, he knew, Aunt Emily also knew. Two little careless words—and then continued to talk of Paris, the Channel crossing, and the weather.

"Didn't he squash her just!" remarked Tim, when they were alone together. "She expected him to thank her awfully and give her a kiss." And, accordingly, none of them were in the least surprised when he suddenly poked his head inside the door as they lay in bed and explained that he had just looked in to say good-night, and when he left them a moment later added gravely from the door: "Mind, you never disturb me, children; because, if you do—!" He shook a warning finger and was gone. He looked enormous in the doorway.

From that moment Uncle Felix became an important factor in their lives. The mysterious compact between them all was signed and sealed, yet none could say who drew it up and worded it. His duties became considerable. He almost took Daddy's place. The Study, indeed, at certain hours of the evening, became their recognised nesting place, and Daddy was as pleased as they themselves were. He seemed relieved. He rarely ground out epics now when his brain was tired and full of Government stationery and sealing-wax. Uncle Felix held the wizard's wand, and what he did with it was this: he raised the sense of wonder in them to a higher level. Daddy had awakened it, and fed it with specimens they could understand. But Uncle Felix poked it into yet greater activity by giving them something that no one could ever possibly understand! He stimulated it so that it worked in them spontaneously and of its own accord. He made it *grow*. And no amount of Aunt Emilies in the world could stop him.

Their father felt no jealousy. When the story-hour came round, he produced a set of sentences he kept slyly up his sleeve for the occasion. "Ask your Uncle Felix; he's better at stories and things than I am. It's his business." This was the model. A variation ran: "Oh, don't bother me just now, children. I've got a lot of figures to digest." But the shortest version was simply, "Run and plague your uncle. I'm too busy."

"Try Mother" was used when Uncle Felix was in hiding. Only it had no result. Mother's mind was too diffuse to carry conviction. It was soaked in servants and things. In another sense it was too exact. The ingredients of her stories were like a cooking recipe. Besides, hers was the unpardonable fault of never forgetting the time. On the very stroke of the clock she broke off abruptly with "Now it's bed-time; you shall hear the rest another night." Daddy forgot, or pleaded for "ten minutes more." Uncle Felix, however, said flatly, "They can't go till it's finished"—and he meant it. His voice was deep and gruff—"like a dog's," according to Maria—and his laugh was like a horse's neigh; it made the china rattle. He was "frightfully strong," too, stronger than Weeden, for he could take a child under each arm and another on his back—and run! He never smiled when he told his stories, and, though this made them seem extra real, it also alarmed deliciously—in the terrible places. Perched on his gigantic knees, they felt "like up the cedar," and when he stretched an arm or leg it was the great cedar branch swaying in the wind.

His manner, too, was stern to severity, and his voice was so deep sometimes that they could "feel it rumbling inside," as though he had "swallowed the dinner gong." He was a very important man somewhere; Daddy was just in the Stationery Office, but Uncle Felix was an author, and the very title necessarily included awe. He wrote "storical-novuls." His name was often in the newspapers. They connected him with the "Govunment." It had to do somewhere with the Police. No one trifled with Uncle Felix. Yet, strange to say, the children never could be properly afraid of him, although they tried very hard. Their audacity, their familiarity, their daring astonished everybody. The gardeners and coachmen, to say nothing of the indoor servants, treated him as though he was some awful emperor. But the children simply pushed him about. He might have been a friendly Newfoundland dog that wore tail-coats and walked on his hind legs, for all they feared reprisals.

He gave them a taste of his quality soon after his arrival.

"No, children, it's impossible now. I'm busy over a scene of my storicalnovul. Ask your father." He growled it at them, frowning darkly.

The parental heels had just that instant vanished round the door.

"Father's got the figures and says he can't."

"Or your mother—" he said, gruffly.

"Mother's doing servants in the housekeeper's room."

"Take your foot out of my waistcoat pocket this instant," he roared.

"Why?" enquired Maria. "How else can I climb up?"

He shook and swayed like the cedar branch, but he did not shake her off. "Because," he thundered, "there's money in it, and you've got holes in your stockings, and toes with you are worse than fingers."

And he strode across the floor, Tim clinging to one leg with both feet off the ground, and Judy pushing him behind as though he were a heavy door that wouldn't open. He was very angry indeed. He told them plainly what he thought about them. He explained the philosophy of authors to them in brutal sentences. "Leave me alone, you little botherations!" he cried. "I'm in the middle of a scene in a storicalnovul." It was disgraceful that a man could lose his temper so. "Leave me alone, or I'll ..."

In the corner of the big nursery sofa there was sudden silence. It was a chilly evening in early spring. Between the bars across the windows the wisteria leaves sifted the setting sunlight. The railway train lay motionless upon the speckled carpet. A cat, so fat it couldn't unroll, lay in a ball of mystery against the high guard of wire netting before the fire. Outside the wind went moaning.

And Time ran backwards, or else the clock stopped dead. Dusk slipped in between the window bars. The cedars on the lawn became gigantic. They heard the haystacks shuffling out of their tarpaulins. The whole house rose into the air and floated off. Mother, Daddy, Nurses, beds dropped from the windows as it sailed away. All were left behind, forgotten details of some stupid and uncomfortable life elsewhere.

"Quite ready," sighed the top of one cedar to the other.

"And waiting, too," an answer came from nowhere.

And then the Universe paused and settled with a little fluttering sound of wonder. The onceuponatime Moment entered the room....

"There was a thing that nobody could understand," began the deep, gruff voice. "And this thing that nobody could understand was something no one understood at all."

"That's twice they couldn't understand it," observed Judy, in the slight pause he made for effect.

"It was alive," he went on, "and very beautiful, so beautiful, in fact, that people were astonished and felt rather ashamed because they couldn't understand it. Some declared it wasn't worth understanding at all; others said it might be worth understanding if they had the time to think about it; and the rest decided that it was nothing much, and promptly forgot that it existed. Their lives grew rather dull in consequence. A few, however, set to work to discover what it was. For the beauty of it set something in them strangely burning."

"It was a firework, I think," remarked Maria, then felt she had said quite an awful thing. For Tim just looked at her. "It's alive, Uncle Felix told you," he stated. She was obliterated— for the moment.

"Yes," resumed the story-teller, "it was alive, and its beauty set the hearts of a few people on fire to know what it meant. It was difficult to find, however, and difficult to see properly when found.

"These people tried to copy it, and couldn't. Though it looked so simple it was impossible to imitate. It went about so quickly, too, that they couldn't catch hold of it and—"

"But have *you* seen it?" asked Judy, her head bobbing up into his face with eager curiosity.

It was a vital question. All waited anxiously for his reply.

"I have," he answered convincingly. "I saw it first when I was about your age, and I've never forgotten it."

"But you've seen it since, haven't you? It's still in the world, isn't it?"

"I've seen it since, and it's still in the world. Only no one knows to this day why it's there. No one can explain it. No one can understand it. It's so beautiful that it makes you wonder, and it's so mysterious that it makes you—"

"What?" asked Tim for the others, while he paused a moment and stared into their gazing faces.

"Wonder still more," he added.

Another pause followed.

"Then is your heart still burning, Uncle Felix?" Judy enquired, prodding him softly. "And does it matter much?"

"It matters a great deal, yes, because I want to find out, and cannot. And the burning goes on and on whenever I see the thing-that-nobody-can-understand, and even when I don't see it but just think about it—which is pretty often. Because, if I found out why it's there, I should know so much that I should give up writing storicalnovuls and become a sort of prophet instead."

They stared in great bewilderment. Their curiosity was immense. They were dying to know what the thing was, but it was against the Rules to ask outright.

"Were their lives *very* dull?"—Maria set this problem, suddenly recalling something at the beginning of the story.

"Oh, very dull indeed. They had no sense of wonder—those who forgot."

"How awful for them!"

"Awful," he agreed, in a long-drawn whisper, shuddering.

And that shudder ran through every one. The children turned towards the darkening room. The gloomy cupboard was a blotch of shadow. The table frowned. The bookshelves listened. The white face of the cuckoo clock peered down upon them dimly from the opposite wall, and the chairs, it seemed, moved up a little closer. But through the windows the stars were beginning to peep, and they saw the crests of the friendly cedars waving against the fading sky.

He pointed. High above the cedars, where the first stars twinkled, the blue was deep and exquisitely shaded from the golden streak below it into a colour almost purple.

"The thing that nobody could understand was even more wonderful than *that*," he whispered. "But no one could tell why it was there; no one could guess; no one could find out. And to this day—no one *can* find out."

His voice grew lower and lower and lower still.

"To-morrow I'll show it to you. You shall see it

for yourselves."

They hardly heard him now. The voice seemed far away. What could it be—this very, very wonderful thing?

"We'll go out and find one...by the stream ...where the willows bend...and shake their pointed leaves.... We'll go to-morrow...."

His voice died away inside his waistcoat. Not a sound was audible. The children were very close against him. In his big hands he took each face in turn and put his lips inside the rim of three small ears.

He told the secret then, while wonder filled the room and hovered exquisitely above the crowded chair....

Awakened by the silence, presently, the ball of black unrolled itself beside the wire fender, it stretched its four black legs. And the children, hushed, happy, and with a mysterious burning in their hearts, went off willingly to bed, to dream of wonder all night long, and to ask themselves in sleep, *"Why God has put blue dust upon the body of a dragon-fly?"*

CHAPTER VI

THE GROWTH OF WONDER

The story of the dragon-fly marked a turning-point in their lives; they realised that life was crammed with things that nobody could understand. Daddy's reign was over, and Uncle Felix had ascended the throne. Wonder—but a growing wonder—ruled the world. The great Stranger they had always been vaguely expecting had drawn nearer; it was not Uncle Felix, yet he seemed the forerunner somehow. That "Some Day" of Daddy's—they had almost forgotten its existence—became more and more a possibility. Life had two divisions now: Before Uncle Felix came—and Now. To Maria alone there seemed no interval. To her it was always Now. She had so much wonder in her that she *knew*.

Outwardly the household ran along as usual, but inwardly this enormous change was registered in three human hearts. The adventures they had before Uncle Felix came were the ordinary kind all children know; they invented them themselves. Their new adventures were of a different order—impossible but true. Their uncle had brought a key that opened heaven and earth.

He did not know that he had brought this key. It was just natural—he let himself in because it was his nature so to do; the others merely went in with him. He worked away in his room, covering reams of paper with nonsense out of his big head; and the trio never disturbed him or knocked at his door, or even looked for him: they knew that his real life ran with theirs, and the moment he had covered so many dozen sheets he would appear and join them. All people had their duties; his duty was to fill so many sheets a day for printers; but his important life belonged to them and they just lived it naturally together. He would never leave the Old Mill House. The funny thing was—whatever had he done with himself before he came there!

Everything he said and did lit up the common things of daily life with this strange, big wonder that was his great possession. Yet his method was simple and instinctive; he never thought things out; he just—knew.

And the effect of his presence upon the other Authorities was significant. Not that the Authorities admitted or even were aware of it, but that the children saw them differently. Aunt Emily, for instance, whom they used to dread, they now felt sorry for. She was so careful and particular that she was afraid of life, afraid of living. Prudence was slowly killing her. Everything must be done in a certain way that made it safe; only, by the time it was safe it was no longer interesting. They saw clearly how she missed everything owing to the excessive caution and preparation in her: by the time she was ready, the thing had simply left. Instead of coming into the hayfield at once and enjoying it, she uttered so many warnings and gave so much advice against disaster—"better take this," and "better not take that"—that by the time they got there the hayfield had lost all its wonder. It was just a damp, untidy hayfield.

Daddy, however, gained in glory. He approved of his big brother. On his return from London every evening the first thing he asked was, "What have you all been up to to-day? Has Uncle Felix given you the moon or rolled the sun and stars into a coloured ball?" Weeden, too, had grown in mystery—he made the garden live, and understood the secret life of every growing thing; while Thompson and Mrs. Horton, each in their separate ways, led lives of strange activity in the lower regions of the house till the kitchen seemed the palace of an ogress and the pantry was its haunted vestibule. "Mrs.

Horton's kitchen" was a phrase as powerful as "Open Sesame"; and "the butler's pantry" edged the world of mighty dream.

Above all, Mother occupied a new relationship towards them that made her twice as splendid as before. Until Uncle Felix came, she was simply "Mother," who loved them whatever they did and made allowances for everything. That was her duty, and unless they provided her with something to make allowances for they had failed in what was expected of them. Her absorption in servants and ordering of meals, in choosing their clothes and warning Jackman about their boots—all this was a chief reason for her existence, and if they didn't eat too much sometimes and wear their boots out and tear their clothes, Mother would have been without her normal occupation. Whereas now they saw her in another light, touched with the wonder of the sun and stars. It was proper, of course, for her to have children, but they realised now that she contrived to make the whole world work somehow for their benefit. Mother not only managed the entire Household, from the dinner-ordering slate at breakfast-time to the secret whisperings with Jackman behind the screen at bedtime, or the long private interviews with Daddy in his study after tea: she led a magnificent and stupendous life that regulated every smallest detail of their happiness. She was for ever thinking of them and slaving for their welfare. The wonder of her enormous love stole into their discerning hearts. They loved her frightfully, and told her all sorts of little things that before they had kept concealed. There were heaps and heaps of mothers in the world, of course; they were knocking about all over the place; but there was only one single Mother, and that was theirs.

Yet, in his own peculiar way, it was Uncle Felix who came first. Daddy believed in a lot of things; Mother believed in many things; Aunt Emily believed in certain things done at certain times and in a certain way. But Uncle Felix believed in everything, everywhere and always. To him nothing was ever impossible. He held, that is, their own eternal creed. He was akin to Maria, moreover, and Maria, though silent, was his spokesman often.

"Why *does* a butterfly fly so dodgy?" inquired Tim, having vainly tried to catch a Painted Lady on the lawn.

Daddy made a grimace and shrugged his shoulders, yet left the insect quite as wonderful as it was before. Mother looked up from her knitting with a gentle smile and said, "Does it, darling? I hadn't noticed." Aunt Emily, balancing her parasol to keep the sun away, observed in an educational tone of voice, "My dear Tim, what foolish questions you ask! It's because its wings are so large compared to the rest of its body. It can't help itself, you see." She belittled the insect and took away its wonder. She explained.

Tim, unsatisfied, moved over to the wicker chair where Uncle Felix sat drowsily smoking his big meerschaum pipe. He pointed to the vanishing Painted Lady and repeated his question in a lower voice, so that the others could not hear:

"Why does it fly like that—all dodgy?" Whatever happened, the boy knew his Uncle would leave the butterfly twice as wonderful as he found it.

But no immediate answer came. They watched it for a moment together in silence. It behaved in the amazing way peculiar to its kind. Nothing in the world flies like a butterfly. Birds and other things fly straight, or sweep in curves, or rise and drop in understandable straight lines. But the Painted Lady obeyed no such rules. It dodged and darted, it jerked and shot, it was everywhere and anywhere, least of all where it ought to have been. The swallows always missed it. It simply doubled—and disappeared round the corner of the building.

Then, puffing at his pipe, Uncle Felix looked at Tim and said, "I couldn't tell you. It's one of the things nobody can understand, I think."

"Yes," agreed Tim, "it must be."

Algernon Blackwood

There was a considerable pause.

"But there must be some way of finding out," the boy said presently. He had been thinking over it.

"There is." The man rose slowly from his chair.

"What is it?" came the eager question.

"Try it ourselves, and see if we can do the same!"

And they went off instantly, hand in hand, and vanished round the corner of the building.

The adventures they had since Uncle Felix came were of this impossible and marvellous order. That strange and lovely cry, "There's some one coming," ran through the listening world. "I believe there is," said Uncle Felix. "Some day he'll come and a tremendous thing will happen," was another form of it, to which the answer was, "I know it will."

It was much nearer to them than before. It was just below the edge of the world, the edge of life. It was in the air. Any morning they might wake and find the great thing was there— arrived in the night while they were sound asleep. So many things gave hints. A book *might* tell of it between the lines; each time a new book was opened a thrill slipped out from the pages in advance. Yet no book they knew had ever told it really. Out of doors, indeed, was the more likely place to expect it. The tinkling stream either ran towards it, or else came from it; that was its secret, the secret it was always singing about day and night. But it was impossible to find the end or beginning of any stream. Wind, moreover, announced it too, for wind didn't tear about and roar like that for nothing. Spring, however, with its immense hope and expectation, gave the clearest promise of all. In winter it hid inside something, or at least went further away; yet even in winter the marvellous something or some one lay waiting underneath the snow, behind the fog, above the clouds. One day, some day, next day, or the day after to-morrow—and it would suddenly be there beside them.

Whence came this great Expectancy they never questioned, nor what it was exactly, nor who had planted it. This was a mystery, one of the things that no one can understand. They felt it: that was all they knew. It was more than Wonder, for Wonder was merely the sign and proof that they were seeking. It was faint and exquisite in them, like some far, sweet memory they could never quite account for, nor wholly, even once, recapture. They remembered almost—almost before they were born.

"We'll have a look now," Uncle Felix would say every walk they took; but before they got very far it was always time to come in again. "That's the bother of everything," he agreed with them. "Time always prevents, doesn't it? If only we could make it stop—get behind time, as it were—we might have a chance. Some day, perhaps, we shall."

He left the matter there, but they never forgot that pregnant remark about stopping time and getting in behind it. No, they never forgot about it. At Christmas, Easter, and the like, it came so near that they could almost smell it, but when these wonderful times were past they looked back and knew it had not really come. The holidays cheated them in a similar way. Yet, when it came, they knew it would be as natural and simple as eating honey, though at the same time with immense surprise in it. And all agreed that it was somehow connected with the Dawn, for the Dawn, the opening of a new day, was something they had heard about but never witnessed. Dawn must be exceedingly wonderful, because, while it happened daily, none of them had ever seen it happen. A hundred times they had agreed to wake and have a look, but the Dawn had always been too quick and quiet. It slipped in ahead of them each time. They had never seen the sun come up.

In some such sudden, yet quite natural way, this stupendous thing they expected would come up. It would suddenly be there. Everybody, moreover, expected it. Grown-ups pretended they didn't, but they did. Catch a grown-up when he wasn't looking, and he *was* looking. He didn't like to be caught, that's all, for as often as not he was smiling to himself, or just going to—cry.

They shared, in other words, the great, common yearning of the world; only they knew they yearned, whereas the rest of the world forgets.

"I think," announced Judy one day—then stopped, as though unsure of herself.

"Yes?" said her Uncle encouragingly.

"I think," she went on, "that the Night-Wind knows an awful lot, if only—" she stopped again.

"If only," he helped her.

"We," she continued.

"Could," he added.

"Catch it!" she finished with a gasp, then stared at him expectantly.

And his answer formed the subject of conversation for fully half an hour in the bedroom later, and for a considerable time after Jackman had tucked them up and taken the candle away. They watched the shadows run across the ceiling as she went along the passage outside; they heard her steps go carefully downstairs; they waited till she had safely disappeared, for the door was ajar, and they could hear her rumbling down into the lower regions of Mrs. Horton's kitchen—and then they sat up in bed, hugged their knees, shuddered with excitement, and resumed the conversation exactly where it had been stopped.

For Uncle Felix had given a marvellous double-barrelled

answer. He had said, "We can." And then he had distinctly added, "We will!"

CHAPTER VII

IMAGINATION WAKES

For the Night-Wind already had a definite position in the mythology of the Old Mill House, and since Uncle Felix had taken to reading aloud certain fancy bits from the storicalnovul he was writing at the moment, it had acquired a new importance in their minds.

These fancy bits were generally scenes of action in which the Night-Wind either dropped or rose unexpectedly. He used the children as a standard. "Thank you very much, Uncle," meant failure, the imagination was not touched; but questions were an indication of success, the audience wanted further details. For he knew it was the child in his audience that enjoyed such scenes, and if Tim and Judy felt no interest, neither would Mr. and Mrs. William Smith of Peckham. To squeeze a question out of Maria raised hopes of a second edition!

A Duke, disguised as a woman or priest, landing at night; a dark man stealing documents from a tapestried chamber of some castle, where bats and cobwebs shared the draughty corridors—such scenes were incomplete unless a Night-Wind came in audibly at critical moments. It wailed, moaned, whistled, cried, sang, sighed, soughed or—sobbed. Keyholes and chimneys were its favourite places, but trees and rafters knew it too. The sea, of course, also played a large part in these adventures, for water above all was the element Uncle Felix loved and understood, but this Night-Wind, being born at sea, was also of distinct importance. The sea was terrible, the wind was sad.

To the children it grew more and more distinct with each appearance. It had a personality, and led a curious and wild existence. It had privileges and prerogatives. Owing to its various means of vocal expression—singing, moaning, and the rest—a face belonged to it with lips and mouth; teeth too, since it whistled. It ran about the world, and so had feet; it flew, so wings pertained to it; it blew, and that meant cheeks of sorts. It was a large, swift, shadowy being whose ways were not the ordinary ways of daylight. It struck blows. It had gigantic hands. Moreover, it came out only after dark—an ominous and suspicious characteristic rather.

"Why isn't there a day-wind too?" inquired Judy thoughtfully.

"There is, but it's *quite* a different thing," Uncle Felix answered. "You might as well ask why midday and midnight aren't the same because they both come at twelve o'clock. They're simply different things."

"Of course," Tim helped him unexpectedly; "and a man can't be a woman, can it?"

The Night-Wind's nature, accordingly, remained a mystery rather, and its sex was also undetermined. Whether it saw with eyes, or just felt its way about like a blind thing, wandering, was another secret matter undetermined. Each child visualised it differently. Its hiding-place in the daytime was equally unknown. Owls, bats, and burglars guessed its habits best, and that it came out of a hole in the sky was, perhaps, the only detail all unanimously agreed upon. It was a pathetic being rather.

This Night-Wind used to come crying round the bedroom windows sometimes, and the children liked it, although they did not understand all its melancholy beauty. They heard the different voices in it, although they did not catch the meaning of the words it sang. They heard its footsteps too. Its way of moving awed them. Moreover, it was for ever trying to get in.

"It's wings," said Judy, "big, dark wings, very soft and feathery."

"It's a woman with sad, black eyes," thought Tim, "that's how I like it."

"It's some one," declared Maria, who was asleep before it came, so rarely heard it at all. And they turned to Uncle Felix who knew all that sort of thing, or at any rate could describe it. He found the words. They lay hidden in his thick back hair apparently—there was little on the top!—for he always scratched his head a good deal when they asked him questions about such difficult matters. "What is it *really*—the Night-Wind?" they asked gravely; "and why does it sound so *very* different from the wind in the morning or the afternoon?"

"There *is* a difference," he replied carefully. "It's a quick, dark, rushing thing, and it moves like—like anything."

"We know *that*," they told him.

"And it has long hair," he added hurriedly, looking into Tim's staring eyes. "That's what makes it swish. The swishing, rushing, hushing sound it makes—that's its hair against the walls and tiles, you see."

"It *is* a woman, then?" said Tim proudly. All looked up, wondering. An extraordinary thing was in the air. A mystery that had puzzled them for ages was about to be explained. They drew closer round the sofa, and Maria blundered against the table, knocking some books off with a resounding noise. It was their way of reminding him that he had promised. "Hush, hush!" said Uncle Felix, holding up a finger and glancing over his shoulder into the darkened room. "It may be coming now... Listen!"

"Yes, but it is a woman, isn't it?" insisted Tim, in a hurried whisper. He had to justify himself before his sisters. Uncle Felix must see to that first.

The big man opened his eyes very wide. He shuddered. "It's a—Thing," was the answer, given in a whisper that increased the excitement of anticipation. "It certainly is a—Thing! Now hush! It's coming!"

They listened then intently. And a sound *was* heard. Out of the starry summer night it came, quite softly, and from very far away—upon discovery bent, upon adventure. Reconnoitering, as from some deep ambush in the shrubberies where the blackbirds hid and whistled, it flew down against the house, stared in at the nursery windows, fluttered up and down the glass with a marvellous, sweet humming—and was gone again.

"Listen!" the man's voice whispered; "it will come back presently. It saw us. It's awfully shy—"

"Why is it awfully shy?" asked Judy in an undertone.

"Because people make it mean so much more than it means to mean," he replied darkly. "It never gets a chance to be just itself and play its own lonely game—"

"We've called it things," she stated.

"But we haven't written books about it and put it into poetry," Uncle Felix corrected her with an audacity that silenced them. "We play our game; it plays its."

"It plays its," repeated Tim, amused by the sound of the words.

"And that's why it's shy," the man held them to the main point, "and dislikes showing itself—"

"But why is its game lonely?" some one asked, and there was a

Algernon Blackwood

general feeling that Uncle Felix had been caught this time without an answer. For what explanation could there possibly be of that? Their faces were half triumphant, half disappointed already.

He smiled quietly. He knew everything—everything in the world. "It's unhappy as well as shy," he sighed, "because nothing will play with it. Everything is asleep at night. It comes out just when other things are going in. Trees answer it, but they answer in their sleep. Birds, tucked away in nests and hiding-places, don't even answer at all. The butterflies are gone, the insects lost. Leaves and twigs don't care about being blown when there's no one there to see them. They hide too. If there are clouds, they're dark and sulky, keeping their jolly sides towards the stars and moon. Nothing will play with the Night-Wind. So it either plays with the tiles on the roof and the telegraph wires—dead things that make a lot of noise, but never leave their places for a proper game—or else just—plays with itself. Since the beginning of the world the Night-Wind has been shy and lonely and unhappy."

It was unanswerable. They understood. Their sense of pity was greatly touched, their love as well.

"Do pigs really see the wind, as Daddy says?" inquired Maria abruptly, feeling the conversation beyond her. She merely obeyed the laws of her nature. But no one answered her; no one even heard the question. Another sound absorbed their interest and attention. There was a low, faint tapping on the window-pane. A hush, like church, fell upon everybody.

And Uncle Felix stood up to his full height suddenly, and opened his arms wide. He drew a long, deep breath.

"Come in," he said splendidly.

The tapping, however, grew fainter and fainter, till it finally ceased. Everybody waited expectantly, but it was not repeated. Nothing happened. Nobody came in. The tapper had retreated.

"It was a twig," whispered Judy, after a pause. "The Virgin Creeper—"

"But it was the wind that shook it," exclaimed Uncle Felix, still standing and waiting as though he expected something. "The Night-Wind—Look out!"

A roaring sound over the roof drowned his words; it rose and fell like laughter, then like crying. It dropped closer, rushed headlong past the window, rattled and shook the sash, then dived away into the darkness. Its violence startled them. A deep lull followed instantly, and the little tapping of the twig was heard again. Odd! Just when the Night-Wind seemed furthest off it was all the time quite near. It had not really gone at all; it was hiding against the outside walls. It was watching them, trying to get in. The tapping continued for half a minute or more—a series of hurried, gentle little knocks as from a child's smallest finger-tip.

"It wants to come in. It's trying," whispered some one.

"It's awfully shy."

"It's lonely and frightfully unhappy."

"It likes us and wants to play."

There was another pause and silence. No one knew quite what to do. "There's too much light. Let's put the lamp out," said a genius, using the voice of Judy.

As though by way of answer there followed instantly a sudden burst of wind. The torrent of it drove against the house; it boomed down the chimney, puffing an odour of soot into the room; it shook the door into the passage; it lifted an edge of carpet, flapping it. It shouted, whistled, sang, using a dozen different voices all at once. The roar fell into syllables. It was amazing. A great throat uttered words. They could scarcely believe their ears.

The wind was shouting with a joyful, boisterous shout: "Open the window! *I'll* put out the light!"

All heard the wonderful thing. Yet it seemed quite natural in a way. Uncle Felix, still standing and waiting as though he knew not exactly what was going to happen, moved forward at once and boldly opened the window's lower sash. In swept the mighty visitor, the stranger from the air. The lamp gave one quick flicker and went out. Deep stillness followed. There was a silence like the moon.

The shy Night-Wind had come into the room.

Ah, there was awe and wonder then! The silence was so unexpected. The whole wind, not merely part of it, was in. It had come so gently, softly, delicately too! In the darkness the outline of the window-frame was visible; Uncle Felix's big figure blocked against the stars. Judy's head could be seen in silhouette against the other window, but Tim and Maria, being smaller, were merged in the pool of shadow below the level of the sill. A large, spread thing passed flutteringly up and down the room a moment, then came the rest. It settled over everything at once. A rustle was audible as of trailing, floating hair.

"It's hiding in the corners and behind the furniture," whispered Uncle Felix; "keep quiet. If you frighten it— whew!"—he whistled softly—"it'll be off above the tree-tops in a second!"

A low soft whistle answered to his own; somewhere in the room it sounded; there was no mistaking it, though the exact direction was difficult to tell, for while Tim said it was through the keyhole, Judy declared positively that it came from the door of the big, broken cupboard opposite. Maria stated flatly, "Chimney."

"Hush! It's talking." It was Uncle Felix's voice breathing very low. "It likes us. It feels we're friendly."

A murmur as of leaves was audible, or as of a pine bough sighing in a breeze. Yet there were words as well—actual spoken words:

"Don't look for me, please," they heard. "I do not want to be seen. But you may touch me. I like that."

The children spread their hands out in the darkness, groping, searching, feeling.

"Ah, your touch!" the sighing voice continued.

"It's like my softest lawn. Your hair feels as my grass feels on the hill-tops, and the skin of your cheeks is smooth and cool as the water-surface of my lily ponds at midnight. I know you" —it raised its tones to singing. "You are children. I kiss you all!"

"I feel you," Judy said in her clear, quiet voice. "But you're cold."

"Not really," was the answer that seemed all over the room at once. "That's only the touch of space. I've come from very high up to-night. There's been a change. The lower wind was called away suddenly to the sea, and I dropped down with hardly a moment's warning to take its place. The sun has been very tiresome all day—overheating the currents."

"Uncle, *you* ask it everything," whispered Tim, "simply everything!"

"Say how we love it, please," sighed Judy. "I feel it closing both my eyes."

"It's over all my face," put in Maria, drawing her breath in loudly.

Algernon Blackwood

"But my hair's lifting!" Judy exclaimed. "Oh, it's lovely, lovely!"

Uncle Felix straightened himself up in the darkness. They could hear him breathing with the effort. "Please tell us what you do," he said. "We all can feel you touching us. Play with us as you play with trees and clouds and sleeping flowers along the hedgerows."

A singing, whistling sound passed softly round the room; there was a whirr and a flutter as when a flight of bees or birds goes down the sky, and a voice, a plaintive yet happy voice, like the plover who cry to each other on the moors, was audible:

"I run about the world at night,
Yet cannot see;
My hair has grown so thick these millions years,
It covers me.
So, like a big, blind thing
I run about,
And know all things by touching them.
I touch them with my wings;
I know each one of you
By touching you;
I touch your *hearts*!"

"I feel you!" cried Judy. "I feel you touching me!"

"And I, and I!" the others cried. "It's simply wonderful!"

An enormous sigh of happiness went through that darkened room.

"Then play with me!" they heard. "Oh, children, play with me!"

The wild, high sweetness in the windy voice was irresistible. The children rose with one accord. It was too dark to see, but they flew about the room without a fault or slip. There was no stumbling; they seemed guided, lifted, swept. The sound of happy, laughing voices filled the air. They caught the Wind, and let it go again; they chased it round the table and the sofa; they held it in their arms until it panted with delight, half smothered into silence, then marvellously escaping from them on the elastic, flying feet that tread on forests, clouds, and mountain tops. It rushed and darted, drove them, struck them lightly, pushed them suddenly from behind, then met their faces with a puff and shout of glee. It caught their feet; it blew their eyelids down. Just when they cried, "It's caught! I've got it in my hands!" it shot laughing up against the ceiling, boomed down the chimney, or whistled shrilly as it escaped beneath the crack of the door into the passage. The keyhole was its easiest escape. It grew boisterous, singing with delight, yet was never for a moment rough. It cushioned all its blows with feathers.

"Where are you now? I felt your hair all over me. You've gone again!" It was Judy's voice as she tore across the floor.

"You're whacking me on the head!" cried Tim. "Quick, quick! I've got you in my hands!" He flew headlong over the sofa where Maria sat clutching the bolster to prevent being blown on to the carpet.

They felt its soft, gigantic hands all over them; its silky coils of hair entangled every movement; they heard its wings, its rushing, sighing voice, its velvet feet. The room was in a whirr and uproar.

"Uncle! Can't *you* help? You're the biggest!"

"But it's blown me inside out," he answered, in a curiously muffled voice. "My fingers are blown off. It's taken all my breath away."

The pictures rattled on the wall; loose bits of paper fluttered everywhere; the curtains flapped out horizontally into the air.

"Catch it! Hold it! Stop it!" cried the breathless voices.

"Join hands," he gasped. "We'll try." And, holding hands, they raced across the floor. They managed to encircle something with their spread arms and legs. Into the corner by the door they forced a great, loose, flowing thing against the wall. Wedged tight together like a fence, they stooped. They pounced upon it.

"Caught!" shouted Tim. "We've got you!"

There was a laughing whistle in the keyhole just behind them. It was gone.

The window shook. They heard the wild, high laughter. It was out of the room. The next minute it passed shouting above the cedar tops and up into the open sky. And their own laughter went out to follow it across the night.

The room became suddenly very still again. Some one had closed the window. The twig no longer tapped. The game was over. Uncle Felix collected them, an exhausted crew, upon the sofa by his side.

"It was very wonderful," he whispered. "We've done what no one has ever done before. We've played with the Night-Wind, and the Night-Wind's played with us. It feels happier now. It will always be our friend."

"It was awfully strong," said Tim in a tone of awe. "It fairly banged me."

"But awfully gentle," Judy sighed. "It kissed me hundreds of times."

"I felt it," announced Maria.

"It's only a child, really," Uncle Felix added, half to himself, "a great wild child that plays with itself in space—"

He went on murmuring for several minutes, but the children hardly heard the words he used. They had their own sensations. For the wind had touched their hearts and made them think. They heard it singing now above the cedars as they had never heard it sing before. It was alive and lovely, it meant a new thing to them. For they had their little aching sorrows too; it had taken them all away: they had their little passionate yearnings and desires; it had prophesied fulfilment. The dreamy melancholy of childhood, the long, long days, the haunted nights, the everlasting afternoons—all these were in its wild, great, windy voice, the sighing, the mystery, the laughter too. The joy of strange fulfilment woke in their wind-kissed hearts. The Night-Wind was their friend; they had played with it. Now everything could come true.

And next day Maria, lost to the Authorities for over an hour, was at length discovered by the forbidden pigsties in a fearful state of mess, but very pleased and happy about something. She was watching the pigs with eyes brimful of questioning wonder and excitement. She was listening intently too. She wanted to find out for certain whether pigs really—really and truly—saw—anything unusual!

CHAPTER VIII

WHERE WONDER HIDES

The children had never been to London, but they knew the direction in which it lay—beyond the crumbling kitchen-garden wall, where the wall-flowers grew in a proud colony. The sky looked different there, a threatening quality in it. Both snow and thunderstorm came that way, and the dirty sign-post "London Road" outside the lodge-gates was tilted into the air significantly.

They regarded London as a terrible place, though a necessity: Daddy's office was there; Christmas and Birthday presents came from London, but also it was where the Radical govunment lived—an enormous, evil, octopus kind of thing that made Daddy poor. Weeden, too, had been known to say dark things with regard to selling vegetables, hay, and stuff. "What can yer igspect when a Radical govunment's in?" And the fact that neither he nor Daddy did anything to move it away proved what a powerful thing it was, and made them feel something hostile to their happiness dwelt London-way beyond that crumbling wall.

The composite picture grew steadily in their little minds. When ominous clouds piled up on that northern horizon, floating imperceptibly towards them, it was a fragment of London that had broken off and come rolling along to hover above the old Mill House. A very black cloud was the Seat of Govunment.

London itself, however, remained as obstinately remote as Heaven, yet the two visibly connected; for while the massed vapours were part of London, the lanes and holes of blue were certainly the vestibule of Heaven. "His seat is in the Heavens" must mean something, they argued. They were quite sweetly reverent about it. They merely obeyed the symbolism of primitive age.

"I shall go to Heaven," Tim said once, when they discussed dying as if it were a game. He wished to define his position, as it were.

"But you haven't been to London yet," came the higher criticism from Judy. "London's a metropolis."

Metropolis! It was an awful thing to say, though no one quite knew why. Part of their dread was traceable to this word. Ever since some one had called it "the metropolis" in their hearing, they had associated vague awe with the place. The ending "opolis" sounded to them like something that might come "ontopofus"—and that, again, brought "octopus" into the mind. It seemed reckless to mention London and Heaven together—yet was right and proper at the same time. Both must one day be seen and known, one inevitably as the other. Thus heavenly rights were included in their minds with a ticket to London, far, far away, when they were much, much older. And both trips were dreaded yet looked forward to.

Maria, however, held no great opinion of either locality. She disliked the idea of long journeys to begin with. Having no objection to moving her eyes, she was opposed to moving her body—unless towards an approved certainty. Puddings, bonfires, and laps at story-time were approved certainties; Heaven and London apparently were not. She was contented where she was. "London's a bother," was her opinion: it meant a rush in the hall when the dog-cart was waiting for the train and Daddy was too late to hear about bringing back a new blue eye for a broken doll. And as for the other place—her ultimatum was hardly couched in diplomatic language, to say

Algernon Blackwood

the least. An eternal Sunday was not her ideal of happiness. Aunt Emily, it was stated, would live in Heaven when she died, and the place had lost its attractiveness in consequence. For Aunt Emily used long words and heard their "Sunday Colics," and the clothes she wore on that seventh workless day reminded them of village funerals or unhappy women who came to see over the house when it was to be let, and asked mysterious questions about something called "the drains." Daddy's top-hat with a black band was another item in the Sunday and Metropolis picture. London and Heaven, as stated, were not looked forward to unreservedly.

There were compensations, though. They knew the joy of deciding who would go there. Stumper, of course, for one: it was the only place he would not come back from: he would be K.C.B. Uncle Felix, too, because it was his original source of origin. Mother repeatedly called him "angel," and even if she hadn't, it was clear he knew all about both places by the way he talked. Stumper's India was not quite believed in owing to the way he described it, but Uncle Felix's London was real and living, while the other marvellous things he told them could only have happened in some kind of heavenly place. His position, therefore, was unshakable, and Mother and Daddy also had immemorial rights. Others of their circle, however, found themselves somewhat equivocally situated. Thompson and Mrs. Horton were uncertain, for since there was "no marriage" there, there could be no families to wait upon and cook for. Weeden, also, was doubtful. Having never been to London, the alternative happiness was not properly within his grasp, whereas the Postman might be transferred from the metropolis to the stars at any minute of the day or night. Those London letters he brought settled his case beyond all argument whatever.

All of which needs mention because there was a place called the End of the World, and the title has of course to do with it. For the End of the World is the hiding-place of Wonder.

Beyond that crumbling kitchen-garden wall was a very

delightful bit of the universe. A battered grey fence kept out the road, but there were slits between the boards through which the Passers-by could be secretly observed. All Passers-by were criminals or heroes on their way to mysterious engagements; the majority were disguised; many of them could be heard talking darkly to themselves. They were a queer lot, those Passers-by. Those who came *from* London were escaping, but those going north were intent upon awful business in the sinister metropolis—explosions, murders, enormous jewel robberies, and conspiracies against the Radicalgovunment. The solitary policeman who passed occasionally was in constant terror of his life. They longed to warn him. Yet he had his other side as well—his questionable side.

This neglected patch of kitchen-garden, however, possessed other claims to charm as well as the tattered fence. It was uncultivated. Some rows of tangled currant bushes offered excellent cover; there was a fallen elm tree whose trunk was "home"; a pile of rubbish that included scrap-iron, old wheel-barrows, broken ladders, spades, and wire-netting, and, chief of all, there was the spot behind the currant bushes where Weeden, the Gardener, burnt dead leaves. It was sad, but mysterious and beautiful too, this burning of the leaves; though, according to Uncle Felix, who gave the Gardener's explanation, it was right and necessary. They loved the smoke, too, hanging in the air above the lawn, with its fragrant smell and shadowy distances:

"Oh, Gardener! How can you let them burn?" "Because," he explained, "they've 'ad their turn, And nobody wants their shade.

> These withered-up messes
> Is worn-out old dresses
> I tuck round the boots
> Of the shiverin' roots
> Till the Spring makes 'em over
> Like roses and clover—
> But nobody wants dead leaves, dead leaves,

Algernon Blackwood

Nor nobody wants their shade!"

A deserted corner, yet crowded gloriously with life. Adventure lurked in every inch. There was danger, too, terror, wonder, and excitement. And since for them it was the beginning of all things, they called it, naturally, The End of the World. To escape to the End of the World, unaccompanied by grown-ups, and, if possible, their whereabouts unknown to anybody, was a daily duty second to no other. It was a duty, wet or fine, they seldom left, neglected.

Besides themselves, two others alone held passes to this sanctuary: Uncle Felix, because he loved to go there (he wrote his adventure stories there, saying anything might happen in such a lonely place), and the Gardener, because he was obliged to. Come-Back Stumper was excluded. They had taken him once, and he had said such an abominable thing that he was never allowed to visit it again. "A messy hole," he called it. Mr. Jinks had never even seen it, but, after his death in the railway accident, his remains, recovered without charge from the Hospital, had been buried somewhere in the scrap-heap. From this point of view alone he knew the End of the World; he was worthy of no other. His epitaph was appalling—too horrible to mention really. Tim composed it, but Uncle Felix distinctly said that it never, *never* must be referred to audibly again:

Here Matthew Jinks
Just lies and st—

"It's *not* nice," he said emphatically, "and you mustn't say it. Always speak well of the dead." And, as they couldn't honestly do that, they obeyed him and left Mr. Jinks in his unhonoured grave, with a broken wheel-barrow for a headstone and a mass of wire-netting to make resurrection difficult. In order to get the disagreeable epitaph out of their minds Uncle Felix substituted a kinder and gentler one, and made them learn it by heart:

Old Jinks lies here

Without a tear;
He meant no wrong,
But we didn't get along;
So Jinks lies here,
And we've nothing more to fear.
He's all right:
Jinks
Sinks
Out of sight!

It was the proud colony of wallflowers that first made Uncle Felix like the place. Their loveliness fluttered in the winds, and their perfume stole down deliciously above the rubbish and neglect. They seemed to him the soul of ruins triumphing over outward destruction. Hence the delicate melancholy in their scent and hence their lofty chosen perch. Out of decay they grew, yet invariably above it. Both sun and stars were in their flaming colouring, and their boldness was true courage. They caught the wind, they held the sunset and the dawn; they turned the air into a shining garden. They stood somehow for a yearning beauty in his own heart that expressed itself in his stories.

"If you pick them," he warned Tim, who climbed like a monkey, and was as destructive as his age, "the place will lose its charm. They grow for the End of the World, and the End of the World belongs to them. This wonderful spot will have no beauty when they're gone." To wear a blossom in the hair or buttonhole was to be protected against decay and ugliness.

Most wonderful of all, however, was the door in the old grey fence; for it was a Gateway, and a Gateway, according to Uncle Felix, was a solemn thing. None knew where it led to, it was a threshold into an unknown world. Ordinary doors, doors in a house, for instance, were not Gateways; they merely opened into rooms and other familiar places. Dentists, governesses, and bedrooms existed behind ordinary, indoor doors; but out-of-doors opened straight into the sky, and in virtue of it were extraordinary. They were Gateways. At the End of the World stood a stupendous, towering door that was a Gateway. Another, even more majestic, rose at the end of life. This door in the grey fence was a solemn, mysterious, and enticing Gateway—into everything worth seeing.

It was invariably kept locked; it led into the high-road that slithered along secretly and sedulously—to London. For the children it was out of bounds. Here the Policeman lived in constant terror of his life, and here went to and fro the strange world of Passers-by. The white road flowed past like a river. It moved. From the lower branches of the horse-chestnut tree they could just see it slide; also when the swing went extra high, and from the end of the prostrate elm. It went in both directions at once. It encircled the globe, going under the sea too. The door leading into it was a quay or port. But the brass knob never turned; the Gardener said there was no key; and from the outer side the handle had long since been removed, lest Passers-by might see it and come in. Even the keyhole had been carefully stuffed up with that stringy stuff the Gardener carried in his pockets.

Till, finally, something happened that made the End of the World seem suddenly a new place. Tim noticed that the stringy stuff had been removed.

The day had been oppressively hot, and tempers had been sorely tried. Mother had gone to lie down with a headache; Aunt Emily was visiting the poor with a basket; Daddy was inaccessible in his study; all Authorities were doing the dull things Authorities have to do. It was September, and the world stood lost in this golden haze of unexpected heat. Very still it stood, the yellow leaves quite motionless and the smoke from the kitchen chimney hanging stiff and upright in the air. There was no breath of wind.

"There's simply *nothing* to do," the children said—when suddenly Uncle Felix arrived, and their listlessness was turned to life and interest. He had gone up in the morning to London, and the suddenness of his return was part of his prerogative. Stumper, Jinks, and other folk were announced days and days beforehand, but Uncle Felix just—came.

"We'll go to the End of the World," he decided gravely, the moment he had changed. "There's something going on there. Quick!" This meant, as all knew, that he had an idea. They stole out, and no one saw them go. Across the lawn and past the lime trees humming busily with tired bees, they crept beneath the shadow of the big horse-chestnut, where the staring windows of the house could no longer see them. They disappeared. The Authorities might look and call for ever without finding them.

"Slower, please, a little," said Maria breathlessly, and was at once picked up and carried. Moving cautiously through the laurel shrubbery, they left the garden proper with its lawns and flower-beds, and entered the forbidden region at the End of the World. They stood upright. Uncle Felix dropped Maria like a bundle.

"Look!" he said below his breath. "I told you so!"

He pointed. The colony of wallflowers were fluttering in the windless air. Nothing stirred but these. The stillness was unbroken. Sunshine blazed on the rubbish-heap. The currant bushes watched. Deep silence reigned everywhere. But the flowers on the crumbling wall waved mysteriously their coloured banners of alarm.

"It looks different," said Judy in a hushed aside.

"Something's happened," whispered Tim, staring round him.

Maria watched them from the ground, prepared to follow in any direction, but in no hurry until a plan was decided.

"The keyhole!" cried Tim loudly, and at the same moment a huge blackbird flew out of the shrubberies behind them, and flashed across the open space toward the orchard on the other side. It whistled a long, shrill scream of warning. It was bigger by far than any ordinary blackbird.

"Home! Quick! Run for your lives!" cried some one, as they dashed for the safety of the elm tree. Even Maria ran. They scrambled on to the slippery, fallen trunk and gasped for breath as they stood balancing in an uneasy row, all holding hands.

"It was bigger than a hen," exclaimed Judy inconsequently. "It couldn't have come through any keyhole." She stared with inquiring, startled eyes at her brother. The bird and the keyhole were somehow lumped together in her mind.

"They've stopped," observed Maria, and sat down in the comfortable niche between the lopped branch and the trunk. It was true. The wallflowers were as motionless now as painted outlines on a nursery saucer.

"Because we're safe," said Uncle Felix. "It was a warning."

And then all turned their attention to Tim's discovery of the keyhole. For the stuffing had been removed. The white, dusty road gleamed through the hole in a spot of shining white.

"Hush!" whispered their guide. "There's something moving."

"Perhaps it's Jinks in his cemetery," thought Judy after a pause to listen.

"No," said Uncle Felix with decision. "It's outside. It's on the—road!"

His earnestness on these occasions always thrilled them; his gravity and the calm way he kept his head invariably won their confidence.

"The London Road!" they repeated. That meant the world.

"Something going past," he added, listening intently. They listened intently with him. All four were still holding hands.

"The great High Road outside," he repeated softly, while they moved instinctively to the highest part of the tree whence they could see over the fence. They craned their necks. The dusty road was flowing very swiftly, and like a river it had risen. Never before had it been so easily visible. They saw the ruts the carts had made, the hedge upon the opposite bank, the grassy ditch where the hemlock grew in feathery quantities. They even saw loose flints upon the edge. But the actual road was higher than before. It certainly was rising.

"Metropolis!" cried Tim. "I see an eye!"

Some one was looking through the keyhole at them.

"An eye!" exclaimed several voices in a hushed, expectant tone.

There was a pause, during which every one looked at every one else.

"It's probably a tramp," said Uncle Felix gravely. "We'll let him in."

The proposal, however, alarmed them, for they had expected something very different. To stuff the keyhole, run away and hide, or at least to barricade the fence was what he ought to have advised. Instead of this they heard the very opposite. The excitement became intense. For them a tramp meant danger, robbery with violence, intoxication, awful dirt, and an under-the-bed-at-midnight kind of terror. It was so long since they had seen the tramp—their own tramp—that they had forgotten his existence.

"They'll kill us at once," said Maria, using the plural with the comprehensive and anticipatory vision of the child.

"They're harmless as white mice," said her Uncle quickly,

"once you know how to treat them, and full of adventures too. I do," he added with decision, referring to the treatment. And he stepped down to unbar the gate.

The children, breathless with interest, watched him go. On the trunk, of course, they felt comparatively safe, for it was "home"; but none the less the "girls" drew up their skirts a little, and Tim felt premonitory thrills run up his spidery legs into his spine. The wallflowers shook their tawny heads as a sudden breath of wind swept past them across the End of the World. It seemed an age before the audacious thing was accomplished and the door swung wide into the road outside. Uncle Felix might so easily have been stabbed or poisoned or suffocated—but instead they saw a shabby, tangled figure come shuffling through that open gate upon a cloud of dust.

"Quick! he's a perjured man!" cried Judy, remembering a newspaper article. "Shut the gate!" She sprang down to help. "He'll be arrested for a highway violence and be incarc-"

There was confusion in her mind. She felt pity for this woebegone shadow of a human being, and terror lest the Policeman, who lived on the white, summery high road, would catch him and send him to the gallows before he was safe inside. Her love was ever with the under dog.

There was a rush and a scramble, the gate was shut, and the Tramp stood gasping before them in the enchanted sanctuary of the End of the World.

"He's ours!" exclaimed Judy. "It's our old tramp!"

"Be very polite to him," Uncle Felix had time to whisper hurriedly, seeing that all three stood behind him. "He's a great Adventurer and a Wanderer too."

CHAPTER IX

A PRIEST OF WONDER

He was a grey and nameless creature of shadowy outline and vague appearance. The eye focused him with difficulty. He had an air of a broken tombstone about him, with moss and lichen in wayward patches, for his face was split and cracked, and his beard seemed a continuation of his hair; but he had soft blue eyes that had got lost in the general tangle and seemed to stray about the place and peep out unexpectedly like flowers hiding in a thick-set hedge. The face might be anywhere; he might move suddenly in any direction; he was prepared, as it were, to move forward, sideways, or backwards according as the wind decided or the road appeared—a sort of universal scarecrow of a being altogether.

Yet, for all his forlorn and scattered attitude, there hung about his rags an air of something noble and protective, something strangely inviting that welcomed without criticism all the day might bring. Homeless himself, and with no place to lay his extraordinary body, the birds might have built their nests in him without alarm, or the furry creatures of fields and woods have burrowed among his voluminous misfit-clothing to shelter themselves from rain and cold. He would gladly have carried them all with him, safely hidden from guns or traps or policemen, glad to be useful, and careless of himself. That, at any rate, was the mixed impression that he gave.

"Thank you," he said in a comfortable sort of voice that

Algernon Blackwood

sounded like wind among telegraph wires on a high road: then added "kindly all."

And instantly the children felt delighted with him; their sympathy was gained; fear vanished; the Policeman, like a scape-goat, took all their sins away. They did not actually move closer to the Tramp but their eyes went nestling in and out among his tattered figure. Judy, however, it was noticeable, looked at him as though spell-bound. To her he was, perhaps, as her Uncle said, the Great Adventurer, the type of romantic Wanderer for ever on the quest of perilous things—a Knight.

It was Uncle Felix who first broke the pause.

"You've come a long way," he suggested.

"Oh, about the same as usual," replied the Tramp, as though all distances and localities were one to him.

"Which means—?"

"From nowhere, and from everywhere."

"And you are going on to—?"

"Always the same place."

"Which is—?"

"The end." He said it in a rumbling voice that seemed to issue from a pocket of the torn old coat rather than from his bearded mouth.

"Oh, dear," sighed Judy, "that is a *very* long way indeed. But, of course, you never get tired out?" Her eyes were brimmed with admiration.

He shrugged his great loose shoulders. It was odd how there seemed to be another thing within all that baggy clothing and behind the hair. The shaggy exterior covered a slimmer thing that was happy, laughing, dancing to break out. "Not tired out," he said, "a bit sleepy sometimes, p'r'aps." He glanced round him carelessly, his strange eyes resting finally on Judy's face. "But there's lots of beds about," he explained to her, "once you know how to make 'em."

"Yes," the child murmured, with a kind of soft applause, "of course there must be."

"And those wot sleeps in ditches dreams the sweetest—that *I* know."

"They must," agreed Judy, as though grass and dock leaves were familiar to her. "And you get up when you're ready, don't you?"

"That's it," replied the wanderer. "Only you always *are* ready."

"But how do you know the time?" asked Tim.

The Tramp turned round slowly and looked at his questioner.

"Time!" he snorted. And he exchanged a mysterious glance of sympathy with Maria, who lifted her eyes in return, but otherwise made no sign whatever. "Sit quiet like," he added, "and everything worth 'aving comes of itself. That's living that is. The 'ole world belongs to you."

"I've got a watch," said Tim, as though challenged. "I've got an alarum clock too. Only you have to wind them up, of course."

"There you are!" the Tramp exclaimed, "you've got to wind 'em up. They don't go of theirselves, do they?"

"Oh, no."

"I never knew 'appiness until I chucked my watch away," continued the other.

"*Your* watch!" exclaimed Tim.

"Well, not igsackly," laughed the Tramp.

"Oh, he didn't mean *that*," Judy put in quickly.

"I was usin' it at the time, any'ow," chuckled their guest, "and wot you're usin' at the time belongs to you. I never knew 'appiness while I kep' it. Watches and clocks only mean 'urry. It's an endless job, tryin' to keep up with 'em. You've got to go so fast for one thing—I never was a sprinter—bah!" he snorted—"there's nothing in it. Life isn't a 'undred yards race. You miss all the flowers on the way at that pace. And what's the prize?" He glanced down contemptuously at his feet. "Worn-out boots. Yer boots wear out—that's all."

He looked round at the children, smiling wonderfully. Maria seemed to understand him best, perhaps. She looked up innocently into his tangled face. "That's it," he said, with another chuckle. "YOU know wot I mean, don't yer, missie?" But Maria made no reply. She merely beamed back at him till her face seemed nothing but a pair of wide blue eyes.

"Stop yer clocks, go slow," the man murmured, half to himself, "and you'll see what I mean. There's twice as much time as before. You can do anything, everything,"—he spread his arms out—"because there's never any 'urry. You'd be surprised."

"You're very hungry, aren't you?" inquired Tim, resenting the man's undue notice of Maria.

The Tramp stared hard into the boy's unwavering eyes. "Always," he said briefly, "but, then, there's always folks to give."

"Rather," exclaimed Judy with enthusiasm, and Tim added eagerly, "I should think so."

They seemed to know all about him, then. Something had

entered with him that made common stock of the five of them. It was wonderful of Uncle Felix to have known all this beforehand.

"We're all alive together," murmured the Tramp below his breath, and then Uncle Felix showed another stroke of genius. "We'll make tea out here to-day," he said, "instead of having it indoors. Tim, you run and fetch a tea-pot, a bottle of milk, and some cups and a kettle full of water; put some sugar in your pockets and bring a loaf and butter and a pot of jam. A basket will hold the lot. And while you're gone we'll get the fire going."

"A big knife and some spoons too," Judy cried after his disappearing figure, "and don't let Aunt Emily see you, mind."

The Tramp looked up sharply. "I had an Aunt Emily once," he said behind his hedged-in face. Expecting more to follow, the others waited; but nothing came. There was a little pause.

"Once?" asked Maria, wondering perhaps if there were two such beings in the world at the same time.

The man of journeys nodded.

"Did she mend your clothes and things—and love to care for you?" Judy wished to know.

He shook his tangled head. "She visited the poor," he told them, "and had no time for the likes of me. And one day I fell out of a big hole in my second suit and took to tramping." He rubbed his hands vigorously together in the air. "And here I am."

"Yes," said Maria kindly. "I'm glad."

Meanwhile, Judy having decided to go and help her brother with the tea-things, the others set to work and made a fire. Maria helped with her eyes, picking up an occasional stick as well, but it was the Tramp who really did the difficult part. Only the way he did it made it appear quite easy somehow. He began with the tiniest fire in the world, and the next minute it seemed ready for the kettle, with a cross-bar arranged adroitly over it and a supply of fresh wood in a pile beside it.

"What do *you* think about it?" asked Tim of his sister, as they struggled back with the laden basket. Apparently a deep question of some kind asked for explanation in his mind.

"It's awful that he has no one to care about him," was the girl's reply. "I think he's a very nice man. He looks magnificent and awfully brown."

"That's dirt," said her brother.

"It's travel," she replied indignantly.

The Tramp, when they got back, looked tidier somehow, as though the effect of refined society had already done him good. His appearance was less uncouth, his hair and beard a shade less hay-fieldy. It was possible to imagine what he looked like when he was young—sure sign of being tidy; just as to be very untidy gives an odd hint of what old age will do eventually to face and figure. The Tramp looked younger.

They all made friends in the simple, unaffected way of birds and animals, for at the End of the World there was no such thing as empty formality. The children, supported by the presence of their important uncle, asked questions, this being their natural prerogative; it came to them as instinctively as tapping the lawn for worms comes to birds, or scratching the earth for holes is a sign of health with rabbits. At first shyly— then in a ceaseless, yet not too inquisitive torrent. Questions are the sincerest form of flattery, and the Tramp, accustomed probably to severer questions from people in uniform, was quite delighted. He smiled quietly behind the scenery of his curious great face, but he answered all: where he lived, how he travelled, what friends he had, where he spent Christmas, what barns and ditches and haystacks felt like, anything and everything, even where he meant to be buried when he died. "'ere, where I've lived so 'appily," and he made a wide gesture with one tattered arm to include the earth and sky. He had no secrets apparently; he was glad they should know all. The children had never known such a delightful creature in their lives before.

"And you eat anything?" inquired Tim, "anything you can, I mean?"

"Anything you can *get*, he means," corrected Judy softly.

He gave an unexpected answer. "I swallow sunsets, and I bite the moon; I nibble stars. I never need a spoon."

He said it as naturally as a duchess describing her latest diet at a smart dinner-party, with an air, too, as of some great personage disguised on purpose so that he might enjoy the simple life.

"That rhymes," stated Maria.

"So does this," he replied; "I live on open hair and bits of bread; the sunlight clothes me, and I lay me 'ead—"

The hissing of the kettle interrupted him. "Water's boiling," cried Uncle Felix; "hand round the cups and cut the loaf." A cup was given to each. The tea was made.

"Do you take sugar, please?" asked Judy of the guest. The quietness of her voice made it almost tender. Such a man, moreover, might despise sweet things. But he said he did.

"Two lumps?" she asked, "or one?"

"Five, please," he said.

She was far too polite to show surprise at this, nor at the fact that he stirred his tea with a little bit of stick instead of with a spoon. She remembered his remark that he had no use for spoons. Tim, saying nothing, imitated all he did as naturally as though he had never done otherwise in his life before. They enjoyed their picnic tea immensely in this way, seated in a row upon the comfortable elm tree, gobbling, munching, drinking, chattering. The Tramp, for all his outward roughness, had the manners of a king. He said what he thought, but without offence; he knew what he wanted, yet without greed or selfishness. He had that politeness which is due to alert perception of every one near him, their rights and claims, their likes and dislikes; for true politeness is practically an expansion of consciousness which involves seeing the point of view of every one else—at once. A tramp, accustomed to long journeys, big spaces, obliged ever to consider the demands of impetuous little winds, the tastes of flowers, the habits and natural preferences of animals, birds, and insects, develops this bigger sense of politeness that crowds in streets and drawing-rooms cannot learn. Unless a tramp takes note of *all*, he remains out of touch with all, and therefore is uncomfortable.

"Is everything all right?" asked Uncle Felix presently, anxious to see that he was well provided for.

"Everything, thank you," the wanderer replied, "and, if you don't mind, I'll 'ave my supper here later too. I've brought it with me." And out of one capacious pocket he produced—a bird. "It's a chickin," he informed them, as they stared with wide-opened eyes. Maria was the first to go on eating her slice of bread and jam. Unordinary things seemed to disturb her less than ordinary ones. Somehow it seemed quite natural that he should go about with a bird for supper in his pocket.

"However did you get it—in there?" asked Tim, modifying his sentence just in time to avoid inquisitive rudeness.

"It gave itself to me," he replied. "That kind of things 'appens sometimes when you're tramping. *They* know," he added significantly. "You see, it's my birthday to-day, and something like this always 'appens on my birthday. Last time it was a fish. I fell into the stream and went right under. When I got out on to the bank again I found a trout in my pocket. The time before I slept beside a haystack, and when I awoke at sunrise I felt something warm and soft against my face like feathers. It *was* feathers. There was a 'en's nest two inches from my nose, and six nice eggs in it all ready for my birthday breakfast. I only ate four of them. You should never take all the heggs out of a nest." He looked round at the group and smiled. "But I think the chickin's best of all," he told them, "and next year I expect a turkey, or a bit of bacon maybe."

"You never, never grow old, do you?" Judy asked. Her admiration was no longer concealed. It seemed she saw him differently a little from the others.

"Oh, jest a nice age," he said.

"You seem to know so much," she explained her question, "everything."

He laughed behind his tea-cup as he fingered the chicken on his lap.

"As to that," he murmured, "there's only a few things worth knowing. If you can just forget the rest, you're all right."

"I see," she replied beneath her breath. "But—but it's got to be plucked and cleaned and cooked first, hasn't it?"

"The chickin?" he laughed. "Oh, dear me, no! Cooked, yes, but not plucked or cleaned in the sense you mean. That's what they do in 'ouses. Out here we have a better way. We just wrap it up in clay and dig a 'ole and light a fire on top, and in a 'arf hour it's ready to eat, tender, juicy, and sweet as a bit of 'oneycomb. Break open the ball of clay, and the feathers all come away wiv it." And then he produced from another pocket a fat, thick roll of yellow butter, freshly made apparently, for it was wrapped in a clean white cloth.

Algernon Blackwood

They stared at that for a long time without a word.

"They go together," he explained, and the explanation seemed sufficient as well as final. "And they come together too," he added with a smile.

"Did the butter give itself to you as well as the chicken?" inquired Judy. The Tramp nodded in the affirmative as he placed it beside him on the trunk ready for use later. And everybody felt in the middle of a delightful mystery. All were the same age together. Bird and butter, sun and wind, flowers and children, tramp and animals—all seemed merged in a jolly company that shared one another's wants and could supply them. The wallflowers wagged their orange-bonneted heads, the wind slipped sighing with delicious perfumes from the trees, the bees were going home in single file, and the sun was sinking level with the paling top—when suddenly there came a disturbing element into the scene that made their hearts beat faster with one accord. It was a sound.

A muffled, ominous beat was audible far away, but slowly coming nearer. As it approached it changed its character. It became sharper and more distinct. Something about the measured intervals between its tapping repetitions brought a threatening message of alarm. Every one felt the little warning and looked up. There was anxiety. The sound jarred unpleasantly upon the peace of the happy company. They listened. It was footsteps on the road outside.

CHAPTER X

FACT AND WONDER—CLASH

Uncle Felix paused over his last bit of bread and jam, Tim and Judy cocked their ears up. Maria's eyes stood still a moment in the heavens, and the Tramp stopped eating. He picked up the butter and replaced it carefully in his pocket.

"I know those steps," he murmured half to himself and half to the others. "They're all over the world. They follow me wherever I go. I hear 'em even in me sleep." He sighed, and the tone of his voice was weary and ill at ease.

"How horrid for you," said Judy very softly.

"It keeps me moving," he muttered, trying to conceal all signs of face behind hair and beard, which he pulled over him like a veil. "It's the Perliceman."

"The Policeman!" they echoed, staring.

"But he can't find you here!"

"He'll never see you!"

"You're quite safe inside the fence with us, for this is the End of the World, you know."

"He's not afraid—never!" exclaimed Judy proudly.

"He goes everywhere and sees everything," whispered the Tramp. "He's been following me since time began. So far he has not caught me up, but his boots are so much bigger than my own—the biggest, strongest boots in the world—that in the hend he is bound to get me."

"But you've done nothing," said Judy.

The wanderer smiled. "That's why," he said, holding up a warning finger. "It's because I do nothing. 'ush!" he whispered. The steps came nearer, and he lowered his voice so that the end of the sentence was not audible.

"'ide me," he said in a whisper. And he waved his arms imploringly, like the branches of some wind-hunted tree.

There was a tarpaulin near the rubbish-heap, and some sacking used for keeping the vegetables warm at night. "That'll do," he said, pointing. "Quick!—Good-bye!" In a moment he was beneath the spread black covering, the children were sitting on its edges, quietly eating more bread and jam, and looking as innocent as stars. Uncle Felix poked the fire busily, a grave and anxious look upon his face.

The steps came nearer, paused, came on again then finally stopped outside the gate. The flowing road that bore them ceased running past in its accustomed way. The evening stopped still too. The silence could be heard. The setting sun looked on. Upon the crumbling wall the orange flowers shook their little warning banners.

And there came a tapping on the wooden gate.

No one moved.

The tapping was repeated. There was a sound of drums about it. The round brass handle turned. The door pushed open, and in the empty space appeared—the Policeman.

"Good evening," he said in a heavy, uncompromising way. He looked enormous, framed there by the open gate, the white road behind him like a sheet. He looked very blue—a great towering shadow against the sunlight. It was very clear that he *knew* he was a policeman and could think of nothing else. He was dressed up for the part, and received many shillings a week from a radculgovunment to look like that. It would have been a dereliction of duty to forget it. He was stuffed with duty. His brass buttons shone.

"Good *evening*," he repeated, as no one spoke.

"*Good* evening," replied Uncle Felix calmly. The Policeman accentuated the word "evening," but Uncle Felix emphasised the adjective "good." From the very beginning the two men disagreed. "This is private property, very private indeed. We are having tea, in fact, privately, upon our own land."

"No property is private," returned the Policeman, "and to the Law no thing nor person either."

For a moment the children felt afraid. It seemed incredible that Uncle Felix could be arrested, and yet things had an appearance of it.

"Kindly close the gate so that we cannot be overheard," he said firmly, "and then be good enough to state your business here." He did not offer him a seat; he did not suggest a cup of tea; he spoke like a brave man who expected danger but was prepared to meet it.

The Policeman stepped back and closed the gate. He then stepped forward again a little nearer than before. From a pocket, hitherto invisible inside his belt, he drew forth a crumpled notebook and a stub of pencil. He was very dignified and very grave. He took a deep breath, held the paper and pencil ready to use, expanded his chest till it resembled a toy balloon in the Park, and said:

Algernon Blackwood

"I am looking for a man." He paused, then added: "Have you seen a man about?"

"About what?" asked Uncle Felix innocently.

"About fifty or thereabouts," replied the other. "Disguised in rags and a wig of hair and a false beard."

"What has he done?" It was like a game of chess, both opponents well matched. Uncle Felix was too big to be caught napping by clever questions that hid traps. The children felt the danger in the air, and watched their uncle with quivering admiration. Only their uncle stood alone, whereas behind the Policeman stretched a line of other policemen that reached to London and was in touch with the Government itself.

"What has he done?" repeated their champion.

"He's disappeared," came the deep-voiced answer.

"There's no crime in that," was the comment, given flatly.

"But he's disappeared with"—the Policeman consulted his notebook a moment—"a chicken and a roll of butter what don't belong to him—"

"Roll *and* butter, did you say?"

"No, sir, roll *of* butter was what I said." He spoke respectfully, but was grave and terrible. "He is a thief."

"A thief!"

"He lives nowhere and has no home. You see, sir, duty is duty, and we're expected to run in people who live nowhere and have no homes."

"Which road did he take?" Uncle Felix clearly was pretending in order to gain time.

The man of law looked puzzled. "It was a roll of butter and a bird, sir," he said, consulting his book again, "and my duty is to run him in—"

"The moment you run into him."

"Precisely," replied the blue giant. "And, having seen him come in here some time ago, I now ask you formally whether you have seen him too, and I call upon you to show me where he's hiding." He thrust one huge foot forward and held his notebook open with the pencil ready. "Anything you say will be used against you later, remember. You must all be witnesses."

"*If* you find him," put in Uncle Felix dryly.

"*When* I find him," said the other. And his eye wandered over to the tarpaulin that was spread out beside the rubbish-heap. For it had suddenly moved.

Everybody had seen that movement. There was no disguising it. Feeling uncomfortable the Tramp had shifted his position. He probably wanted air.

"I saw it move," the Policeman growled, moving a step towards the rubbish-heap. "He's under there all right enough, and the sooner he comes out the better for him. That's all I've got to say."

It was a most disagreeable and awkward moment. No one knew quite what was best to do. Maria turned her eyes as innocently upon the tarpaulin as she could manage, but it was obvious what she was really looking at. Her brother held his breath and stared, expecting a pistol might appear and some one be shot dead with a marvellous aim, struck absolutely in the mathematical centre of the heart. Uncle Felix, upon whom fell the burden of rescue or defence, sat there with a curious look upon his face. For a moment it seemed he knew not what to do.

The Policeman, approaching still nearer to the tarpaulin, glared at him.

"You're an accessory," he said sternly, "both before and after the fact."

"I didn't say he *wasn't* there."

"You didn't say he *was*," was the severe retort. It was unanswerable.

"He'll hang by the neck till he's dead," thought Tim, "and afterwards they'll bury the body in a lime-kiln so that even his family can't visit the grave." He looked wildly about him, thinking of possible ways of escape he had read or heard about, and his eye fell upon his sister Judy.

Now Judy was a queer, original maid. She believed everything in the world. She believed not only what was told her but also what she thought. And among other things she believed herself to be very beautiful, though in reality she was the ugly duckling of the brood. "All God has made is beautiful," Aunt Emily had once reproved her, and, since God had made everything, everything must be beautiful. It was. God had made her too, therefore she was simply lovely. She enjoyed numerous romances; one romance after another flamed into her puzzled life, each leaving her more lovely than it found her. She was also invariably good. To be asked if she was good was a blundering question to which the astonished answer was only an indignant "Of course." And, similarly, all she loved herself was beautiful. Her romances had included gardeners and postmen, stable-boys and curates, age of no particular consequence provided they stimulated her creative imagination. And the latest was—the Tramp.

Something about the woebegone figure of adventure had set on fire her mother instinct *and* her sense of passionate romance. She saw him young, without the tangled beard, without the rags, without the dilapidated boots. She saw him in her mind as a warrior hero, storming difficulty, despising danger, wandering beneath the stars, a being resplendent as a prince and fearless as a deity. He was a sun of the morning, and the dawn was in his glorious blue eyes.

And Tim now saw that this sister of his, alone of all the party, was about to do something unexpected. She had left her place upon the fallen trunk and stepped up in front of the Policeman.

"Stand aside, missy," this individual said, and his voice was rough, his gesture very decided. It was, in fact, his "arresting" manner. He was about to do his duty.

"Just wait a moment," said Judy calmly; and she placed herself directly in his path, her legs apart, her arms akimbo on her hips. "You say the man you want to find is old and ragged and looks like a tramp?"

"That's it," replied the Policeman, greatly astonished, and pausing a moment in spite of himself. "You'll see him in a moment. Jest help me to lift a corner o' this 'ere tarpaulin, and I'll show him to you." He pushed her deliberately aside.

"All right," said Judy, her eyes shining brilliantly, her gestures touched with a confidence that surprised everybody into silence, "but first I want to tell you that the person underneath this old sheet thing is not a tramp at all—"

"You don't say so," interrupted the other, half impudently, half sarcastically. "What is he then, I'd like to know?"

The girl drew herself up and looked the great blue figure straight in the eyes.

"He's my brother," she said, in a clear strong voice, "and he's not a thief."

"Your brother!" repeated the man, a trifle taken aback.

Algernon Blackwood

He guffawed.

"He's young and noble," she went on, half singing the words in her excitement and belief, "and he's dressed all in gold. He walks like wind about the world, has curly hair, and wears a sword of silver. He's simply beautiful, and he's *got no beard at all!*"

"And he's your brother, is he?" cried the Policeman, laughing rudely, "and he jest wears all that get-up for fun, don't he?" And he stooped down and pulled the tarpaulin violently to one side.

"He is my brother, and I love him, and he is beautiful," she answered, dancing lightly round him and flinging her arms in the air to the complete amazement of policeman, Uncle Felix, and her brother and sister into the bargain. "There! You can see for yourself!"

The Policeman stood aghast and stared. He drew a long, deep breath; he whistled softly; he pushed his big, spiked helmet back. He staggered. "Seems there's a mistake," he stammered stupidly, "a kind of mistake somewhere, as it were. I—" He stuck fast. He wiped his lips with his thick brown hand.

"A mistake everywhere, I think," said Uncle Felix sternly. "Your mistake."

The two men faced each other, for Uncle Felix had risen to his feet. The children held back and stared in silence. They were not quite sure what it was they saw. On Judy's face alone was a radiant confidence.

For, in place of the bedraggled and unkempt figure that had crawled beneath the sheet ten minutes before, there rose before them all apparently a tall young stripling, clean and white and shining as a fair Greek god. His hair was curly, he was dressed in gold, a silver sword hung down beside him, and his beardless face and beauty in it that made it radiant as a glad spring day. The sunlight was very dazzling just at that moment.

"You said," continued Uncle Felix, in a voice of deadly quiet, "that the man you wanted had a wig of hair and a beard—a false beard?"

The Policeman stared as though his eyes would drop out upon the tarpaulin. But he said no word. He consulted his note-book in a dazed, flustered kind of way. Then he looked up nervously at the astonishing figure of the "Tramp." Then he looked back at his book again.

"And old?" said Uncle Felix.

"And old," repeated the officer thickly, poring over the page.

"About fifty, I think, you mentioned?"

"'Bout fifty—did I?" He said it faintly, like a man not sure of a lesson he ought to know by heart.

"Disguised into the bargain!" Uncle Felix raised his voice till it seemed to thunder out the words.

"Them was my instructions, sir," the man was heard to mumble sulkily.

Uncle Felix, to the children's immense delight and admiration, took a step nearer to the man of law. The latter moved slowly backwards, glancing half fiercely, half suspiciously at the glorious figure of the person he had expected to arrest as a dangerous thief and tramp.

"And, following what you stupidly call your instructions," cried Uncle Felix, looking sternly at him, "you have broken in our gate, trespassed on our private property, disturbed our guests, and removed forcibly our tarpaulin from its rightful place."

The crestfallen and amazed Policeman gasped and raised his hands with a gesture of despair. He looked like a ruined man. Had there been a handkerchief in his bulging coat, he must have cried.

"And you call yourself an Officer of the Law?" boomed the Defender of Personal Liberty. He went still nearer to him. His voice, to the children, sounded simply magnificent. "A uniformed and salaried representative of the Government of England!"

"Oo calls me orl that?" asked the wretched man in a trembling tone. "I gets twenty-five shillings a week, and that's orl I know."

There came a pause then, while the men faced each other.

"Uncle, let him go, please," said Judy. "He couldn't help it, you know. And he's a married man with a family, I expect. Some day—"

A forgiving smile softened the features of both men at these gentle words.

"This time, then," said Uncle Felix slowly, "I won't report you; but don't let it occur again as long as you live. A day will come, perhaps, when you will understand. And here," he added, holding out his hand with something in it, "is another shilling to make it twenty-six. I advise you—if you're still open to friendly advice—to buy a pair of glasses with it."

The discredited official took the shilling meekly and pocketed it with his note-book. He cast one last hurried glance of amazement and suspicion at the man who had been beneath the tarpaulin, and began to slink back ignominiously towards the gate. At the last minute he turned.

"Good *evenin'*," he said, as he vanished into the road.

"*Good* evening," Uncle Felix answered him, as he closed the gate behind him.

Then, how it happened no one knew exactly. Judy, walking up to the shining figure, took him by the hand and led him slowly through the gate on to the long white road. There was a blaze of sunset pouring through the trees and the shafts of slanting light made it difficult to see what every one was doing. In the general commotion he somehow vanished. The gate was closed. Judy stood smiling and triumphant just inside upon the mossy path.

"You saved his life," said some one.

"It's all right," she said—and burst into tears.

But children are not much impressed by the tears of others, knowing too well how easily they are produced and stopped. Tim went burrowing to find the bird, and Maria just mentioned that the Tramp had taken the butter away in his pocket. By the time this fact was thoroughly established the group was ready to leave, the tea-things all collected, the fire put out, and the sun just dipping down below the top of the old grey fence.

Then, and not till then, did the affair of the Tramp come under discussion. What seemed most puzzling was why the Policeman had not arrested him after all. They could not make it out at all; it seemed a mystery. There was something quite unusual about it altogether. Uncle Felix and Judy had been wonderful, but—

"Did you see him blink," said Tim, "when Judy went up and gave it him hot?"

"Yes," observed Maria, who had done nothing herself but stare. "I did."

The brother, however, was not so sure. "I think he really

believed her," he declared with assurance, proud of her achievement. "He really saw him young and with a sword and curly hair and all that."

Judy looked at him with surprise. Her tears had ceased flowing by this time.

"Of course," she said. "Didn't *you?*" There was pain in her voice in addition to blank astonishment.

"Of course we did," said Uncle Felix quickly with decision. "Of course we did."

As they went into the house, however, Uncle Felix lingered behind a moment as though he had forgotten something. His face wore a puzzled expression. He seemed a little bewildered. He walked into the hat-rack first, then into the umbrella-stand, then stopped abruptly and put his hand to his head.

"Headache?" asked Tim, who had been watching him.

His uncle did not hear the question, at least he did not answer. Instead he pulled something hurriedly out of his waistcoat pocket, held it to his ear, listened attentively a moment, and then gave a sudden start.

"What is it, Uncle?"

"Oh, nothing," was the reply; "my watch has stopped, that's all." He stood still a moment or two, reflecting deeply. His eyebrows went up and down. He pursed his lips. "Odd," he continued, half to himself; "I'm sure I wound it up last night...!" he added, "it's going again now. It stopped—only for a moment!"

"Aha," said Tim significantly, and looked about him. He waited breathlessly for something more to happen. But nothing did happen—just then.

Only, when at last Uncle Felix looked down, their eyes met and a flash of knowledge too enormous ever to be forgotten passed noiselessly between the two of them.

"Perhaps...!" murmured his uncle.

"I wonder...!"

That was all.

Algernon Blackwood

CHAPTER XI

JUDY'S PARTICULAR ADVENTURE

Adventure means saying Yes, and being careless; children say Yes to everything and are very careless indeed: even their No is usually a Yes, inverted or deferred. "I won't play," parsed by a psychologist, means "I'll play when I'm ready." The adventurous spirit accepts what offers regardless of consequences; he who hesitates and thinks is but a Policeman who prevents adventure. Now everything offers itself to children, because they rightly think that everything belongs to them. Life is conditionless, if only people would let them accept it as it is. "Don't think; accept!" expresses the law of their swift and fluid being. They act on it. They take everything they can—get. But it is the Policeman who adds the "get," changing the whole significance of life with one ugly syllable.

Each of the children treasured an adventure of its very own; an adventure-in-chief, that could not possibly have happened to anybody else in the world. These three survivals in an age when education considers childhood a disease to be cured as hurriedly as possible—took their adventure the instant that it came, and each with a complete assurance that it was unique. To no one else in the world could such a thing have happened, least of all to the other two. Each took it characteristically, according to his or her individual nature—Judy, with a sense of Romance called deathless; Tim, with a taste for Poetic Drama, a dash of the supernatural in it; and Maria, with a magnificent inactivity that ruled the world by waiting for things to happen, then claiming them as her own. Her masterly instinct for repose ran no risk of failure from misdirected energy. And to all three secrecy, of course, was essential: "Don't never tell the others, Uncle! Promise faithfully!"

For to every adventure Uncle Felix acted as audience, atmosphere, and chorus. He watched whatever happened—audience; believed in its reality—atmosphere; and explained without explaining away—chorus. He had the unusual faculty of being ten years young as well as forty years old, and a real adventure was not possible without him.

The secrecy, of course, was not preserved for long; sooner or later the glory must be shared so that "the others" knew and envied. For only then was the joy complete, the splendour properly fulfilled. And so the old tired world went round, and life grew more and more wonderful every day. For children are an epitome of life—a self- creating universe.

That week was a memorable one for several reasons. Daddy, overworked among his sealing-wax, went for a change to Switzerland, taking Mother with him; Aunt Emily, in her black silk dress that crackled with disapproval, went to Tunbridge Wells—an awful place in another century somewhere; and Uncle Felix was left behind to "take charge of ''em"—"em" being the children and himself. It was evidence of monumental trust and power, placing him in their imaginations even above the recognised Authorities. His sway was never for a moment questioned.

"No lessons, then!" he had insisted as a condition of acceptance, and after much confabulation the point was yielded with reluctance. It was to be a fortnight's holiday all round. They had the house and grounds entirely to themselves, and with the departure of the elders a sheet was pulled by some one off the world, a curtain rolled away, another drop-scene fell, the word No disappeared. They saw invisible things.

Algernon Blackwood

Another reason, however, made the week memorable—the daisies. It was extraordinary. The very day after the grown-ups left the daisies came. Like thousands of small white birds, with bright and steady eyes, they arrived and settled, thick and plentiful. They appeared in sheets and crowds upon the grass, all of their own accord and unexplained. In a night the lawns turned white. It seemed a prearranged invasion. Judy, first awake that morning, looked out of her window to watch a squirrel playing, and noticed them. Then she told the others, and Maria, one eye above the blankets, ejaculated "Ah!" She claimed the daisies too.

Now, whereas a single daisy has no smell and seems a common, unimportant thing, a bunch of several hundred holds all the perfume of the spring. No flowers lie closer to the soil or bring the smell of earth more sweetly to the mind; upon the lips and cheeks they are as soft as a kitten's fur, and lie against the skin closer than tired eyelids. They are the common people of the flower world, yet have, in virtue of that fact, the beauty and simplicity of the common people. They own a subdued and unostentatious strength, are humble and ignored, are walked upon, unnoticed, rarely thought about and never praised; they are cut off in early youth by mowing machines; yet their pain in fading is unreported, their little sufferings unsung. They cling to earth, and never aspire to climb, but they hold the sweetest dew and nurse the tiniest little winds imaginable. Their patience is divine. They are proud to be the carpet for all walking, running things, and in their universal service is their strength. The rain stays longer with them than with grander flowers, and the best sunlight goes to sleep among them in great pools of fragrant and delicious heat. The daisies are a stalwart little people altogether.

But they have another quality as well—something elfin, wayward, mischievous. They peep and whisper. It is said they can cast spells. To sleep upon a daisied lawn is to run a certain risk. There is this hint of impudence in their attitude, half audacity, half knavery, that shows itself a little in the way they stare unwinkingly all day at everything above them—at the stately things that tower proudly in the air—then just shut up at sunset without a word of explanation or apology. They see everything, but keep their opinions to themselves. Because people notice them so little, and even tread upon their tiny and inquiring faces, they are up to things all the time—undiscovered things. They know, it is said, the thoughts of Painted Ladies and Clouded Brimstones, as well as the intentions of the disappearing golden flies; why wind often runs close to the ground when the tree-tops are without a single breath; but, also, they know what is going on *below* the surface. They live, moreover, in every country of the globe, and their system of intercommunication is so perfect that even birds and flying things can learn from it. They prove their breeding by their perfect taste in dress, the well-bred ever being inconspicuous; and their simplicity conceals enormous, undecipherable wonder. One daisy out of doors is worth a hundred shelves of text-books in the house. Their mischief, moreover, is not revenge, though some might think it so—but a natural desire to be recognised and thought and talked about a little. Daisies, in a word, are—daisies.

And it was by way of the daisies that Judy's great adventure came to her, the particular adventure that was her very own. For she had deep sympathy with flowers, a sympathy lacking in her brother and sister, and it was natural that her adventure in chief should come that way. She could play with flowers for long periods at a time; she knew their names and habits; she picked them gently, without cruelty, and never merely for the "fun" of picking them; while the way she arranged them about the house proved that she understood their silent, inner natures, their likes and dislikes—in a word, their souls. For Judy connected them in her mind with birds. Born in the air, they seemed to her.

As has been seen, she was the first to notice the arrival of the daisies. From the bedroom window she waved her arm to them, and showed plainly the pleasure that she felt. They arrived in troops and armies. Risen to the surface of the lawn like cream, she saw them staring with suspicious innocence at

Algernon Blackwood

the sky. They stared at *her*.

"Just when the others have gone away!" was her instant thought, though unexpressed in words. There was meaning somewhere in this calculated arrival.

"They *are* alive," she asked that afternoon, "aren't they? But why do they all shut up at night? Who—" she changed the word—"what closes them?"

She was alone with Uncle Felix, and they had chosen with great difficulty a spot where they could lie down without crushing a single flower with their enormous bodies. After considerable difficulty they had found it. Having done a great many things since lunch—a feast involving several second helpings—they were feeling heavy and exhausted. So Judy chose this moment for her simple question. The world required explanation.

"There's life in everything," he mumbled, with his face against the grass, "everything that grows, especially." And having said it, he settled down comfortably again to doze. His pipe was out. He felt rather like a log.

"But stopping growing isn't dying," she informed him sharply.

"Oh, no," he agreed lazily, "you're alive for a long time after that."

"*You* stopped growing before I was born."

"And I'm not quite dead yet."

"Exactly," she said, "so daisies *are* alive."

It was absurd to think of dozing at such a time. He rolled round heavily and gazed at her through half-closed eyelids. "A daisy breathes," he murmured, "and drinks and eats; sap circulates in its little body. Probably it feels as well. Delicate threads like nerves run through it everywhere. It knows when it is being picked or walked on. Oh, yes, a daisy is alive all right enough." He sighed like a big dog that has just shaken a fly off its nose and lies waiting for the next attack. It came at once.

"But who knows it?" she asked. "I mean—there's no good in being alive unless some one else knows it too!"

Then he sat up and stared at her. Judy, he remembered, knew a lot of things she could tell to no one, not even to herself—and this seemed one of them. The question was a startling one.

"An intellectual mystic at twelve!" he gasped. "How on earth did you manage it?"

"I may be a mystillectual insect," she replied, proud of the compliment. "But what's the good of being alive, even like a daisy, unless others know it—*us*, for instance?"

He still stared at her, sitting up stiffly, and propped by his hands upon the grass behind him. After prolonged reflection, during which he closed his eyes and opened them several times in succession, sighing laboriously while he did so, low mumbled words became audible.

"Forgive my apparent slowness," he said, "but I feel like a mowing-machine this afternoon. I want oiling and pushing. The answer to your inquiry, however, is as follows: We could—*if* we took the trouble."

"Could know that daisies are alive?" she cried.

His great head nodded.

"If we thought about them very hard indeed," he went on, "and for a very, very long time we could feel as they feel, and so understand them, and know exactly *how* they are alive."

And the way he said it, the grave, thoughtful, solemn way, convinced her, who already was convinced beforehand.

"I do believe we could," she answered simply.

"I'm sure of it," he said.

"Let's try," she whispered breathlessly.

For a minute and a half they stared into each other's eyes, knowing themselves balanced upon the verge of an immense discovery. She did not doubt or question; she did not tell him he was only humbugging. Her heart thrilled with the right conditions—expectation and delight. Her dark-brown eyes were burning.

He murmured something that she did not properly understand:

> Expect and delight
> Is the way to invite;
> Delight and expect,
> And you'll know things direct!

"Let's try!" she repeated, and her face proved that she fulfilled his conditions without knowing it; she was delighted, and she expected—everything.

He scratched his head, wrinkling up his nose and pursing his lips for a moment. "There's a dodge about it," he explained. "To know a flower yourself you must feel exactly like it. Its life, you see, is different to ours. It doesn't move and hurry, it just lives. It feels sun and wind and dew; it feels the insects' tread; it lifts its skin to meet the rain-drops and the whispering butterflies. It doesn't run away. It has no fear of anything, because it has the whole green earth behind it, and it feels safe because millions of other daisies feel the same"—

"And smells because it's happy," put in Judy. "Then what *is* a daisy? What is it really?"

She was "expecting" vividly. Her mind was hungry for essentials. This mere description told her nothing real. She wanted to feel "direct."

What is a daisy? The little word already had a wonderful and living sound—soft, sweet, and beautiful. But to tell the truth about this ordinary masterpiece was no easy matter. An ostentatious lily, a blazing rose, a wayward hyacinth, a mass of showy wisteria—advertised, notorious flowers—presented fewer difficulties. A daisy seemed too simple to be told, its mystery and honour too humble for proud human minds to understand. So he answered gently, while a Marble White sailed past between their very faces: "Let's think about it hard; perhaps we'll get it that way."

The butterfly sailed off across the lawn; another joined it, and then a third. They danced and flitted like winged marionettes on wires that the swallows tweaked; and, as they vanished, a breath of scented air stole round the trunk of the big lime tree and stirred the daisies' heads. A thousand small white faces turned towards them; a thousand steady eyes observed them; a thousand slender necks were bent. A wave of movement passed across the lawn as though the flowers pressed nearer, aware at last that they were being noticed. And both humans, the big one and the little one, felt a sudden thrill of happiness and beauty in their hearts. The rapture of the Spring slipped into them. They concentrated all their thoughts on daisies....

"I'm beginning to feel it already," whispered the Little Human, turning to gaze at him as though that breath of air impelled her too.

The wind blew her voice across his face like perfume; he looked, but could not see her clearly; she swayed a little; her eyes melted together into a single lovely circle, bright and steady within their fringe of feathery lashes. He tried to speak—"Delight and expect, and we'll know it direct"—but his voice spread across whole yards of lawn. It became a single word that rolled and floated everywhere about him, rising and falling like a wave upon a sea of green: "Daisy, daisy, daisy." On all sides, beneath, above his head as well, it passed with the music of the wandering wind, and he kept repeating it— "Daisy, daisy!" *She* kept repeating it, too, till the sound multiplied, yet never grew louder than a murmur of air and grass and tiny leaves—"Daisy, daisy, daisy." It broke like a sea upon the coast-line of another world. It seemed to contain an entire language in itself, nothing more to be said but those two soft syllables. It was everywhere.

But another vaster sound lay underneath. As the crest of a breaking wave utters its separate note of foam above the general booming of the sea that bears it, so the flying wave of daisy-tones rose out of this deeper sound beneath. Both humans became aware that it was but a surface-voice they imitated. They heard this other foundation-sound that bore it—deep, booming, thunderous, half lost and very far away. It was prodigious; yet there was safety and delight in it that brought no hint of fear. They swam upon the pulse of some enormous, gentle life that rose about and through them in a swelling tide. They felt the heave of something that was strong enough to draw the moon, yet soft enough to close a daisy's eyes. They heard the deep, lost roar of it, rising and coming nearer.

"The Earth!" he whispered. "And the Spring is rising through it. Listen!"

"We're growing together," replied the Little Human. "We're rising with the Spring!"

Ah, it was exquisite. They were in the Daisy World.... He tried to move and reach her, but found that he could not take a step in any direction, and that his feet were imbedded in the soft, damp soil. The movement which he tried to make spread wide among a hundred others like himself. They rose on every side. All shared his movements as they had shared his voice. He heard his whole body murmuring "Daisy, daisy, daisy...." And she leaned over, bending towards him a slim form in a graceful line of green that formed the segment of a circle. A little shining face came close for a moment against his own, rimmed with delicate spears of pink and white. It sang as it shone. The Spring was in it. There were hundreds like it everywhere, yet he recognised it as one he knew. There were thousands, tens of thousands, yet this one he distinguished because he loved it.

Their faces touched like the fringes of two clouds, and then withdrew. They remained very close together, side by side among thousands like themselves, slowly rising on the same great tide. The Earth's round body was beneath them. They felt quite safe—but different. Already they were otherwise than they had been. They felt the big world flying.

"We're changing," he murmured, seizing some fragments of half-remembered speech. "We're marvellously changed!"

"Daisies," he heard her vanishing reply, "we're two daisies on the lawn!"

And then their voices went. That was the end of speech, the end of thinking too. They only felt....

Long periods passed above their heads and then the air about them turned gorgeous as a sunset sky. It was a Clouded Yellow that sailed lazily past their faces with spreading wings as large as clouds. They shared that saffron glory. The draught of cool air fanned them. The splendid butterfly left its beauty in them before it sailed away. But that sunset sky had lasted for hours; that cool wind fanning them was a breeze that blew steadily from the hills, making "weather" for half an afternoon. Time and duration as humans measure them had passed away; there was existence without hurry; end and beginning had not been invented yet. They did not know things in the stupid sense of having names for them; all that there was they shared; that was enough. They knew by feeling.

Algernon Blackwood

For everything was plentiful and inexhaustible—the heavens emptied light and warmth upon them without stint or measure; space poured about them freely, for they had no wish to move; they felt themselves everywhere, for all they needed came to them without the painful effort of busy things that hunt and search outside themselves; both food and drink slipped into them unawares from an abundant source below that equally supplied whole forests without a trace of lessening or loss. All life was theirs, full, free, and generous beyond conception. They owned the world, without even the trouble of knowing that they owned it. They lived, simply staring at the universe with eyes of exquisitely fashioned beauty. They knew joy and peace, and were content with that.

They did communicate. Oh, yes, they shared each other's special happiness. There was, it is true, no sound of broken syllables, no speech which humans use to veil the very thing they would express; but there was that simpler language which all Nature knows, which cannot lie because it is unconscious, and by which constellations converse with buttercups, and cedars with the flying drops of rain—there was gesture. For gesture and attitude can convey all the important and necessary things, while speech in the human sense is but an invention of some sprite who wanted people to wonder what they really meant. In sublimest moments it is never used even in the best circles of intelligence; it drops away quite naturally; souls know one another face to face in dumb but eloquent—gesture.

"The sun is out; I feel warm and happy; there is nothing in the world I need!"

"You are beside me," he replied. "I love you, and we cannot go far apart. I smell you even when no wind stirs. You are sweetest when the dew has gone and left you moist and shiny."

A little shiver of enjoyment quivered through her curving stem. His petals brushed her own. She answered:

"Wet or fine, we stand together, and never stop staring at each other till we close our faces—"

"In the long darkness. But even then we whisper as we grow—"

"And open our eyes together at the same moment when the light comes back—"

"And feel warm and soft, and smell more delicious than ever in the dawn."

These two brave daisies, growing on the lawn, had lives of concentrated happiness, asking no pity for their humble station in the universe. All treated them with unadulterated respect, and everything made love to them because they were so tender and so easily pleased. They knew, for instance, that their splendid Earth was turning with them, for they felt the swerve of her, sharing from their roots upwards her gigantic curve through space; they knew the sun was part of them, because they felt it drawing their sweet-flavoured food up all their dainty length till it glowed in health upon their small, flushed faces; also they knew that streams of water made a tumbling fuss and sent them messages of laughter, because they caught the little rumble of it through miles of trembling ground. And some among them—though these were prophets and poets but half believed, and looked upon as partly mad and partly wonderful—affirmed that they felt the sea itself far leagues away, bending their heads this way and that for hours at a stretch, according to the thundering vibrations that the tide sent through the soil from distant shores.

But all, from the tallest spread-head to the smallest button-face—all knew the pleasure of the uncertain winds; all knew the game of holding flying things just a moment longer, by fascinating them, by drowsing them into sleepiness, by nipping their probosces, or by puffing perfume into their nostrils while they caught their feet with the pressure of a hundred yellow rods....

Algernon Blackwood

Enormous periods passed away. A cloud that for a man's "ten minutes" hid the sun, wearied them so that they simply closed their eyes and went to sleep. Showers of rain they loved, because it washed and cooled them, and they felt the huge satisfaction of the earth beneath them as it drank: the sweet sensation of wet soil that sponged their roots, the pleasant gush that sluiced their bodies and carried off the irritating dust. They also felt the heavier tumbling of the swollen streams in all directions. The drops from overhanging trees came down and played with them, bringing another set of perfumes altogether. A summer shower was, of course, "a month" to them, a day of rain like weeks of holiday by the sea.... But, most of all, they enjoyed the rough-and-tumble nonsense of the violent weather, when they were tied together by the ropes of running wind; for these were visiting days—all manner of strangers dropped in upon them from distant walks in life, and they never knew whether the next would be a fir-cone or one of those careless, irresponsible travellers, a bit of thistle-down....

Yet, for all their steadiness, they knew incessant change—the variety of a daisy's existence was proverbial. Nor was the surprise of being walked upon too alarming—it did not come to all—for they knew a way of bending beneath enormous pressure so that nothing broke, while sometimes it brought a queer, delicious pleasure, as when the bare feet of some flying child passed lightly over them, leaving wild laughter upon a group of them. They knew, indeed, a thousand joys, proudest of all, however, that the big Earth loved them so that she carried millions of them everywhere she went.

And all, without exception, communicated their knowledge by the movements, attitudes, and gestures they assumed; and since each stood close to each, the enjoyment spread quickly till the entire lawn felt one undivided sensation by itself. Anything passing across it at such a moment, whether insect, bird, loose leaf or even human being, would be aware of this, and thus, for a fleeting second, share another world. Poets, it is said, have received their sweetest inspirations upon a daisied lawn in the flush of spring. Nor is it always a sight of prey that makes the swallows dart so suddenly sideways and away, but some chance message of joy or warning intercepted from the hosts of flowers in the soil.

And from this region of the flower-life comes, of course, the legend that fairies have emotions that last for ever, with eternal youth, and with loves that do not pass away to die. This, too, they understood. Because the measurement of existence is a mightier business than with over-developed humans-in-a-hurry. For knowledge comes chiefly through the eye, and the eye can perceive only six times in a second—things that happen more quickly or more slowly than six times a second are invisible. No man can see the movement of a growing daisy, just as no man can distinguish the separate beats of a sparrow's wing: one is too slow, and the other is too quick. But the daisy is practically all eye. It is aware of most delightful things. In its short life of months it lives through an eternity of unhurrying perceptions and of big sensations. Its youth, its loves, its pleasures are—to it—quite endless....

"I can see the old sun moving," she murmured, "but you will love me for ever, won't you?"

"Even till it sinks behind the hills," he answered, "I shall not change."

"So long we have been friends already," she went on. "Do you remember when we first met each other, and you looked into my opening eyes?"

He sighed with joy as he thought of the long, long stretch of time.

"That was in our first reckless youth," he answered, catching the gold of passionate remembrance from an amber fly that hovered for an instant and was gone. "I remember well. You were half hidden by a drop of hanging dew, but I discovered you! That lilac bud across the world was just beginning to open." And, helped by the wind, he bent his shining head, taller than hers by the sixtieth part of an inch, towards the lilac trees beside the gravel path.

"So long ago as that!" she murmured, happy with the exquisite belief in him. "But you will never change or leave me—promise, oh, promise that!"

His stalk grew nearer to her own. He leaned protectively towards her eager face.

"Until that bud shall open fully to the light and smell its sweetest," he replied—the gesture of his petals told it plainly—"so long shall you and I enjoy our happy love."

It was an eternity to them.

"And longer still," she pleaded.

"And longer still," he whispered in the wind. "Even until the blossom falls."

Ah, it was good to be alive with such an age of happiness before them!

He felt the tears in her voice, however; he knew there was something that she longed to tell.

"What is your sadness?" he asked softly, "and why do you put such questions to me now? What is your little trouble?"

A moment's hesitation, a moment's hanging of the graceful head the width of a petal's top nearer to his shoulder—and then she told him.

"I was in darkness for a time," she faltered, "but it was a long, long time. It seemed that something came between us. I lost your face. I felt afraid."

And his laughter—for just then a puff of wind passed by and shook his sides for him—ran across many feet of lawn.

"It was a Bumble Bee," he comforted her. "It came between us for a bit, its shadow fell upon you, nothing more! Such things will happen; we must be prepared for them. It was nothing in myself that dimmed your world."

"Another time I will be braver, then," she told him, "and even in the darkness I shall know you close, ah, very close to me...."

For a long, long stretch of time, then, they stood joyfully together and watched the lilac growing. They also saw the movement of the sun across the sky. An eternity passed over them.... The vast disc of the sun went slowly gliding....

But all the enormous things that happened in their lives cannot be told. Lives crammed with a succession of such grand and palpitating adventures lie beyond the reach of clumsy words. The sweetness sometimes was intolerable, and then they shared it with the entire lawn and so obtained relief—yet merely in order to begin again. The humming of the rising Spring continued with the thunderous droning of the turning Earth. Never uncared for, part of everything, full of the big, rich life that brims the world in May—ah, almost fuller than they could hold sometimes—they passed with existence along to their appointed end.

"We began so long ago, I simply can't remember it," she sighed.

Yet the sun they watched had not left half a degree behind him since they met.

"There was no beginning," he reproved her, smiling, "and there will never be any end."

And the wind spread their happiness like perfume everywhere until the whole white lawn of daisies lay singing their rapture to the sunshine....

The minute underworld of grass and stalks seemed of a sudden to grow large; yet, till now, they had not realised it as "large"—but simply natural. A beetle, big and broad as a Newfoundland dog, went lumbering past them, brushing its polished back against their trembling necks; yet, till now, they had not thought of it as "big"—but simply normal. Its footsteps made a grating sound like the gardener's nailed boots upon the gravel paths. It was strange and startling. Something was different, something was changing. They realised dimly that there was another world somewhere, a world they had left behind long, long ago, forgotten. Something was slipping from them, as sleep slips from the skin and the eyes in the early morning when the bath comes "pinging" upon the floor. What did it mean?

Big and little, far and near, above, below, inside and outside—all were mixed together in a falling rush.

They themselves were changing.

They looked up. They saw an enormous thing rising behind them with vast caverns of square outline opening in its sides—a house. They saw huge, towering shapes whose tops were in the clouds—the familiar lime trees. Big and tiny were inextricably mixed together.

And that was wrong. For either the forest of grass was as big as themselves—in which case they still were daisies; or else it was tiny and far below them—in which case they were hurrying humans again. There was an odd confusion...while consciousness swung home to its appointed centre and Adventure brought them back towards the old, familiar starting-place again.

There came an ominous and portentous sound that rushed towards them through the air, and through the solid ground as well. They heard it, and grew pale with terror. Across the entire lawn it rumbled nearer, growing in volume awfully. The very earth seemed breaking into bits about them. And then they knew.

It was the End of the World that their prophets had long foretold.

It crashed upon them before they had time to think. The roar was appalling. The whole lawn trembled. The daisies bowed their little faces in a crowd. They had no time even to close their innocent eyes. Before a quarter of their sweet and happy life was known, the End swept them from the world, unsung and unlamented. Two of them who had planned Eternity together fell side by side before one terrible stroke....

"I do believe—" said Judy, brushing her tumbled hair out of her eyes.

"Not possible!" exclaimed Uncle Felix, sitting up and stretching himself like a dog. "It's a thing I never do, *never, NEVER!* I think my stupid watch has stopped again...."

They stared at each other with suspiciously sleepy eyes.

"Promise," she whispered presently, "promise never to tell the others!"

"I promise faithfully," he answered. "But we'd better get up, or we shall have our heads cut off like—all the other daisies."

He pulled her to her feet—out of the way of the heavy mowing machine which Weeden was pushing with a whirring, droning noise across the lawn.

CHAPTER XII

TIM'S PARTICULAR ADVENTURE

Tim's "particular adventure" was of another kind. It was a self-repeater—of some violence, moreover, when the smallness of the hero is considered. Whether in after-life he become an astronomer-poet or a "silver-and-mechanical engineer"—both dreams of his—he will ever be sharp upon rescuing something. A lost star or a burning mine will be his objective, but with the essential condition that it be—unattainable. Achievement would mean lost interest. For Tim's desire was, is, and ever will be insatiable. Profoundest mystery, insoluble difficulty, and endless searching were what his soul demanded of life. For him all ponds were bottomless, all gipsies older than the moon. He felt the universe within him, and was born to seek its inexplicable "explanation"—outside. The realisation of such passion, however, is not necessarily confined to writers of epics and lyrics. Tim was a man of action before he was a poet. "Forever questing" was his unacknowledged motto. Besides asking questions about stars and other inaccessible incidents of his Cosmos, he liked to "go busting about," as he called it—again with one essential condition that the thing should never come to an end by merely happening. Its mystery must remain its beauty.

"I want to save something from an awful, horrible death," he announced one evening, looking up from *Half-hours with English Battles* for a sign of beauty in distress.

"Not so easy," his uncle warned him, equally weary of another overrated book—his own.

"But I feel like it," he replied. "Come on."

Uncle Felix still held back. "That you feel like it doesn't prove that there's anything that *wants* rescuing," he objected.

The boy stared at him with patient tolerance and surprise.

"I promised," he said simply.

It was the other's turn to stare. "And when, pray?" They had been alone for the last half hour. It seemed strange.

"Oh—just now," replied the boy carelessly. "A few minutes ago—about."

"Indeed!" It seemed stranger still. No one had come in. Yet Tim never prevaricated.

"Yes," he said, "I gave my wordy honour." It was so gravely spoken that, while pledges involving life and death were obviously not new to him, this one was of exceptional kind.

"Who, then, did you promise—whom, I mean?" the man demanded, fixing him with his stern blue eyes.

And the answer came out pat: "Myself!"

"Aha!" said the other, with a sigh and a raising of the eyebrows, by way of apology. "That settles it—"

"Of course."

"Because what you think and say, you must also act," the man continued. "If you promise yourself a thing, and then don't do it, you've simply told a lie." And he drew another sigh. He scented action coming.

"Let's go at once and find it," said Tim, putting a text-book into seven words. He hitched his belt up, and looked round to make sure his sisters were not within reach of interference. There was a moment's pause, during which Uncle Felix hitched his will up. They rose, then, standing side by side. They left the room arm in arm on their way into the garden. The dusk was already laying its first net of shadows to catch the Night.

"Hadn't you better change first?" asked Tim, thoughtfully, on his way down. He glanced at his companion's white flannel suit. "You're so awfully visible."

"Visible!" It was not his bulk. Tim was never deliberately rude. Was it the risk of staining that he meant?

"Any one can see you miles away like that."

The other understood instantly. In an adventure everything sees, everything has eyes, everything watches. The world is alive and full of eyes. He hesitated a moment.

"Oh, that's all right," he replied. "To be easily seen is the best way. It disarms curiosity at once. Tell all about yourself and nobody ever thinks anything. It's trying to hide that makes the world suspect you. Keep nothing back and show yourself is the best way to go about unnoticed. I've tried it."

"Ah," exclaimed Tim, in an eager whisper, "same as walking into the strawberry-bed without asking—"

"So my white clothes are just the thing," said the other, avoiding the pit laid for him.

"Of course, yes." Tim still chased the big idea in his mind. "Besides," he added, full of another splendid thought, "like that they won't expect you to do very much. They'll watch *you* instead of me."

There was confusion in the utterance, but things were rather crowding in upon him, to tell the truth, and imagination leaped ahead upon two trails at once. He looked at his big companion with more approval. "You'll do," he signified, pulling his cap over his eyes, thrusting both hands in his pockets, and slithering rapidly down the bannisters in advance.

"Thanks," said Uncle Felix, following him, three steps at a time, with effort.

In the hall they paused a moment—a question of doors.

"Back," said Uncle Felix.

"Front's better," decided the boy. "Then nobody'll think anything, you see." He was quick to put the new principle into practice.

On the lawn there was another pause, this time a question of direction.

"The wood, of course!" And they set off together at a steady trot. Few words were wasted when Tim went "busting about" in this way. Uncle Felix resigned himself and looked to him for guidance; there was some one to be rescued; there was danger to be run; the risk was bigger than either of them realised; but more than that he knew not.

"Got a handkerchief with you?" the boy asked presently.

"Yes, thanks; got everything," panted the other.

"For signalling," was offered three minutes later by way of explanation, "in case we get lost—or anything like that."

"Quite so."

"Is it a clean one?"

"Yes."

"Good!"

They climbed the swinging gate of iron, rushed the orchard, crossed the smaller hayfield in the open, heedless of the rabbits that rolled like fat balls into pockets made to fit them, slipped out of sight behind a stack of straw whose threatening lopsidedness seemed to support a ladder, and so eventually came to a breathless and perspiring halt upon the edges of a— wood.

It was a very ordinary wood, small, inconspicuous, and unimposing. No big trees towered; there was no fence of thick, black trunks. It was not mysterious, like the dense evergreens on the other side of the grounds where the west wind shook half a mile of dripping branches in stormy weather:

> Where the yew trees are gigantic,
> And the yellow coast of "Spain,"
> Breasting on the dim "Atlantic,"
> Stores the undesired rain.

It grew there in a kind of untidy muddle, on the very outskirts of the estate, meekly—rather disappointingly, Uncle Felix thought. There was no hint of anything haunted or terrible about it. Round rabbits fussed busily about its edges, darting as though pulled by wires, and the older wood-pigeons, no doubt, slept comfortably in its middle. But game despised it heartily, and traps were never laid. There was not even a trespassers' board, without which no wood is properly attractive. Indeed, for most people it was simply not worth the trouble of entering at all. Apparently no one ever bothered about it.

Yet, precisely for these very reasons, it was real. Tim described it afterwards as a "naked" wood. It had no fence to hold it together, it was not dressed up by human beings, it just grew naturally. To this very openness and want of concealment it owed its deep security, its safety was due entirely to the air of innocence it wore. But in reality it was disguised. It was a forest—without a middle, without a heart.

"This is our wood," announced Tim in a low voice, as they stood and mopped their faces. His tone suggested that they would enter at their peril.

"And is it a big wood?" the other asked with caution, as though he had not noticed it before.

"Much bigger than it looks," the boy replied. "You can easily get lost." Then added, with the first touch of awe about him, "It has no centre."

"That's the worst kind," said his companion shivering slightly. "Like a pond that has no bottom."

Tim nodded. His face had grown a trifle paler. He showed no immediate anxiety to make the first advance, reserving that privilege for his comrade. A breath of wind stole out and set the dry leaves rustling.

"We must look out," he said at length. "There'll be a sign."

Uncle Felix listened attentively to every word. The boy had moved up closer to him. "And if anything happens one of us must climb a tree and signal. *You've* got the clean handkerchief. You see, it's at the centre that it gets rather nasty—because anybody who gets there simply disappears and is never heard of again. That's why there's no centre at all *really*. It's a terrible rescue we've got to do."

The adventure fulfilled the desire of his heart, for, since there was no centre, the search would last for ever.

"Keep a sharp look-out for the sign," replied the man, feeling a small hand steal into his own. "We'd better go in before it gets any darker."

"Oh, that's nothing," was the whispered comment. "The great thing is not to lose our way. Just follow me!"

They then went into this wood without a centre, without a middle, without a heart. Into this heartless wood they moved stealthily, Uncle Felix singing under his breath to keep his courage up:

"A wood is a mysterious place,
It never looks you in the face,
But stares *behind* you all the time.
Your safest plan is just to—climb!
For, otherwise you lose your way,
The week, the month, the time of day;
It turns you round, it makes you blind,
And in the end you lose your mind!
Avoid the centre,
If you enter!

"It grows upon you—grows immense,
Its peace is *not* indifference,
It sees you—and it takes offence,
It knows you're interfering.
Its sleepliness is all pretence,
With trunks and twigs and foliage dense
It's watching you, alert, intense,
It's furious; it's peering.

"Upon the darkening paths below,
Whichever way you try to go
You'll meet with strange resistance.
So climb a tree and wave your hand,
The birds will see and understand,
And *may* bring you assistance.
Avoid the centre,
If you enter,
For once you're there
You—disappear!
Smothered by depth and distance!"

Tim listened without a sign of interest. Every one has his peculiarity, he supposed, and, provided his companion did not dance as well as sing, it was all right. The noise was unnecessary, perhaps, still—the sound of a human voice was not without its charm. The house was a very long way off; the gardeners never came this way. A wood *was* a mysterious place! "Is that all?" he asked—but whether glad or sorry, no man could possibly have told.

"For the present," came the reply, and the sound of both their voices fell a little dead, muffled by the density of the undergrowth. "Are we going right?"

"There'll be a sign," Tim explained again. And the way he said it, the air of positive belief in tone and manner, stung the man's consciousness with a thrill of genuine adventure. It began to creep over him. He kept near to the comforting presence of the boy, aware in quite a novel way of the Presence of the Wood. This very ordinary wood, without claim to particular notice, much less to a notice-board, changed his normal feelings by arresting their customary flow. An unusual sensation replaced what he meant to feel, expected to feel. He was aware of strangeness. He felt included in the purpose of a crowd of growing trees. "But it's just a common little wood," he assured himself, realising as he said it that both adjectives were wrong. For nothing left to itself is ever common, and as for "little"—well, it had suddenly become enormous.

Outside, in what was called the big world, things were going on with frantic hurry and change, but in here the leisured calm was huge, gigantic, so much so that the other dwindled into a kind of lost remoteness. "Smothered by depth and distance," he could almost forget it altogether. Out there nations were at war, republics fighting, empires tottering to ruin; great-hearted ladies were burning furniture and stabbing lovely pictures (not their own) to prove themselves intelligent enough to vote; and gallant gentlemen were flying across the Alps and hunting for the top and bottom of the earth instead of hurrying to help them. All manner of tremendous things were happening at a

Algernon Blackwood

frightful pace—while this unnoticed wood just stood and grew, watching the sun and stars and listening to the brushing winds. Its unadvertised foliage concealed a busy universe of multitudinous, secret life.

How still the trees were—far more imposing than in a storm! Still, quiet things are much more impressive than things that draw attention to themselves by making a noise. They are more articulate. The strength of all these trees emerged in their silence. Their steadiness might easily wear one down.

And now, into its quiet presence, a man and a boy from that distressful outer world had entered. They moved with effort and difficulty into its untrodden depths. Uninvited and unasked, they sought its hidden and invisible centre, the mysterious heart of it which the younger of the adventurers could only describe by saying that "It isn't there, because when you get there, you disappear!" Two ways of expressing the same thing, of course! Moreover, entering involved getting out again. Escape and Rescue—the Wood always in opposition—took possession of the man's slow mind....

It was already thick about them, and the trees stood very still. The branches drooped, motionless in the warm evening air. The twigs pointed. Each leaf had an eye, but a hidden, lidless eye. The saplings saw them, but the heavier trunks *observed* them. It was known in what direction they were going, the direction, however, being chosen and insisted on by the Wood. Their very steps were counted. The whole business of the trees was suspended while they passed. They were being watched. And the stillness was so deep that it forced them, too, to make as little noise as possible. They moved with the utmost caution, pretending that a snapping twig might betray their presence, yet knowing quite well that each detail of their blundering advance was marked down with the accuracy of an instantaneous photograph. Tim, usually in advance, looked round from time to time, with a finger on his lips; and though he himself made far more noise than his companion, he stared with reproach when the latter snapped a stick or let a leafy branch swish through the air too loudly.

"Oh, hush!" he whispered. "Please do hush!" and the same moment caught his own foot in a root, placed cunningly across the path, and sprawled forward with the noise of an explosion. But he made no reference to the matter. His own noises did no harm apparently. He was perfectly honest about it, not merely putting the blame elsewhere to draw attention from himself. His uncle's size and visibility were co-related in his mind. Being convinced that he moved as stealthily and soundlessly as a Redskin, it followed obviously that his companion *didn't*.

The dusk had noticeably deepened when at length they reached a little clearing and stood upright, perspiring freely, and both a little flustered. The silence was really extraordinary. It seemed they had entered a private place, a secret chamber where they had no right, and were intruders. The clearing formed a circle, and from the open sky overhead a grey, mysterious light fell softly on the leafy walls. They paused and peered about them.

"Hark! What's that?" asked Tim in a whisper.

"Nothing," replied the other.

"But I heard it," the boy insisted; "something rushing."

"I'm rather out of breath, perhaps."

The boy looked at him reproachfully. His expression suggested "Why *are* you so noisy and enormous? It's hopeless, really!" But aloud he merely said, "It's got awfully dark all of a sudden."

"It's the wood does that," replied Uncle Felix. "Outside it's only twilight. I think we'd better be getting on."

"We're getting there," observed the boy.

"But we shan't be able to see the sign if this darkness gets worse," said the other apprehensively.

The answer gave him quite a turn. "It's been—ages and ages ago!"

The idea of rescue meanwhile had merged insensibly into escape, but neither remarked upon the change. It was only that the original emotion had spread a bit. Tim and Uncle Felix stood close together in this solemn clearing, waiting, peering about them, listening intently. But Tim had seen the sign; he knew what he was doing all the time; he was in more intimate relations with the Being of the Wood than his great floundering Uncle possibly could be.

"Which way, do *you* think?" asked the latter anxiously.

There seemed no possible exit from the clearing, no break anywhere in the leafy walls; even the entrance was covered up and hidden. The Wood blocked further advance deliberately.

"We're lost," said Tim bluntly, turning round and round. His eyes opened to their widest. "You've simply taken a wrong turning somewhere."

And before Uncle Felix could expostulate or say a word in self-defence, the inevitable reward of his mistake was upon him.

"*You've* got the handkerchief!"

Already the boy was looking about him for a suitable tree.

"But *you* saw the sign, Tim," he began excuses; "and it's *your* wood; I've never been here before—"

"That one looks the easiest," suggested Tim, pointing to a beech. It had one low branch, but the trunk was smooth and slippery as ice. He pushed aside the foliage with his hands to make an opening towards it. "I'll help you up." Tim spoke as though there was no time to lose.

But help came just then unexpectedly from another quarter—there was a sudden battering sound. Something went past them through the branches with a crashing noise. It was terrific, the way it smashed and clattered overhead, making a clapping rattle that died away into the distance with strange swiftness. They jumped; their hearts stood still a moment. It was so horribly close. But the stillness that followed the uproar was far worse than the noise. It felt as though the Wood had stretched a hand and aimed a crafty blow at them from behind the shield of foliage. A quiver of visible silence ran across the leafy walls. They stood stock still, staring blankly into each other's eyes.

"A wood-pigeon!" whispered Uncle Felix, recovering himself first. "We've been *seen*!"

A faint smile passed over Tim's startled face. There was no other expression in it. The tension was distressingly acute. One sentence, however, came to the lips of both adventurers. They uttered it under their breath together:

"It's—disappeared!"

Instinctively they held hands then. Tim stood, rooted to the ground.

"The *centre!*" They whispered it almost inaudibly. The horror of the spot where people vanished was upon them both. The power of the Wood had worn them down.

"Yes, but don't *say* it," cried Uncle Felix; "above all, don't say it aloud." And he clapped one hand upon his own mouth, and the other upon the boy's, as Tim came cuddling closer to his comforting expanse of side. "That only wakes it up, and—"

He did not finish the sentence. Instead, his mind began to think tremendously. They were both badly frightened. What was the best thing to be done? At first he thought: "Keep perfectly still, and make no slightest movement; a quiet person is not noticed." But, the next instant, came the truer wisdom: "If anything unusual occurs, go on doing exactly what you were doing before. Hold the atmosphere, as it were." And on this latter inspiration he decided to act at once—

Only to discover that Tim had realised it before him. The boy was pulling at him. "*Do* come on, Uncle!" he was saying. "We shall go mad with fright if we keep on standing here—we shall be raving lunatics!"

They set off wildly then, plunging helter-skelter into the silent, heartless wood. The trees miraculously opened up a way for them as they dived and stooped and wriggled forward. In which direction they were going neither of them had the least idea, but as neither one nor the other disappeared, it was clear they had not reached the actual centre. They gasped and spluttered, their breath grew shorter, the darkness increased. They came to all sorts of curious places that deceived them; ways opened invitingly, then closed down again and blocked advance; there were clearings that were obviously false, open places that were plainly sham; and a dozen times they came to spots that seemed familiar, but which really they had never seen before. Sense of direction left them, for they continually changed the angle, compelled by the undergrowth to do so. Twigs leaped at them and stung their faces, Tim's cheeks were splashed with mud, Uncle Felix's clean white flannels showed irregular lines of dirty water to his knees. It was altogether a tremendous affair in which rescue and escape were madly mingled with furious attack and terrified retreat. Everything was moving, and in all directions at once. They rushed headlong through the angry Wood. But the Wood itself rushed ever past them. It was roused.

The confusion and bewilderment had got a little more than they could manage, indeed, when—quite marvellously and unexpectedly—the darkness lifted. They saw trees separately instead of in a whirling mass. The trunks stood more apart from one another. There were patches of faint light. More—there was a line of light. It shone, grey and welcome, some dozen yards in front of them.

"Come on!" cried Tim. "Follow me!"

And two minutes later they found themselves outside, torn, worn, and breathless, upon the edge—standing exactly at the place where they had entered three-quarters of an hour before. They had made an enormous circle. Panting and half collapsed, they stood side by side in an exhausted heap.

"We're out," said Tim, with immense relief. Profoundly satisfied with himself, he looked round at his bedraggled Uncle. It was plain that he had rescued some one from "an awful-anorrible death."

"At last!" replied the other gratefully, aware that he was the rescued one. "But only just in time!"

And they moved away in the deepening dusk towards the house, whose welcome lights shone across the intervening hayfield.

Algernon Blackwood

CHAPTER XIII

TIME HESITATES

Meanwhile the coveted fortnight drew towards a close. It had begun on a Friday, and that left two full, clear weeks ahead. It had seemed an inexhaustible period—when it started. There was the feeling that it would draw out slowly, like an ordinary lesson-week; instead of which it shot downhill to Saturday with hardly a single stop. On looking back, the children almost felt unfairness; somebody had pushed it; they had been cheated.

And, of course, they *had* been cheated. Time had played his usual trick upon them. The beginning was so prodigal of reckless promises that they had really believed a week would last for ever. Childhood expects, quite rightly, to have its cake and eat it, for there is no true reason why anything should ever end at all. The devices are various: a titbit is set aside to enjoy later, thus deceiving Time and checking its ridiculous hurry. But in the long run Time invariably wins. After Thursday the week had shot into Saturday without a single pause. It whistled past. And the titbit, Saturday, had come.

Yet without the usual titbit flavour; for Saturday, as a rule, wore splashes of gold and yellow upon its latter end, being a half-holiday associated with open air and sunshine, but now, Monday already in sight, with lessons and early bed and other prohibitions by the dozen, hearts sank a little, a shadow crept upon the sun. They had a grievance; some one had cheated them of a final joy. The collapse was unexpected, therefore wrong. And the arch-deceiver who had humbugged them, they knew quite well, was Time. He was in their thoughts. He mocked them all day long. Clocks grinned; *Saturday, June* 3, flaunted itself insolently in their faces.

"The day after to-morrow," remarked some one, noticing a calendar staring on the wall; and from the moment that phrase could be used it meant the day was within measurable distance.

"Aunt Emily leaves Tunbridge Wells" was mentioned too, sounding less unpleasant than "Aunt Emily comes back." But the climax was reached when somebody stated bluntly without fear of contradiction:

"To-morrow's Sunday."

For Sunday had no particular colour. Monday was black, and Saturday was gold, but Sunday never had been painted anything. Though a buffer-day between a vanished week and a week of labour coming, it was of uncertain character. Queer, grave people came back to lunch. There were collects and a vague uneasiness about the heathen being unfed and naked. There was a collection, too—pennies emerged from stained leather purses and dropped clicking into a polished box with a slit in the top. Greenland's icy mountains also helped to put a chill into the sunshine. A pause came. Time went slower than usual—God rested, they remembered, on the seventh day—yet nothing happened much, and with their Sunday clothes they put on a sort of dreadful carefulness that made play seem stiff, unnatural, and out of place.

Daddy, too, before the day was over, invariably looked worried, the servants bored, Mother drowsy, and Aunt Emily "like a clergyman's wife." Time sighed audibly on Sunday.

"It's our last day, anyhow," they agreed, determined to live in the present and enjoy Saturday to the full.

Algernon Blackwood

It was then Uncle Felix, having overheard their comments upon Time, looked round abruptly and made one of his startling remarks. "To-morrow," he said, "is one of the most wonderful days that was ever invented. You'll see."

And the way he said it provided the very thrill that was needed to chase the shadow from the sun. For there was a hint of promise in his voice that almost meant he had some way of delaying the arrival of Black Monday.

"You'll see," he repeated significantly, shading his eyes with both hands and peering up at the sun.

Tim and Judy watched him with keen faces. They noticed that he said "to-morrow" instead of "Sunday." But before they could squeeze out a single question, there came a remarkable interruption from below. From somewhere near the ground it came. Maria, seated on a flower-pot whose flower didn't want to grow, opened her mouth and spoke. As is already known, this did not often happen. It was her characteristic to keep it closed. Even at the dentist's she never could be got to open her mouth, because he had once hurt her; she flatly refused to do so, and no amount of "Now open, please," ever had the least effect on her firm decision. She was taken in vain to see the dentist.

This last Saturday of the week, however, she opened.

"I've not had *my* partickler adventure," was what she said.

At the centre of that circle where she lived in a state of unalterable bliss, the fact had struck her, and she mentioned it accordingly.

Tim and Judy turned upon her hungrily, but before they could relieve their feelings by a single word their Uncle had turned upon her too. Lowering his eyes from the great circular sun that moved in a circle through the sky, he let them fall upon the circular Maria who reposed calmly upon the circle of the earth, which itself swung in another circle round the sun.

"Exactly," he said, "but it's coming. Your father told you a day would come. It is!"

He said no more than that, but it was enough to fill the remainder of the day with the recurrent thrill of a tremendous promise. Each hour seemed pregnant with a hint of exceptional delivery. There were signs and whispers everywhere, and everybody was aware of it. Uncle Felix looked "bursting with it," as though he could hardly keep it in, and even the Lesser Authorities had as much as they could do to prevent it flying out of them in sudden sentences. Jackman wore a curious smile, which Judy declared was "just the face she made the day Maria was born"; Mrs. Horton left her kitchen and was seen upon the lawn actually picking daisies; and even Thompson—well, when Tim and his sister came upon him basking with a pipe against the laundry window, wearing a discarded tweed coat of their father's, and looking "exactly like the Pope asleep," he explained his position to Tim with the extraordinary remark that "even the Servants' Hall 'as dreams," and went on puffing his pipe precisely as before. But Weeden betrayed it most. They knew by the smell—"per fumigated," as they called it—that he was in the passages, watering the flowers or arranging new ones on the window-sills, and when Tim said, "Seen any more water-rats to pot at, Weeden?" the man just smiled and replied, "Good mornin', Master Tim; it's Saturday."

The inflection of his tone was instantly noticed. "Oh, I say, Weeden, how do you know? *Do* tell me. I won't say a word, I promise." But the Head Gardener kept his one eye—the other was of glass—upon the spout of his watering-can, and answered in a voice that issued from his boots—"Because to-morrow's Sunday, Master Tim, unless something 'appens to prevent it." He then went quickly from the room, as though he feared more questions; he took the secret with him; he was nervous about betraying what he knew. But Judy agreed with Tim that "his answer proved it, because why should he have said it unless he knew!"

Meanwhile, that fine morning in early June slipped along its sunny way; a heavy treacle-pudding luncheon was treated properly; Uncle Felix lit his great meerschaum pipe, and they all went out on the lawn beneath the lime trees. The undercurrent of excitement filled the air. Something was going to happen, something so wonderful that they could not speak about it. They did not dare to ask questions lest they should somehow stop it. It was a most delicately poised affair. The least mistake might send it racing in the opposite direction. But their imaginations were so actively at work inside that they could not help whispering among themselves about it. The silence of their Uncle piled up the coming wonder in an enormous heap.

"Something *is* coming," affirmed Judy in an undertone for the twentieth time, "but *I* think it will be after tea, don't you?"

"Prob'ly," assented her brother, very full of treacle pudding. He sighed.

"Or p'r'aps it's *somebody*, d'you think?"

Tim shrugged his shoulders carefully, conscious of insecurity within.

"I shouldn't be surprised, would you?" Judy insisted. Of course she knew as much as he did, but she wanted to make him say something definite.

"It's both," he said grandly. "Things like this always come together."

"Yes, but it's *quite* new. It's never happened before."

He looked sideways at her with the pity of superior knowledge.

"How could it?" So great was his private information that he almost added "stupid." But he kept back the word for later. He repeated instead: "However could it?"

"Well, but—" she began.

"Don't you see, it's what Daddy always told us," he reminded her with an air. And instantly, with overwhelming certainty, those Wonder Sentences of their father's, first spoken years ago, crashed in upon their minds: Some day; a day is coming; a day will come.

Tim's assurance hurt her vanity a little, for it was only fair that she should know something too, however little. But the force of the discovery at once obliterated all lesser personal emotions.

"Tim!" she gasped, overcome with admiration. "Is it really *that*?"

Tim never forgot that moment of proud ascendancy. He felt like a king or something.

"Look out," he whispered quickly. "You'll spoil it all if *he* knows we've guessed." And he nodded his head towards Uncle Felix in his wicker-chair. "It's Maria's adventure, too, remember."

Judy smiled and flushed a little.

"He's not listening," she whispered back, ignoring Maria's claim. She was not quite so stupid as her brother thought her. "But how on earth did you know? It's too wonderful!" She flung the hair out of her eyes and wriggled away some of her suppressed excitement on the grass. Tim held his breath in agony while he watched her. But the smoke from his Uncle's pipe rose steadily into the sunny air, and his face was hidden by a paper that he held. The moment of danger passed. The boy leaned over towards his sister's ear.

"Where it comes *from*," he whispered, "is what I want to know," and straightened up again with the air of having delivered an ultimatum that no girl could ever possibly reply to.

"*From?*" she repeated. She seemed a little disappointed. "D'you mean that may stop it coming?"

"Of course not," he said contemptuously. "But everything must come from somewhere, mustn't it?"

Judy stared at him speechless, while he surveyed her with an air of calm omnipotence. To ask a thing no one could answer was the same as knowing the answer oneself.

"Mustn't it?" he repeated with triumph.

And, in the inevitable pause that followed, they both instinctively glanced up at Uncle Felix. The same idea had occurred to both of them. Although direct questions about what was coming were obviously impermissible, an indirect question seemed fairly within the rules. The fact was, neither of them could keep quiet about it any longer. The strain was more than human nature could stand. They simply *must* find out. They would get at it that way.

"Try him," whispered Judy. And Tim turned recklessly towards his Uncle and drew a long, deep breath.

CHAPTER XIV

MARIA STIRS

"Uncle," he began with a rush lest his courage should forsake him, "where does everything come from? Everything in the world, I mean?"—then waited for an answer that did not come.

Uncle Felix neither moved nor spoke, and the question, like a bomb that fails to explode, produced no result after considerable effort and expense. The boy looked down again at the alarum clock he had been trying to mend, and turned the handle. It was too tightly wound to go. A stopped clock has the sulkiest face in the world. He stared at it; the handle clicked beneath the pressure of his hand. "It must come from somewhere," he added with decision, half to himself.

"From the East, of course," advanced Judy, and tried to draw her Uncle by putting some buttercups against his cheek and mentioning loudly that he liked butter.

Then, since neither sound nor movement issued from the man in the wicker-chair, the children continued the discussion among themselves, but *at* the man, knowing that sooner or later he must become involved in it. Judy's answer, moreover, so far as it went, was excellent. The sun rose in the East, and the wind most frequently mentioned came also from that quarter. Easter, when everything rose again, was connected with the same point of the compass. The East was enormously

Algernon Blackwood

far away with a kind of fairyland remoteness. The dragon-rugs in Daddy's study and the twisted weapons in the hall were "Easty" too. According to Tim, it was a "golden, yellow, crimson-sort-of, mysterious, blazing hole of a place" of which no adequate picture had ever been shown to them. China and Japan were too much photographed, but the East was vague and marvellous, the beginning of all things, "Camel-distant," as they phrased it, with Great Asia upon its magical frontiers. For Asia, being equally unphotographed, still shimmered with uncommon qualities.

But, chiefly, it was a vast hole where travellers disappeared and left no trace; and to leave no trace was simply horrible.

"The easier you go the less chance there is," maintained Judy. She said this straight into the paper that screened her uncle's face—without the smallest result of any kind whatsoever. Then Tim recalled something that Colonel Stumper had said once, and let fly with it, aiming his voice beneath the paper's edge.

"East is east," he announced with considerable violence, but might as well have declared that it was south for all the response obtained. It was very odd, he thought; his Uncle's mind must be awfully full of something. For he remembered Come-Back Stumper saying the same thing once to Daddy at the end of a frightful argument about missionaries and idols, and Daddy had been unable to find any reply at all. Yet Uncle Felix did not stir a finger even. Accordingly, he made one more effort. He recited in a loud voice the song that Stumper had made up about it. If that had no effect, they must try other means altogether:

> The East is just an endless place
> That lies beyond discovery,
> Where travellers who leave no trace
> Are lost without recovery.
> Both North and South have got a pole—
> Men stand on the equator;
> But the East is just an awful hole—

You're never heard of later!

It had no effect. Goodness! he thought, the man must be ill. Or, perhaps, like the alarum clock, he was too tightly wound to go, and the burden of the secret he contained so wonderfully up his sleeve half choked him. The boy grew impatient; he nudged Judy and made an odd grimace, and Judy, belonging to the sex that took risks and thought little of personal safety when a big end was to be obtained, stood up and put the buttercups against her own cheek.

"But I like it ever so much more than *you* do," she said in a loud voice.

The move was not a bad one; the paper wobbled, sank a quarter of an inch, revealed the bridge of the reader's nose, then held severely steady again. Whereupon Tim, noticing this sign of weakening, followed his sister's lead, rose, kicked the tired clock like a ball across the lawn, and exclaimed in a tone of challenge to the universe: "But where did everything come from before that—before the East, I mean?" And he glared at his immobile Uncle through the paper with an air of fearful accusation, as though he distinctly held he was to blame. If that didn't let the cat out of the bag, nothing would!

The big man, however, rested heavily with his legs crossed, as though still he had not heard. Doubtless he felt as heavy as he looked, for the afternoon was warm, and luncheon—well, at any rate, he remained neutral and inactive. Something might happen to divert philosophical inquiry into other channels; a rat might poke its nose above the pond; a big fish might jump; an awfully rare butterfly come dancing; or Maria, as on rare occasions she had been known to do, might stop discussion with a word of power. The chances were in his favour on the whole. He waited.

But nothing happened. No rat, nor fish, nor butterfly did the things expected of them; they were on the children's side. Maria sat blocked and motionless against the landscape; and

Algernon Blackwood

the round world dozed. Yes—but the music of the world was humming. The bees droned by, there was a whisper among the unruffled leaves.

Tim tapped him sharply on the knee. The man shuffled, then looked over the top of his illustrated paper with an air of shocked surprise.

"Eh, Tim," he asked. "Where we all come from, did you say?"

"Everything, not only us," was the clean reply.

"That's it," Judy supported him.

"Now, then," Maria added quietly, as if she had done all the work.

Uncle Felix laid down his entertaining pictures of public men in misfit-clothing furiously hitting tiny balls over as much uncultivated land as possible—and sighed. Their violent attitudes had given him a delightful sensation of repose. They were the men who governed England, and this savage hitting was proof of their surplus energy. He resigned himself, but with an air.

"Well," he said vaguely, "I suppose—it all just—began somehow—of itself." And he stole a sideways glance at a picture of a stage Beauty attired like a female Guy Fawkes.

"It was created in six days, of course, us last," said Tim, regarding him with patient dignity. "We remember all that. But where it came *from* is what we thought *you'd* know." He closed the illustrated paper and moved it out of reach, while the man brushed from his beard the grass and stuff that Judy had arranged there cleverly in a decorative pattern.

"From?" repeated Uncle Felix, as though the word were unfamiliar.

"Your body and mind," the boy resumed, ignoring the pretence that laziness offered in place of information, "and all that kind of thing; trees and mountains, and birds and caterpillars and people like Aunt Emily, and clergymen and volcanoes and elephants—oh, everything in the world everywhere?"

There was another sigh. And another pause dropped down upon creation, while they watched a looper caterpillar that clung to the edge of the illustrated paper and made futile circles in the air with the knob it called its head. Some one had forgotten to let down the ladder it expected, or perhaps it, too, was asking unanswerable questions of the sun.

"I believe," announced Judy, still smarting under a sense of recent neglect, "it just came from nowhere. It's all in a great huge circle. And we go round and round and rounder," she went on, as no one met her challenge, "till we're finished!"

She avoided her brother's eye, but glanced winningly at Uncle Felix, remembering that she had gained support from him before by a similar device. At Maria she looked down. "You know nothing anyhow," her expression said, "so you *must* agree."

"I don't finish," said Maria quietly, whereupon Tim, feeling that the original question was being shelved, made preparation to obliterate her—when Uncle Felix intervened with a longer observation of his own.

"It's not such a bad idea," he said, glancing sideways at Maria with approval, "that circle business. Everything certainly goes *round*. The earth is round, and the sun is round, and, as Maria says, a circle never finishes." He paused, reflecting deeply.

"But who made the circle," demanded Tim.

"That *is* the point," agreed Uncle Felix, nodding his head. "Some one must have made it—some day—mustn't they?"

They stared at him, as probably the animals stared at Adam, wondering what their splendid names were going to be. The yearning in their eyes was enough to make a rock produce sweet-scented thyme. Even the looper steadied its pin-point head to listen. But nothing happened. Uncle Felix looked dumber than the clock. He looked hot, confused, and muddled too. He kept his eyes upon the grass. He fumbled in his pockets for a match. He spoke no word.

"What?" asked Tim abruptly, by way of a hint that something further was expected of him.

Uncle Felix looked up with a start. Like Proteus who changed his shape to save himself the trouble of prophesying, he swiftly changed the key to save himself providing accurate information that he didn't possess.

"It wasn't a circle, exactly," he said slowly; "it was a thought, a great, white, wonderful, shining thought. That's what started the whole business first," and he looked round hopefully at the eager faces. "Somebody thought it all," he went on, recklessly, "and it all came true that way. See?"

They waited in silence for particulars.

"Somebody thought it all out first," he elaborated, "and so it simply *had* to happen."

There was an interval of some thirty seconds, and then Tim asked:

"But who thought *him*?" He said it with much emphasis.

Uncle Felix sat up with energy and lit his pipe. His listeners drew closer, with the exception of Maria, whose life seemed concentrated in her fixed and steady eyes.

"It's like this, you see," the man explained between the puffs; "if you go into the schoolroom, you find a lot of things lying about everywhere—blocks, toys, engines, and all sorts of things—don't you?"

"Yes," they agreed, without enthusiasm.

"Well," he continued, "what's the good of them until you *think* something about them—think them into something—some game or meaning or other? They're nothing but a lot of useless stuff just lying untidily upon the floor. See what I mean?"

They nodded, but again without enthusiasm.

"With our End of the World place," he went on, seeing that they listened attentively, "it's the same again. It was nothing but a rubbish-heap until we thought it into something wonderful—which, of course, it is," he hastened to add. "But by thinking about it, we discovered—we *created* it!"

They nodded again. Somebody grunted. Maria watched the caterpillar crawling up his sleeve.

"The things—the place and the toys," he resumed hopefully, "were there all the time, but they meant nothing—they weren't alive—until we thought about them." He blew a cloud of smoke. "So, you see," he continued with an effort, "if we could only *think out* what everything meant, we could—er—find out what—what everything meant—and where it came from. Everything would be all right, don't you see?"

Judy's expression was distraught and puzzled. Maria's eyes were closed so tightly that her entire face seemed closed. The pause drew out.

"Yes, but where does everything come from?" inquired Tim calmly.

He valued the lengthy explanation at just exactly—nothing!

"Because there simply must be a beginning somewhere," added Judy.

They were at the starting-point again. They had merely made a circle.

And Uncle Felix found himself in difficulties of his own creating. Where everything came from puzzled him as much as it puzzled the children, or the looper caterpillar that was now crawling from his flannel collar to his neck and contemplating the thicket of his dense back hair. Why ask these terrible questions? he thought, as he looked around at the sunshine and the trees. Life would be no happier if he knew. Since everything was already here, going along quite pleasantly and usefully, it really couldn't help matters much to know precisely where it all came from. Possibly not. But it would have helped him enormously in his relations with the children—his particular world at the moment—if he could have provided them with a satisfactory explanation. And he knew quite well what they expected from him. That dreadful "Some Day" hung in the balance between success and failure.

And it was then that assistance came from a most unlikely quarter—from Maria. There was no movement in the stolid head. The eyes merely rolled round like small blue moons upon the expanse of the expressionless face. But the lips parted and she spoke. She asked a question. And her question shifted the universe back upon its ultimate foundations. It set a problem deeper far than the mere origin of everything. It touched the *cause*.

"Why?" she inquired blandly.

It seemed a bomb-shell had fallen among them. Maria had closed her eyes again. Her face was calm as a cabbage, still as a mushroom in a storm. She claimed the entire discussion somehow as her own. Yet she had merely exercised her prerogative of being herself. Having gone into the root of the matter with a monosyllable, she retired again into her eternal centre. She had nothing more to offer—at the moment.

Why?

They had never thought of Why there should be anything. It was far more interesting than Where. Why was a deeper question than whence. It made them feel more important, for one thing. Somebody—but Somebody who was not there—owed them a proper explanation about it. The burden of apology or excuse was lifted instantly from Uncle Felix's shoulders, for, obviously, he had nothing to do with the reason for their being in the world.

Without a moment's hesitation he flung his arms out, let the pipe fall from his lips, and—burst into song:

> Why should there be anything?
> Why should we be here?
> It isn't where we come from,
> But why should we appear?
> It's really inexplicable,
> Extr'ordinary, queer:
> Why *should* we come and talk a bit,
> And then—just disappear?

"Why, why, why?" shouted the two elder children. The air was filled with flying "whys." They tried to sing the verse.

"Let's dance it," cried Judy, leaping to her feet. "Give us the words again, please." She picked up the clock and plumped it down into Maria's uncertain lap. "You beat time," she ordered. "It's the tune of 'Onward Christian Soldiers.'"

Maria, disinclined to budge unless obliged to, did nothing.

"It's a beastly tune," Tim supported her. "I hate those Sunday hymn tunes. They're not real a bit."

He watched Judy and his Uncle capering hand in hand among

Algernon Blackwood

the flower-beds. He didn't feel like dancing himself. He looked at the clock that, like Maria and himself, refused to go. He looked at Maria, fastened immovably upon the lawn. The clock lay glittering in the sunshine. Maria sat like a shining ball beside it. He felt the afternoon was a failure somewhere. Things weren't going quite as he wanted, the clock wasn't going either. And when they did go they went of their own accord, independent of himself, of his direction, guidance, wishes. He was out of it. This was *not* the time to dance. What was the meaning of it all? It had to do somehow with the clock that wouldn't go. It had to do with Maria, who wouldn't budge. The clock had stopped of its own accord. That lay at the bottom of it all, he felt. Some day things would be different, more satisfactory—more real.... Some day!

And strange, new ideas, very vague and dim, very far away, very queer, and very wonderful, poured through his searching, questioning little mind.

"Beat time!" shouted Judy to her motionless sister. "I told you to beat time. You're doing nothing. You never do!"

Tim stood watching them, while the words rang on in his head: "You are doing nothing! You never do!" How wonderful it was! Maria never did anything, yet was always there *in* everything. And the others—how funny they were, too! They looked like an elephant and a bird, he thought, for Judy hopped and fluttered, while his Uncle moved heavily, making holes in the soft lawn with his great feet. "Beat time, beat time!" cried Judy at intervals.

What a queer phrase it was—to *beat* time. Why beat it? It wasn't there unless it was beaten. Poor Time; and Maria refused to beat it. His eye wandered from Maria to the dancers, and a kind of reverie stole over him. What was the use of dancing unless there was something to dance round? Maria was round; why didn't they dance round her? His thoughts returned to Maria. How funny Maria was! She just sat there doing nothing at all. Maria was dull and unenterprising, yet somehow everything came round to her in the end. It was just because she waited, she never hurried. She was a sort of centre. Only it must be rather stupid just to be a centre. Then, suddenly, two ideas struck him at the same instant, scattering his dreamy state of reverie. The first was—Everything comes from a centre like Maria; *that's* where everything comes from! The second, bearing no apparent relation to it, found expression in words:

He cried out: "I know what! Let's go to the End of the World and make a fire and burn things!"

And he looked at Maria as though he had discovered America.

"Beat time, oh, *do* beat time," cried Judy breathlessly.

"We're going to make a fire," he shouted; "there's lots of things to burn." He looked about him as though to choose a place. But he couldn't find one. He pointed vaguely, first at Maria, as though she was the thing to burn, and then at the landscape generally. "Then you can dance *round* it," he added convincingly to clinch the matter.

But the bird and the elephant continued their gymnastic exercises on the lawn, while Maria turned her eyes without moving her head and watched them too.

Then, while the tune of "Onward Christian Soldiers" filled the air, Tim and Maria began an irrelevant argument about things in general. Tim, at least, told her things, while she laid the clock down upon the grass and listened. But the flood of language rolled off her as minutes roll from the face of the sun, producing no effect. There was wonder in her big blue eyes, wonder that never seemed to end. But minutes don't decrease merely because the rising and setting of the sun sends them flying, and there are not fewer words in a boy's vocabulary merely because he uses up a lot in saying things. Both words and minutes seemed a circle without beginning or end. It was most odd and strange—this feeling of endlessness that was everywhere in the air. And, long before Tim had got even to the middle of his enormous speech, he had forgotten all about the fire, forgotten about dancing, about burning things, forgotten about everything everywhere, because his roving eye had fallen again upon the—clock. The clock absorbed his interest. It lay there glittering in the sunshine beside Maria. It wasn't going; Maria wasn't going either. It had stopped. He realised abruptly, realised it without rhyme or reason, that a stopped clock, a clock that isn't going, was a—mystery.

And the tide of words dried up in him; he choked; something was wrong with the universe; for if the clock stopped—*his* clock—time—time must—he was unable to think it out—but time must surely get muddled and go wrong too.

And he moved over to Maria just as she was about to burst into tears. He sat down beside her. At the same moment Judy and Uncle Felix, thinking a quarrel was threatening, stopped their dancing, and joined the circle too. They stood with arms akimbo, panting, silent, waiting for something to happen so that they could interfere and set it right again.

But nothing did happen. There was deep silence only. The slanting sunshine lay across the lawn, the wind passed sighing through the lime trees, and the clock stared up into their faces, motionless, a blank expression on it—stopped. They formed a circle round it. No one moved or spoke. There was a queer, deep pause. The sun watched them; the sky was listening; the entire afternoon stood still. Something else beside the clock, it seemed, was slowing up.

"To-morrow's Sunday. Time's getting awfully short," was in the air inaudibly.

"Let's sit down," whispered Tim, already seated himself, but anxious to feel the others close. Judy and Uncle Felix obeyed. They all sat round in a circle, staring at the shining disc of the motionless, stopped clock. It might have been a Lucky Bag by the way they watched it with expectant faces.

But Maria also was in that circle, sitting calmly in its centre.

Then Uncle Felix cautiously lifted the glittering round thing and held it in his hand. He put his ear down to listen. He shook his head.

"It hasn't gone since this time yesterday," said Tim in a low tone. "That's twenty-four hours," he added, calculating it on the fingers of both hands.

"A whole day," murmured Judy, as if taken by surprise somehow; "a day and a night, I mean."

She exchanged a glance of significant expectation with her brother, but it was at their uncle they looked the moment after, because of the strange and sudden sound that issued from his lips. For it was like a cry, and his face wore a flushed and curious expression they could not fathom. The face and the cry were signs of something utterly unusual. He was startled—out of himself. A marvellous idea had evidently struck him. "It's either something," thought Judy, "or else he's got a pain." But Tim's mind was quicker. "He's got it," the boy decided, meaning, "We've got it out of him at last!" Their manoeuvres had taken so long of accomplishment that their original purpose had almost been forgotten.

"A day, a whole day," Uncle Felix was mumbling to himself in a dazed kind of happy way, "an entire day, I do declare!" He looked round solemnly, yet with growing excitement, into the children's faces. "Twenty-four hours! An entire day," he went on, half beneath his breath.

"*Some day;* of course..." Tim said in a low voice, catching the mood of wonder, while Judy added, equally stirred up, "A day will come..." and then Uncle Felix, breaking out of his queer reverie with an effort, raised his voice and looked as if the end of the world had come.

"But do you realise what it means?" he asked them sharply.

Algernon Blackwood

"D'you understand what's happened?"

He drew a long, deep breath that quivered with suppressed amazement, and waited several seconds for their answers—in vain. The children gazed at him without uttering a word; they made no movement either. The arresting tone of his voice and a certain huge expression in his eyes made everything in the world seem different. It was a moment of real life; he had discovered something stupendous. But, explanation being beyond them, they attempted no immediate answer to his question. The pressure of interest blocked every means of ordinary expression known to them.

Then Uncle Felix spoke again; his big eyes fixed Tim piercingly like a pin. "When did it stop?" he inquired gravely. He meant to make quite sure of his discovery before revealing it. There must be no escape, no slip, no carelessness. "When did it stop, I ask you, Tim?" he repeated.

Tim was a trifle vague. "I was asleep," he whispered. "When I woke up—it wasn't going."

"You wound it?"

"Oh, yes, I wound it right enough."

"What time was it?"

"The clock—or the day, Uncle?" He was confused a little; he wished to be awfully accurate.

Uncle Felix explained that he desired to know what time the clock had stopped. The importance of the answer could be judged by the intentness of his expression while he waited.

"The finger-hands were at four," said the boy at length.

Uncle Felix gave a jump. "Ha, ha!" he exclaimed triumphantly, "then it stopped of its own accord!" They could have screamed with excitement, though without the least idea what they were excited about. You could have heard a butterfly breathing.

"It stopped at dawn!" he continued, louder.

"Dawn!" piped Tim, unable to think of anything else, but obliged to utter something.

"Dawn, yes," cried Uncle Felix louder still. "It stopped of its own accord at dawn! Just at the beginning of a new day it stopped! It's marvellous! Don't you see? It's marvellous!"

"Goodness!" cried Judy, her mind obfuscated, yet thrilled with a transport of inexplicable delight. "It's marvellous!"

"I say!" Tim shouted, dropping his voice suddenly because he too was at a loss for any more intelligible relief in words.

They sat and stared at their amazing uncle. There was a hush upon the entire universe; there was marvel, mystery, but at first there was also muddle. They waited, holding their breath with difficulty. Some one, it seemed, must either explode or—or something else, they knew not exactly what. It would hardly have surprised them if Judy had suddenly flown through the air, Tim vanished down a hole, or Maria gleamed at them from the inside of a quivering bubble of soap. There was this kind of intoxicating feeling, delicious and intense. Even To-morrow might *not* be Sunday after all: it felt strange and wonderful enough for that!

The possibility that *Some Day* was coming—was close at hand—had in some mysterious way become a probability. It was clear at last why Uncle Felix had been so heavy and preoccupied.

"You see what's happened?" he continued after the long pause. "You see what it all means—this strange stopping of the clock—at Dawn?"

Algernon Blackwood

They admitted nothing; the least mistake on their part might prevent, might spoil or cripple it. The depth and softness of his tone warned them. They stared and waited. He gathered them closer to him with both arms. Even Maria wriggled slightly nearer—an inch or so.

"It means," he said in still lower tones, "the calendar,"—then stopped abruptly to examine the effect upon them.

Now, ordinarily, they knew quite well what a calendar was; but this new, strange emphasis he put upon it robbed the word suddenly of all its original meaning. Their minds went questioning at once:

"What *is* a calendar?" asked Judy carefully—"exactly?" she added, to make her meaning absolutely clear. It sounded almost like a nonsense word.

"Exactly," he repeated cautiously, yet with some great emotion working in him, "what is a calendar? That's the whole question. I'll try and tell you what a calendar is." He drew a deeper breath, a great effort being evidently needed. "A calendar," he went on, while the word sounded less real each time it was uttered, "is an invention of clever, scientific men to note the days as they pass; it records the passing days. It's a plan to measure Time. It's made of paper and has the date and the name of the day stamped in ink on separate sheets. When a day has passed you tear off a sheet. That day is done with—gone. There are three hundred and sixty-five of these separate sheets in a year. It's just an invention of scientific men to measure the passing of—Time, you see?"

They said they saw.

"Another invention," he resumed, his face betraying more and more emotion, "is a clock. A clock is just a mechanical invention that ticks off the movements of the sun into seconds and minutes and hours. Both clocks and calendars, therefore, are mere measuring tricks. Time goes on, or does not go on, just the same, whether you possess these inventions or whether you do not possess them. Both clocks and calendars go at the same rate whether Time goes fast or slow. See?"

A tremendous discovery began to poke its nose above the edge of their familiar world. But they could not pull it up far enough to "see" as yet. Uncle Felix continued to pull it up for them. That he, too, was muddled never once occurred to them.

"Scientific men, like all other people, are not always to be relied upon," he went on. "They make mistakes like—you, or Thompson, or Mrs. Horton, or—or even me. Clocks, we all know, are full of mistakes, and for ever going wrong. But the same thing has happened to calendars as well. Calendars are notoriously inaccurate; they simply cannot be depended upon. No calendar has ever been entirely veracious, nor ever will be. Like elastic, they are sometimes too long and sometimes too short—imperfectly constructed."

He paused and looked at them. "Yes," they said breathlessly, aware dimly that accustomed foundations were already sliding from beneath their feet.

"Half the calendars of the world are simply wrong," he continued, more boldly still, "and the people who live by them are in a muddle consequently—a muddle about Time. England is no exception to the rest. Is it any wonder that Time bothers us in the way it does—always time to do this, or time to do that, or not time enough to finish, and so on?"

"No," they said promptly, "it isn't."

"Of course," he resumed. "Well, sometimes a nation finds out its mistake and alters its calendar. Russia has done this; the Russian New Year and Easter are not the same as ours. Pope Gregory, the thirteenth, ordered that the day after October 4, 1582, should be called October 15. He called it the Gregorian Calendar; but there are lots of other calendars besides—there's the Jewish and Mohammedan, and a variety of calendars in the East. All of them can't be right. The result is that none of them are right, and the world is in confusion. Some calendars mark off too many days, others mark off too few. Half the world is ahead of Time, and the other half behind it. The Governments know this quite well, but they dare not say anything, because their officials are muddled enough as it is. There is everywhere this fearful rush and hurry to keep up with Time. All are terrified of being late—too late or too early."

"Naturally."

"And the extraordinary result of all these mistakes," he went on marvellously, "is simply this: that a considerable amount of Time has never been recorded at all by any of them. There are a lot of extra days, unused, unrecorded days, still at large—if only we could find them."

"Extra Days!" they gasped. Tim and Judy's mouths were open now, and slowly opening wider every minute. Only Maria's mouth kept closed. Her great blue eyes were closed as well. She looked as if she could have told them all this in a couple of words!

"Knocking about on the loose," he explained further, then paused and stared into the upturned faces; "sort of escaped days that have never been torn off calendars or ticked away by clocks—unused, unfilled, unlived—slipped out of Time, that is—"

"Then when Daddy said, 'A day is coming,' and all that—?" Tim managed to squeeze out as though the pain of the excitement hurt his lips.

"Of course," replied Uncle Felix, nodding his great head, "of course. Sooner or later one of these lost Extra Days is bound to crop up. And what's more—" he glanced down significantly at the stopped alarum-clock—"I think—"

He broke off in the middle of the sentence. They all stood up. Tim picked up the clock and handed it to his uncle, who held it tightly against his chest a moment, then put it into his capacious pocket.

"I think," he went on enormously, "it's come!"

An entire minute passed without a sound.

"We can fill it with anything we like?" asked Judy, overawed a little.

"Anything we like," came the sublime reply.

"And do things over and over again—sort of double—and no hurry?" Tim whispered.

"Anything, anywhere, anyhow, and no end to it all," he answered gloriously. "No hurry either!" It was too much to think about all at once, too big to realise. They all sat down again beside Maria, who had not moved an inch in any direction at all. She was a picture of sublime repose.

"We have only got to find it, then climb into it, then sail away," murmured Uncle Felix, with a strange catch in his breath they readily understood.

"When will it begin?" both children asked in the same breath.

"At dawn," he said.

"To-morrow morning?"

"At dawn to-morrow morning."

"But to-morrow's Sunday," they objected.

"To-morrow's—an Extra Day," he said amazingly.

They hesitated a moment, stared, frowned, smiled, then opened their eyes and mouths still wider than before.

"Oh, like that!" they exclaimed.

"Like that, yes," he said finally. "It means getting in behind Time, you see. There's no Time in an Extra Day because it's never been recorded by calendar or clock. And that means getting behind the great hurrying humbug of a thing that blinds and confuses everybody all the world over—it means getting closer to the big Reality that—"

He broke off sharply, aware that his own emotion was carrying him out of his depth, and out of their depth likewise. He changed the sentence: "We shall be in Eternity," he whispered very softly, so softly that it was scarcely audible perhaps.

And it was then that Maria, still seated solidly upon the lawn, looked up and asked another baffling and unexpected question. For this was *her* private and particular adventure: and, living ever at the centre of the circle, Maria claimed even Eternity as especially her own. Her question was gigantic. It was infinitely bigger than her original question, "Why?" It was the greatest question in the universe, because it answered itself adequately at once. It was the question the undying gods have flung about the listening cosmos since Time first began its tricky cheating of delight—and still fling into the echoing hearts of men and children everywhere. The stars and insects, the animals and birds, even the stones and flowers, all keep the glorious echo flying.

"Why not?" she asked.

It was unanswerable.

CHAPTER XV

"A DAY WILL COME"

They went into the house as though wafted—thus does a shining heart deduct bodily weight from life's obstructions; they had their tea; after tea they played games as usual, quite ordinary games; and in due course they went to bed. That is, they followed a customary routine, feeling it was safer. To do anything unusual just then might attract attention to their infinite Discovery and so disturb its delicate equilibrium. Its balance was precarious. Once an Authority got wind of anything, the Extra Day might change its course and sail into another port. Aunt Emily, even from a distance...! In any case, they behaved with this intuitive sagacity which obviated every risk—by taking none.

Yet everything was different. Behind the routine lay the potent emphasis of some strange new factor, as though a lofty hope, a brave ideal, had the power of transmuting common duties into gold and crystal. This new factor pushed softly behind each little customary act, urging what was commonplace over the edge into the marvellous. The habitual became wonderful. It felt like Christmas Eve, like the last night of the Old Year, like the day before the family moved for the holidays to the sea— only more so. Even To-morrow-will-be-Sunday had entirely disappeared. A thrill of mysterious anticipation gilded everything with wonder and beauty that were impossible, yet true. Some Day, *the* Thing that Nobody could Understand— Somebody—was coming at last.

Uncle Felix was in an extraordinary state; his acts were normal enough, but his speech betrayed him shamefully; they had to warn him more than once about it. He seemed unable to talk ordinary prose, saying that "Everything *ought* to rhyme, At such a time," and, instead of walking like other people, his feet tried to keep in time with his language. "But you don't understand," he replied to Tim's grave warnings; "you don't understand what a gigantic discovery it is. Why, the whole world will thank us! The whole world will get its breath back! The one thing it's always dreaded more than anything else— being too late—will come to an end! We ought to dance and sing—"

"Oh, please hush!" warned Judy. "Aunt Emily, you know—" Even at Tunbridge Wells Aunt Emily might hear and send a telegram with No in it.

"Has it lost its breath?" Tim asked, however. But, though it was in the middle of tea, Uncle Felix could not restrain himself, and burst into one of his ridiculous singing fits, instead of answering in a whisper as he should have done. "Burst" described it accurately. And his feet kept time beneath the table. It was the proper place for Time, he explained.

The clocks are stopped, the calendars are wrong, Time holds gigantic finger-hands Before his guilty face. Listen a moment! I can hear the song That no one understands—

"It's the blue dragon-fly," interrupted Tim, remembering the story of long ago.

"It's the Night-Wind—out by day," cried Judy.

"It's both and neither," sang the man,
"This song I hear. It first began
Before the hurrying race
Of ticking, and of tearing pages
Deafened the breathless ages:
It is the happy singing

Of wind among the rigging
Of our Extra Day!"

"It's something anyhow," decided Judy, rather impressed by her uncle's fit of bursting.

And, somehow, Dawn was the password and Tomorrow the key. No one knew more than that. It had to do with Time, for Uncle Felix had taken the stopped clock to his room and hidden it there lest somebody like Jackman or Thompson should wind it up. Later, however, he gave it for safer keeping to Maria, because she moved so rarely and did so little that was unnecessary that she seemed the best repository of all. Also, this was *her* particular adventure, and what risk there was belonged properly to her. But beyond this they knew nothing, and they didn't want to know. In the immediate future, just before the gateway of To-morrow's dawn, a great gap lay waiting, a gap they had discovered alone of all the world. The scientists had made a mistake, the Government had been afraid to deal with it, the rest of the world lay in ignorance of its very existence even. It satisfied all the conditions of real adventure, since it was unique, impossible, and had never happened to any one before. They, with Uncle Felix, had discovered it. It belonged to them entirely—the most marvellous secret that anybody could possibly imagine. Maria, they took for granted, would share it with them. A hole in Time lay waiting to receive them. A *Day Will Come* at last was actually coming.

"We'd better pack up," said Judy after tea. She said it calmly, but the voice had a whisper of intense expectancy in it.

"Pack up nothing," Uncle Felix reproved her quickly. "The important thing is—don't wind up. Just go on as usual. It will be best," he added significantly, "if you all hand over your timepieces to me at once." And, without a word, they recognised his wisdom and put their treasures into his waistcoat pockets—watches of silver, tin, and gunmetal. His use of the strange word "timepieces" was convincing. The unusual was in the air.

"There's Thompson's and Jackman's and Mrs. Horton's," Judy reminded him, her eyes shining like polished door-knobs.

"Too wrong to matter," decided Uncle Felix. "They're always slow or fast."

"Then there's the kitchen clock," Tim mentioned; "the grandfather thing."

Uncle Felix reflected a moment. His reply was satisfactory and conclusive:

"I'll go down to-night," he explained in a low voice, "when the servants are in bed. I'll take the weights off."

Judy and Tim appreciated the seriousness of the occasion more than ever.

"Into Mrs. Horton's kitchen?" they whispered.

"Into Mrs. Horton's kitchen," he agreed, beneath his breath.

Maria, meanwhile, said nothing. Her eyes kept open very wide, but no audible remark got past her lips. She paid no attention to the singing nor to the whispered conversation; she ate an enormous tea, finishing up all the cakes that the others neglected in their excitement and preoccupation; but she appeared as calm and unconcerned as the tea-cosy that concealed the heated, stimulating teapot beneath it. She looked more circular and globular than ever. Even the knowledge that this was the eve of her own particular adventure did not rouse her. Her expression seemed to say, "I never *have* believed in Time; at the centre where *I* live, clocks and calendars are not recognised"; and later, when Judy blew the candle out and asked as usual, "Are you all right, Maria?" her reply came floating across the darkened room without the smallest alteration in tone or accent: "I'm alright." The stopped alarum-clock was underneath her pillow; Uncle Felix had tucked them up, each in turn; everything was all right. She fell asleep, the others fell asleep, Time also fell asleep.

And above the Old Mill House that warm June night the darkness kept the secret faithfully, yet offered little signs and hints to those who did not sleep too heavily. The feeling that something or somebody was coming hung in the very air; there was a gentle haze beneath the stars; and a breeze that passed softly through the lime trees dropped semi-articulate warnings. There were curious, faint echoes flying between the walls and the Wood without a Centre; the daisies heard them and opened half an eyelid; the Night-Wind whispered and sighed as it bore them to and fro. Maria's question entered the dream of the entire garden: "Why not? Why not? Why not?"

An owl in the barn beyond the stables heard the call and took it up, and told it to some swallows fast asleep below the eaves, who woke with sudden chattering and mentioned it to a robin in the laurel shrubberies below. The robin pretended not to be at all surprised, but felt it a duty to inform a coot who lived a quarter of a mile away among the reeds of the lower pond. When it returned from its five-minute flight, the swallows had gone to sleep again, and only the owl went on hooting softly through the summer darkness. "It really needn't go on so long about it," thought the robin, then fell asleep again with its head between exactly the same feathers as before. But the news had been distributed; the garden was aware; the birds, as natural guardians of the dawn, had delivered the message as their duty was. "Why not? Why not?" hummed all night long through the dreams of the Mill House garden. Weeden turned in his sleep and sighed with happiness.

Nothing could now prevent it; a day was coming at last, an extra, unused, unrecorded day. The immemorial expectancy of childhood, the universal anticipation, the promise that something or somebody was coming—all this would be fulfilled. This promise is really but the prelude to creation. God felt it before the world appeared. And children have stolen it from heaven. Conceived of wonder, born of hope, and realised by belief, it is the prerogative of all properly-beating

Algernon Blackwood

hearts. Everything living feels it, and—everything lives. The Postman; the Figure coming down the road; the Visitor on the pathway; the Knock upon the door; even the Stranger in the teacup—all are embodiments of this exquisite scrap of heaven, divine expectancy. It may be Christmas, it may be only To-morrow, but equally it may be the End of the World. Something is coming—into the heart—something satisfying. It is the eternal beginning. It is the—dawn.

Long after the children had retired to bed Uncle Felix sat up alone in the big house thinking. He made himself cosy in the library, meaning to finish a chapter of the historical novel he had sadly neglected these past days, and he set himself to the work with a will. But, try as he would, the story would not run; he fixed his mind upon the scene in vain; he concentrated hard, visualised the place and characters as his habit was, reconstructed the incidents and conversation exactly as though he had seen them happen and remembered them—but the imagination that should have given them life failed to operate. It became a mere effort of invention. The characters would not talk of their own accord; the incidents did not flow in a stream as when he worked successfully; life was not in them. He began again, wrote and rewrote, but failed to seize the atmosphere of reality that alone could make them interesting. Interest—he suddenly realised it—had vanished. He felt no interest in the stupid chapter. He tore it up—and knew it was the right thing to do, because he heard the characters laughing.

"I'm not in the mood," he reflected. "It's artificial. William Smith of Peckham would skip this chapter. There's something bigger in me. I wonder...!"

He lit his pipe and sat by the open window, watching the stars and sniffing the scented summer night. He let his thoughts go wandering as they would, and the moment he relaxed attention a sense of pleasant relief stole over him. He discovered how great the effort had been. He also discovered the reason. It offered itself in a flash to his mind that was no longer blocked by the effort and therefore unreceptive.

"A man can't live adventure and write it too," he, realised sharply. "He writes what he would like to live. I'm living adventure. The desire to live it vicariously by writing it has left me. Of course!"

It was a sweet and rich discovery—that the adventures of the last ten days had been so real and meant so much to him. No man of action, leading a deep, full life of actual experience, felt the need of scribbling, painting, fiddling. "Glorious, by Jove!" he exclaimed between great puffs of smoke. "I've struck a fact!" He had been so busily creating these last days that he had lost the yearning to describe merely what others did. The children had caught him body and soul in their eternal world of wonder and belief. Judy and Tim had taught him this.

Yet, somehow, it was the inactive, calm Maria who loomed up in his thoughts as the principal enchantress. Maria's apparent inactivity was a blind; she did not do very much in the sense of rushing helter-skelter after desirable things, but she obtained them nevertheless. She got in their way so that they ran into her—then she claimed them. She knew beforehand, as it were, the way they would take. She was always there when anything worth happening was about. And though she spoke so little— during a general conversation, for instance—she said so much. At the end of all the talk, it was always Maria who had said the important thing. Her "why" and "why not" that very afternoon were all that he remembered of the intricate and long discussion. It left the odd impression on his mind that talk, all the world over, said one thing only; that the millions of talkers on the teeming earth, eagerly chattering in many languages, said one and the same thing only. There *was* only one thing to be said.

That is—they were all trying to say it. Maria *had* said it....

A whirring moth flew busily past the open window and vanished into the night. He thought of his own books; for writers, painters, preachers, musicians, these were trying to say it too. "If I could describe that moth exactly," he murmured to himself, "give the sensation of its flight, its unconscious attraction to the light, its plunge back into the darkness, its precise purpose in the universe, its marvellous aim and balance—its life, I could—er—"

The thought broke off with a jagged end. With a leap then it went on again:

"Touch reality," and he heard his own voice saying it. He had uttered it aloud. The sound had an odd effect upon him. He realised the uselessness of words. No words touched reality. To be known, reality had to be lived, experienced. Maria managed this in some extraordinary way. She had reality.... Time did not humbug her. Nor did space.... Goodness!

The moth whirred into the room, softly banging itself against the ceiling, and through the smoke from his pipe he saw that a dozen more were doing the same thing with tireless energy. They felt or saw the light; all obeyed the one driving desire to get closer into it. He saw millions and millions of people, the whole world over, rushing about on two legs and behaving similarly. How they did run about and fuss, to be sure! What was it all about? What were they after? People had to earn their living, of course, but it seemed more than that, for all were after something, and the faster they went the better pleased they were. Apparently they thought speed was of chief importance—as though speed killed Time. They banged themselves into obstacles everywhere; they screamed and disagreed, and accused each other of lying and being blind, but the thing they were after either hid itself remarkably well, or went at incredible speed, for no one ever came up with it or found it. Time invariably blocked them. Only one or two—Maria sort of people—sat still and waited....

He watched them all and wondered. One rushed up to an office in a train, while another built the train he rushed in; one wore black and preached a sermon, another wore blue and guarded a street, a third wore red and killed, a fourth wore very little and danced; all in the end were nothing and—

disappeared. Some lived in a room and read hundreds of books; another wrote them; one spent his days examining the stars through a telescope, another hurried off to find the Poles; hundreds were digging into the ground, ferreting in the air or under the water. A large number fed animals, then killed and cooked them when they had been fed enough. Hens laid eggs and eggs produced hens that laid more eggs. There were always thousands hurrying along the roads, then coming back again. The millions of living beings were everywhere extremely busy after something, yet hardly any two of them agreed exactly what it was they sought. There were sects, societies, religions by the score, each one cocksure it knew and had found Reality, yet proving by the continuous busy searching that it had not found it. Yet all, oddly enough, fitted in together fairly well, as in a gigantic Dance, though obviously none knew exactly what the tune was, nor who played it. Would they never know? Would all die before they found it? Were they all after the same thing, or after a lot of different things? And why, in the name of goodness, couldn't they all agree about it? Wasn't it, perhaps, that they looked in different ways—all for the same thing? Surely the world had existed long enough for *that* to be settled finally—Reality! Time prevented always....

A moth fell with a soft and disconcerting plop upon the top of his head, cannonaded thence against the window-sill, and shot out into the night again. He came back with a start to *his* reality: that he had promised the children an Extra Day, that for twenty-four hours, in spite of the paradox, Time should cease its driving hurry—and that, for the moment at any rate, he was very sleepy and must go upstairs to bed.

He rose, shook himself free of the curious reverie with a mighty yawn, and looked at the gold watch from his waistcoat pocket. Out came a number of other timepieces with it! And it was then that the personality of Maria entered the room, and stood beside him, and said distinctly, "This is *my* particular adventure, please remember."

And he understood that whatever happened, it would happen

according to the gospel of Maria. Getting behind Time meant getting a little nearer to Reality, one stage nearer at any rate. It meant entering the region where she dwelt so serenely. It was her doing, and not his. He realised in a flash that in her quiet way she was responsible and had drawn them in, seduced them. All gravitated to her and into her mysterious circle. Maria claimed them. It was certainly her particular adventure. Only she would share it with them all.

CHAPTER XVI

TIME HALTS

He looked at his watch a second time, and found that it was later than he had supposed—eleven o'clock. In the act of winding it, however, he paused; something he had forgotten came back to him, and a curious smile broke over his face. He stroked his beard, glanced at the ceiling where the moths still banged and buzzed, then strolled over to the open window, and said "Hm!" He put his head and shoulders out into the air. And then he again said "Hm—m—m"—only longer than the first time. It seemed as if some one answered him. That "Hm" floated off to some one who was listening for it. Perhaps it was an echo that came floating back. Perhaps it wasn't.

But any grown-up person who hesitates in an empty room of a country house at eleven o'clock at night and murmurs "Hm" into the open air is not in an ordinary state of mind. The normal thing is to put the lights out and go up more or less briskly to bed. Uncle Felix was no exception to this rule. His emotions, evidently, were not quite normal.

He listened. The night was very still. The stars, like a shower of golden rain arrested in full flight, paused in a flock and looked at him, but in so deliberate a way that he was conscious of being looked at. It was rather a delightful sensation, he thought; never before had they seemed so intimate, so interested in his life. He was aware that a friendly relationship existed between him and those far, bright, twinkling eyes.

"Hm" he murmured softly once again, then heard a sound of wings rush whirring past his face, and next a chattering of birds somewhere overhead among the heavy eaves. "So I'm not the only one awake," he thought, and, for some odd reason, felt rather pleased about it. "Sounds like swallows. I wonder!"

But he saw no movement anywhere; no wind stirred the ivy on the wall, the limes were motionless, the earth asleep. Even the stream beyond the laurel shrubberies ran silently. Dimly he made out the garden lying at attention, the flower-beds like folded hands upon its breast; and further off, the big untidy elms in pools of deeper shadow, their outlines blurred as dreams blur the mind. Yet, though he could detect no slightest movement, he was keenly aware that other things beside the stars were looking at him. The night was full of carefully-screened eyes, all fixed upon him. Framed in the lighted window, he was so easily visible. Night herself, calm and majestic, gazed down upon him through wide-open lids that filled the entire sky. He felt the intentness of her steadfast gaze, and paused. He stopped. It seemed that everything stopped too. So striking, indeed, was the sensation, that he gave expression to it half aloud:

"It's slowing up," he murmured, "stopping!... I do believe! Hm!..."

There was no answer this time, no sign of echo anywhere, but he heard an owl calling its muffled note from the Wood without a Centre.

"It's probably seen me too," he thought, and then it also stopped.

He waited a moment, hoping it would begin again, for he loved the atmosphere of childhood that the sound invoked in him. But the flutey call was not repeated. He drew his head in, closed and bolted the window, fastened the shutters carefully and pulled the curtains over; then he extinguished the lamps, lit his candle, and moved out softly into the hall on his way upstairs. And for the first time in his life he felt that in shutting the window he had not shut the beauty out. The beauty of that watching, listening night had not gone away from him by closing down the shutters. It was not lost. It stopped there. This novel realisation was very queer and very exquisite. Regret did not operate.

And he went along the passage, murmuring "Hm" over and over to himself, for there seemed nothing more adequate that he could think of. The servants had long since gone to bed; he alone was awake in the whole big house. He moved cautiously down the long corridor towards the green baize doors, fully aware that it was not the proper way upstairs. He pushed them, and they swung behind him with a grunt that repeated itself several times, lessening and shortening until it ended in an abrupt puffing sound—and he found himself in a chilly corridor of stone. It was very dark; the candle threw the shadow of his hand down the gaping length in front of him. He went stealthily a few steps further, then stopped opposite a closed door of white. For a moment he held his breath, examining the panels by the light of the raised candle; then turned the knob of brass, threw it wide open, and found himself—in Mrs. Horton's kitchen.

The room was very warm. There was the curious, familiar smell of brooms and aprons, of soap and soda, flavoured with brown sugar, treacle, and a dash of toast and roasted coffee. The ashes still glowed between the bars of the range like a grinning mouth. He put the candle down and looked about him nervously. There was an awful moment when he thought a great six-foot cook, with red visage and bare arms, would rise and strike him with a ladle or a rolling-pin. In the faint light he made out the white deal table in the centre, the rows of pots and pans gleaming in mid-air, dish-cloths hanging on a string to dry, layers of plates of various sizes on the shelves, and jugs suspended by their handles at an angle ready for pouring out. He saw the dresser with its huge, capacious drawers—the only drawers in the world that opened easily, and were deep enough to be of value.

Also—there was a sound, the sound all kitchens have, steadily tapping, clicking, ticking. He turned; he saw the familiar object whence the sound proceeded. At the end of the great silent room, upright like a sentry placed against the wall, stiff and rigid, he saw a figure with a round and pallid face, staring solemnly at him through the gloom. He stiffened and stood rigid too, listening to the tapping noise that issued from its hollow interior of wood and iron. Watching him with remorseless mien, the kitchen clock asked him for the password. "Why not? Why not?" its ticking said distinctly.

The warmth was comforting. He sat down on the white deal table, knowing himself an intruder, but boldly facing the tall monster that guarded the deserted room and challenged him. "*You* haven't stopped," he answered in his beard. "Why not?" And as he said it, a new expression stole upon its hardened countenance, the challenge melted, the obdurate stare relaxed. The quaint, grandfatherly aspect of benevolence shone over it like a smile; it looked not only kind, but contrite. He saw it as it used to be, ages and ages ago, when he was a boy, sliding down the banisters towards it, or towards its counterpart in the hall. It winked.

The ticking, too, became less aggressive and relentless, less sure of itself, almost as though it were slowing up. There was a plaintive note behind the metallic sharpness. The great kitchen clock also was aware of a conspiracy hatching against Time....

And as he sat and listened to the machinery tapping away the seconds, he heard a similar tapping in his brain that swung gradually into rhythm with the clock. A pendulum in his mind was swinging, each swing a little shorter than the one before; and he remembered that a dozen pendulums in a room, starting at different lengths, ended by swinging all together. "We're slowing up together—stopping!" murmured the two pendulums. "Why not? Why not? Why not?..."

Presently both would cease, yet ceasing would be the beginning, not the end. A state without end or beginning would supervene. Ticking meant time, and time meant becoming; but beyond becoming lay the bottomless sea of being, which was eternity. Maria floated there—calm, quiet, serene, little globular Maria, circular, the perfect form.

The Kitchen Spell rolled in upon him, smothering mind and senses.

It came at first so gradually he hardly noticed it, but it rose and rose and rose, till at length he sat dipped to the eyes in it, and then finally his eyes went under too. He was immersed, submerged. The parochial vanished; he swam in the universal. He felt drowsy, soothed, and very happy; his heart beat differently. Consciousness ran fluttering along the edge of something hard that hitherto had seemed an unsurpassable barrier. The barrier melted and let him through.

He rubbed his eyes and started. "That's the clock in Mrs. Horton's kitchen," he tried to say, but the words had an empty and ridiculous sound, as if there was no meaning in them. They flew about him in the air like little butterflies trying to settle. They settled on one meaning, only to flit elsewhere the next minute and settle on another meaning. They could mean anything and everything. They did mean everything. They meant *one* thing. Finally they settled back into his heart. And their meaning caught him by the throat in a most delicious way. The air was full of tiny fluttering wings; he heard pattering feet and little voices; hair tied with coloured ribbons brushed his cheeks; and laughing, mischievous eyes like stars floated loose about the ceiling. The Kitchen Spell grew mighty—irresistible... rising over him out of a timeless Long Ago.

From the direction of the ghostly towel-horse it seemed to come. But beyond the towel-horse was the window, and beyond the window lay the open fields, and beyond the fields lay miles and miles of country asleep beneath the stars; and this country stretched without a break right up to the lonely wolds of distant Yorkshire where an old grey house contained another kitchen, silent and deserted in the night. All the empty kitchens of England were at this moment in league together, but this old Yorkshire kitchen was the parent of them all—and thence the Spell first issued. It was his own childhood kitchen.

And Uncle Felix travelled backwards against the machinery of Time that cheats the majority so easily with its convention of moving hands and ticking voice and bullying, staring visage. He slid swiftly down the long banister-descent of years and reached in a flash that old sombre Yorkshire kitchen, and stood, four-foot nothing, face smudged and fingers sticky, beside the big deal table with the dying embers in the grate upon his right. His heart was beating. He could just reach the juicy cake without standing on a chair. He ate the very slice that he had eaten forty years ago. It *was* possible to have your cake and eat it too!...

He gulped it down and sucked the five fingers of each hand in turn—then turned to attack the staring monster that had tried to make him believe it was impossible. He crossed the stone floor on tiptoe, but with challenge in his heart, looked straight into its humbugging big face, opened its carefully buttoned jacket—and took off the weights.

"Hm!" he murmured, with complacent satisfaction that included victory, "I've stopped you!"

There was a curious, long-drawn sound as the machinery ran down; the chains quivered, then hung motionless. There was disaster in the sound, but laughter too—the laughter of the culprit caught in the act, unmasked, exposed at last. "But I've had a good time these last hundred years," he seemed to hear, with the obvious answer this insolence suggested: "Caught! You're It!"—in a tone that was not wholly unlike Maria's.

He turned and left the kitchen as stealthily as he had entered it. He went along the cold stone corridor, through the green baize doors, and so up the softly carpeted stairs to his bedroom. He undressed and rolled solemnly between the sheets. He sighed deeply, but he did not move again. He fell instantly into the right position for sleep.

But while he slept, the timeless night brought up its mystery. Moored outside against the walls an Extra Day lay swinging from the stars. The waves of Time washed past its sides, yet could not move it. The wind was in the rigging; it lay at anchor, filling the sky with a beauty of eternity. And above the old Mill House the darkness, led by the birds, flowed on to meet the quivering Dawn.

CHAPTER XVII

A DAY HAS COME

MARIA'S PARTICULAR ADVENTURE

The day was hardly born, and still unsure of itself, when a robin with its tail cocked up stood up alertly on the window-sill of Uncle Felix's bedroom, peeped in through the open sash, and noticed the objects in front of it with a certain deliberation.

These objects were half in shadow, but, unlike those it was most familiar with, they did not move in the breeze that stirred the world outside. The robin had just swung up from a lilac branch below. Its toes were spread to their full extent for balancing purposes. It peeped busily in all directions. Then, suddenly, a big object at the far end of the darkened room moved slowly underneath a mass of white, as Uncle Felix, aware that some one was watching him, rolled over in his bed, opened his sleepy eyes, and stared. At the same moment the robin twitched, and fixed its brilliant glance upon him. It had found the particular object that it sought.

Uncle Felix, somewhat dazed by sleep and dreams, saw the tight, fat body of the bird outlined against the open sky, but thought at first it was an eagle or a turkey, until perspective righted itself, and enabled him to decide that it was a robin only. He saw its scut tail pointing. And, from the attitude of the bird, of its cocked-up tail, the angle of its neck and head, to say nothing of the inquisitive way it peeped sideways at him over the furniture, he realised that it had come in with a definite purpose—a purpose that concerned himself. In a word, it had something to communicate.

"Odd!" he thought drowsily, as he met its piercing eye. "A robin in my room at dawn! I wonder what it's up to?"

Then, remembering vaguely that he expected somebody or something out of the ordinary, he made a peculiar noise that seemed to meet the case: he tried to whistle at it. But his lips, being rather dry, made instead a hissing sound that would have frightened most robins out of the room at once. On this particular bird, however, the effect was just the opposite. It hopped self-consciously on to the dressing-table, fluttered next to the arm-chair, and the same second dropped out of sight behind the end of the four-poster bed. It acted, that is, with decision; it was making distinct advances.

He sat up then in order to see it better, and discovered it perched saucily upon the toe of his evening shoe, looking deliberately into his face as it rose above the bed-clothes.

"Come along," he said, making his voice as soft as possible, "and tell me what you want."

His expression tried to convey that he was harmless, and he smiled to counteract the effect of his bristling hair which stuck out at right angles as it only can stick out on waking. He felt complimented by the visit of the bird, and did not wish to frighten it. But the Robin, accustomed to seeing scarecrows in the dawn, showed not the slightest fear; on the contrary, it showed interest and a simple, innocent affection too. It fluttered up on to the rail between the bed-posts, almost within reach of his stretched-out hand; its flexible toes clutched the bar as though it were a twig; it moved first two inches to the right, then two inches to the left again, then held steady. It next flicked its tail, and cocked its small head sideways, as if about to deliver a speech or message it had learned by heart; stared intently into the bearded human visage close in front of it; abruptly opened its wings; whirred them with a rapidity that made a sound like a shower of peas striking a taut sheet; and then, with a single, exquisitely-chosen curve—vanished through the open window and was gone.

"Well," murmured the confused and astonished man, "if anything means anything, that does. Only, I wonder what it *does* mean!"

He was a little startled, and he remained in a sitting position for some minutes, staring at the open window, and hoping the robin would return. Somehow he did not think it would, but he hoped it might. The robin, however, made no sign. And, meanwhile, the dawn slipped higher up the sky, showing the groups of trees with greater sharpness. A draught of morning air came in.

"The dawn!" he thought; "how marvellous! Perhaps the robin came to show me that." He sniffed the fresh perfume of dew and leaves and earth that rise for a moment with the early light, then fade away. "Or that!" he added, pausing to enjoy the delicate fragrance. "But for the bird I should have slept, and missed them both. I wonder!"

He wished he were dressed and out upon the lawn; but the bed was enticing, and it was no easy thing to get up and wash and put on eleven separate articles of clothing. What a pity he was not dressed like a bird in one garment only! What a pity he could not wash himself by flying through a rushing shower of sweet rain! By the time his clothes were on, and he had made his way downstairs, and unlocked the big chained doors, all this strange, wild emotion would have evaporated. If only he could have landed with a single curve among the flower-beds, as the robin did! Besides, he would feel hungry, and a worm...!

The warmth of the bed crept upwards towards his eyes; the eyelids dropped of their own accord; his weight sank slowly downwards; the pillow was smooth as cream. He remembered

Judy saying once that, if a war came, she would go out and "soothe pillows." A pillow was, indeed, a very soothing thing. His head sank backwards into a mass of feathery sensations like a flock of dreams. He drew a long, deep breath. He began to forget a number of things, and to remember a number of other things. They mingled together, they became indistinguishable. What were they? He could make a selection—choose those he liked best, and leave the others—couldn't he? Why not, indeed? Why not?

One was that the clocks had stopped for twenty-four hours and that an extra, unused day was dawning; another, that To-day was Sunday. He could make his choice. Yet all days, surely, were unused till they came! True; but clocks decreed and regulated their length. *This* Extra Day, having been overlooked long ago, was beyond the reach of measuring clocks. No clocks had ever ticked it into passing. It could never pass. Only the present passed. The Past, to which this day belonged, remained where it was, endless, beginningless, self-repeating. He chose it without more ado. And the robin had come to mention something about it. Its small round body was full, its head tight packed with what it had to tell. It was bursting with information. But what—?

And then he realised abruptly another thing: It *had* delivered its message.

The presence of the bird had announced a change of conditions in the room, a change in his heart and brain as well. But how? He was too drowsy to decide quite; yet in some way the robin had brought in with it the dawn of an unusual day, a kind of bird-day, light as a feather, swift as a flashing wing, spontaneous—air, freedom, escape, sweet brilliance, a thing of flowers, winds, and beauty, a thing of innocence and captivating loveliness, a happy, dancing day. He felt a new sort of knowledge pass darting through him, a new point of view, almost a bird's-eye aspect of old familiar things—joy. That neat, sharp beak had pricked his imagination into swifter life. The meaning of the bird's announcement flowed with delicate

Algernon Blackwood

power all through his drowsy body. It summed itself up in this:—Somebody, Something, long expected, at last was coming....

And then he incontinently fell asleep. He lost consciousness. But, while he lay heavily upon his soothing pillow, the marvellous Dawn slid higher up the sky, and the robin popped up once upon the window-sill again, glanced sideways at him with approval, then flashed away so close above the soaking lawn that the dew-drops quivered as it passed. Apparently, it was satisfied.

At the same moment, in another part of the old house, Tim found his sleep disturbed in a similar fashion; a shrill twittering beneath the eaves mingled with his dreams. He shook a toe and wrinkled up his nose. He woke. His bedroom, being on the top floor, was lighter than those below; there were no trees to cast shadows or obstruct the dawn.

Tim rubbed his eyes, yawned, scratched, then pattered over to the window to see what all the noise was about. In his night-shirt he looked like a skinny bird with folded wings of white, as he leaned forward and stuck his head out into the morning air. Upon the strip of back-lawn below, the swallows, who had been chattering so loudly overhead, stood in an active group. Clutching the cold iron bars, and resting his chin upon the topmost one, he watched them. He had never before seen swallows on the ground like that; he associated them with the upper sky. It was odd to see them standing instead of flying; their behaviour seemed not quite normal; there was commotion of an unusual kind among them. A grey cat, stalking them warily down the stable path, came near yet did not trouble them; they felt no alarm. They strutted about like a lot of black-frocked parsons at a congress; they looked as if they had hands tucked behind their pointed coat-tails. They were talking among themselves—discussing something. And from time to time they shot upward glances at the window just above them—at himself.

"I believe they want me to look at something or other," the boy thought vaguely. It seemed as if he had picked them out of a dream and put them there upon the lawn. He felt dazed and happy; he had been dreaming of curious wild things. Where was he? What had happened? "It feels just like something coming," he decided, "or somebody. Some one's about in the grounds, perhaps...!"

It was very exciting to be awake at such an unearthly hour; the sun was still below the edge of the gigantic earth! A great, slow thrill stole up into his heart. He noticed the streaks of colour in the sky, and felt the chilly wind. "It's sunrise!" he exclaimed, rubbing one naked foot against the other; "that's what it is. And I'm up to see it!"

The thrill merged into a deep, huge sense of wonder that enthralled him. At the same moment the swallows, disturbed by his voice, looked up with one accord, then rose in a single sweep and whirled off into the upper air, wings faintly tinged with gold. They scattered. Tim watched them for a little while, dimly aware that he watched something "perfectly magnificent." His eyes followed one bird after another, caught in a sudden little rapture he could not understand... then turned and saw his bed, flushed with early pink, across the room. With a running jump he landed among the sheets, rolled himself up into a ball, and promptly fell asleep again. It was not yet four o'clock.

Across the landing, meanwhile, Judy, wakened by a brush of feathery wind, was at her window too. She felt very sure of something, although she didn't in the least know what. It was the same thing that Tim and Uncle Felix knew, only they knew they didn't know it, whereas she didn't know she knew it. Her knowledge, therefore, was greater than theirs.

The room was touched with soft grey light; it was to the west, and the night still clung about the furniture. Like a ball in a saucer, Maria lay asleep in bed against the opposite wall, her neutrality to all that was going on absolute as usual. But Judy did not wake her, she preferred to live alone; she knew that she was alive in her night-gown between night and morning, and that was an unusual pleasure she wished to enjoy without interference. For months she had not waked before half-past seven. The excitement of the unfamiliar was in her heart. She had caught the earth asleep—surprised it. For the first time in her life she saw "the Earth." She discovered it.

She knelt on a chair beside the open window, peering out, and as she did so, a strange, wild cry came sounding through the stillness. It was like a bugle-call, but she knew no human lips had made it. She glanced quickly in the direction whence it came—the pond—and the next instant the reeds about the edge parted and the thing that had emitted the curious wild cry emerged plainly into view. It was a pompous-looking creature. It came out waddling.

"It's the up-and-under bird," exclaimed Judy in a whisper. "Something's happening!"

It was a water-fowl, a creature whose mysterious habit of living upon the surface of the pond as well as underneath made the children's nick-name a necessity. And now it was attempting a raid on land as well. But land was not its natural place. Something certainly had happened, or was going to happen.

"It's a snopportunity," decided Judy instantly. Far more than an opportunity, a snopportunity was something to be snapped up quickly, the sort of thing that ordinarily happened behind one's back, usually discovered too late to be made use of. "I've caught it!" She remembered that the clocks had stopped, yet not knowing why she remembered it. It was the thing she didn't know she knew. She knew it before it happened. That was a snopportunity.

She watched the heavy bird for a considerable time as it slowly appropriated the land it had no right to. It moved, she thought, like a twisted drum on very short drumsticks. It had a water-logged appearance. It was bird and fish ordinarily, but now it was pretending to be animal as well—a thing that flew, swam, walked. Its webbed feet patted the ground complacently. It came laboriously towards the wall of the house, then halted. It paused a moment, then turned its eyes up, while Judy turned hers down. The pair of creatures looked at one another steadily for several seconds.

"You're not out for nothing," exclaimed Judy audibly. "So now I know!"

The reply was neither in the affirmative nor in the negative. The up-and-under bird said nothing. It made no sign. It just turned away, stalked heavily back across the lawn without once looking either to right or left, launched itself upon the water, uttered its queer bugle-call for the last and second time, and promptly disappeared below. The tilt of its vanishing tail expressed sublime indifference to everything on land. And Judy, reflecting vaguely that she, too, was something of an up-and-under creature, followed its example, though without the same dispatch or neatness of execution. She tumbled sideways into bed and disappeared beneath the sheets, aware that the bird had left her richer than it found her. It had communicated something that lay beyond all possible explanation. She had no tail, nor did she express indifference. On the contrary, she hugged herself, making sounds of pleasurable anticipation in her throat that lay plunged among depths of soothing pillows.

It seems, then, that the entire household, the important portion of it, at any rate, had been duly notified that something unusual was afoot, and that the dawn of the day just breaking through a ghostly sky was distinctly out of the ordinary. The birds, always the first to wake, and provided with the most sensitive apparatus for recording changes, had caught the mysterious whisper from the fading night; they had instantly communicated it to the best of their ability to their established friends. The robin, the swallows, and the up-and-under bird, having accomplished their purpose, disappeared from view in order to attend to breakfast and the arrangement of their own subsequent adventures. Earth, air, and water had delivered messages. The news had been flashed. Those who deserved it had been warned. The day could now begin.

Maria, alone, meanwhile, slept on soundly, secure in that stodgy immobility that takes no risks. Oblivious, apparently, of all secret warnings of excitement or alarm, she lay in a tight round ball, inactive, undisturbed. Even her breathing revealed her peculiar idiosyncrasy: no actual movement on her surface was discernible. Her breathing involved the least possible disturbance of the pink and white contours that bulged the sheets and counterpane. Her face was calm, expressionless, and even dull, yet wore a certain look as though she knew so much that she had no need to maintain her position by the least assertion. Exertion would have been a denial of her right to exist. And exist she certainly did. The weight of her personality lent balance to the quivering uncertainty of this mysterious dawn. Maria remained an unassailable reality, an immovable centre round which anything might happen, yet never end, and certainly no disaster come. And Judy, glancing at her as she disappeared below her own sheets, noted this fact without understanding that she did so. This was another aspect of the thing she didn't know she knew.

"Maria's asleep," she felt, "so there's no need to get up yet. It's all right!" In spite of the marvellous thing she knew was coming, that is, she felt herself anchored safely to the firm reality of calm Maria, soundly, peacefully asleep. And five minutes later she was in the same desirable condition herself.

But, hardly were they all asleep, than a figure none of them had noticed, yet all perhaps had vaguely felt, rose out of the little ditch this side of the laurel shrubberies, and advanced slowly towards the old Mill House. The shape was shadowy and indeterminate at first; it might have been a bush, a sheaf of straw, a clump of high-grown weeds, for birds fluttered just above it, and the swallows darted down without alarm. A shaggy thing, it seemed part of the natural landscape.

Half-way across the lawn, however, it paused and stretched itself; it rubbed its eyes; it yawned; and, as it shook the sleep from face and body, the outline grew distinctly clearer. The thing that had looked like a bundle of hay or branches resolved itself into a human being; the loose untidiness gave place to definite shape, as leaves, grass, twigs, and wisps of straw fell fluttering from it to the ground. It was a pathetic and yet wonderful sight, beauty, happiness, and peace about it somewhere, together with a soft and tender sweetness that tempered the wildness of its aspect. Indescribably these qualities proclaimed themselves. It was a man.

"They've seen me twice," he mentioned to the dipping swallows. "This is my third appearance. They'll recognise me without a word. The Day has come."

He stood a moment, shaking the extras of the night from hair and clothing, then laughed with a sound like running water as the birds swooped down and carried the straws and twigs away with a great business of wings. Next, glancing up at the open windows of the house, he started forward with a light but steady step. "They will not be surprised," he said, "for they have always believed in me. They knew that some day I should come, and in the twinkling of an eye!" He paused and chuckled in his beard. "I'm not *the* one thing they're expecting, but I'm next door to it, and I can show them how to look at any rate."

And he began softly humming the words of a little song he had evidently made up himself, and therefore liked immensely. He neared the walls; the sunrise tipped a happy, glorious face; he disappeared from view as though he had melted through the old grey stone. And a flight of swallows, driven by the fresh dawn wind, passed high overhead across the heavens, leading the night away. They swung to the rhythm of his little song:

My secret's in the wind and open sky,
There is no longer any Time—to lose;
The world is young with laughter; we can fly

Among the imprisoned hours as we choose.

The rushing minutes pause; an unused day
Breaks into dawn and cheats the tired sun;
The birds are singing. Hark! Come out and play!
There is no hurry! Life has just begun!

THE EXTRA DAY

BEHIND *TIME*

I

The day broke. It broke literally. The sky gave way and burst asunder, scattering floods of radiant sunshine. This was the feeling in Uncle Felix's heart as he came downstairs to breakfast in the schoolroom. A sensation of feathery lightness was in him, of speed as well: he could rise above every obstacle in the world, only—there were no obstacles in the world to rise above. Boredom, despair, and pessimism, he suddenly realised, meant deficiency of energy merely. "Birds can rise above everything—and so can I!"—as though he possessed a robin's normal temperature of 110 degrees!

Although it was Sunday morning, and a dark suit was his usual custom, he had slipped into flannels and a comfortable low collar, without thinking about it one way or the other. "It's a jolly day," he hummed to himself, "and I'm alive. We must do all kinds of things—everything! It's all one thing really!" It seemed there was a new, uplifting sense of joy in merely being alive. He repeated the word again and again—"alive, alive, alive!" Of course a robin sang: it was the natural thing to do.

He looked out of the window while dressing, and caught the startling impression that this life emanated from the world of familiar trees and grass and flowers spread out before his eyes. Everything was singing. Beauty had dropped down upon the

Algernon Blackwood

earth; the earth, moreover, knew that she was beautiful—she was obviously enjoying herself, both as a whole and in every tiniest nook and corner of her gigantic being. Yet without undue surprise he noted this; the marvel was there as always, but he did not pause to say, "How marvellous!" It was as natural as breathing, and as easily accepted. He was always breathing, but he never stopped and thought, "Good Lord, I'm breathing! How dreadful if it stopped!" He simply went on breathing. And so, with the beauty of this radiant morning, it never occurred to him "This will not last, the sun will set, the shadows fall, the marvel pass and die." That this particular day could end did not even suggest itself.

On his way down the passage, Judy and Tim came dancing from their rooms to meet him. They, too, were dressed in their everyday-adventure things, no special sign of Sunday anywhere about them—slipped into their summery clothing as naturally as birds and flowers grow into the bright and feathery stuff that covers them. This notion struck him, but faintly; it was not a definite thought. He might as well have noticed, "Ah, the sky is dressed in light, or mist! The wind blows it into folds and creases!" Yet the notion did strike him with its little dream-like hammer, because with it came a second tiny blow, producing, it seemed, a soft blaze of light behind his eyes somewhere: "I've recovered the childhood sense of reality, the vivid certainty, the knowledge!... Somebody's coming.... Somebody's here— hiding still, perhaps, yet nearer..." It flashed like a gold-fish in some crystal summer fountain... and was gone again.

In the passage Judy touched his hand, and said confidingly, "You will take me to the end of the world to-day, Uncle."

It was true and possible. No special preparation was required for any journey whatsoever. They were already prepared for anything—like birds. And some one, it seemed, had taken his name away!

"We'll do everything at once," said Tim, with the utmost assurance in tone and manner.

"Of course," was his obvious and natural reply to each, no explanations or conditions necessary. Things would happen of themselves, spontaneously. There was only one thing to do! "We're alive," he added. They just looked at him as he said it, then pulled him down the passage a little faster than before. Yet the way they ran dancing along that oil-cloth passage held something of the joy and confidence with which birds launch themselves into flight across the earth. There was this sense of spontaneous excitement and delight about.

"He's here already," Judy whispered, as they neared the breakfast room. "I can feel it."

"Came in while we were asleep," her brother added. "I know it," and he clapped his hands.

"At dawn, yes," agreed Uncle Felix, saying it on the spur of the moment. He was perplexed a little, perhaps, but did not hesitate. He had not *quite* the assurance of the others. He meant to let himself go, however.

There was not the slightest doubt or question anywhere; *they* believed because they knew; what they had expected for so long had happened. The Stranger in the Tea-cup had arrived at last. They went down the long corridor of the Old Mill House, every window open to the sunshine that came pouring in. The very walls seemed made of transparent, shining paper. The world came flowing in. A happiness of the glowing earth sang in their veins. At the door they paused a second.

"I know exactly who he is," breathed Judy softly.

"I know what he looks like," whispered Tim.

"There was never time to see him properly before," said Uncle Felix. "Things went by so fast. He whizzed and vanished. But now—of course-"

They pushed the door open and went in.

Breakfast was already laid upon the shining cloth; hot dishes steamed; there were flowers upon the table, and climbing roses peeped in round the grey walls of sun-baked stone. A bird or two hopped carelessly upon the window-sill, and a smell of earth and leaves was in the air. Sunshine, colour, and perfume filled the room to overflowing, yet not so full that there was not ample space for the "somebody" who had brought them. For somebody certainly was there—some one whom the children, moreover, took absolutely for granted.

There had been surprise outside the door, but there was none when they were in. Something like a dream, it seemed, this absence of astonishment, though, of course, no one took it in that way. For, at first, no one spoke at all. The children went to their places, lifting the covers to see what there was to eat. They did the normal, natural thing; eyed and sniffed the porridge, cream, brown sugar, and especially approved the dish of comfortable, fat poached eggs on toast. They were satisfied with what they saw; everything was as it ought to be— plentiful, available, on hand. There was enough for everybody.

But Uncle Felix paused a moment just inside the open door, and stared; he looked about him as though the incredible thing had really happened at last. A rapt expression passed over his face, and his eyes seemed fixed upon something radiant that hung upon the air. He sighed, and caught his breath. His heart grew amazingly light within him. Every thought and feeling that made up his personality—so it felt, at least—had wings of silver tipped with golden fire.

"At last!" he murmured softly to himself, "at last!"

He moved forward slowly into the room, his eyes still fixed on vacancy. The face showed exquisite delight, but the lips were otherwise dumb. He looked as if he had caught a glimpse of something he could not utter.

"Porridge, please, Uncle," he heard a voice saying, as some one put a large silver spoon into his hand. "I like the hard lumps."

And another voice added, "I like the soupy, slippery stuff, please." He pulled himself together with an effort.

"Ah," he mumbled, peeping from the dishes at the children's faces, "the tea has stopped turning in the cup at last. He's come up to the surface."

And they turned and looked at him, but without the least surprise again; it was perfectly natural, it seemed, that there should be this Presence in the room; their Uncle's remark was neither here nor there. He had a right to express his own ideas in his own way if he wanted to. Their own remarks outside the door they had apparently forgotten. That, indeed, was already a very long time ago now. In the full bliss of realisation, anticipation was naturally not remembered. The excitement in the passage belonged to some dim Yesterday—almost when they were little.

They began immediately to talk *at* the Stranger in the room.

"I didn't *hear* anybody come," remarked Tim, as he mixed cream and demerara sugar inside an artificial pool of porridge, "but it's all the same—now. Our Somebody's here all right." And then, between gulps, he added, "The swallows laid an awful lot of eggs in the night, I think."

"On tiptoe just at dawn," remarked Judy casually, following her own train of thought, and intent upon chasing a slippery poached egg round and round her plate at the same time. "The birds were awake, of course."

The birds! As she said it, a memory of some faint, exquisite dream, of years and years ago it seemed, fled also on tiptoe through the bright, still air, and through three listening hearts as well. The robin, the swallows, and the up-and-under bird made secret signs and vanished.

"They know everything first, of course," said Uncle Felix aloud; "they're up so early, aren't they?" To himself he said,

"I'm dreaming! This is a dream!" his reason still fluttering a little before it died. But he kept his secret about the robin tightly in its hiding-place.

"Before they've happened—*really*," Tim mentioned. "They do a thing to-morrow long before to-morrow's come." He knew something the others could not possibly know.

"Everything comes from the air, you see," advanced Judy, secure in the memory of her private morning interview. "But it can disappear under—underneath when it wants to."

"Or into a hole," agreed Tim.

And somebody in that breakfast-room, somebody besides themselves, heard every word they spoke, listened attentively, and understood the meanings they thought they hid so cleverly. They knew, moreover, that he did so.

"Let's pretend," Tim suddenly exclaimed, catching his sister's eye just as it was wandering into the pot of home-made marmalade.

"All right," she said at once, "same as usual, I suppose?"

Tim nodded, glancing across the table. "Sitting next to *you*, Uncle"—he pointed to the unoccupied chair and unused plate—"in that empty place."

"Thank you," murmured the man, still hovering between reality and dream. He said it shyly. It was all too marvellous to ask questions about, he felt.

"It's a lovely morning," continued Judy politely, smiling at the empty place. "Will you have tea and coffee, or milkhot-waterandsugar?" She listened attentively for the answer, the smile of a duchess on her rosy face, then bowed and handed a lump of sugar to Tim, who set it carefully in the middle of the plate.

"Butter or honey?" inquired the boy, "or butter and honey?" He, too, waited for the inaudible reply, then asked his Uncle to pass the pot of honey *and* the butter-dish. The Stranger, apparently, liked sweet things best—at any rate, natural things.

They went on with their breakfast then, eating as much as ever they could hold, talking about everything in the world as usual, and occasionally bowing to the empty chair, addressing remarks to it, and listening to—answers! Sometimes they passed things, too—another lump of sugar, more drops of honey, a thick blob of clotted cream as well. It was obvious to them that somebody occupied that chair, so real, indeed, that Uncle Felix found himself passing things and making observations about the weather and even arranging a few crumbs of bread in a row beside the other delicacies. It was the right thing to do evidently; acting spontaneously, he had performed an inspired action. And the odd thing was that the food, lying in the blaze of sunlight on the plate, slowly underwent a change: the sugar got smaller in size, the honey-drops diminished, the blob of cream lost its first circumference, and even the bread-crumbs seemed to dwindle visibly.

"It's very hot this morning," said Judy after a bit. "The sun's hungrier than usual," and she pushed the plate into the shade. But it was clear that she referred to some one other than the sun, although the sun belonged to what was going on. "Thirsty, too," she added, "although there are bucketsful of dew about."

"And extra bright into the bargain," declared Tim. "I love shiny stuff like that to wear and dress in. It fits so easily—no bothering buttons."

"And doesn't wear out or stain, does it?" put in Uncle Felix, saying the first thing that came into his head—and again behaving in the appropriate, spontaneous manner. It was clear that the Stranger—to them, at least—was clothed in the gold and silver of the brilliant morning. There was a delicate perfume, too, as of wild flowers and sweet little roadside blossoms. The very air of the room was charged with some living light and beauty brought by the invisible guest. It was passing wonderful. The invading Presence seemed all about them like a spreading fire of loveliness and joy—yet natural as sunshine.

Then, suddenly, Tim sprang up from his chair, and ran to the empty seat. His face shone with keen and eager expectancy, but wore a touch of shyness too.

"I want to be like you," he said in a hushed voice that had all the yearning of childhood breaking through it. "Please put your hand on me." He lowered his head and closed his eyes. He made an odd grimace, half pleasure and half awe, like a boy about to plunge into a pool of water,—then stood upright, proud and delighted as any victorious king. He drew a long breath of relief. He seemed astonished that it had been so easily accomplished.

"I'm full of it!" he cried. "I'm burning! He touched me on the head!"

"Touched!" cried Judy, full herself of joy and happy envy.

The boy nodded his head, as though he would nod it off on to the tablecloth. He looked as if any minute he might burst into flame with the sheer enjoyment of it. "Warm all over," he gasped. "I could strike a match on my trousers now like Weeden."

Then, while Uncle Felix rubbed his eyes and did his best to see the invisible, Judy sprang lightly from her chair, ran up to the vacant place, put out her arms and bent her face down so that her falling torrent of hair concealed it for a moment. She certainly put her arms round—something. The next minute she straightened up again with triumph and tumult in her shining eyes.

"I kissed him," she announced, flushed like any rose, "and he kissed me back. He blew the wind into my hair as well. I'm flying! I'm lighter than a feather!" And she went, dancing and flitting, round the table like a happy bird.

Then Uncle Felix rose sedately from his seat. He did not mean to be left out of all this marvellous business merely because his body was a little older and more worn. He stretched his arm across the table, missing the cream-jug by a narrow margin, but knocking the toast-rack over in his eagerness. He held his hand out to the empty chair.

"Please take my hand," he said, "and let me have something too."

He went through the pantomime of shaking hands, but to his intense amazement it seemed that there was an answering clasp. A smooth, soft running touch closed gently on his own; it was cool and yielding, delicate as the down upon a robin's breast, yet firm as steel. And in that moment he knew that his glimpse on entering the room was not a trick, but had been a passing glimpse of what the children always believed in, hoped for—saw.

"Thank you," he murmured, withdrawing his hand and examining it, "very much indeed. This *is* a beautiful day."

An extraordinary power came into him, a feeling of confidence and security and joy he had never known before. Yet all he could find to say was that it was a very beautiful day. The commonest speech expressed exactly what he felt. Ordinary words at last had meaning, small words could tell it.

"It's all right?" remarked Tim, in an excited but quite natural tone.

"It *is*," he answered.

"Then let's go out now and do all sorts of things. There's

simply heaps to do."

"Out into the sun," cried Judy. "Come on. We'll get into our old garden boots." And she dragged her brother headlong out of the room.

THE STRANGER WHO IS WONDER

II

And Uncle Felix moved forward into the pool of sunlight that blazed upon the faded carpet pattern. It was composed of round, fat trees, this pattern, with birds like goblin peacocks flying in mid-air between them. The sunshine somehow lifted them, so that they floated upon the quivering atmosphere; the pattern seemed to hover between him and the carpet. And he too felt himself lifted—in mid-air—part of the day and sunshine.

He closed his eyes; he tried to realise who and where he was; all he could remember, however, went into a single sentence and kept repeating itself on the waves of his singing, dancing blood: "Clock's stopped, clock's stopped,—stopped clocks, stopped clocks...!" till it sounded like a puzzle sentence—then lost all meaning.

He sat down in a chair, but the chair was next to the "empty" one, and from it something poured into him, over him, round him, as wind pours about a bird or tree. He became enveloped by it; his mind began to rush, yet rushed in a circle, so that he never entirely lost sight of it. Another set of words replaced the first ones: "Behind Time, behind Time," jostling on each other's heels, tearing round and round like a Catherine Wheel, shining and dancing as they spun.

He opened his eyes and looked about him. The room was full

Algernon Blackwood

of wonder. It glistened, sparkled, shone. A million things, screened hitherto from sight by thick clouds of rushing minutes, paused and offered themselves; things that were commonplace before stood still, revealed in startling glory. They no longer raced past at headlong speed. Visible at last, unmasked, they showed themselves as they really were, in naked beauty. This beauty settled on everything in golden rain, it settled on himself as well. All that his eyes rested on looked— distinguished....

And, like snow-flakes, words and thoughts came thickly crowding, like flakes of fire too. He snatched at them, caught them in bunches, tried to sort them into sentences. They were everywhere about him, showering down as from a box of cardboard letters overturned in the sky. The reality he sought hid among them as a whole—he knew that—but no mere sequence of words and letters could quite capture this reality.

He plunged his hands among the flying symbols....

In a flash a number of things—an enormous number of things—became extraordinarily clear and simple; they became one single thing. Then, while reason and vision still fluttered to and fro, like a pair of butterflies, first one and then the other leading, he dashed in between them. He seized handfuls of the flying letters and made the queerest sentences out of them, longer and faster-moving than the first ones.

"Time *is* the arch-deceiver. It drives things past us in a hurrying flock. We snatch at them. And those we miss seem lost for ever because some one calls out, in a foolish voice of terror and regret, 'Too late!' Yet, in reality, *we* stand still; the rush of the hours is a sham. We see things out of proportion, like trees from the window of a train, their beauty hidden in a long, thick smudge. *We* do not move; it is the train that hurries us along: the trees are always steadily there—and beautiful. There is enough of everything for everybody—no need to try and get there first. To hurry is to chase your tail, which some one has suggested does not belong to you. It can never be captured by pursuit. But pause—stand still—it instantly presents itself, twitches its tip, and laughs: 'I've been here all the time. I'm part of you!'"

He turned towards the empty chair and smiled. The smile, he felt, came marvellously back to him from the sunshine and the open world of sky and trees beyond. There was some one there who smiled—invisibly.

"You're real, quite real," the letters danced instantly into new sentences. "But you are so awfully close to me—so close I cannot see you."

He felt the invisible Stranger suddenly as real as that. There was only one thing to see—only one thing everywhere. The beauty of the discovery put reason utterly and finally to flight. But that one thing was hiding. The Stranger concealed himself—he hid on purpose. He wanted to be looked for—found. And the heart grew "warm" or "cold" accordingly: when it was warm that mysterious anticipation stirred—"Some one is coming!"

And Uncle Felix, sitting in the sunlight of that breakfast-room, understood that the entire universe formed a conspiracy to hide "him." Some one, indeed, had come, slipped into the gorgeous and detailed clothing of the entire world as easily as birds and trees slip into their own particular clothing, planning with Time to hide him, wanting to play a little—to play at Hide-and-Seek. "Let them all look for me! I'm hiding!..."

Yet so few would play! Instead of coming out to find him where he hid so simply in the open, they built severe and gloomy edifices; invented Rules of the game by which each could prove himself right and all the others wrong.... Oh, dear!... And all the time, *he* hid there in the open before their very eyes—in the wind, the stream, the grass, in the sunlight and the song of birds, and especially behind little careless things that took no thought ... waiting to play and let himself be found... while songs and poems and fairy-tales, even

Algernon Blackwood

religious too, cried endlessly across the world, "Look and you'll find him." There *was* only one thing to say: "Search in the open; he hides there!"

Everything became clear and simple—one thing, Life was a game of Hide-and-Seek. There were obstacles placed in the way on purpose to make it more interesting. One of them was Time. But everything was one thing, and one thing only; a peacock and a policeman were the same, so were an elephant and a violet, an uncle and a bee, a Purple Emperor and a child like Tim or Judy: all did, said, lived one and the same thing only. They looked different—because one looked *at* them differently.

Smiling happily to himself again as the letters grouped themselves swiftly into these curious sentences, he heard the birds singing in the clean, great sky... and it seemed to him that the Stranger blew softly upon his eyes and hair. The sentences instantly telescoped: "Come, look for me! There is no hurry; life has just begun...." And he barely had time to realise that the entire complicated mass of them had, after all, only this one thing to say... when the returning children bursting into the room scattered his long reverie, and the last cardboard letter disappeared like magic into empty space.

"Where is he?" cried Tim at once, staring impatiently about him. There was rebuke and disappointment in his eyes. "Uncle, you've been arguing. He's gone!"

Judy was equally quick to seize the position of affairs. "You've frightened him away!" she declared with energy. "Quick! We must go out and look!"

"Yes," muttered their uncle a little guiltily, and was about to add something by way of explanation when he felt Judy pull his sleeve. "Look!" she whispered. "He can't have gone so *very* far!"

She pointed to the plate with the sugar, honey, cream, and

crumbs upon it; a bird was picking up the crumbs, a wasp was on the lump of sugar, a bee beside it, standing on its head, was drinking at the drop of honey; all were unafraid, and very leisurely about it; there seemed no hurry; there was enough for every one. Then, as the trio of humans stared with delight, they saw another guest arrive and dance up gaily to the feast. A gorgeous butterfly sailed in, hovered above the crowded plate a moment, then settled comfortably beside its companions and examined the blob of cream. The others moved a little to make room for it. It was a Purple Emperor, the rarest butterfly in all England, whose home was normally high above the trees.

"Of course," Judy whispered to her brother, as she watched the bee make room for its larger neighbour; "they belong to him—"

"He sent them," replied Tim below his breath, "just to let us know—"

"Yes," mumbled Uncle Felix for the second time, a soft amazement stealing over him. "He brought them. And they're all the same thing really."

There was the perfume of a thousand flowers in the room. A faint breeze floated through the open window and touched his eyes. He heard the world outside singing in the sunshine. "Come along," he said in a low, hushed whisper; "let's go and look." And he moved eagerly—over the tree-and-peacock pattern.

They tiptoed out together, while the bird cocked up its head to watch them go; the bee, still drinking, raised its eyes; and all four fluttered their wings as though they laughed. They seemed to say "There is no hurry! We're all alive together! There's enough for all; no need to get there first!" *They* knew. The golden day lay waiting outside with overflowing beauty, and he who had brought them in stood just behind this beauty that hid and covered them. When they had eaten and drunk, they, too, would come and join the search. Exceedingly

Algernon Blackwood

beautiful they were—the shy grace of the dainty bird, the brilliant wasp in black and gold, the soft brown bee, the magnificent Purple Emperor, fresh from the open spaces above the windy forest: all said the same big, joyful thing, "We are alive!... No hurry!..."

The trio flew down the passage, took the stairs in leaps and bounds, raced across the hall where the back-door, standing open, framed the lawn and garden in a blaze of sunshine.

And as Uncle Felix followed, half dancing like the other two, he saw a little thing that vaguely reminded him of—another little thing. The memory was vague and far away; there was a curious distance in it, like the distance of a dream recalled in the day-light, no longer what is called quite real. For his eye caught something gleaming on the side-table below the presentation clock, and the odd, ridiculous word that sprang into his mind was "salver." It was the silver salver on which Thompson brought in visitors' cards. But it was a plate as well; and, being a plate, he remembered vaguely something about a collection. The association of ideas worked itself out in a remote and dreamlike way; he felt in his pocket for a shilling, a sixpence, or a threepenny bit, and wondered for a second where the big, dark building was to which all this belonged. Something was changed, it seemed. His clothes, this dancing sunshine, joy and laughter. The world was new. What did it mean?...

"No bells are ringing," flashed back the flying letters in a spray.

He was on the point of catching something by the tail... when he saw the children waiting for him on the sunny lawn outside. He ran out instantly to join them. They had noticed nothing odd, apparently. It had never even occurred to them. And in himself the memory dived away, its very trail obliterated as though it had not been.

For this was Sunday morning, yet Sunday had not—happened.

HIDE-AND-SEEK

III

The garden clung close and soft about the Old Mill House as a mood clings about the emotion that has summoned it. Uncle Felix, Tim, and Judy were as much a part of it as the lilac, hyacinths, and tulips. Any minute, it seemed, the butterflies and bees and birds might settle on them too.

For a bloom of exquisite, fresh wonder lay upon the earth, lay softly and secure as though it need never pass away. No fading of daylight could dim the glory of all the promises of joy the day contained, no hint of waning anywhere. "There is no hurry," seemed written on the very leaves and blades of grass. "We're all alive together! Come and—look!" The garden, lying there so gently in its beauty, hid a secret.

Yet, though all was so calm and peaceful, there was nowhere the dulness of stagnation. Life brimmed the old-world garden with incessant movement that flashed dancing and rhythm even into things called stationary. The joy of existence ran riot everywhere without check or hindrance; there was no time—to pause and die. For the sunlight did not merely lie upon the air—it poured; wind did not blow—it breathed, ambushed one minute among the rose-trees just above the ground, and cantering next through the crests of the busy limes. The elms and horse-chestnuts that ordinarily grew now leaped—leaped upwards to the sun; while all flying things—birds, insects, bees, and butterflies—passed in and out like darting threads of colour, pinning the beauty into a patterned tapestry for all to see. The entire day was charged with the natural delight of endless, sheer existence. It was visible.

Each detail, moreover, claimed attention, as though never seen properly before; no longer dulled by familiarity, but shaking off its "ordinary" appearance, proud to be looked at, naked and alive. The rivulet ran on, but did not run away; the gravel paths, soft as rolled brown sugar, led somewhere, but led in both directions, each of them inviting; the blue of the sky did not stay "up there and far away," but dropped down close in myriad flakes, lifting the green carpet of the lawn to meet it. The day seemed like a turning circle that changed every moment to show another aspect of its gorgeous pattern, yet, while changing, only turned, unable to grow older or to pass away. There was something real at last, something that could be known, enjoyed—something of eternity about it. It was real.

"Wherever has he got to?" exclaimed Judy, trying to pierce the distances of earth and sky with distended eyes. "He can't be very far away, because—I kissed him."

Tim, sitting beside her on the grass, felt the exquisite mystery of it too. It was marvellous that any one could vanish in such a way. But he hesitated too. He felt uncertain about something. His thoughts flew off to that strange wood he loved to play in. He remembered the warning: "Beware the centre, if you enter; For once you're *there*, you disappear!" But this explanation did not appeal to him as likely now. He stared at Judy and his uncle. Some one *had* touched him, making him warm and happy. He remembered that distinctly. He had caught a glimpse—though a glimpse too marvellous to be seen for long, even to be remembered properly. "But there's no good looking unless we know where to look," he remarked. "Is there?"

"He's just gone out like a candle," whispered Judy.

"Extror'nary," declared her brother, hugging the excitement

that thrilled his heart. "But he can't be really lost. I'm sure of that!"

And a great hush fell upon them all. Some one, it seemed, was listening; some one was watching; some one was waiting for them to move.

"Uncle?" they said in the same breath together, then hung upon his answer.

This authority hesitated a moment, looking about him expectantly as though for help.

"I think," he stated shyly, "I think—he's—hiding."

Nothing more wonderful ever fell from grown-up lips. They had heard it said before—but only said. Now they realised it.

"Hiding!" They stood up; they could see further that way. But they waited for more detail before showing their last approval.

"Out here," he added.

They were not quite sure. They expected a disclosure more out of the ordinary. It *might* be true, but—

"Hide-and-seek?" they repeated doubtfully. "But that's just a game." They were unsettled in their minds.

"Not *that* kind," he replied significantly. "I mean the kind the rain plays with the wind and leaves, the stream with the stones and roots along its bank, the rivers with the sea. That's the kind of hide-and-seek I mean!"

He chose instinctively watery symbols. And his tone conveyed something so splendid and mysterious that it was impossible to doubt or hesitate a moment longer.

"Oh," they exclaimed. "It never ends, you mean?"

"Goes on for ever and ever," he murmured. "The moment the river finds the sea it disappears and the sea begins to look. The wind never really finds the clouds, and the sun and the stars—"

"*We* know!" they shouted, cutting his explanations short.

"Come on then!" he cried. "We've got the hunt of our lives before us." And he began to run about in a circle like an animal trying to catch its tail.

"But are we to look for him, or he for us?" inquired the boy, after a preliminary canter over the flower-beds.

"We for him." They sprang to attention and clapped their hands.

"It's an enormous hide," said Tim. "We may get lost ourselves. Better look out!"

And then they waited for instructions. But the odd thing was that their uncle waited too. There was this moment's hesitation. They looked to him. The old fixed habit asserted itself: a grown-up must surely know more than they did. How could it be otherwise? In this case, however, the grown-up seemed in doubt. He looked at them. It *was* otherwise.

"It's so long since I played this kind of hide-and-seek," he murmured. "I've rather forgotten—"

He stopped short. There certainly was a difficulty. Nobody knew in what direction to begin.

"It's a snopportunity," exclaimed Judy. "I'm sure of that!"

"We just look—everywhere!" cried Tim.

A light broke over their uncle's face as if a ray of sunshine touched it. His mind cleared. Some old, forgotten joy, wonderful as the dawn, burst into his heart, rose to fire in his eyes, flooded his whole being. A glory long eclipsed, a dream interrupted years ago, an uncompleted game of earliest youth—all these rose from their hiding-place and recaptured him, soul and body. He glanced at the children. These things he had recaptured, they, of course, had never lost; this state and attitude of wonder was their natural prerogative; he had recovered the ownership of the world, but they had possessed it always. They knew the whole business from beginning to end—only they liked to hear it stated. That was obviously his duty as a grown-up: to stick the label on.

"Of course," he whispered, deliciously enchanted. "You've got it. It's *the* snopportunity! The great thing is to—look."

And, as if to prove him right, a flock of birds passed sweeping through the air above their heads, paused in mid-flight, wheeled, fluttered noisily a second, then scattered in all directions like leaves whirled by an eddy of loose, autumn wind.

"Come on," cried Tim, remembering perhaps the "dodgy" butterfly and trying to imitate it with his arms and legs. "I know where to go first. Just follow me!"

"And there'll be signs, remember," Uncle Felix shouted as he followed. "Whoever finds a sign must let the others know at once."

They began with the feeling that they would discover the Stranger in a moment, sure of the places where he had tried cleverly to conceal himself, but soon began to realise that this was no ordinary game, and that he certainly knew of mysterious spots and corners they had never dreamed about. It was as Tim declared, "an enormous hide." Come-Back Stumper's cunning dive into bed was nothing compared to the skill with which this hider eluded their keen searching. There was another difference too. In Stumper's case their interest had waned, they felt they had been cheated somehow, they knew themselves defeated and had given up the search. But here the interest was unfailing; it increased rather than diminished; they were ever on the very edge of finding him, and more than once they shrieked with joy, "I've got him!"—only to find they had been "very hot" but not quite hot enough. It was, like everything else upon this happy morning, endless.

It continued and continued, as naturally as the rivulet that ran for ever downhill to find the sea, that nothing, it seemed, could put a stop to, much less an end. The feeling that time was passing utterly disappeared; weeks, months, and years lay waiting somewhere near, but could be left or taken, used or not used, as they pleased. To take a week and use it was like picking a flower that looked much prettier growing sweetly in the sunny earth. Why pick it? It came to an end that way! The minutes, the hours and days, morning, noon and night as well, the very seasons too, offered themselves, and—vanished. They did not come and go, they were just "there"; and to steal into one or other of them at will was like stealing into one mood after another as the heart decreed. They were mere counters in the gorgeous and unending game. They helped to hide the mysterious Stranger who was evidently in the centre round which all life lay grouped so marvellously. They hid and covered him as moods hide and cover the heart that wears them—temporarily. Uncle Felix and the children used them somewhat in this way, it seems, for while they looked and hunted in and out among them, any minute, day or season was recoverable at will. They did not pass away. It was the seekers who passed through them. To Uncle Felix, at any rate, it seemed a fact—this joyous sensation of immense duration, yet of nothing passing away: the bliss of utter freedom. He gasped to realise it. But the children did not gasp. They had always known that nothing ever really came to an end. "The weather's still here," he heard Judy calling across the lawn to Tim—as though she had just been looking among December snowdrifts and had popped back again into the fragrance of midsummer hayfields. "The Equator's made of golden butterflies, all shining," the boy called back, having evidently just been round the world and seen its gleaming waist....

But none of them had found what they were looking for....

They had looked in all the difficult places where a clever player would be most likely to conceal himself, yet in vain; there was no definite sign of him, no footprints on the flower-beds or along the edge of the shrubberies. The garden proper had been searched from end to end without result. The children had been to the particular hiding-places each knew best, Tim to the dirty nook between the ilex and the larder window, and Judy to the scooped-out trunk of the rotten elm, and both together to the somewhat smelly channel between the yew trees and a disused outhouse—all equally untenanted.

In the latter gloomy place, in fact, they met. No sunlight pierced the dense canopy of branches; it was barely light enough to see. Judy and Tim advanced towards each other on tiptoe, confident of discovery at last. They only realised their mistake at five yards' distance.

"You!" exclaimed Tim, in a disappointed whisper. "I thought it was going to be a sign." "I felt positive he'd be in here somewhere," said Judy.

"Perhaps we're both signs," they declared together, then paused, and held a secret discussion about it all.

"He's got a splendid hide," was the boy's opinion. "D'you think Uncle Felix knows anything? You heard what he said about signs...!"

They decided without argument that he didn't. He just went "thumping about" in the usual places. He'd never find him. They agreed it was very wonderful. Tim advanced his pet idea—it had been growing on him: "I think *he* knows some special place we'd never look in—a hole or something." But Judy met the suggestion with superior knowledge: "He moves about," she announced. "He doesn't stop in a hole. He flies at an awful rate—from place to place. That's—signs, I expect."

"Wings?" suggested Tim.

Judy hesitated. "You remember—at breakfast, wasn't it?—ages and ages ago—all had wings—those things—"

She broke off and pointed significantly at the figure of Uncle Felix who was standing with his head cocked up at an awkward angle, staring into the sky. Shading his eyes with one hand, he was apparently examining the topmost branches of the tall horse-chestnuts.

"He couldn't have got up a tree, could he, or into a bird's nest?" said the girl. She offered the suggestion timidly, yet her brother did not laugh at her. There was this strange feeling that the hider might be anywhere—simply anywhere. This was no ordinary game.

"There's such a lot," Tim answered vaguely.

She looked at him with intense admiration. The wonder of this marvellous game was in their hearts. The moment when they would find him was simply too extraordinary to think about.

Judy moved a step closer in the darkness. "Can he get small, then—like that?" she whispered.

But the question was too much for Tim.

"Anyhow he gets about, doesn't he?" was the reply, the vagueness of uncertain knowledge covering the disappointment. "There are simply millions of trees and nests and—and rabbit-holes all over the place."

They were silent for a moment. Then Judy asked, still more timidly:

"I say, Tim?"

"Well."

"What does he really look like? I can't remember quite. I mean—shall we recognise him?"

Tim stared at her. "My dear!" he gasped, as though the question almost shocked him. "Why, he touched me—on the head! I felt it!"

Judy laughed softly; it was only that she wanted to remind herself of something too precious to be forgotten.

"*I* kissed him!" she whispered, a hint of triumph in her voice and eyes.

They stood staring at one another for a little while, weighing the proofs thus given; then Tim broke the silence with a question of his own. It was the result of this interval of reflection. It was an unexpected sort of question:

"Do you know what it is we want?" he asked. "I do," he added hurriedly, lest she should answer first.

"What?" she said, seeing from his tone and manner that it was important.

"We shall never, never find him this way," he said decisively.

"What?" she repeated with impatience.

Tim lowered his voice. "What we want," he said with the emphasis of true conviction, "is—a Leader."

Judy repeated the word after him immediately; it was obvious; why hadn't she thought of it herself? "Of course," she agreed. "That's it exactly."

"We're looking wrong somewhere," her brother added, and they both turned their heads in the direction of Uncle Felix who was still standing on the lawn in a state of bewilderment, examining the treetops. He expected something from the air, it seemed. Perhaps he was looking for rain—he loved water so. But evidently he was not a proper leader; he was even more bewildered than themselves; he, too, was looking wrong somewhere, somehow. They needed some one to show them how and where to look. Instinctively they felt their uncle was no better at this mighty game than they were. If only somebody who knew and understood—a leader—would turn up!

And it was just then that Judy clutched her brother by the arm and said in a startled whisper, "Hark!"

They harked. Through the hum of leaves and insects that filled the air this sweet June morning they heard another sound—a voice that reached them even here beneath the dense roof of shrubbery. They heard words distinctly, though from far away, rising, falling, floating across the lawn as though some one as yet invisible were singing to himself.

For it was the voice of a man, and it certainly was a song. Moreover, without being able to explain it exactly, they felt that it was just the kind of singing that belonged to the kind of day: it was right and natural, a fresh and windy sound in the careless notes, almost as though it was a bird that sang. So exquisite was it, indeed, that they listened spellbound without moving, standing hand in hand beneath the dark bushes. And Uncle Felix evidently heard it too, for he turned his head; instead of examining the tree-tops he peered into the rose trees just behind him, both hands held to his ears to catch the happy song. There was both joy and laughter in the very sound of it:

> My secret's in the wind and open sky;
> There is no longer any Time—to lose;
> The world is young with laughter; we can fly
> Among the imprisoned hours as we choose.
> The rushing minutes pause; an unused day
> Breaks into dawn and cheats the tired sun.

The birds are singing. Hark! Come out and play!
There is no hurry; life has just begun.

The voice died away among the rose trees, and the birds burst into a chorus of singing everywhere, as if they carried on the song among themselves. Then, in its turn, their chorus also died away. Tim looked at his sister. He seemed about to burst—if not into song, then into a thousand pieces.

"A leader!" he exclaimed, scarcely able to get the word out in his excitement. "Did you hear it?"

"Tim!" she gasped—and they flew out, hand in hand still, to join their uncle in the sunshine.

"Found anything?" he greeted them before they could say a word. "I heard some one singing—a man, or something—over there among the rose trees—"

"And the birds," interrupted Judy. "Did you hear them?"

"Uncle," cried Tim with intense conviction, "it's a sign. I do believe it's a sign—"

"That's exactly what it is," a deep voice broke in behind them "—a sign; and no mistake about it either."

All three turned with a start. The utterance was curiously slow; there was a little dragging pause between each word. The rose trees parted, and they found themselves face to face with some one whom they had seen twice before in their lives, and who now made his appearance for the third time therefore—the man from the End of the World: the Tramp.

THE LEADER

IV

He was a ragged-looking being, yet his loose, untidy clothing became him so well that his appearance seemed almost neat— it was certainly natural: he was dressed in the day, the garden, the open air. Judy and Tim ran up fearlessly and began fingering the bits of stuff that clung to him from the fields and ditches. In his beard were some stray rose leaves and the feather of a little bird. The children had an air of sheltering against a tree trunk—woodland creatures—mice or squirrels chattering among the roots, or birds flown in to settle on a hedge. They were not one whit afraid. For nothing surprised them on this marvellous morning; everything that happened they— accepted.

"He's shining underneath," Judy whispered in Tim's ear, cocking her head sideways so that she could catch her brother's eye and at the same time feel the great comfort of the new arrival against her cheek.

"And awfully strong," was the admiring reply.

"So soft, too," she declared—though whether of mind or body was not itemized—"like feathers."

"And smells delicious," affirmed Tim, "like hay and rabbits."

Each child picked out the quality the heart desired and

approved; almost, it seemed, each felt him differently. Yet, although not one whit afraid, they whispered. Perhaps the wonder of it choked their utterance a little.

The Tramp smiled at them. All four smiled. The way he had emerged from among the rose trees made them smile. It was as natural as though he had been there all the time, growing out of the earth, waving in the morning air and sunlight. There was something simple and very beautiful about him, perhaps, that made them smile like this. Then Uncle Felix, whom the first shock of surprise had apparently deprived of speech, found his voice and observed, "Good-morning to you, good-morning." The little familiar phrase said everything in a quite astonishing way. It was like a song.

"*Good*-morning," replied the Tramp. "It is. I was wondering how long it would be before you saw me."

"Ah!" said Judy and Tim in the same breath, "of course."

"The fact is," stammered Uncle Felix, "you're so like the rest of the garden—so like a bit of the garden, I mean—that we didn't notice you at first. But we heard—" he broke off in the middle of the sentence—"That *was* you singing, wasn't it?" he asked with a note of hushed admiration in his voice.

The smile upon the great woodland face broadened perceptibly. It was as though the sun burst through a cloud. "That's hard to say," he replied, "when the whole place is singing. I'm just like everything else—alive. It's natural to sing, and natural to dance—when you're alive and looking—and know it."

He spoke with a sound as though he had swallowed the entire morning, a forest rustling in his chest, singing water just behind the lips.

"*Looking!*" exclaimed Uncle Felix, picking out the word. He moved closer; the children caught his hands; the three of them sheltered against the spreading figure till the four together seemed like a single item of the landscape. "Looking!" he repeated, "that's odd. We've lost something too. You said too,—just now—something about—a sign, I think?" Uncle Felix added shyly.

All waited, but the Tramp gave no direct reply. He smiled again and folded two mighty arms about them. Two big feathery wings seemed round them. Judy thought of a nest, Tim of a cozy rabbit hole, Uncle Felix had the amazing impression that there were wild flowers growing in his heart, or that a flock of robins had hopped in and began to sing.

"Lost something, have you?" the Tramp enquired genially at length; and the slow, leisurely way he said it, the curious half-singing utterance he used, the words falling from his great beard with this sound as of wind through leaves or water over sand and pebbles—somehow included them in the rhythm of existence to which he himself naturally belonged. They all seemed part of the garden, part of the day, part of the sun and earth and flowers together, marvellously linked and caught within some common purpose. Question and answer in the ordinary sense were wrong and useless. They must *feel*—feel as he did—to find what they sought.

It was Uncle Felix who presently replied: "Something— we've—mis-laid," he said hesitatingly, as though a little ashamed that he expressed the truth so lamely.

"Mis-laid?" asked the Tramp. "Mis-laid, eh?"

"Forgotten," put in Tim.

"Mis-laid or forgotten," repeated the other. "That all?"

"Some*body*, I should have said," explained Uncle Felix yet still falteringly, "somebody we've lost, that is."

"Hiding," Tim said quickly.

"About," added Judy. There was a hush in all their voices.

The Tramp picked the small feather from his beard—apparently a water-wagtail's—and appeared to reflect a moment. He held the soft feather tenderly between a thumb and finger that were thick as a walking-stick and stained with roadside mud and yellow with flower-pollen too.

"Hiding, is he?" He held up the feather as if to see which way it fluttered in the wind. "Hiding?" he repeated, with a distinct broadening of the smile that was already big enough to cover half the lawn. It shone out of him almost like rays of light, of sunshine, of fire. "Aha! That's his way, maybe, just a little way he has—of playing with you."

"You know him, then! You know who it is?" two eager voices asked instantly. "Tell us at once. You're leader now!" The children, in their excitement, almost burrowed into him; Uncle Felix drew a deep breath and stared. His whole body listened.

And slowly the Tramp turned round his shaggy head and gazed into their faces, each in turn. He answered in his leisurely, laborious way as though each word were a bank-note that he dealt out carefully, fixing attention upon its enormous value. There was certainly a tremor in his rumbling voice. But there was no hurry.

"I've—seen him," he said with feeling, "seen him—once or twice. My life's thick with memories—"

"Seen him!" sprang from three mouths simultaneously.

"Once or twice, I said." He paused and sighed. Wind stirred the rose trees just behind him. He went on murmuring in a lower tone; and as he spoke a sense of exquisite new beauty stole across the old-world garden. "It was—in the morning—very early," he said below his breath.

"At dawn!" Uncle Felix whispered.

"When the birds begin," from Judy very softly.

"To sing," Tim added, a single shiver of joy running through all three of them at once. The enchantment of their own dim memories of the dawn—of a robin, of swallows, and of an up-and-under bird flashed magically back.

The Tramp nodded his great head slowly; he bowed it to the sunlight, as it were. There was a great light flaming in his eyes. He seemed to give out heat.

"Just seen him—and no more," he went on marvellously, as though speaking of a wonderful secret of his own. "Seen him a-stealing past me—in the dawn. Just looked at me—and went—went back again behind the rushing minutes!"

"Was it long ago? How long?" asked Judy with eager impatience impossible to suppress. They did not notice the reference to Time, apparently.

The wanderer scratched his tangled crop of hair and seemed to calculate a moment. He gazed down at the small white feather in his hand. But the feather held quite still. No breath of wind was stirring. "When I was young," he said, with an expression half quizzical, half yearning. "When I first took to the road— as a boy—and began to look."

"As long ago as that!" Tim murmured breathlessly. It was like a stretch of history.

The Tramp put his hand on the boy's shoulder. "I was about your age," he said, "when I got tired of the ordinary life, and started wandering. And I've been wandering and looking ever since. Wandering—and wondering—and looking—ever since," he repeated in the same slow way, while the feather between his great fingers began to wave a little in time with the dragging speech.

The wonder of it enveloped them all three like a perfume rising from the entire earth.

"We've been looking for ages too," cried Judy.

"And we've seen him," exclaimed her brother quickly.

"Somebody," added Uncle Felix, more to himself than to the others.

The Tramp combed his splendid beard, as if he hoped to find more feathers in it.

"This morning, wasn't it?" he asked gently, "very early?"

They reflected a moment, but the reflection did not help them much. "Ages and ages ago," they answered. "So long that we've forgotten rather—"

"Forgotten what he looks like. That's it. Same trouble here," and he tapped his breast. "We're all together, doing the same old thing. The whole world's doing it. It's the only thing to do." And he looked so wise and knowing that their wonder increased to a kind of climax; they were tapping their own breasts before they knew it.

"Doing it everywhere," he went on, weighing his speech as usual; "only some don't know they're doing it." He looked significantly into their shining eyes, then finished with a note of triumph in his voice. "We do!"

"Hooray!" cried Tim. "We can all start looking together now."

"Maybe," agreed the wanderer, very sweetly for a tramp, they thought.

They glanced at their Uncle first for his approval; the Tramp glanced at him too; his face was flushed and happy, the eyes very bright. But there was an air of bewilderment about him too. He nodded his head, and repeated in a shy, contented voice—as though he surrendered himself to some enchantment too great to understand—"I think so; I hope so; I—wonder!"

"We've looked everywhere already," Tim shouted by way of explanation—when the Tramp cut him short with a burst of rolling laughter:

"But in the wrong kind of places, maybe," he suggested, moving forward like a hedge or bit of hayfield the wind pretends to shift.

"Oh, well—perhaps," the boy admitted.

"Probly," said Judy, keeping close beside him.

"Of course," decided Uncle Felix; "but we've been pretty warm once or twice all the same." He lumbered after the other three, yet something frisky about him, as about a pony released into a field and still uncertain of its bounding strength.

"Have you really?" remarked their leader, good-humouredly, but with a touch of sarcasm. "Good and right, so far as it goes; only 'warm' is not enough; we want to be hot, burning hot and steaming all the time. That's the way to find him." He paused and turned towards them; he gathered them nearer to him with his smiling eyes somehow. "It's like this," he went on more slowly than ever: "A good hider doesn't choose the difficult places; he chooses the common ordinary places where nobody would ever think of looking." He kept his eyes upon them to make sure they understood him. "The little, common places," he continued with emphasis, "that no one thinks worth while. He hides in the open—bang out in the open!"

"In the open!" cried the children. "The open air!"

"In the open!" gasped Uncle Felix. "The open sea!"

The Tramp almost winked at them. He looked like a lot of

ordinary people. He looked like everybody. He looked like the whole world somehow. He smiled just like a multitude. He spoke, as it were, for all the world—said the one simple thing that everybody everywhere was trying to say in millions of muddled words and sentences. The wind and trees and sunshine said it with him, for him, after him, before him. He said the thing—so Uncle Felix felt, at any rate,—that was always saying itself, that was everywhere heard, though rarely listened to; but, according to the children, the thing they knew and believed already. Only it was nice to hear it stated definitely—*they* felt.

And the tide of enchantment rose higher and higher; in a tide of flowing gold it poured about all three.

"That's it," the Tramp continued, as though he had not noticed the rapture his very ordinary words had caused. "Sea and land and air together. But more than that—he hides deep and beautiful."

"Deeply and beautifully," murmured the writer of historical novels, all of them entirely forgotten now.

"Deep and beautiful," repeated the other, as though he preferred the rhythm of his own expression. He drew himself up and swallowed a long and satisfying draught of air and sunshine. He waved the little wagtail's feather before their eyes. He touched their faces with its tip. "Deep, tender, kind, and beautiful," he elaborated. "Those are the signs—signs that he's been along—just passed that way. The whole world's looking, and the whole world's full of signs!"

For a moment all stood still together like a group of leafy things a passing wind has shaken, then left motionless; a wild rose-bush, a climbing vine, a clinging ivy branch—all three kept close to the stalwart figure of their big, incomparable leader.

And Judy knew at last the thing she didn't know; Tim felt

himself finally in the eternal centre of his haunted wood; in the eyes of Uncle Felix there was a glistening moisture that caught the sunlight like dew upon the early lawn. He staggered a little as though he were on a deck and the sea was rolling underneath him.

"How ever did you find it out?" he asked, after an interval that no one had cared to interrupt. "What in the world made you first think of it?" And though his voice was very soft and clear, it was just a little shaky.

"Well," drawled the Tramp, "maybe it was just because I thought of nothing else. On the road we live sort of simply. There's never any hurry; the wind's a-blowing free; everything's sweet and careless—and so am I." And he chuckled happily to himself.

"Let's begin at once!" cried Tim impatiently. "I feel warm already—hot all over—simply burning."

The Tramp signified his agreement. "But you must each get a feather first," he told them, "a feather that a bird has dropped. It's a sign that we belong together. Birds know everything first. They go everywhere and see everything all at once. They're in the air, and on the ground, and on the water, and under it as well. They live in the open—sea or land. And if you have a feather in your hand—well, it means keeping in touch with everything that's going. They go light and easy; we must go light and easy too."

They stared at him with wonder at the breaking point. It all seemed so obviously and marvellously true. How had they missed it up till now?

"So get a feather," he went on quietly, "and then we can begin to look at once."

No one objected, no one criticised, no one hesitated. Tim knew where all the feathers were because he knew every nest in the garden. He led the way. In less than two minutes all had small, soft feathers in their hands.

"Now, we'll begin to look," the Tramp announced. "It's the loveliest game on earth, and the only one. It's Hide-and-Seek behind the rushing minutes. And, remember," he added, holding up a finger and chuckling happily, "there's no hurry, the wind's a-blowing free, the sun is warm, everything's sweet and careless—and so are we."

THE COMMON SIGNS

V

"But has he called yet?" asked Tim, remembering suddenly that it wasn't fair to begin till the hider announced that he was ready. "He's got to hoot first, you know. Hasn't he?" he added doubtfully.

"Listen!" replied the man of the long white roads. And he held his feather close against his ear, while the others copied him. Fixing their eyes upon a distant point, they listened, and as they listened, their lips relaxed, their mouths opened slowly, their eyebrows lifted—they heard, apparently, something too wonderful to be believed.

To Uncle Felix, still fumbling in his mind among unnecessary questions, it seemed that the power of hearing had awakened for the first time, or else had grown of a sudden extraordinarily acute. The children merely listened and said "Oh, oh, oh!"; the sound they heard was familiar, though never fully understood till now. For him, it was, perhaps, the recovery of a power he had long forgotten. At any rate he—heard. For the air passed through the tiny fronds of the feather—through the veined web of its delicate resistance—round the hollow stem and across the fluffy breadth of it—with a humming music as of wind among the telegraph wires, only infinitely sweet and far away. There were several notes in it, a chord—the music that accompanies all flying things, even a butterfly or settling leaf, and ever fills the air with unguessed melody.

It opened their power of hearing to a degree as yet undreamed of even by the all-believing children. Their feathers became wee, accurate, tuning-forks for all existence. They understood that everything in the whole world sang; that no rose leaf fluttered to the earth, no rabbit twitched its ears, no mouse its tail, no single bluebell waved a head towards its bluer neighbour, without this exquisite accompaniment of fairy music.

"Listen, listen!" the Tramp repeated softly from time to time, watching their faces keenly. "Listen, and you'll hear him calling...!"

And this fairy humming, having so marvellously attuned their hearing, then led them on to the larger, louder sounds; they pricked their ears up, as the saying goes; they noticed the deeper music everywhere. For the morning breeze was rustling and whispering among the leaves and blades of grass with a thousand happy voices. It was the ordinary summer sound of moving air that no one pays attention to.

"Oh, that!" exclaimed Uncle Felix. "I hadn't noticed it." He felt ashamed. He who had taught them the beauty of the self-advertising Night-Wind, had somehow missed and overlooked the wonder—the searching, yearning beauty—of this meek, incomparable music: because it was so usual. For the first time in his life he heard the wind as it slipped between the leaves, shaking them into rapture.

"And that," laughed the Tramp, cocking his great head to catch the murmur of the stream beyond the lawn, "if the dust of furniture and houses ain't blocked your ears too thickly." They stooped to listen. "Like laughter, isn't it?" he observed, "singing and laughing mixed together?"

They straightened up again, too full of wonder to squeeze out any words.

"It's everywhere," said Uncle Felix, "this calling—these calling voices. Is that where you got *your* song from?"

"It's everywhere and always," replied the other evasively. "The birds get their singing from it. They get everything first, of course, then pass it on. The whole world's music comes from that, though there's nothing—*nothing*," he added with emphasis, "to touch the singing of a bird. He's calling everywhere and always," he went on as no one contradicted him or ventured upon any question; "only you've got to listen close. He calls soft and beautiful. He doesn't shout and yell at you."

"Soft and beautiful, yes," repeated Uncle Felix below his breath, "the small, still voices of the air and sea and earth." And, as he said it, they caught the murmur of the little stream; they heard singing in the air as well. The blackbirds whistled in one direction, the thrushes trilled and gurgled in another, and overhead, both among the covering leaves and from the open sky, a chorus of twittering and piping filled the chambers of the day. Judy recalled, as of long ago, the warning bugle-call of an up-and-under bird; Tim faintly remembered having overheard some swallows "discussing" together; Uncle Felix saw a robin perched against a sky of pearly grey at the end of an interminable corridor that stretched across whole centuries.... Then, close beside the three of them, a bumble-bee, a golden fly, and a company of summer gnats went by—booming, trumpeting, singing like a tiny carillon of bells respectively.

"Hark and listen," exclaimed the Tramp with triumph in his voice, and looking down at Tim particularly. "He's calling all the time. It's the little ordinary sounds that give the hints."

"It's an enormous hide; I mean to look for ever and ever," cried the delighted boy.

"I can hear everything in the world now," cried Judy.

"Signs, " said Uncle Felix, after a pause. This time he did not make a question of his thought, but merely dropped the word out like a note of music into the air. His feather answered it and took it further.

The Tramp caught the word flying before it reached the ground:

"Deep, tender, kind and beautiful," he said, "but above all— beautiful." He turned his shaggy head and looked about him carelessly. "There's one of them, for instance," he added, pointing across the lawn. "There's a sign. It means he's passed that way! He ain't too far away—may-be."

They followed the direction of his eyes. A dragon-fly paused hovering above the stream, its reflection mirrored in the clear running water underneath. Against the green palisade of reeds its veined and crystal wings scattered the sunlight into shining flakes. The blue upon its body burned—a patch of flaming beauty in mid-air. They watched it for a moment. Then, suddenly—it was gone, the spot was empty. But the speed, the poise, the perfect movement, the flashing wings, above all the flaming blue upon its tail still held them spellbound. Somehow, it seemed, they had borrowed that speed, that flashing beauty, making the loveliness part and parcel of themselves. Swiftly they turned and stared up at the Tramp. There was a rapt look upon his tangled face.

"A sign," he was saying softly. "He's passed this way. He can't be hiding very far from here." And, drawing a long, deep breath, he gazed about him into endless space as though about to sing again.

The dragon-fly had vanished, none knew whither, gone doubtless into some new hiding-place; it just gave the hint, then slipped away upon its business. But the wonder and the beauty it had brought remained behind, crept into every heart. The mystery of life, the reality that lay hiding at the core of things, the marvel and the dream—all these were growing clearer. All lovely things were "signs." And there fell a sudden hush upon the group, for the Thing that Nobody could Understand crept up and touched them.

Abruptly, then, lest the wonder of it should prove more than they could bear perhaps, a blackbird whistled with a burst of flying laughter at them from the shrubberies. Laughter and dancing both were part of wonder. The Tramp at once moved forward, chuckling in his beard; he waved his arms; his step was lighter, quicker; he was singing softly to himself: they only caught stray sentences, but they loved the windy ringing of his voice. They knew not where he borrowed words and tune: "The world is young with laughter; we can fly.... Among the imprisoned hours as we choose.... The birds are singing.... Hark! Come out and play.... There is no hurry.... Life has just begun...."

"Come on!" cried Tim. "Let's follow him; we're getting frightfully warm!"

He seized Judy and his uncle by the hands and cleared the rivulet with a running leap. The Tramp, however, preferred to wade across. "Get into everything you can," he explained in mid-stream with a laugh. "It keeps you in touch; it's all part of the looking."

He led them into the field where the blackbird still went on whistling its heart out into the endless summer morning. But to them it seemed that he led them out across the open world for ever and ever....

It grew very marvellous, this game of hide and seek. Sometimes they forgot it was a game at all, forgot what they were looking for, forgot that they were looking for anything or any one at all. Yet the mighty search continued subconsciously, even when passing incidents drew their attention from their chief desire. Always, at the back of thought, lay this exquisite, sweet memory in their hearts, something they half remembered, half forgot, but very dear, very marvellous. Some one was hiding somewhere, waiting, longing to play with them, expecting to be found.

It may be that intervals went by, those intervals called years and months; yet no one noticed them, and certainly no one named them. They knew one feeling only—the joy of endless search. Some one was hiding, some one was near, and signs lay scattered everywhere. This some one lay in his wonderful hiding-place and watched their search with laughter in his eyes. He remained invisible; perhaps they would never see him actually; but they felt his presence everywhere, in every object, every tree and flower and stone, in sun and wind, in water and in earth. The power and loveliness of common things became insistent. They were aware of them. It seemed they brushed against this shining presence, pushing for ever against a secret door of exit that led into the final hiding-place. Eager to play with them, yet more eager still to be discovered, the wonderful hider kept just beyond their sight and touch, while covering the playground with endless signs that he was near enough for them to know for certain he was—there. For among the four of them there was no heart that doubted. None explained. None said No.... Nor was there any hurry.

"*I* believe," announced Tim at length, with the air of a sage about him, "the best way is to sit still and wait; then he'll just come out like a rabbit and show himself." And, as no one contradicted, he added confidently, "that's *my* idea." His love was evidently among the things of the soil, rabbits, rats and hedgehogs, both hunter and adventurer strong in him.

"A hole!" cried Judy with indignation. "Never! He's in the air. I heard a bird just now that—"

"Whew!" whistled Uncle Felix, interrupting her excitedly. "He's been along here. Look! I'm sure of it." And he said it with such conviction that they ran up, expecting actual footprints.

"How do you know?" Tim asked dubiously, seeing no immediate proof himself. All paused for the reply; but Uncle

Felix also paused. He had said a thing it seemed he could not justify.

"Don't hesitate," said the Tramp, watching him with amusement. "Don't think before you speak. There's nothing to think about until you've spoken."

Uncle Felix wore an expression of bewilderment. "I meant the flowers," he stammered, still unsure of his new powers.

"Of course," the other chuckled. "Didn't I tell you 'tender and beautiful,' and 'bang out in the open'?"

"Then you're right, Uncle; they *are* signs," cried Judy, "and you *do* like butter," and she danced away to pick the dandelions that smothered the field with gold. But the Tramp held out his feather like a wand.

"They're our best signs, remember," he cried. "You might as well pick a feather out of a living bird."

"Oh!"—and she pulled herself up sharply, a little flush running across her face and the wind catching at her flying hair. She swayed a moment, nearly overbalancing owing to the interrupted movement, and looking for all the world like a wild young rose tree, her eyes two shining blossoms in the air. Then she dropped down and buried her nose among the crowd of yellow flowers. She smelt them audibly, drawing her breath in and letting it out again as though she could almost taste and eat the perfume.

"That's better," said the Tramp approvingly. "Smell, then follow," and he moved forward again with his dancing, happy step. "All the wild, natural things do it," he cried, looking back over his shoulder at the three who were on their knees with faces pressed down against the yellow carpet. "It's the way to keep on the trail. Smell—then follow."

Something flashed through the clearing mind of the older

man, though where it came from he had less idea than the dandelions: a mood of forgotten beauty rushed upon him—

"O, follow, follow!
Through the caverns hollow,
As the song floats thou pursue,
Where the wild bee never flew—"

and he ran dancing forward after the great Tramp, singing the words as though they were his own.

Yet the flowers spread so thickly that the trail soon lost itself; it seemed like a paper-chase where the hare had scattered coloured petals instead of torn white copy-books. Each searcher followed the sign of his or her own favourite flower; like a Jack-in-the-Box each one bobbed up and down, smelling, panting, darting hither and thither as in the mazes of some gnat—or animal-dance, till knees and hands were stained with sweet brown earth, and lips and noses gleamed with the dust of orange-tinted pollen.

"Anyhow, I'd rather look than find," cried Tim, turning a somersault over a sandy rabbit-mound.

The swallows flashed towards Judy, a twittering song sprinkling itself like liquid silver behind them as they swooped away again.

"I expect," the girl confessed breathlessly, "that when we do find him—we shall just die—!"

"Of happiness, and wonder," ventured Uncle Felix, watching a common Meadow Brown that perched, opening and closing its wings, upon his sleeve. And the Tramp, almost invisible among high standing grass and thistles, laughed and called in his curious, singing voice, "There is no hurry! Life has just begun!"

"Then we might as well sit down," suggested Uncle Felix, and suiting the action to the word, chose a nice soft spot upon the mossy bank and made himself comfortable as though he meant to stay; the Tramp did likewise, gathering the children close about his tangled figure. For one thing a big ditch faced them, its opposite bank overgrown with bramble bushes, and for another the sloping moss offered itself invitingly, like a cushioned sofa. So they lay side by side, watching the empty ditch, listening to the faint trickle of water tinkling down it. Slender reeds and tall straight grasses fringed the nearer edge, and, as the wind passed through them with a hush and whisper, they bent over in a wave of flowing green.

"He's certainly gone that way," Judy whispered, following with her eyes the direction of the bending reeds. She was getting expert now.

"Along the ditch, I do believe," agreed Tim. There were no flowers in it, and few, perhaps, would have found beauty there, yet the pointing of the reeds was unmistakable. "It's chock full of stuff," he added, "but a rat could get along, so I suppose—"

"The signs are very slight sometimes," murmured the Tramp, his head half buried in the moss, "and sometimes difficult as well. You'd be surprised." He flung out his arms and legs and continued laughingly. "When things are contrary you may be sure you're getting somewhere—getting warm, that is."

The children heard this outburst, but they did not listen. They were absorbed in something else already, for the movements of the reeds were fascinating. They began to imitate them, swaying their heads and bodies to and fro in time, and crooning to themselves in an attempt to copy the sound made by the wind among the crowded stalks.

"Don't," objected Uncle Felix, half in fun, "it makes me dizzy." He was tempted to copy them, however, and made an effort, but the movement caught him in the ribs a little. His body, like his mind, was not as supple as theirs. An oak tree or an elm, perhaps, was more his model.

"Do," the Tramp corrected him, swaying as he said it. "Swing with a thing if you want to understand it. Copy it, and you catch its meaning. That's rhythm!" He made an astonishing mouthful of the word. The children overheard it.

"How do you spell it?" Judy asked.

"I don't," he replied; "I do it. Once you get into the"—he took a great breath—"rhythm of a thing, you begin to like it. See?"

And he went on swaying his big shoulders in imitation of the rustling reeds. All four swayed together then, holding their feathers before them like little flying banners. More than ever, they seemed things growing out of the earth, out of the very ditch. The movement brought a delicious, soothing sense of peace and safety over them; earth, air, and sunshine all belonged to them, plenty for everybody, no need to get there first and snatch at the best places. There was no hurry, life had just begun. They seemed to have dug a hole in space and curled up cosily inside it. They whispered curious natural things to one another. "A wren is settling on my hair," said Judy: "a butterfly on my neck," said Uncle Felix: "a mouse," Tim mentioned, "is making its nest in my trousers pocket." And the Tramp kept murmuring in his voice of wind and water, "I'm full of air and sunlight, floating in them, floating away... my secret's in the wind and open sky... there is no longer any Time—to lose...."

A bright green lizard darted up the sun-baked bank, vanishing down a crack without a sound; it left a streak of fire in the air. A golden fly hovered about the tallest reed, then darted into another world, invisibly. A second followed it, a third, a fourth—points of gold that pinned the day fast against the moving wall of green. A wren shot at full speed along the bed of the ditch, threading its winding length together as upon a woven pattern. All were busy and intent upon some purpose common to the whole of them, and to everything else as well; even the things that did not move were doing something.

"I say," cried Tim suddenly, "they're covering him up. They're hiding him better so that we shan't find him. We've got too warm."

How long they had been in that ditch when the boy exclaimed no one could tell; perhaps a lifetime, or perhaps an age only. It was long enough, at any rate, for the Tramp to have changed visibly in appearance—he looked younger, thinner, sprightlier, more shining. He seemed to have shed a number of outward things that made him bulky—bits of beard and clothing, several extra waistcoats, and every scrap of straw and stuff from the hedges that he wore at first. More and more he looked as Judy had seen him, ages and ages ago, emerging from the tarpaulin on the rubbish-heap at the End of the World.

He sprang alertly to his feet at the sound of Tim's exclamation. The sunlit morning seemed to spring up with him.

"We have been very warm indeed," he sang, "but we shall get warmer still before we find him. Besides, those things aren't hiding him—they're looking. Everything and everybody in the whole wide world is looking, but the signs are different for everybody, don't you see? Each knows and follows their own particular sign. Come on!" he cried, "come on and look! We shall find him in the end."

COME-BACK STUMPER'S SIGN

VI

The steep bank was easily managed. They were up it in a twinkling, a line of dancing figures, all holding hands.

First went the Tramp, shining and glowing like a mirror in the sunshine—fire surely in him; next Judy, almost flying with the joy and lightness in her—as of air; Tim barely able to keep tight hold of her hand, so busily did his feet love the roots and rabbit-holes of—earth; and finally, Uncle Felix, rolling to and fro, now sideways, now toppling headlong, roaring as he followed like a heavy wave. Fire, air, earth, and water—they summarised existence; owned and possessed the endless day; lived it, were one with it. Their leader, who apparently had swallowed the sun, fused and unified them in this amazing way with—fire.

And hardly had they passed the line of shy forget-me-nots on the top of the bank, than they ran against a curious looking object that at first appeared to be an animated bundle of some kind, but on closer inspection proved to be a human figure stooping. It was somebody very busy about the edges of a great clump of bramble bushes. At the sound of their impetuous approach it straightened up. It had the face of a man—yellowish, patched with red, breathless and very hot. It was Come-back Stumper.

He glared at them, furious at being disturbed, yet with an

Algernon Blackwood

uneasy air, half comical, half ashamed, as of being—caught. He took on a truculent, aggressive attitude, as though he knew he would have to explain himself and did not want to do so. He turned and faced them.

"Mornin'," he grunted fiercely. "It's a lovely day."

But they all agreed so promptly with him that he dropped the offensive at once. His face was *very* hot. It dripped.

"Energetic as usual," observed Uncle Felix, while Tim poked among the bushes to see what he had been after, and Judy offered him a very dirty handkerchief to mop his forehead with. His bald head shone and glistened. Wisps of dark hair lay here and there upon it like the feathers of a crow's torn wing.

"Thanks, dear," he said stiffly, using the few inches of ragged cambric and then tucking the article absent-mindedly into a pocket of his shooting coat. "I've been up very early—since dawn. Since dawn," he repeated in a much louder voice, "got up, in fact, with the sun." He meant to justify his extreme and violent activity. He glanced at the Tramp with a curious air of respect. Tim thought he saluted him, but Judy declared afterwards he was only wiping "the hot stuff off the side of his dear old head."

"Wonderful moment,—dawn, ain't it, General?" said the Tramp. "Best in the whole day when you come to think of it."

"It is, sir," replied Stumper, as proud as though a Field-Marshal had addressed him, "and the first." He looked more closely at the Tramp; he rubbed his eyes, and then produced the scrap of cambric and rubbed them again more carefully than before. Perhaps he, too, had been hoping for a leader! Something very proud and happy stole upon his perspiring face of ochre. He moved a step nearer. "Did you notice it this morning?" he asked in a whisper, "the dawn, I mean? Never saw anything like it in me life before. Thought I was in the

Himalayas or the Caucasus again. Astonishin', upon me word—the beauty of it! And the birds! Did you hear 'em? Expect you usually do, though," he added with a touch of unmistakable envy and admiration in his tone.

"Uncommon," agreed the Tramp, "and no mistake about it. *They* knew, you see." They no longer called each other "Sir" and "General"; they had come to an understanding apparently.

"Umph!" said Stumper, and looked round shyly at the others.

Stumper was evidently under the stress of some divine emotion he was half ashamed of. An unwonted passion stirred him. He seemed a prey to an unusual and irrepressible curiosity. Only the obvious fact that his listeners shared the same feelings with him loosened his sticky tongue and stole self-consciousness away. He had expected to be laughed at. Instead the group admired him. The Tramp—his manner proved it—thought of him very highly indeed.

"Never knew such a day in all me life before," Stumper admitted frankly. "Couldn't—simply couldn't stay indoors."

He still retained a trace of challenge in his tone. But no one challenged. Judy took his arm. "So you came out?" she said softly.

"Like us," said Uncle Felix.

"Of course," Tim added. But it was the Tramp who supplied the significant words they had all been waiting for, Stumper himself more eagerly than any one else. "To look," he remarked quite naturally.

Stumper might have just won a great world-victory, judging by the expression that danced upon his face. He dropped all pretence at further concealment. He put his other arm round Tim's shoulder, partly to balance himself better against Judy's pushing, and partly because he realised the companionship of both children as very dear just then. He had a great deal to say, and wanted to say it all at once, but words never came to him too easily; he had missed many an opportunity in life for the want of fluent and spontaneous address. He stammered and halted somewhat in his delivery. A new language with but a single word in it would have suited him admirably.

"Yes," he growled, "I came out—to look. But when I got out—I clean forgot what it was—who, I mean—no, *what*," he corrected himself again, "I'd come out to look for. Can't make it out at all." He broke off in a troubled way.

"No?" agreed Judy sympathetically, as though *she* knew.

"But you want to find it awfully," Tim stated as a fact.

"Awfully," admitted Stumper with a kind of fierceness.

"Only you can't remember what it looks like quite?" put in Uncle Felix.

Stumper hesitated a moment. "Too wonderful to remember properly," he said more quietly; something like that. "But the odd thing is," he went on in a lower tone, "I've seen it. I *know* I've seen it. Saw it this mornin'—very early—when the pigeon woke me up—at dawn."

"Pigeon!" exclaimed Tim and Judy simultaneously. "Dawn!"

"Carrier-pigeon—flew in at my open window—woke me," continued the soldier in his gruff old voice. "I've used 'em—carrier-pigeons, you know. Sent messages—years ago. I understand the birds a bit. Extraordinary thing, I thought. Got up and looked at it." He blocked again.

"Ah!" said some one, by way of encouragement.

"And it looked back at me." By the way he said it, it was clear he hardly expected to be believed.

"Of course," said Uncle Felix.

"Naturally," added Tim.

"And what d'you think?" Stumper went on, a note of yearning and even passion in his voice. "What d'you think?" he whispered: "I felt it had a message for me—brought *me* a message—something to tell me—"

"Round its neck or foot?" asked Tim.

Stumper drew the boy closer and looked down into his face. "Eyes," he mumbled, "in its small bright eyes. There was a flash, I saw it plainly—something strange and marvellous, something I've been looking for all my life."

No one said a single word, but the old soldier felt the understanding sympathy rising like steam from all of them.

"Then, suddenly, it was gone—out into the open sky—bang into the sunrise. And I saw the dawn all over everything. I dressed—rushed out—and—"

"Had it laid an egg?" Tim asked, remembering another kind of hunting somewhere, long ago.

"How could it?" Judy corrected him quickly. "There was—no time—" then stopped abruptly. She turned towards Come-Back Stumper; she gave him a hurried and affectionate hug. "And then," she asked, "what happened next?"

Stumper returned the hug, including Tim in it too. "I found *this*—fluttering in my hand," he said, and held up a small grey feather for them to admire. "It's the only clue I've got. The pigeon left it."

While they admired the feather and exhibited their own, Tim crying, "We've got five now, nearly a whole wing!" Stumper was heard to murmur above their heads, "And since I—came out to look—I've felt—quite different."

"Your secret's in the wind and open sky!" cried Judy, dancing round him with excitement. Her voice came flying from the air.

"You're awfully warm—you're hot—you're burning!" shouted Tim, clapping his hands. His voice seemed to rise out of the earth.

"We've all seen it, all had a glimpse," roared Uncle Felix with a sound of falling water, rolling up nearer as he spoke. "It's too wonderful to see for long, too wonderful to remember quite. But we shall find it in the end. We're all looking!" He began a sort of dancing step. "And when we find it—" he went on.

"We'll change the world," shouted Stumper, as though he uttered a final word of command.

"It's a he, remember," interrupted Tim. "Come along!"

And then the Tramp, who had been standing quietly by, smiling to himself but saying nothing, came nearer, opened his great arms and drew the four of them together. His voice, his shining presence, the warm brilliance that glowed about him, seemed to envelop them like a flame of fire and a fire of—love.

"We're thinking and arguing too much," he drawled in his leisurely, big voice, "we lose the trail that way, we lose the rhythm. Just love and look and wonder—then we'll find him. There is no hurry, life has just begun. But keep on looking all the time." He turned to Stumper with a chuckle. "You said you had a flash," he reminded him. "What's become of it? You can't have lost it—with that pigeon's feather in your hand!"

"It's waggling," announced Tim, holding up his own, while the others followed suit. The little feathers all bent one way— towards the bramble clump. Their tiny, singing music was just audible in the pause.

"Yes," replied Come-Back Stumper at length. "I've had a flash—flashes, in fact! What's more," he added proudly, "I was after a couple of them—just when you arrived."

Everybody talked at once then. Uncle Felix and the children fell to explaining the signs and traces they had already discovered, each affirming vehemently that their own particular sign was the loveliest—the dragon-fly, the flowers, the wind, the bending reeds, even the lizard and the bumble-bee. The chorus of sound was like the chattering of rooks among the tree-tops; in fact, though the quality of tone of course was different, the resemblance to a concert of birds, all singing together in a summer garden, was quite striking. Out of the hubbub single words emerged occasionally—a "robin," "swallows," an "up-and-under bird"—yet, strange to say, so far as Stumper was concerned, only one thing was said; all said the same one thing; he heard this one thing only—as though the words and sentences they used were but different ways of pronouncing it, of spelling it, of uttering it. Moreover, the wind in the feather said it too, for the sound and intonation were similar. It was the thing that wind and running water said, that flame roared in the fireplace, that rain-drops pattered on the leaves, even house-flies, buzzing across the window-panes—everything everywhere, the whole earth, said it.

He stood still, listening in amazement. His face had dried by now; he passed his hand across it; he tugged at his fierce military moustache.

"Hiding—near us—in the open—everywhere," he muttered, though no one heard him; "I've had my flashes too."

"Different people get different signs, of course," the Tramp made himself heard at length, "but they're all the same. All lie along the trail. The earth's a globe and circle, so everything leads to the same place—in the end."

"Yes," said Stumper; "thank you"—as though he knew it already, but felt that it was neatly put.

"Follow up your flash," added the Tramp. "Smell—then follow. That is—keep on looking."

Stumper turned, pirouetting on what the children called his "living leg." "I will," he cried, with an air of self-abandonment, and promptly diving by a clever manoeuvre out of their hands, he fell heavily upon all fours, and disappeared beneath the dense bramble bushes just behind them. Panting, and certainly perspiring afresh, he forced his way in among the network of thick leaves and prickly branches. They heard him puffing; it seemed they heard him singing too, as he reached forward with both arms into the dark interior. Caught by his whole-hearted energy, they tried to help; they pushed behind; they did their best to open a way for his head between the entwining brambles.

"Don't!" he roared inside. "You'll scratch my eyes out. I shan't see—anything!" His mouth apparently was full of earth. They watched the retreating soles of his heavy shooting-boots. Slowly the feet were dragged in after him. They disappeared from sight. Stumper was gone.

"He'll come back, though," mentioned Judy. The performance had been so interesting that she almost forgot its object, however. Tim reminded her. "But he won't find anything in a smelly place like that," he declared. "I mean," he added, "it can't be a beetle or a grub that we're—looking for." Yet there was doubt and wonder in his voice. Stumper, a "man like that," and a soldier, a hunter too, who had done scouting in an Indian jungle, and met tigers face to face—a chap like that could hardly disappear on all fours into a clump of bramble bushes without an excellent reason!

An interval of comparative silence followed, broken only by the faint murmur of the wind that stirred their humming feathers. They stood in a row and listened intently. Hardly a sound came from the interior of the bramble bushes. The soldier had justified his title. He had retired pletely. To Judy it occurred that he might be suffocated, to Tim that he might have been eaten by some animal, to Uncle Felix that he might have slipped out at the other side and made his escape. But no one expressed these idle thoughts in words. They believed in Stumper really. He invariably came back. This time would be no exception to the rule.

And, presently, as usual, Stumper did come back. They heard him grunting and panting long before a sign of him was visible. They heard his voice, "Got him! Knew I was right! Bah! Ugh!" as he spluttered earth and leaves from his mouth apparently. He emerged by degrees and backwards; backed out, indeed, like an enormous rabbit. His boots, his legs, his hands planted on the ground, his neck and then his face, looking out over his shoulder, appeared successively. "Just the kind of place he *would* choose!" he exclaimed triumphantly, collapsing back upon his haunches and taking a long, deep breath. Beside the triumph in his voice there was a touch of indescribable, gruff sweetness the children knew was always in his heart—no amount of curried-liver trouble could smother *that*. Just now it was more marked than usual.

"Show us!" they cried, gathering round him. Judy helped him to his feet; he seemed a little unsteady. Purple with the exertion of the search, both cheeks smeared with earth, neck-tie crooked, and old grey shooting-coat half-way up his back, Come-Back Stumper stood upright, and looked at them with shining eyes. He was the picture of a happy and successful man.

"There!" he growled, and held out a hand, palm upwards, still trembling with his recent exertions. "Didn't I tell you?"

They crowded round to examine a small object that lay between two smears of earth in the centre of the upturned palm. It was round and had a neat little opening on its under side. It was pretty, certainly. Their heads pressed forward in a bunch, like cabbages heaped for market. But no one spoke.

"See it?" said Stumper impatiently; "see what it is?" He bent forward till his head mixed with theirs, his big aquiline nose in everybody's way.

"We see it—yes," said Uncle Felix without enthusiasm. "It's a snail shell—er—I believe?" The shade of disappointment in his voice was reflected in the children's faces too, as they all straightened up and gazed expectantly at the panting soldier. "Is that all?" was the sentence no one liked to utter.

But Stumper roared at them. "A snail shell!" he boomed; "of course it's a snail shell! But did you ever see such a snail shell in your lives before? Look at the colour! Look at the shape! Put it against your ears and hear it singing!" He was furious with their lack of appreciation.

"It's the common sort," said Uncle Felix, braver than the others, "something or other vulgaris—"

"Hundreds of them everywhere," mentioned Tim beneath his breath to Judy.

But Stumper overheard them.

"Common sort! Hundreds everywhere!" he shouted, his voice almost choking in his throat; "look at the colour! Look at the shape, I tell you! Listen to it!" He said the last words with a sudden softness.

They lowered their heads again for a new examination.

"What more d'you want, I'd like to know? There's colour for you! There's wonder! There's a sheer bit of living beauty!" and he lowered his head again so eagerly that it knocked audibly against Tim's skull.

"Please move your nose away," said Tim, "I can't see."

"Common indeed!" growled the soldier, making room willingly enough, while they obeyed his booming orders. They felt a little ashamed of themselves for being so obtuse, for now that they looked closer they saw that the shell was certainly very beautiful. "Common indeed!" he muttered again. "Why, you don't know a sign when it's straight before your noses!"

Judy pulled the fingers apart to make it roll towards her; she felt it all over, stroking the smooth beauty of its delicate curves. It was exquisitely tinted. It shone and glistened in the morning sunlight. She put it against her ear and listened. "Oh!" she exclaimed. "It *is* singing," as the murmur of the wind explored its hollow windings.

"That's the Ganges," explained Stumper in a softer voice. "The waves of the Ganges breaking on the yellow sands of India. Wind in the jungle too." His face looked happy as he watched her; his explosions never lasted long.

She passed it over to her brother, who crammed it against his ear and listened with incredible grimaces as though it hurt him. "I can hear the tigers' footsteps," he declared, screwing up his eyes, "and birds of paradise and all sorts of things." He handed it on reluctantly to his uncle, who listened so deeply in his turn that he had to shut both eyes. "I hear calling voices," he murmured to himself, "voices calling, calling every-where....it's wonderful... like a sea of voices from the other side of the world... the whole world's singing...!"

"And look at the colour, will you?" urged Stumper, snatching it away from the listener, who, seemed in danger of becoming entranced. "Why, he's not only passed this way—he's actually touched it. That's his touch, I tell you!"

"That's right," mumbled the Tramp, watching the whole performance with approval. "Folks without something are always sharper than the others." But this reference to a wooden leg was also too low for any one to hear it.

Besides Stumper was saying something wonderful just then; he lowered his voice to say it; there was suppressed excitement in

Algernon Blackwood

him; he frowned and looked half savagely at them all:

"I found other signs as well," he whispered darkly. "Two other signs. In the darkness of those bushes I saw—another flash—two of 'em!" And he slowly extended his other hand which till now he had kept behind his back. It was tightly clenched. He unloosed the fingers gradually. "Look!" he whispered mysteriously. And the hand lay open before their eyes. "He's been hiding in those very bushes, I tell you. A moment sooner and we might have caught him."

His enthusiasm ran all over them as they pressed forward to examine the second grimy hand. There were two things visible in it, and both were moving. One, indeed, moved so fast that they hardly saw it. There was a shining glimpse—a flash of lovely golden bronze shot through with blue—and it was gone. Like a wee veiled torch it scuttled across the palm, climbed the thumb, popped down the other side and dropped upon the ground. Vanished as soon as seen!

"A beetle!" exclaimed Uncle Felix. "A tiny beetle!"

"But dipped in colour," said Stumper with enthusiasm, "the colour of the dawn!"

"Another sign! I never!" He was envious of the soldier's triumph.

"He looks in the unlikely places," muttered the Tramp again, approvingly. "You've been pretty warm this time." But, again, he said it too low to be audible. Besides, Stumper's other "find" engrossed everybody's attention. All were absorbed in the long, dainty object that clung cautiously to his hand and showed no desire to hurry out of sight after the brilliant beetle. It was familiar enough to all of them, yet marvellous. It presented itself in a new, original light.

They watched it spellbound; its tiny legs moved carefully over the wrinkles of the soldier's skin, feeling its way most delicately, and turning its head this way and that to sniff the unaccustomed odour. Sometimes it looked back to admire its own painted back, and to let its distant tail know that all was going well. The coloured hairs upon the graceful body were all a-quiver. It fairly shone. There was obviously no fear in it; it had perfect control of all its length and legs. Yet, fully aware that it was exploring a new country, it sometimes raised its head in a hesitating way and looked questioningly about it and even into the great faces so close against its eyes.

"A caterpillar! A common Woolly Bear!" observed Tim, yet with a touch of awe.

"It tickles," observed Stumper.

"I'll get a leaf," Judy whispered. "It doesn't understand your smell, probly." She turned and picked the biggest she could find, and the caterpillar, after careful observation, moved forward on to it, turning to inform its following tail that all was safe. Gently and cleverly they restored it to the bush whence Stumper had removed it. It went to join the snail-shell and the beetle. They stood a moment in silence and watched the quiet way it hid itself among the waves of green the wind stirred to and fro. It seemed to melt away. It hid itself. It left them. It was gone.

And Stumper turned and looked at them with the air of a man who has justified himself. He had certainly discovered definite signs.

But there was bewilderment among the group as well as pleasure. For signs, they began to realise now, were everywhere indeed. The world was smothered with them. There was no one clear track that they could follow. All Nature seemed organised to hide the thing they looked for. It was a conspiracy. It was, indeed, an "enormous hide," an endless game of hide-and-seek. The interest and the wonder increased sensibly in their hearts. The thing they sought to find, the Stranger, "It," by whatever name each chose to call the mysterious and evasive "hider," was so marvellously hidden. The glimpse they once had known seemed long, long ago, and very far away. It lay like a sweet memory in each heart, half forgotten, half remembered, but always entirely believed in, very dear and very exquisite. The precious memory urged them forward. They would search and search until they re-discovered it, even though their whole lives were spent in the looking. They were quite positive they would find him in the end.

All this lay somehow in the expression on Stumper's face as he glared at them and ejaculated a triumphant "There! I told you so!" And at that moment, as though to emphasize the thrill of excited bewilderment they felt, a gorgeous brimstone butterfly sailed carelessly past before their eyes and vanished among the pools of sunlight by the forest edge. Its presence added somehow to the elusive and difficult nature of their search. Its flamboyant beauty was a kind of challenge.

"That's what the caterpillar gets into," observed Tim dreamily.

"Let's follow it," said Judy. "*I* believe the flying signs are best."

"Puzzlin' though," put in the Tramp behind them. They had quite forgotten his existence. "Let's ask the gardener what *he* thinks."

He pointed to a spot a little further along the edge of the wood where the figure of a man was visible. It seemed a good idea. Led by the Tramp, Uncle Felix and Stumper following slowly in the rear, they moved forward in a group. Weeden might have seen something. They would ask him.

WEEDEN'S SIGN

VII

John WEEDEN—the children always saw his surname in capitals—was probably the most competent Head Gardener of his age, or of any other age: he supplied the household with fruit and vegetables without grumbling or making excuses. When asked to furnish flowers at short notice for a dinner-party he made no difficulty, but just produced them. Neither did he complain about the weather; wet or dry, it was always exactly what his garden needed. All weather to him was Fine Weather. He believed in his garden, loved it, lived in it, was almost part of it. To make excuses for it was to make excuses for himself. WEEDEN was a genius.

But he was mysterious too. He was one-eyed, and the loss endeared him to the children, relating him also, once or twice removed, to Come-Back Stumper; it touched their imaginations. Being an artist, too, he never told them how he lost it, a pitchfork and a sigh were all he vouchsafed upon the exciting subject. He understood the value of restraint, and left their minds to supply what details they liked best. But this wink of pregnant suggestion, while leaving them divinely unsatisfied, sent them busily on the search. They imagined the lost optic roaming the universe without even an attendant eyelid, able to see things on its own account—invisible things. "Weeden's lost eye's about," was a delightful and mysterious threat; while "I can see with the Gardener's lost eye," was a claim to glory no one could dispute, for no one could deny it.

Its chief duty, however, was to watch the "froot and vegebles" at night and to keep all robbers—two-foot, four-foot, winged, or wriggling robbers—from what Aunt Emily called "destroying everything."

A source of wonder to the children, this competent official was at the same time something of an enigma to the elders. His appearance, to begin with, was questionable, and visitors, being shown round the garden, had been known to remark upon it derogatively sometimes. It was both in his favour and against him. For, either he looked like an untidy parcel of brown paper, loose ends of string straggling out of him, or else—in his Sunday best—was indistinguishable from a rose-bush wrapped up carefully in matting against the frost. Yet, in either aspect, no one could pretend that he looked like anything but a genuine Head Gardener, the spirit of the kitchen-garden and the potting-shed incarnate.

It was the way he answered questions that earned for him the title of enigma—he avoided a direct reply. (He was so cautious that he would hesitate even when he came to die.) He would think twice about it. The decision to draw the final breath would incapacitate him. He would feel worse—and probably continue alive instead, from sheer inability to make his mind up. In all circumstances, owing to his calling doubtless, he preferred to hedge. If Mrs. Horton asked for celery, he would intimate "I'll have a look." When Daddy enquired how the asparagus was doing, he obtained for reply, "Won't you come and see it for yourself, sir?" Upon Mother's anxious enquiry if there would be enough strawberries for the School Treat, WEEDEN stated "It's been a grand year for the berries, mum." Then, just when she felt relieved, he added, "on the 'ole."

For the children, therefore, the Gardener was a man of mystery and power, and when they saw his figure in the distance, their imagination leaped forward with their bodies, and WEEDEN stood wrapped in a glory he little guessed. He was bent double, digging (as usual in his spare time) for truffles beneath the beech trees. These mysterious delicacies with the awkward name he never found, but he liked looking for them.

At first he was so intent upon his endless quest that he did not hear the approach of footsteps.

"No hurry," said the Tramp, as they collected round the stooping figure and held their feathers up to warn his back. For the wandering eye had a way of seeing what went on behind him. An empty sack, waiting for the truffles, lay beside him. He looked like an untidy parcel, so he was *not* in his Sunday clothes.

At the sound of voices he straightened slowly and looked round. He seemed pleased with everything, judging by the expression of his eye, yet doubtful of immediate success.

"Good mornin'," he said, touching his speckled cap to the authorities.

"Found any?" enquired Uncle Felix, sympathetically.

"It seems a likely spot, maybe," was the reply. "I'm looking." And he closed the mouth of the sack with his foot lest they should see its emptiness.

But the use of the verb set the children off at once.

"I say," Tim exploded eagerly, "we're looking too—for somebody who's hiding. Have you seen any one?"

"Some one very wonderful?" said Judy. "Has he passed this way? It's Hide-and-Seek, you know."

WEEDEN looked more mysterious at once. It was strange how a one-eyed face could express so big a meaning. He scratched his head and smiled.

"All my flowers and vegitubles is a-growin' nicely," he said at length. "It is a lovely mornin' for a game." His eye closed and opened. The answer was more direct than usual. It meant volumes. WEEDEN was in the know. They felt him somehow related to their leader—a kind of organised and regulated tramp.

"You *have* seen him, then?" cried Judy.

"With your gone eye!" exclaimed Tim. "Which way? And what signs have you got?"

"Flowers, beetles, snail-shells, caterpillars—anything beautiful is a sign, you know," went on Judy, breathlessly.

"Deep, tender, kind and beautiful," interposed the Tramp, laying the accent significantly on the first adjective, as if for Weeden's special benefit.

WEEDEN looked up. "Sounds like my garden things," he said darkly, more to himself than to the others. He gazed down into the hole he had been digging. The moist earth glistened in the sunlight. He sniffed the sweet, rich odour of it, and scratched his head in the same spot as before—just beneath the peak of his speckled cap. His nose wrinkled up. Then he looked again into the faces, turning his single eye slowly upon each in turn. The Tramp's remark had reached his cautious brain.

"There's no sayin' where anybody sich as you describe him to be might hide hisself a day like this," he observed deliberately, his optic ranging the sunny landscape with approval. "I never saw sich a beautiful day before—not like to-day. It's endless sort of. Seems to me as if I'd been at this 'ole for weeks."

He paused. The others waited. WEEDEN was going to say something real any moment now, they felt.

"No hurry," the Tramp reminded him. "Everything's light and careless, and so are we. There is no longer any Time—to lose."

His voice half sang, half chanted in the slow, windy way he had, and the Gardener looked up as if a falling apple had struck him on the head. He shifted from one leg to the other; he seemed excited, moved. His single eye was opened—to the sun. He looked as if his body was full of light.

"*You* was the singer, was you?" he asked wonderingly, the tone low and quiet. "It was you I heard a-singin'—jest as dawn broke!" He scratched his head again. "And me thinkin' all the time it was a bird!" he added to himself.

The Tramp said nothing.

WEEDEN then resumed his ordinary manner; he went on speaking as before. But obviously—somewhere deep down inside himself—he had come to a big decision.

"Gettin' nearer and nearer," he resumed his former conversation exactly where he had left it off, "but never near enough to get disappointed—ain't it? When you gets to the end of anything, you see, it's over. And that's a pity."

Uncle Felix glanced at Stumper; Stumper glanced down at the end of his "wooden" leg; the Tramp still said nothing, smiling in his beard, now combed out much smoother than before.

"It comes to this," said Weeden, "my way of thinkin' at least." He scratched wisdom from another corner of his head. "There's a lot of 'iding goin' on, no question about *that*; and the great thing is—my way of thinkin' at any rate—is—jest to keep on lookin'."

The children met him eagerly at this point, using two favourite words that Aunt Emily strongly disapproved of: "deslidedly," said one; "distinkly," exclaimed the other.

"That's it," continued WEEDEN, pulling down his cap to hide, perhaps, the spot where wisdom would leak out. "And, talking of signs, I say—find out yer own pertickler sign, then follow it blindly—till the end."

He straightened up and looked with an air of respectful candour at the others. The decision of his statement delighted them. The children felt something of awe in it. Something of their Leader's knowledge evidently was in him.

"Miss Judy, she gets 'er signs from the air," he said, as no one spoke. "Master Tim goes poking along the ground, looking for something with his feet. He feels best that way, feels the earth—things a-growin' up or things wot go down into 'oles. Colonel Stumper—and no offence to you, sir—chooses dark places where the sun forgets to shine—"

"Dangerous, jungly places," whispered Tim, admiringly.

"And Mr. Felix—" he hesitated. Uncle Felix's easiest way of searching seemed to puzzle him. "Mr. Felix," he went on at length, "jest messes about all over the place at once, because 'e sees signs everywhere and don't know what to foller in partickler for fear of losin' hisself."

Come-Back Stumper chuckled audibly, but Uncle Felix asked at once—"And you, WEEDEN? What about yourself, I wonder?"

The Gardener replied without his usual hesitation. It was probably the most direct reply he had ever made. No one could guess how much it cost him. "Underground," he said. "My signs lies underground, sir. Where the rain-drops 'ides theirselves on getting down and the grubs keeps secret till they feel their wings. Where the potatoes and the reddishes is," he added, touching his cap with a respectful finger. He went on with a hint of yearning in his tone that made it tremble slightly: "If I could find igsackly where and 'ow the potatoes gets big down there"—he pointed to the earth—"or how my roses get colour out of the dirt—I'd know it, wouldn't I, sir? I'd—'ave him, fair!"

The effort exhausted him, it seemed. So deeply was he moved that he had almost gone contrary to his own nature in making such an explicit statement. But he had said something very real at last. It was clear that he was distinctly in the know. Living among natural growing things, he was in touch with life in a deeper sense than they were.

"And me?" the Tramp mentioned lightly, smiling at his companion of the outdoor life. "Don't leave me out, please. I'm looking like the rest of you."

WEEDEN turned round and gazed at him. He wore a strange expression that had respect in it, but something more than mere respect. There was a touch of wonder in his eye, a hint of worship almost. But he did not answer; no word escaped his lips. Instead of speaking he moved up nearer; he took three cautious steps, then halted close beside the great burly figure that formed the centre of the little group.

And then he did a curious and significant little act; he held out both his hands against him as a man might hold out his hands to warm them before a warm and comforting grate of blazing coals.

"Fire," he said; then added, "and I'm much obliged to you."

He wore a proud and satisfied air, grateful and happy too. He put his cap straight, picked up his spade, and prepared without another word to go on digging for truffles where apparently none existed. He seemed quite content with—looking.

A pause followed, broken presently by Tim: a whisper addressed to all.

"He never finds any. That shows how real it is."

"They're somewhere, though," observed Judy.

They stood and watched the spade; it went in with a crunching sound; it came out slowly with a sort of "pouf," and a load of rich, black earth slid off it into the world of sunshine. It went in again, it came out again; the rhythm of the movement caught them. How long they watched it no one knew, and no one cared to know: it might have been a moment, it may have been a year or two; so utterly had hurry vanished out of life it seemed to them they stood and watched for ever...when they became aware of a curious sensation, as though they felt the whole earth turning with them. They were moving, surely. Something to which they belonged, of which they formed a part—was moving. A windy voice was singing just in front of them. They looked up. The words were inaudible, but they knew it was a bit of the same old song that every one seemed singing everywhere as though the Day itself were singing.

The Tramp was going on.

"Hark!" said Tim. "The birds are singing. Let's go on and look."

"The world is wild with laughter," Judy cried, snatching the words from the air about her. "We can fly—" She darted after him.

"Among the imprisoned hours as we choose," boomed the voice of Uncle Felix, as he followed, rolling in behind her.

"We can play," growled Stumper, hobbling next in the line. "*My* life has just begun."

Their Leader waited till they all came up with him. They caught him up, gathering about him like things that settled on a sunny bush. It almost seemed they were one single person growing from the earth and air and water. The Tramp glowed there between them like a heart of burning fire.

"*He* ought to be with us, too," said Judy, looking back.

"No hurry," replied the Tramp. "Let him be; he's following *his* sign. When he's ready, he'll come along. It's a lovely day."

They moved with the rhythm of a flock of happy birds across the field of yellow flowers, singing in chorus something or other about an "extra day." A hundred years flowed over them, or else a single instant. It mattered not. They took no heed, at any rate. It was so enormous that they lost themselves, and yet so tiny that they held it between a finger and a thumb. The important thing was—that they were getting warmer.

Then Judy suddenly nudged Tim, and Tim nudged Uncle Felix, and Uncle Felix dug his elbow into Come-Back Stumper, and Stumper somehow or other caught the attention of the Tramp—a sort of panting sound, half-whistle and half-gasp. They paused and looked behind them.

"He's ready," remarked their Leader, with a laughing chuckle in his beard. "He's coming on!"

WEEDEN, sure enough, had quietly shouldered his shovel and empty sack, and was making after them, singing as he came. Judy was on the point of saying to her brother, "Good thing Aunt Emily isn't here!" when she caught a look in his eyes that stopped her dead.

AUNT EMILY FINDS—HERSELF

VIII

"My dear!" he exclaimed in his tone of big discovery.

Judy made a movement like a swan that inspects the world behind its back. She tried to look everywhere at once. It seemed she did so.

"Gracious me!" she cried. She instinctively chose prohibited words. "*My* gracious me!"

For the places of the world had marvellously shifted and run into one another somehow. A place called "Somewhere Else" was close about her; and standing in the middle of it was—a figure. Both place and figure ought to have been somewhere else by rights. Judy's surprise, however, was quite momentary; swift, bird-like understanding followed it. Place was a sham and humbug really; already, without leaving the schoolroom carpet, she and Tim had been to the Metropolis and even to the East. This was merely another of these things she didn't know she knew; she understood another thing she didn't understand. She believed.

The rest of the party had disappeared inside the wood; only Tim remained—pointing at this figure outlined against the trees. But these trees belonged to a place her physical eyes had never seen. Perhaps they were part of her mental picture of it. The figure, anyhow, barred the way.

It was a woman, the last person in the world they wished to see just then. The face, wearing an expression as though it tried to be happy when it felt it ought not to be, was pointed; chin, ears, and eye-brows pointed; nose pointed too—round doors and into corners—an elastic nose; there was a look of struggling sweetness about the thin, tight lips; the entire expression, from the colourless eyes down to the tip of the decided chin, was one of marked reproach and disapproval that at the same time fought with an effort to be understanding, gentle, wise. The face wanted to be very nice, but was prevented by itself. It was pathetic. Its owner was dressed in black, a small, neat bonnet fastened carefully on the head, an umbrella in one hand, and big goloshes on both feet. There were gold glasses balanced on the nose. She smiled at them, but with a smile that prophesied rebuke. Before she spoke a word, her entire person said distinctly NO.

"Bother!" Tim muttered beneath his breath, then added, "It's her!" Already he felt guilty—of something he had not done, but might do presently. The figure's mere presence invited him to break all rules.

"We thought," exclaimed Judy, trying to remember what rules she had just disobeyed, and almost saying "hoped,"—"we thought you were at Tunbridge Wells." Then with an effort she put in "Aunty."

Yet about the new arrival was a certain flustered and uneasy air, as though she were caught in something that she wished to hide—at any rate something she would not willingly confess to. One hand, it was noticed, she kept stiffly behind her back.

"Children," she uttered in an emphatic voice, half-surprised remonstrance, half-automatic rebuke; "I am astonished!" She looked it. She pursed her lips more tightly, and gazed at the pair of culprits as though she had hoped better things of them and *again* had been disappointed. "You know quite well that this is out of bounds." It came out like an arrow, darting.

Algernon Blackwood

"We were looking for some one," began Tim, but in a tone that added plainly enough "it wasn't you."

"Who's hiding, you see," quoth Judy, "but expecting us—at once." The delay annoyed her.

"You are both well aware," Aunt Emily went on, ignoring their excuses as in duty bound, "that your parents would not approve. At this hour of the morning too! You ought to be fast asleep in bed. If your father knew—!"

Yet, strange to say, the children felt that they loved her suddenly; for the first time in their lives they thought her lovable. A kind of understanding sympathy woke in them; there was something pitiable about her. For, obviously, she was looking just as they were, but looking in such a silly way and in such hopelessly stupid places. All her life she had been looking like this, dressed in crackling black, wearing a prickly bonnet and heavy goloshes, and carrying a useless umbrella that of course must bother her. It was disappointment that made her talk as she did. But it was natural she should feel disappointment, for it never rained when she had her umbrella, and her goloshes were always coming off.

"She's stuck in a hole," thought Tim, "and so she just says things at us. She hurts herself somewhere. She's tired."

"She has to be like that," thought Judy. "It's really all pretending. Poor old thing!"

But Aunt Emily was not aware of what they felt. They were out of bed, and it was her duty to find fault; they were out of bounds, and she must take note of it. So she prepared to scold a little. Her bonnet waggled ominously. She gripped her umbrella. She spoke as though it was very early in the morning, almost dawn—as though the sun were rising. There was confusion in her as to the time of day, it seemed. But the children did not notice this. They were so accustomed to being rebuked by her that the actual words made small impression.

She was just "saying things"; they were often very muddled things; the attitude, not the meaning, counted. And her attitude, they divined, was subtly different.

"You know this is forbidden," she said. "It is damp and chilly. It's sure to rain presently. You'll get your feet wet. You should keep to the gravel paths. They're plain enough, are they not?" She looked about her, sniffing—a sniff that usually summoned disasters in a flock.

"Oh, yes," said Tim; "and they look like brown sugar, *we* thought."

"It does not matter what you thought, Timothy. The paths are made on purpose to be walked upon and used—"

"They're beautifully made," interrupted Judy, unable to keep silent longer. "WEEDEN made them for us."

"And we've used them all," exclaimed Tim, "only we came to an end of them. We've done with them—paths!" The way he uttered the substantives made it instantly sound ridiculous.

Aunt Emily opened her mouth to say something, then closed it again without saying it. She stared at them instead. They watched her. All fear of her had left their hearts. A new expression rose struggling upon her pointed features. She fidgeted from one foot to the other. They felt her as "Aunty," a poor old muddled thing, always looking in ridiculous places without the smallest notion she was wrong. Tim saw her suddenly "all dressed up on purpose" as for a game. Judy thought "She's bubbling inside—really."

"There's WEEDEN in there," Tim mentioned, pointing to the wood behind her.

Something uncommonly like a smile passed into Aunt Emily's eyes, then vanished as suddenly as it came. Judy thought it was like a bubble that burst the instant it reached the sunlight on the surface of a pond.

"And how often," came the rebuke, automatically rather, "has your Mother told you *not* to be familiar with the Gardener? Play if you want to, but do not play with your inferiors. Play with your Uncle Felix, with Colonel Stumper, or with me—"

Another bubble had risen, caught the sunshine, reflected all the colours of the prism, then burst and vanished into airy spray.

"But they're looking with us," Tim insisted eagerly. "We're all looking together for something—Uncle Felix, Come-Back Stumper, everybody. It's wonderful. It never ends."

Aunt Emily's hand, still clutching the umbrella, stole up and put her bonnet straight. It was done to gain a little time apparently. There was a certain hesitation in her. She seemed puzzled. She betrayed excitement too.

"Looking, are you?" she exclaimed, and her voice held a touch of mellowness that was new. "Looking!"

She stopped. She tried to hide the mellowness by swallowing it.

"Yes," said Tim. "There's some one hiding. It's Hide-and-Seek, you see. We're the seekers. It's enormous."

"Will you come with us and look too?" suggested Judy simply. Then while Aunt Emily's lips framed themselves as from long habit into a negative or a reprimand, the child continued before either reached delivery: "There are heaps of signs about; anything lovely or beautiful is a sign—a sign that we're getting warm. We've each got ours. Mine's air. What's yours, Aunty?"

Aunt Emily stared at them; her bewilderment increased apparently; she swallowed hard again. The children returned her stare, gazing innocently into her questioning eyes as if she were some strange bird at the Zoo. The new feeling of kinship with her grew stronger in their hearts. They knew quite well she was looking just as they were; *really* she longed to play their game of Hide-and-Seek. She was very ignorant, of course, they saw, but they were ready and willing to teach her how to play, and would make it easy for her into the bargain.

"Signs!" she repeated, in a voice that was gentler than they had ever known it. There was almost a sound of youth in it. Judy suddenly realised that Aunt Emily had once been a girl. A softer look shone in the colourless eyes. The lips relaxed. In a hat she might have been even pretty. No one in a bonnet could be jolly. "Signs!" she repeated; "deep and beautiful! Whatever in the world—?"

She stopped abruptly, started by the exquisite trilling of a bird that was perched upon a branch quite close behind her. The liquid notes poured out in a stream of music, so rich, so lovely that it seemed as if no bird had ever sung before and that they were the first persons in the world who had ever heard it.

"My sign!" cried Judy, dancing round her disconcerted and bewildered relative. "One of my signs—that!"

"Mine is rabbits and rats and badgers," Tim called out with ungrammatical emphasis. "Anything that likes the earth are mine." He looked about him as if to point one out to her. "They're everywhere, all over the place," he added, seeing none at the moment. "Aunty, what's yours? Do tell us, because then we can go and look together."

"It's *much* more fun than looking alone," declared Judy.

No answer came. But, caught by the astounding magic of the singing bird, Aunt Emily had turned, and in doing so the hand behind her back became visible for the first time since their meeting. The children saw it simultaneously. They nudged each other, but they said no word. The same moment, having failed to discover the bird, Aunt Emily turned back again. She looked caught, they thought. But, also she looked as if she had

Algernon Blackwood

found something herself. The secret joy she tried to hide from them by swallowing it, rose to her wrinkled cheeks and shone in both her eyes, then overflowed and rippled down towards her trembling mouth. The lips were trembling. She smiled, but so softly, sweetly, that ten years dropped from her like a dissolving shadow. And the hand she had so long kept hidden behind her back stole forth slowly into view.

"How did you guess that I was looking for anything?" she inquired plaintively in an excited yet tremulous tone. "I thought no one knew it." She seemed genuinely surprised, yet unbelievably happy too. A great sigh of relief escaped her.

"We're all the same," one of them informed her; "so you are too! Everybody's looking." And they crowded round to examine the objects in her hand—a dirty earth-stained trowel and a fern. They knew she collected ferns on the sly, but never before had they seen her bring home such a prize. Usually she found only crumpled things like old bits of wrinkled brown paper which she called "specimens." This one was marvellously beautiful. It had a dainty, slender stalk of ebony black, and its hundred tiny leaves quivered like a shower of green water-drops in the air. There was actual joy in every trembling bit of it.

"That's my sign," announced Aunt Emily with pride: "Maidenhair! It'll grow again. I've got the roots." And she said it as triumphantly as Stumper had said "snail-shell."

"Of course, Aunty," Judy cried, yet doubtfully. "*You* ought to know." She twiddled it round in her fingers till the quivering fronds emitted a tiny sound. "And you can use it as a feather too." She lowered her head to listen.

"We've each got a feather," mentioned Tim. "It's a compass. Shows the way, you know. You hear him calling—that way."

"The Tramp explained that," Judy added. "He's Leader. Come on, Aunty. We ought to be off; the others went ages ago.

We're going to the End of the World, and they've already started."

For a moment Aunt Emily looked as rigid as the post beside a five-barred gate. The old unbending attitude took possession of her once again. Her eyes took on the tint of soapy water. Her elastic nose looked round the corner. She frowned. Her black dress crackled. The mention of a tramp and the End of the World woke all her savage educational instincts visibly.

"He's a singing tramp and shines like a Christmas Tree," explained Judy, "and he looks like everybody in the world. He's extror'iny." She turned to her brother. "Doesn't he, Tim?"

Tim ran up and caught his Aunt by the umbrella hand. He saw her stiffening. He meant to prevent it if he could.

"Everybody rolled into one," he agreed eagerly; "Daddy and Mother and the Clergyman and you."

"And me?" she asked tremulously.

"Rather!" the boy said vehemently; "as you are now, all rabbity and nice."

Aunt Emily slowly removed one big golosh, then waited.

"Cleaned up and young," cried Judy, "and smells delicious— like flowers and hay—"

"And soft and warm—"

"And sings and dances—"

"And is positive that if we go on looking we shall find—exactly what we're looking for."

Aunt Emily removed the other golosh—a shade more quickly

Algernon Blackwood

than the first one. She kicked it off. The stiffness melted out of her; she smiled again.

"Well," she began—when Judy stood on tip-toe and whispered in her ear some magic sentence.

"Dawn!" Aunt Emily whispered back. "At dawn—when the birds begin to sing!"

Something had caught her heart and squeezed it.

Tim and Judy nodded vehemently in agreement. Aunt Emily dropped her umbrella then. And at the same moment a singing voice became audible in the trees behind them. The song came floating to them through the sunlight with a sound of wind and birds. It had a marvellous quality, very sweet and very moving. There was a lilt in it, a laughing, happy lilt, as though the Earth herself were singing of the Spring.

And Aunt Emily made one last vain attempt: she struggled to put her fingers in her ears. But the children held her hands. She crackled and made various oppressive and objecting sounds, but the song poured into her in spite of all her efforts. Her feet began to move upon the grass. It was awful, it was shocking, it was forbidden and against all rules and regulations: yet—Aunt Emily danced!

And a thin, plaintive voice, like the voice of her long-forgotten youth, slipped out between her faded lips—and positively sang:

"The world is young with laughter; we can fly
Among the imprisoned hours as we choose...."

But to Tim and Judy it all seemed merely right and natural.

"Come on," cried the boy, pulling his Aunt towards the wood.

"We can look together now. You've got your sign," exclaimed

Judy, tugging at her other hand. "Everything's free and careless, and so are we."

"Aim for a path," Tim shouted by way of a concession. "Aunty'll go quicker on a path."

But Aunty was nothing if not decided. "I know a short-cut," she sang. "Paths are for people who don't know the way. There's no time—to lose. Dear me! I'm warm already!" She dropped her umbrella.

And, actually dancing and singing, she led the way into the wood, holding the fern before her like a wand, and happy as a girl let out of school.

But as they went, Judy, knowing suddenly another thing she didn't know, made a discovery of her own, an immense discovery. It was bigger than anything Tim had ever found. She felt so light and swift and winged by it that she seemed almost to melt into the air herself.

"I say, Tim," she said.

"Yes."

She took her eyes from the sky to see what her feet were doing; Tim lifted his from the earth to see what was going on above him in the air.

Judy went on: "I know what," she announced.

"What?" He was not particularly interested, it seemed.

Judy paused. She dropped a little behind her dancing Aunt. Tim joined her. It all happened as quickly as a man might snap his fingers; Aunt Emily, her heart full of growing ferns, noticed nothing.

"We've found her out!" whispered Judy, communicating her

immense discovery. "What she really is, I mean!"

He agreed and nodded. It did not strike him as anything wonderful or special. "Oh, yes," he answered; "rather!" He did not grasp her meaning, perhaps.

But his sister was bursting with excitement, radiant, shivering almost with the wonder of it.

"But don't you see? It's—a sign!" she exclaimed so loud that Aunt Emily almost heard it. "She's found herself! She was hiding—from herself. That's part of it all—the game. It's the biggest sign of all!"

She was so "warm" that she burned all over.

"Oh, yes," repeated Tim. "I see!" But he was not particularly impressed. He merely wanted his Aunt to find an enormous fern whose roots were growing in the sweet, sticky earth *he* loved. Her sign was a fern; his was the ground. It made him understand Aunt Emily at last, and therefore love her; he saw no further than that.

Judy, however, *knew.* She suddenly understood what the Tramp meant by "deep." She also knew now why Stumper, WEEDEN, Uncle Felix too, looked at him so strangely, with wonder, with respect, with love. Something about the Tramp explained each one to himself. Each one found—himself. And she—without realising it before, had acquired this power too, though only in a small degree as yet. The Tramp believed in everybody; she, without knowing it, believed in her Aunt. It was another thing she didn't know she knew.

And the real, long-buried, deeply-hidden Aunt Emily had emerged accordingly. All her life she had been hiding—from herself. She had found herself at last. It was the biggest sign of all.

Tim caught her hand and dragged her after him. "Come on,"

he cried, "we're getting frightfully warm. Look at Aunty! Listen, will you?"

Aunt Emily, a little way in front of them, was digging busily with her dirty trowel. Her bonnet was crooked, her skirts tucked up, her white worsted stockings splashed with mud, her elastic-sided boots scratched and plastered. And she was singing to herself in a thin but happy voice that was not unlike an old and throaty corncrake: "The birds are singing....Hark! Come out and play....Life is an endless search....*I've* just begun...!"

They listened for a little while, and then ran headlong up to join her.

SIGNS EVERYWHERE!

IX

And it was somewhere about here and now—the exact spot impossible to determine, since it was obviously a circular experience without beginning, middle or end—that the gigantic character of the Day declared itself in all its marvellous simplicity. For as they dived deeper and deeper towards its centre, they discovered that its centre, being everywhere at once, existed—nowhere. The sun was always rising—somewhere.

In other words, each seeker grasped, in his or her own separate way, that the Splendour hiding from them lay actually both too near and far away for any individual eye to see it with completeness. Someone, indeed, had come; but this Someone, as Judy told herself, was "simply all over the place." To see him "distinkly is an awful job," according to Uncle Felix; or as Come-Back Stumper realised in the middle of another clump of bramble bushes, "Perspective is necessary to proper vision." "He" lay too close before their eyes to be discovered fully. Tim had long ago described it instinctively as "an enormous hide," but it was more than that; it was a universal hide.

Alone, perhaps, Weeden's lost optic, wandering ubiquitously and enjoying the bird's-eye view, possessed the coveted power. But, like the stars, though somewhat about, it was invisible. WEEDEN made no reference to it. He attended to one thing at a time, he lived in the present; one eye was gone; he just looked for truffles—with the other.

Yet this did not damp their ardour in the least; increased it rather: the gathering of the clues became more and more absorbing. Though not seen, the hider was both known and felt; his presence was a certainty. There was no real contradiction.

For signs grew and multiplied till the entire world seemed overflowing with them, and hardly could the earth contain them. They brimmed the sunny air, flooded the ponds and streams, lay thick upon the fields, and almost choked the woods to stillness. They trickled out, leaked through, dripped over everywhere in colour, shape, and sound. The hider had passed everywhere, and upon everything had left his exquisite and deathless traces. The inanimate, as well as the animate world had known the various touch of his great passing. His trail had blazed the entire earth about them. For the very clouds were dipped in snow and gold, and the meanest pebble in the lane wore a self-conscious gleam of shining silver. So-called domestic creatures also seemed aware that a stupendous hiding-place was somewhere near—the browsing cow, contented and at ease, the horse that nuzzled their hands across the gate, the very pigs, grubbing eternally for food, yet eternally unsatisfied; all these, this endless morning, wore an unaccustomed look as though they knew, and so were glad to be alive. Some knew more than others, of course. The cat, for instance, defending its kittens single-pawed against the stable-dog who pretended to be ferocious; the busy father-blackbird, passing worms to his mate for the featherless mites, all beak and clamour in the nest; the Clouded Yellow, sharing a spray of honeysuckle with a Bumble-bee, and the honeysuckle offering no resistance—one and all, they also were aware in their differing degrees. And the seekers, noting the signs, grew warmer and ever warmer. An ordinary day these signs, owing to their generous profusion, might have called for no remark. They would, probably, have drawn no attention to themselves, merely lying about unnoticed, undiscovered because familiar. But this was not an ordinary day. It was unused, unspoilt and

Algernon Blackwood

unrecorded. It was the Some Day of humanity's long dream—
an Extra Day. Time could not carry it away; it could not end;
all it contained was of eternity. The great hider at the heart of
it was real. These signs—deep, tender, kind and beautiful—
were part of him, and in knowing, recognising them, they
knew and recognised him too. They drew near, that is,
brushed up closer, to his hiding-place from which *he* saw them.
They approached within knowing distance of a Reality that
each in his or her particular way had always yearned for. They
held—oh, distinkly held—that they were winning. They won
the marvellous game as soon as it began. They never had a
doubt about the end.

But their supreme, superb discovery was this: They had always
secretly longed to find the elusive hider; they now realised that
he—wanted them to find him, and that from his hiding-place
he saw them easily. That was the most wonderful thing of
all....

To describe the separate adventures of each seeker would
involve a series of bulky trilogies no bookshelves in the world
could carry; they can, besides, be adequately told in three
simple words that Tim used—shouted with intense
enthusiasm when he tripped over a rabbit-hole and tumbled
headlong against that everlasting Tramp: "I'm still looking!"
He dived away into another hole. "I'm looking still." "So am
I," the Tramp answered, also in three words. "I'm *very* warm,"
growled Stumper; "I'm getting on," Aunt Emily piped; and
while Judy was for ever shouting out "I've found him!" Uncle
Felix, puffing and panting, could only repeat with rapture each
time he met another seeker: "A lovely day! A *lovely* day!" They
said so little—experienced and felt so much!

From time to time, too, others joined them in the tremendous
game. It seemed the personality of the Tramp attracted them.
Something about him—his sincerity, perhaps, or his
simplicity—made them realise suddenly what they were about:
as though they had not noticed it before, not understood it
quite, at any rate. They found themselves. He did and said so

little. But he possessed the unique quality of a Leader—natural persuasion.

Thompson, for instance, cleaning the silver at the pantry window, looked up and saw them pass. They caught him unawares. His pompous manner hung like a discarded mask on a nail beside his livery. He wore his black and white striped waistcoat, and an apron. Of course he looked proper, as an old family servant ought to look, but he looked cheerful too. He was humming to himself as he polished up the covers and the candelabra.

"Well, I never!" he exclaimed, as the line of them filed by. "I never did. And Mr. Weeden with 'em too!"

The Tramp passed singing and looked through the open window at the butler. No more than that. Their eyes met between the bars. They exchanged glances. But something incalculable happened in that instant, just as it had happened to Stumper, Aunt Emily, and the rest of them. Thompson put several questions into his look of sheer astonishment.

"Why not?" the Tramp replied, chuckling as he caught the butler's eye. "It's a lovely morning. We're just looking!"

Thompson was flabbergasted—as if all the old-fashioned families of the world had suddenly praised him. All his life he had never done anything but his ordinary duty.

"It's 'oliday time," said Weeden, coming next, "and all my flowers and vegitubles is a-growin' nicely." He too seemed singing, dancing. Something had happened. The whole world seemed out and playing.

Thompson forgot himself in a most unusual way, forgot that he was an old family servant, that the apron-string met round his middle with difficulty, that the Authorities were away and his responsibilities increased thereby; forgot too, that for twenty years he had been answering bells, over-hearing conversations without pretending to do so, and that visitors wanted hot water and early tea at "7:30 sharp." He remembered suddenly that he was a man—and that he was very fond of some one. The birds were singing, the sun was shining, the flowers were out upon the lawn, and it was Spring.

An amazing longing in him woke and stirred to life. There was a singular itching in his feet. Something in his butler-heart began to purr. "Looking, eh!" he thought. "There's something I've been looking for too. I'd forgot about it."

"No one can make the silver shine as I can," he mumbled, watching the retreating figures, "but it is about finished now,"—he glanced down at it with pride—"and fit to set on the table. Why shouldn't I take a turn in the garden too?"

He looked out a moment. The magic of the spring came upon him suddenly like a revelation. He knew he was alive, that there was something he wanted somewhere, something real and satisfying—if only he could find it—find out what it was. For twenty years he had been living automatically. Alfred Thompson suddenly felt free and careless. The butler—yearned!

He hesitated, gave the dish-cover an extra polish, then called through the door to Mrs. Horton:

"There's a tramp in the garden, Bridget, and Mr. Weeden's with him. Mr. Felix is halso taking the air, and Master Tim—"

He stopped, hearing a step in the pantry. Mrs. Horton stood behind him with a shawl about her shoulders. Her red face was smiling.

"Alfred, let's go out and take a look," she said. "Mary can see to the shepherd's-pie. I've been as quick as I could," she added, as if excusing herself. Moreover, she said distinctly, "shepherd's-*poie*."

"*I* haven't been 'calling,'" replied the butler, "except only just now—just this minute." He spoke as though he was being scolded for not answering a bell. But he cast an admiring glance, half wild, half reckless, at the cook.

"An' you shouting to me to come this last 'arf hour and more!" cried Mrs. Horton. She, too, apparently, was in a "state."

"You are mistaken, Bridget, I have been singing, as I often do when attending to the silver, but as for—"

"You can do without a hat," she interrupted. "Come on! I want to go and look for—for—" She broke off, taking his arm as though they were going down the Strand or Oxford Street. Her red face beamed. She looked very proud and happy. She wanted to look for something too, but she could not believe the moment had really come. She had put it away so long—like a special dish in a cupboard.

"I don't know what's come over me," she went on very confidentially, as she moved beside him through the scullery door, "but—but I don't feel satisfied—not satisfied with meself as I used to be."

"No, Bridget?" It was in his best "7:30" manner. There was a struggle in him.

"No," said Mrs. Horton, with decision. "I give satisfaction—that I know—"

"We both do that," said Thompson proudly. "And no one can do a suet pudding to a turn as you can. Only the other day I heard Sir William a-speaking of it—"

She held his arm more tightly. They were on the lawn by now. The flood of sunlight caught them, showed up the worn and shabby places in his suit of broadcloth, gleamed on her bursting shoes she "fancied" for her kitchen work. They heard the birds, they smelt the flowers, the air bathed them all over like a sea.

"And the silver, Alfred," she said in a lower tone. "Who in the world can make it look as you do? But what I've been feeling lately—since this morning, that is to say—and feeling for the first time in me life, so to speak—"

"Bridget, dear, you've got it!" he interrupted with excitement, "I've felt it too. Felt it this morning first, when I woke up and remembered that nobody wanted hot-water nor early tea, and I said to myself, 'There's more than that in it. I'm not doing all this just only for a salary. I'm doing it for something else. What is it?'"

He spoke very rapidly for a butler. He looked down at her red and smiling face.

"What is it?" he repeated, curiously moved.

She looked up at him without a word.

"It's something 'idden," he said, after a pause. "That's what it is."

"That's it," agreed Mrs. Horton. "Like a recipe."

There was another pause. The butler broke it. They stood together in the middle of the field, flowers and birds and sunshine all about them.

"A mystery—inside of us," he said, "I think—"

"Yes, Alfred," the cook murmured softly.

"*I* think," he continued, "it's a song and dance we want. A little life." He broke off abruptly, noticing the sudden movement of her bursting shoes. She took a long step forwards, then sideways. She opened her arms to the air and sun. She almost pirouetted.

"Life!" she cried, "'ot and fiery. Life! That's it. Hark, Alfred, d'ye hear that singing far away?" She felt the Irish break out of her. "Listen!" she cried, trying to drag him faster. "Listen, will ye? It makes me wild entirely! Give me yer hand! Come on and dance wid me! It's in me hearrt I feel it, in me blood. To the devil with me suet puddings and shepherd-poies—that singing's real, that's loife, that's lovely as a dhream! It's what I've been looking for iver since I can remember. I've got it!"

And Thompson felt himself spinning through the air. Old families were forgotten. The world was young with laughter. They could fly. They did.

The silver was beautifully cleaned. He had earned his holiday.

"That singing!" he gasped, feeling his heart grow big. He followed her across the flowered world. "I believe it is a bird! It would not surprise me to be told—"

"A birrd!" cried Mrs. Horton, turning him round and round. "It's a birrd from Heaven then! I've heard it all the morning. It's been singing in me heart for ages. Now it's out! Come follow it wid me! We'll go to the end of the wurrld to foinde it."

Her kitchen energy—some called it temper—had discovered a greater scope than puddings.

"There is no hurry," the butler panted, moving along with her, and trying hard to keep his balance. "We'll look together. We'll find it!" And as they raced across the field among the flowers after the line of disappearing figures, the Tramp looked back at them and waved his hand.

"It's a lovely morning," he said, as they came up with the rest of the party. "So you're looking too?"

Too much out of breath to answer, they just nodded, and the group accepted them without more to-do. Their object

Algernon Blackwood

evidently was the same. Aunt Emily glanced up from her ferns, nodded and said, "Good morning, it's a lovely day"—and resumed her digging again. It was like shaking hands! They all went forward happily, eagerly, across the wide, wide world together.

The absence of surprise the children knew had now become a characteristic everybody shared. All were in the same state together. The whole day flowed, there were no limitations or conditions, least of all surprise. Even WEEDEN had forgotten hedges and artificial boundaries. No one, therefore, ejaculated nor exclaimed when they ran across the Policeman. He, too, was looking for some one, but, having mislaid his notebook and pencil stub, was unable to mention any names, and was easily persuaded to join the body of eager seekers. Being a policeman, he was naturally a seeker by profession; he was always looking for somebody somewhere—somebody who was going in the wrong direction.

"That's just it," he said, the moment he saw the Tramp, taking his helmet off as though an odd respect was in him. "That's just what I've always felt," he went on vaguely. "I'm looking for some one wot's a'looking for something else—only looking wrong."

"In the wrong places," suggested Stumper, remembering his Indian scouting days.

"In the wrong way," put in Uncle Felix, full of experience by now.

The Policeman listened attentively, as though by rights he ought to enter these sentences laboriously in his notebook.

"That's it, per'aps," he stated. "It takes 'em longer, but they finds out in the end. If I was to show 'em the right way of looking instead of arresting 'em—I'd be *reel*!" And then he added, as if he were giving evidence in a Court of Justice and before a County Magistrate , "There's no good looking for anything where it ain't, now is there?"

"Precisely," agreed Colonel Stumper, remembering happily that his pockets were full of snail-shells. He knew *his* sign.

Thompson, Mrs. Horton, Weeden, and the Policeman glanced at him gratefully. But it was the last mentioned who replied:

"Because every one," he said with conviction at last, "has his own way of looking, and even the burgular is only looking wrong." He, too, it seemed, had found himself.

Their search, their endless hunt, their conversation and adventures thus might be reported endlessly, if only the book-shelves of the world were built more stoutly, and everybody could find an Extra Day lying about in which to read it all. Each seeker held true to his or her first love, obeying an infallible instinct. The adventure and romance that hid in Tim and Judy, respectively, sent them headlong after anything that offered signs of these two common but seductive qualities. Judy lived literally in the air, her feet, her heart, her eyes all off the ground; Tim, filled with an equally insatiable curiosity, found adorable danger in every rabbit-run, and rescued things innumerable. Off the ground he felt unsafe, unsure, and lost himself. Stumper, faithful to his scouting passion, disappeared into all kinds of undesirable places no one else would have dreamed of looking in, yet invariably—came back; and while Uncle Felix tried a little of everything and found "copy" in a puddle or a dandelion, Weeden carried his empty sack without a murmur, knowing it would be filled with truffles at the end. Aunt Emily, exceedingly particular, but no longer interfering with the others, was equally sure of herself. A touch of fluid youth ran in her veins again, and in her heart grew a fern that presently she would find everywhere outside as well—a maiden-hair.

Each, however, in some marvellous way, shared the adventures of the others, as though the Tramp merged all seven of them into one single being, unified them, at any rate, into this one harmonious, common purpose with himself. For, while everybody had a different way of looking, everybody's way—for that particular individual—was exactly right.

"Smell, then follow," was the secret. "Find your own sign and stick to it," the clue. Each sign, though by different routes, led straight towards the marvellous hiding-place. To urge one's own sign upon another was merely to delay that other; but to point out better signs of his own particular kind was to send him on faster than before. Thus there was harmony among them all, for every seeker, knowing this, had—found himself.

REALITY

X

But, while there was no hurry, no passing, and, most certainly of all, no passing away, there was a sense of enormous interval. There were epochs, there were interludes, there was—duration.

Though everything had only just begun, it was yet complete, if not completed.

At any point of an adventure that adventure could be taken over from the very start, the experience holding all the thrill and wonder of the first time.

Cake could be had and eaten too. Tim, half-way down a rabbit-hole, could instantly find himself at the opening again, bursting with all the original excitement of trembling calculations. With the others it was similar.

There was no end to anything. Yet—there was this general consciousness of gigantic interval. It turned in a circle round them—everywhere....

They came together, then, all eight of them, into that place of singular enchantment known as the End of the World, sitting in a group about the prostrate elm that on ordinary days was Home. What they had been doing each one knew assuredly, even if no one mentioned it. Tim, who had been to India with Come-Back Stumper, had a feeling in his heart that expressed itself in one word, "everywhere," accompanied by a sigh of happy satisfaction; Judy felt what she knew as "Neverness"; she had seen the Metropolis inside out, with Uncle Felix apparently. And these two couples now sat side by side upon the tree, gazing contentedly at the colony of wallflowers that flamed in the sunshine just above their heads. WEEDEN, cleaning his spade with a great nailed boot, turned his good eye affectionately upon the sack that lay beside him, full now to bursting. Aunt Emily breathed on her gold-rimmed glasses, rubbed them, and put them on her elastic nose, then looked about her peacefully yet expectantly, ready, it seemed, to start again at any moment—anywhere. She guarded carefully a mossy bundle in her black silk lap. A little distance from her Thompson was fastening a flower into Mrs. Horton's dress, and close to the gate stood the Policeman, smoking a pipe and watching everybody with obvious contentment. His belt was loose; both hands stuck into it; he leaned against the wooden fence.

On the ground, between the tree and the fence, the Tramp had made a fire. He lay crouched about it. He and the fire belonged to one another. It seemed that he was dozing.

And this sense of lying in the heart of an enormous circular interval touched everybody with delicious peace; each had apparently found something real, and was content merely to lie and—be with it. All came gradually to sitting or reclining postures. Yet there was no sense of fatigue; any instant they would be up again and looking.

Occasionally one or other of them spoke, but it was not the kind of speech that struggled to express difficult ideas with tedious sentences of many words. There was very little to *say*: mere statements of indubitable reality could be so easily and briefly made.

"Now," said Tim, unafraid of contradiction.

"Then," said Judy, equally certain of herself.

"Now then," declared Uncle Felix, positive at last of something.

"Naturally," affirmed Aunt Emily.

"Of course," growled Come-Back Stumper. And while WEEDEN, looking contentedly at his bursting sack, put in "Always," the Policeman, without referring to his notebook, added from the fence, "That's right." The remarks of Thompson and Mrs. Horton were not audible, for they were talking to one another some little distance away beside the Rubbish Heap, but their conversation seemed equally condensed and eloquent, judging by the satisfied expression on their faces. Thompson probably said, "Well," the cook adding, "I never!"

The Tramp, stretched out beside his little fire of burning sticks, however, said more than any of them. He also said it shortly—as shortly as the children. There was never any question who was Leader.

"Yes," he mentioned in a whisper that flowed about them with a sound like singing wind.

It summed up everything in a single word. It made them warm, as though a little flame had touched them. All the languages of the world, using all their sentences at once, could have said no more than that consummate syllable—in the way *he* said it: *"Yes!"* It was the word the whole Day uttered.

For this was perfectly plain: Each of the group, having followed his or her particular sign to the end of the world, now knew exactly where the hider lay. The supreme discovery was within reach at last. They were merely waiting, waiting in order to enjoy the revelation all the more, and—waiting in an ecstasy of joy and wonder. Seven or eight of them were gathered together; the hiding-place was found. It was now, and then, and natural, and always, and right: it was Yes, and life had just begun....

There happened, then, a vivid and amazing thing—all rose as one being and stood up. The Tramp alone remained lying beside his little fire. But the others stood—and listened.

The precise nature of what had happened none of them, perhaps, could explain. It was too marvellous; it was possibly the thing that nobody understands, and possibly the thing they didn't know they knew; yet *they* both knew and understood it. To each, apparently, the hiding-place was simultaneously revealed. Their Signs summoned them. The hider called!

Yet all they heard was the singing of a little bird. Invisible somewhere above them in the sea of blazing sunshine, it poured its heart out rapturously with a joy and a passion of life that seemed utterly careless as to whether it was heard or not. It merely sang because it was—alive.

To Judy, at any rate, this seemed what they heard. To the others it came, apparently—otherwise. Their interpretations, at any rate, were various.

Thompson and Mrs. Horton were the first to act. The latter looked about her, sniffing the air. "It's burning," she said. "Mary don't know enough. That's my job, anyhow!" and moved off in the direction of the house with an energy that had nothing of displeasure nor of temper in it. It was apparently crackling that she heard. Thompson went after her, a willing alacrity in his movements that yet showed no sign of undignified hurry. "I'll be at the door in no time," he was heard to say, "before it's stopped ringing, I should not wonder!" There was a solemn joy in him, he spoke as though he heard a bell. WEEDEN turned very quietly and watched their disappearing figures. He shouldered his heavy sack of truffles and his spade. No one asked him anything aloud, but, in answer to several questioning faces, he mumbled cautiously, though in a satisfied and pleasant voice, "My garden wants me—maybe; I'll have a look"—obviously going off to water the apricots and rose trees. He heard the dry leaves rustling possibly.

"Keep to the gravel paths," began Aunt Emily, adjusting her gold glasses; "they're dry"—then changed her sentence, smiling to herself: "They're so beautifully made, I mean." And gathering up her bundle of living ferns, she walked briskly over the broken ground, then straight across the lawn, waving her trowel at them as she vanished in the shade below the lime trees. The shade, however, seemed deeper than before. It concealed her quickly.

"I'll be moving on now," came the deep voice of the Policeman. He opened the gate in the fence and consulted a notebook as he did so. He passed slowly out of sight, closing the gate behind him carefully. His heavy tramp became audible on the road outside, the road leading to the Metropolis. "There's some one asking the way—" his voice was audible a moment, before it died into the distance. The road, the gateway, the fence were not so clear as hitherto—a trifle dim.

These various movements took place so quickly, it seemed they all took place at once; Judy still heard the bird, however. She heard nothing else. It was singing everywhere, the sky full of its tender and delicious song. But the notes were a little—just a little—further away she thought, nor could she see it anywhere.

And it was then that Come-Back Stumper, limping a trifle as usual, approached them. He looked troubled rather, and though his manner was full of confidence still, his mind had mild confusion in it somewhere. He joined Uncle Felix and the children, standing in front of them.

"Listen!" he said in low, gruff voice. He held out an open palm, three snail-shells in it, signifying that they should take one each. "Listen!" he repeated, and put the smallest shell against his own ear. "D'you hear that curious sound?" His head was cocked sideways, one ear pressed tight against the shell, the other open to the sky. "The Ganges..." he mumbled to himself after an interval, "but the stones are moving— moving in the river bed.... That long, withdrawing roar!" He was just about to add "down the naked shingles of the world," when Uncle Felix interrupted him.

"Grating," he said, listening intently to his shell; "a metallic, grating sound. What is it?" There was apprehension in his tone, a touch of sadness. "It's getting louder too!"

"Footsteps," exclaimed Tim. "Two feet, not four. It's *not* a badger or a rabbit." He went on with sudden conviction— "and it's coming nearer." There was disappointment and alarm in him. "Though it might be a badger, p'r'aps," he added hopefully.

"But I hear singing," cried Judy breathlessly, "nothing but singing. It's a bird." Her face was radiant. "It *is* a long way off, though," she mentioned.

They put their shells down then, and listened without them. They glanced from one another to the sky, all four heads cocked sideways. And they heard the sound distinctly, somewhere in the air about them. It had changed a little. It was louder. It *was* coming nearer.

"Metallic," repeated Uncle Felix, with an ominous inflection.

"Machinery," growled Stumper, a fury rising in his throat.

"Clicking," agreed Tim. He looked uneasy.

"I only hear a bird," Judy whispered. "But it comes and goes— rather." And then the Tramp, still lying beside his little fire of burning sticks, put in a word.

"It's *we* who are going," he said in his singing voice. "We're moving on again."

They heard him well enough, but they did not understand quite what he meant, and his voice died into the distance oddly, far away already, almost on the other side of the fence.

And as he spoke they noticed another change in the world about them. Three of the party noticed it—the males, Uncle Felix, Tim, and Come-Back Stumper.

For the light was fading; it was getting darker; there was a slight sense of chill, a growing dimness in the air. They realised vaguely that the Tramp was leaving them, and that with him went the light, the heat, the brilliance out of their happy day.

They turned with one accord towards him. He still lay there beside his little fire, but he seemed further off; both his figure and the burning sticks looked like a picture seen at the end of a corridor, an interminable corridor, edged and framed by gathering shadows that were about to cover it. They stretched their hands out; they called to him; they moved their feet; for the first time this wonderful day, there was hurry in them. But the receding figure of the Tramp withdrew still further and further, until an inaccessible distance intervened. They heard him singing faintly "There is no hurry, Life has just begun...The world is young with laughter...We can fly..." but the words came sighing towards them from the inaccessible region where he lay, thousands of years ago, millions of miles away, millions of miles....

"You won't forget," were the last words they caught. "You know now. You'll never forget...!"

When a sudden cry of joy and laughter sounded close behind them, and they turned to see Judy standing on tiptoe, stretching her thin, slim body as if trying to reach the moon. The light was dim; it seemed the sun had set and moonlight lay upon the world; but her figure, bright and shining, stood in a patch of radiant brilliance by herself. She looked like a white flame of fire ascending.

"I've got it!" she was crying rapturously, "I've got it!" Her voice was wild with happiness, almost like the singing of a bird.

The others stared—then came up close. But, while Tim ran,

Stumper and Uncle Felix moved more slowly. For something in them hesitated; their attitudes betrayed them; there was a certain confusion in the minds of the older two, a touch of doubt. The contrast between the surrounding twilight and the brilliant patch of glory in which Judy stood bewildered them. The long, slim body of the child, every line of her figure, from her toes to the crown of her flying hair, pointing upwards in a stream of shining aspiration, was irresistible, however. She looked like a lily growing, nay rushing, upwards to the sun.

They followed the direction of her outstretched arms and hands. But it was Tim who spoke first. He did not doubt as they did:

"Oh, Judy, where?" he cried out passionately. "Show me! Show me!"

The child raised herself even higher, stretching her toes and arms and hands; her fingers lengthened; she panted; she made a tremendous effort.

"There!" she said, without looking down. Her face was towards the sky, her throat stretched till the muscles showed and her hair fell backwards in a stream.

Then, following the direction of her eyes and pointing fingers, the others saw for the first time what Judy saw—a small wild rose hung shining in the air, dangling at the end of a little bending branch. The bush grew out of the rubbish-heap, clambering up the wall. No one had noticed it before. At the end of the branch hung this single shining blossom, swinging a little in the wind. But it was out of reach—just a shade too high for her eager fingers to take hold of it. Beyond it grew the colony of wall-flowers, also in the curious light that seemed the last glory of the fading day. But it was the rose that Judy wanted. And from somewhere near it came the sweet singing of the unseen bird.

"Too high," whispered Uncle Felix, watching in amazement.

"You can't manage it. You'll crick your back! oh—oh!" The sight of that blossom drew his heart out.

"Impossible," growled Stumper, yet wondering why he said it. "It's out of reach."

"Go it!" cried Tim. "You'll have it in a second. Half an inch more! There—you touched it that time!"

For an interval no one could measure they watched her spellbound; in each of them stirred the similar instinct—that they could reach it, but that she could not. A deep, secret desire hid in all of them to pick that gleaming wild rose that swung above them in the air. And, meanwhile, the darkness deepened perceptibly, only Judy and the blossom framed still in shining light.

Then, suddenly, the child's voice broke forth again like a burst of music.

"I've got it! I've got it!"

There was a breathless pause. Her finger did not stretch a fraction of an inch—but the rose was nearer. For the bird that still sang invisibly had fluttered into view and perched itself deliberately upon the prickly branch. It lowered the rose towards the human hands. It hopped upon the twig. Its weight dropped the prize—almost into Judy's fingers. She touched it.

"I've found him!" gasped the child.

She touched it—and sank with the final effort in a heap upon the ground. The bird fluttered an instant, and was gone into the darkness. The twig, released, flew back. But at the end of it, swinging out of reach, still hung the lovely blossom in mid-air—unpicked.

There was confusion then about the four of them, for the light faded very quickly and darkness blotted out the world; the rose

Algernon Blackwood

was no longer visible, the bush, the wall, the rubbish-heap, all were shrouded. The singing-bird had gone, the Tramp beside his little fire was hidden, they could hardly see one another's faces even. Voices rose on every side. "She missed it!" "It was too lovely to be picked!" "It's still there, growing....I can smell it!"

Yet above them all was heard Judy's voice that sang, rose out of the darkness like a bird that sings at midnight: "I touched it! My airy signs came true! I know the hiding-place! I've—found him!"

The voice had something in it of the Tramp's careless, windy singing as well.

"Look! He's touched me...! Look...!"

For in that instant when the rose swung out of reach again, in that instant when she touched it, and before the fading light hid everything—all saw the petal floating down to earth. It settled slowly, with a zigzag, butterfly course, fluttering close in front of their enchanted eyes. And it was this petal, perhaps, that brought the darkness, for, as it sank, it grew vast and spread until it covered the entire sky. Like a fairy silken sheet of softest coloured velvet it lay on everything, as though the heavens lowered and folded over them. They felt it press softly on their faces. A curtain, it seemed—some one had let the curtain down.

Beneath it, then, the confusion became extraordinary. There was tumult of various kinds. Every one cried at once "I've found him! Now *I* know!" At the touch of the petal, grown so vast, upon their eyelids, each knew his "sign" had led him to the supreme discovery. This flower was born of the travail of a universe. Child of the elements, or at least blessed by them, this petal of a small wild-rose made all things clear, for upon its velvet skin still lay the morning dew, air kissed it, its root and origin was earth, and the fire of the sun blazed in its perfect colouring.... Yet in the tumult and confusion such curious behaviour followed. For Come-Back Stumper, crying that he saw a purple beetle pass across the world, proceeded to curl up as though he crawled into a spiral snail-shell and meant to go to sleep in it; Tim shouted in the darkness that he was riding a huge badger down a hole that led to the centre of the earth; and Uncle Felix begged every one to look and see what he saw, darkness or no darkness—"the splash of misty blue upon the body of a dragon-fly!"

They might almost have been telling their dreams at breakfast-time....

But while the clamour of their excited voices stirred the world beneath the marvellous covering, there rose that other sound—increasing until it overpowered every word they uttered. In the world outside there was a clicking, grating, hard, metallic sound—as though machinery was starting somewhere....

And Judy, managing somehow or other to lift a corner and peer out, saw that the dawn was breaking in the eastern sky, and that a new day was just beginning. The sun was rising.... She went back again to tell the others, but she could not find them. She did not try very hard; she did not look for them. She just closed her eyes.... The swallows were chattering in the eaves, a robin sang a few marvellous bars, then ceased, and an up-and-under bird sent forth its wild, high bugle-call, then dived out of sight below the surface of the pond.

Judy did likewise—dived down and under, drawing the soft covering against her cheek, and although her eyes were already closed she closed them somehow a second time. "Everything's all right," she had a butterfly sort of thought; "there's no hurry. It's not time... yet...!"—and the petal covered her again from head to foot. She had noticed, a little further off, a globular, round object lying motionless beneath another corner of the covering. It gave her a feeling of comfort and security. She slid away to find the others. It seemed she floated, rather. "Everything's free and careless...and so are—so am I...for we shall never...never forget...!" she remembered sweetly—and was gone, fluttering after the up-and-under bird ...into some hidden world she had discovered....

The old Mill House lay dreaming in the dawn. Transparent shades of pink and gold stole slowly up the eastern sky. A stream of amber diffused itself below the paling stars. Rising from a furnace below the horizon it reached across and touched the zenith, painting mid-heaven with a mystery none could understand; then sank downwards and dipped the crests of the trees, the lawn, the moss-grown tiles upon the roof in that sea of everlasting wonder which is light.

Dawn caught the old sleeping world once more in its breathless beauty. The earth turned over in her sleep, gasped with delight—and woke. There was a murmur and a movement everywhere. The spacious, stately life that breathes o'er ancient trees came forth from the wood without a centre; from the lines emanated that gracious, almost tender force they harvest in the spring. There was a little shiver of joy among the rose trees. The daisies blinked and stared. And the earth broke into singing.

Then, in this chorus, came a pause; the thousand voices hushed a moment; the robin ceased its passionate solo in the shrubbery. All listened—listened to another and far sweeter song that stirred with the morning wind among the rose trees. It was very soft and tender, it died away and returned with a faint, mysterious murmur, it rose and fell so gently that it may have been only the rustling of their thousand leaves that guard the opening blossoms.

Yet it ran with power across the entire waking earth:

My secret's in the wind and open sky,
There is no longer any Time—to lose;
The world is young with laughter; we can fly
Among the imprisoned hours as we choose.
The rushing minutes pause; an unused day
Breaks into dawn and cheats the tired sun.

The birds are singing: Hark! Come out and play!
There is no hurry; life has just begun.

And as it died away the sun itself came up and shouted it aloud
as with a million golden trumpets.

CHAPTER XVIII

TIME GOES ON AGAIN—-

Hardly had Judy closed her eyes for the second time, however, than the globular object she had noticed in the corner stirred. It turned, but turned all over, as though it were a ball. It made a sideways movement too, a movement best described as budging. And, accompanying the movements, was a comfortable, contented, satisfied sound that some people call deep breathing, and others call a sigh.

The globular outline then grew slightly longer; one portion of it left the central mass, but left it slowly. The lower part prolonged itself. Slight cracks were audible like sharp reports, muffled but quite distinct. Next, the other end of the ball extended itself, twisted in a leisurely fashion sideways, rose above the general surface and plainly showed itself. It, too, was round. It emerged. Upon its surface shone two small pools of blue. It was a face. Even in the grey, uncertain light this was beyond dispute. It was Maria's face.

Maria awoke. She looked about her calmly. Her mind, ever unclouded because it thought of one thing only, took in the situation at a glance. It was dawn, she was in bed and sleepy, it was not time to get up. Dawn, sleep, bed and time belonged to her. There certainly was no hurry.

The pools of blue then disappeared together, the smaller ball sank down into the pillow to join the larger one, the lower portion that had stretched itself drew in again, and a peaceful sigh informed the universe that Maria intended to resume her interrupted slumbers. She became once more a mere globular outline, self-contained, at rest.

But, in accepting life as it really was by lying down again, the lesser ball had imperceptibly occupied a new position. Maria's head had shifted. Her ear now pressed against another portion of the pillow. And this pressure, communicating itself to an object that lay beneath the pillow, touched a small brass handle, jerked it forward, released a bit of quivering wire connected with a set of wheels, and set in motion the entire insides of this hidden object. There was a sound of grating. This hard, metallic sound rose through the feathers, a clicking, thudding noise that reached her brain. It was—she knew instantly—the stopped alarum clock. It had been overwound. The weight of her head had started it again.

Maria, as usual, by doing nothing in particular, had accomplished much. By yielding herself to her surroundings, she united her insignificant personal forces with the gigantic purposes of Life. She swung contentedly in rhythm with the universe. Maria had set the clock going again!

There was excitement in her then, but certainly no hurry. Disturbing herself as little as possible, she pushed one hand beneath the pillow, drew out the ticking clock, looked at it quietly, remembered sleepily that it had stopped at dawn— Uncle Felix had said so—put it on the chair beside her bed, and promptly retired again into her eternal centre.

"Tim's clock," she realised, "but I've got it." There was no expression on her face whatever. Another child might have taken the trouble—felt interested, at any rate—to try and see what time it was. But Maria, aware that the dim light would make this a difficult and tedious operation, did nothing of the sort. It could make no difference anyhow to any one, anywhere! She was content to know that it was some time or other, and that the clock was going again. Her plan of life was:

Algernon Blackwood

interfere with nothing. She did not know, therefore, that the hands pointed with accuracy to 4 A. M., because she merely did not care to know. But, not caring to know placed her on a loftier platform of intelligence than the rest of the world— certainly above that of her sister, Judy, who was snoring softly among the shadows just across the room. Maria didn't know that she didn't know. No one could rebuke her with "You might have known," much less "You didn't know,"—because she didn't know she didn't know! It was the biggest kind of knowledge in the world. Maria had it.

But before she actually regained her absolute centre, and long before she lost sight of herself within its depths, dim thoughts came floating through her mind like pictures that moonlight paints upon high summer clouds. She saw these pictures; that is, she looked at them and recognised their existence; but she asked no questions. They reached her through the ticking of the busy clock beside the bed; the ticking brought them; but it brought them back. Maria remembered things. And chief among them were the following: That Uncle Felix had promised everybody an Extra Day, that he had stopped all the clocks to let it come, that this Extra Day was to be her own particular adventure, that last night was Saturday, and that this was, therefore, Sunday morning, very early.

And the instant she remembered these things, they were real— for her. She accepted them, one and all, even the contra- dictions in them. If this was actually an Extra Day it could not be Sunday morning too, and *vice versa*. But yet she knew it was. Both were. The confusion was a confusion of words only. There were too many words about.

"Why not?" expressed her attitude. The clock might tick itself to death for all she cared. The Extra Day was her adventure and she claimed it. But she did not bother about it.

Above all, she asked no questions. Nothing really meant anything in particular, because everything meant everything. To ask questions, even of herself, involved hearing a lot of answers and listening to them. But answers were explanations, and explanations muddled and obscured. Explanations were a new set of questions merely. People who didn't know asked questions, and people who didn't understand gave explanations. Aunt Emily explained—because she didn't understand. Also, because she didn't understand, she didn't know. To ask a question was the same thing as to explain it. Everything was one thing. She, Maria, both knew and understood.

She did not say all this, she did not think it even; she just felt it all: it was her feeling. Believing in her particular adventure of an Extra Day, she had already experienced it. She had shared it with the others too. It was *her* Extra Day, so she could do with it what she pleased. "They can have it," she gave the clock to understand. "I'm going to sleep again." All life was an extra day to her.

She went to sleep; sleep, rather, came to her. Happy dreams amused and comforted her. And, while she dreamed, the dawn slid higher up the sky, ushering in—Sunday Morning.

CHAPTER XIX

—AS USUAL

Consciousness was first—unconsciousness; the biggest changes are unconscious before they are conscious. They have been long preparing. They fall with a clap; and people call them sudden and exclaim, "How strange!" But it is only the discovery and recognition that are sudden. It all has happened already long ago—happened before. The faint sense of familiarity betrays it. It is there the strangeness lies.

And it was this delicate fragrance of an uncommunicable strangeness that floated in the air when Uncle Felix and the children came down to breakfast that Sunday morning and heard the sound of bells in the wind across the fields. They came down punctually for a wonder, too; Maria, last but not actually late, brought the alarum clock with her. "It's going," she stated quietly, and handed it to her brother.

Tim took it without a word, looked at it, shook it, listened to its ticking against his ear, then set it on the mantelpiece where it belonged. He seemed pleased to have it in his possession again, yet something puzzled him. An expression of wonder flitted across his face; the eyes turned upwards; he frowned; there was an effort in him—to remember something. He turned to Maria who was already deep in porridge.

"Did *you* wind it up?" he asked. "I thought it'd stopped—last night."

"It's going," she said, thinking of her porridge chiefly.

"It wasn't, though," insisted Tim. He reflected a moment, evidently perplexed. "I wound it and forgot," he added to himself, "or else it wound itself." He went to his place and began his breakfast.

"Wound itself," mentioned Maria, and then the subject dropped.

It was Sunday morning, and everybody was dressed in Sunday things. The excitement of the evening before, the promise of an Extra Day, the detailed preparation—all this had disappeared. Being of yesterday, it was no longer vital: certainly there was no necessity to consult it. They looked forward rather than backward; the mystery of life lay ever just in front of them, what lay behind was already done with. They had lived it, lived it out. It was in their possession therefore, part of themselves.

No one of the four devouring porridge round that breakfast table had forgotten about the promise, any more than they had forgotten giving up their time-pieces, the conversation, and all the rest of it. It was not forgetfulness. It was not loss of interest either that led no one to refer to it, least of all, to clamour for fulfilment. It was quite another motive that kept them silent, and that, even when Uncle Felix handed back the watches, prevented them saying anything more than "Thank you, Uncle," then hanging them on to belt and waistcoat.

Expectation—an eternal Expectation—was established in them.

But there was also this sense of elusive strangeness in their hearts, the certainty that an enormous interval had passed, almost the conviction that an Extra Day—had been. Somewhere, somehow, they had experienced its fulfilment: It was now inside them. A strange familiarity hung about this Sunday morning.

Algernon Blackwood

Yet there were still a million things to do and endless time in which to do them. Expectation was stronger than ever before, but the sense of Interval brought a happy feeling of completion too. There was no hurry. They felt something of what Maria felt, living at the centre of a circle that turned unceasingly but never finished. It was Maria's particular adventure, and Maria had shared it with them. Wonder and expectation made them feel more than usually—alive.

They talked normally while eating and drinking. If things were said that skirted a mystery, no one tried to find its name or label it. It was just hiding. Let it hide! To find it was to lose the mystery, and life without mystery was unthinkable.

"That's bells," said Tim, "it's church this morning"; but he did not sigh, there was no sinking of the heart, it seemed. He spoke as if it was an adventure he looked forward to. "I've decided what I'm going to be," he went on—"an engineer, but a mining engineer. Finding things in the earth, valuable things like coal and gold." Why he said it was not clear exactly; it had no apparent connection with church bells. He just thought of life as a whole, perhaps, and what he meant to do with it. He looked forward across the years to come. He distinctly knew himself alive.

"I shall put sixpence in, I think," observed Judy presently. "It's a lot. And I shall wear my blue hat with the pheasant's feather—"

"Pheasants feather," repeated Tim in a single word, amused as usual by a curious sound.

"And a wild rose *here*," she added, pointing to the place on her dress, though nobody felt interested enough to look. Her remark about the Collection was more vital than the other. Collections in church were made, they believed, to "feed the clergyman." And Sunday was the clergyman's day.

"I've got sixpence," Tim hastened to remind everybody. "I've got a threepenny bit as well."

"It's sixpence to-day, I think," Judy decided almost tenderly. Behind her thought was a caring, generous impulse; the motherly instinct sent her mind to the collection for the clergyman's comfort. But romance stirred too; she wanted to look her best. Her two main tendencies seemed very much alive this Sunday morning. The hat and the sixpence—both were real.

Maria, as usual, had little or nothing to say. She spoke once, however.

"I dreamed," she informed the company. She did not look up, keeping her head bent over the bread and marmalade upon her plate; her blue eyes rolled round the table once, then dropped again. No one asked for details of her dream, she had no desire to supply them. She announced her position comfortably, as it were, set herself right with life, and quietly went on with the business of the moment, which was bread and marmalade.

Uncle Felix looked up, however, as she said it.

"That reminds me," he observed, "I dreamed too. I dreamed that you dreamed."

"Yes," Maria replied briefly, moving her eyes in his direction, but not her head. No other remarks were made; the statement was too muddled to stimulate interest particularly.

When breakfast was over they went to the open window and threw crumbs to a robin that was obviously expecting to be fed. They all leaned out with their heads in the sunlight, watching it. It hopped from a twig on to the ground, its body already tight to bursting. It looked like a toy balloon—as though it wore a dress of red elastic stretched to such a point that the merest pinprick must explode it with a sharp report; and it hopped as though springs were in its feet. The earth, like a taut sheet, made it bounce. Tim aimed missiles of bread

Algernon Blackwood

rolled into pellets at its head, but never hit it.

"It's a lovely morning," remarked Uncle Felix, looking across the garden to the yellow fields beyond. "A perfect day. We'll walk to church." He brushed the breakfast crumbs from the waistcoat of his neat blue suit, lit his pipe, sniffed the air contentedly, and had an air generally of a sailor on shore-leave.

Judy sprang up. "There's button-holes to get," she mentioned, and flew out of the room like a flash of sunlight or a bird.

Tim raced after her. "Wallflower for me!" he cried, while Judy's answer floated back from halfway down the passage: "I'll have a wild rosebud—it'll match my hat!"

Uncle Felix and Maria were left alone, gazing out of the window side by side upon the "lovely morning." She was just high enough to see above the edge, and her two hands lay sprawled, fingers extended, upon the shining sill.

"Yes," she mentioned quietly, as to herself, "and I'll have a forget-me-not." Her eyes rolled up sideways, meeting those of her uncle as he turned and noticed her.

For quite suddenly he "noticed" her, became aware that she was there, discovered her. He stared a moment, as though reflecting. That "yes" had a queer, familiar sound about it, surely.

"Maria," he said, "I believe you will. Everything comes to you of its own accord somehow."

She nodded.

"And there's another thing. You've got a secret—haven't you?" It occurred to him that Maria was rather wonderful.

"I expect so," she answered, after a moment's pause. She looked wiser than an owl, he thought.

"What is it? What *is* your secret? Can't you tell me?"

For it came over him that Maria, for all her inactivity, was really more truly alive than both the other children put together. Their tireless, incessant energy was nothing compared to some deep well of life Maria's outer calm concealed.

He continued to stare at her, reflecting while he did so. Through her globular exterior, standing here beside him, rose this quiet tide whose profound and inexhaustible source was nothing less than the entire universe. Finding himself thus alone with her, he knew his imagination singularly stirred. The full stream of this imagination—usually turned into sea—and history-stories—poured now into Maria. It was the way she had delivered herself of the monosyllable, "Yes," that first enflamed him.

The child, obviously, was quite innocent that her uncle's imagination clothed her in such wonder; she was entirely unselfconscious, and remained so; but, as she kept silent as well, there was nothing to interrupt the natural process of his thought. "You're a circle, a mystery, a globe of wonder," his mind addressed her, gazing downwards half in play and half in earnest. "You're always going it. Though you seem so still— you're turning furiously like a little planet!"

For this abruptly struck him, flashing the symbol into his imagination—that Maria lived so close to the universe that her life and movements were akin to those of the heavenly bodies. He saw her as an epitome of the earth. Fat, peaceful, little, calm, rotund Maria—a miniature earth! She had no call to hurry nor rush after things. Like the earth she contained all things within herself. It made him smile; he smiled as he looked down into her face; she smiled as she rolled her blue eyes upwards into his.

Yet her calm was not the calm of sloth. In that mysterious centre where she lived he felt her as tremendously alive.

For the earth, apparently so calm and steady, knows no pause. She moves round her axis without stopping. She rushes with immense rapidity round the sun. Simultaneously with these two movements she combines a third; the sun, carrying her and all his other planets with him, hurries at a prodigious rate through interstellar space, adventuring new regions never seen before. Calm outwardly, and without apparent motion, the earth—at this very moment, as he leaned across the window-sill—was making these three gigantic, endless movements. This peaceful summer morning, like any other peaceful summer morning, she was actually spinning, rushing, rising. And in Maria—it came to him—in Maria, outwardly so calm, something also—spun—rushed—rose! This amazing life that brimmed her full to bursting, even as it brimmed the robin and the earth, overflowed and dripped out of her very eyes in shining blue. There was no need for her to dash about. She, like the earth, was—carried.

All this flashed upon him while the alarum clock ticked off a second merely, for imagination telescopes time, of course, and knows things all at once.

"What *is* your secret, Maria?" he asked again. "I believe it's about that Extra Day we meant to steal. Is that it?"

Her eyes gazed straight before her across the lawn where Tim and Judy were now visible, searching busily for button-holes.

"It was to be your particular adventure, wasn't it?"

"Yes," she told him at length, without changing her expression of serene contentment.

His imagination warned him he was getting "at her" gradually. He possibly read into her a thousand things that were not there. Certainly, Maria was not aware of them. But, though Uncle Felix knew this perfectly well, he persisted, hoping for a sudden disclosure that would justify his search—even expecting it, perhaps.

"And what sort of a day would it be, then, this Extra Day of yours?" he went on. "It would never end, of course, for one thing, would it? There'd be no time?"

She nodded quietly by way of effortless agreement and consent.

"So that, in a sense, you'd have it always," he said, aware of distinct encouragement. He felt obliged to help her. This was her peculiar power—that everything was done for her while she seemed to do it all herself. "You would live it over and over again, for ever and ever. *That's* your secret, I expect, isn't it?"

"I expect so," the child answered quietly. "I've always got it." She moved in a little closer to his side as she said it. The disclosure he expected seemed so near now that excitement grew in him. Across the lawn he saw the hurrying figures of Tim and Judy, racing back with their button-holes. There was no time to lose.

He put his arm about her, tilting her face upwards with one hand to see it plainly. The blue dyes came up with it.

"Then, what kind of a day *would* you choose, Maria? Tell me—in a whisper."

And then the disclosure came. But it was not whispered. Uncle Felix heard the secret in a very clear, decided voice and in a single word:

"Birthday."

At the same moment the others poured into the room; they came like a cataract; it seemed that a dozen children rushed upon them in a torrent. The air was full of voices and flowers suddenly. A smell of the open world came in with them. Button-holes were fastened into everybody, accompanied by a breathless chorus of where and how they had been found, who got the best, who got it first, and all the rest. From the End of

Algernon Blackwood

the World they came, apparently, but while Tim had climbed the wall for his, Judy picked hers because a bird had lowered the branch into her very hand. For Uncle Felix she brought a spray of lilac; Tim brought a bit of mignonette. Eventually he had to wear them both.

"And here's a forget-me-not, Maria," cried Judy, stooping down to poke it into her sister's blue and white striped dress. "That suits you best, I thought."

"Thank you," said Maria, moving her eyes the smallest possible fraction of an inch.

And they scampered out of the room again, Maria ambling slowly in the rear, to prepare for church. There were prayer-books and things to find, threepenny bits and sixpences for the collection. There was simply heaps to do, as they expressed it, and not a moment to lose either. Uncle Felix listened to the sound of voices and footsteps as they flew down the passage, dying rapidly away into the distance, and finally ceasing altogether. He puffed his pipe a little longer before going to his room upon a similar errand. He watched the smoke curl up and melt into the outer air; he felt the pleasant sunshine warm upon his face; he smelt the perfume rising from his enormous button-hole. But of these things he did not think. He thought of what Maria said. The way she uttered that single word remained with him: "Birthday."

He had half divined her secret. For a birthday was the opening of life; it was the beginning. Maria had "got it always." All days for her were birthdays, Extra Days.

And while they walked along the lane to church he still was thinking about it.

The conversation proved that he was absent-minded rather; yet not that his mind was absent so much as intent upon other things. The children found him heavy; he seemed ponderous to them. And pondering he certainly was—pondering the meaning of existence. The children, he realised, were such brilliant comments upon existence; their unconscious way of living, all they said and thought and did, but especially all they believed, offered such bright interpretations, such simple solutions of a million things. They lived so really, were so really—alive. They never explained, they just accepted; and the explanations given they placed at their true value, still asking, "Yes, but what is the meaning of all that?" So close to Reality they lived—before reason, cloaked and confused it with a million complex explanations. That "Yes" and "Birthday" of Maria's were illuminating examples.

Of this he was vaguely pondering as they walked along the sunny lanes to church, and his conversation proved it. For conversation with children meant answering endless questions merely, and the questions were prompted by anything and everything they saw. Reality poked them; they gave expression to it by a question. And nothing real was trivial; the most careless detail was important, all being but a single question— an affirmation: "We're alive, so everything else is too!"

His conversation proved that he had almost reached that state of time-less reality in which they lived. He felt it this morning very vividly. It seemed familiar somehow—like his own childhood recovered almost.

He answered them accordingly. It didn't matter what was said, because all the words in the world said one thing only. Whether the words, therefore, made sense or not, was of no importance.

"Have you ever seen a rabbit come *out* of its hole?" asked Tim. "They do that for safety," he added; and if there was confusion in his language, there was none in his thought. "Then no one can tell which its hole is, you see. Because each rabbit—"

He broke off and glanced expectantly at his uncle. At junctures like this his uncle usually cleared things up with an easy word or two. He would not fail him now.

"Come *out*, no," was the reply; "no one ever sees a rabbit come out. But I've seen them go *in*; and that's the same thing in the end. They go down the wrong hole on purpose. *They* know right enough. Rabbits are rabbits."

"Of course," exclaimed Judy, "everything's itself and knows its own sign—er—business, I mean."

"Yes," Maria repeated.

And before anything further could be mentioned—if there *was* anything to mention—they arrived at the porch of the church, passed under it without speaking, walked up the aisle and took their places in the family pew, Maria occupying the comfortable corner against the inner wall.

CHAPTER XX

—BUT DIFFERENTLY!

Church was very—that is, they enjoyed the service very much, without knowing precisely why they liked it. They joined in the hymns with more energy than usual, because they felt "singy" and knew the tunes as well. Colonel Stumper handed round one of the bags at the end of a long pole—and, though the clergyman didn't look at all as if he required feeding, the threepenny bits dropped in without the least regret on the part of the contributors. Tim's coin, however, having been squeezed for several minutes before the bag came round, stuck to his moist finger, and Stumper, thinking he had nothing to put in, drove the long handle past him towards Maria. That same instant the coin came un-stuck, and dropped with a rattle into the aisle. Come-Back Stumper stooped to recover it. Whereupon, to Judy, Tim and Uncle Felix, watching him, came a sudden feeling of familiarity, as though all this had happened before. The bent figure, groping after the hidden coin, seemed irresistibly familiar. It was very odd, they thought, very odd indeed. Where—when—had they seen him groping before like that, almost on all fours? But no one, of course, could remark upon it, and it was only Tim and Judy who exchanged a brief, significant glance. Maria, being asleep, did not witness it, nor did she contribute to the feeding of the clergyman either.

There followed a short sermon, of which they heard only the beginning, the end, and certain patches in the middle when

Algernon Blackwood

the preacher raised his voice abruptly, but the text, they all agreed, was "Seek and ye shall find." During the delivery of the portions that escaped them, Tim scratched his head and thought about rabbits, while Judy's mind hesitated between various costumes in the pews in front of her, unable to decide which she would wear when she reached the age of its respective owner.

And so, in due course, feeling somehow that something very real had been accomplished, they streamed out with the rest of the congregation into the blazing summer sunshine. Expectant, inquisitive and hungry, they stood between the yew trees and the porch, yawning and fidgeting until Uncle Felix gave the signal to start. The sunlight made them blink. There was something of pleasurable excitement in knowing themselves part of a "Congregation," for a Congregation was distantly connected with "metropolis" and "govunment," and an important kind of thing at any time.

They stood and watched it. It scattered slowly, loth to separate and go. There was no hurry certainly. People talked in lowered voices, as if conversation after service was against the rules, and the church and graves might overhear; they smiled, but not too gaily; they seemed subdued; yet really they wanted to sing and dance—once safely out of hearing and sight, they would run and jump and stand on their heads. The children, that is, attributed their own feelings to them.

Several—all "Members" of the Congregation—approached and asked unreal questions, to which Judy, as the eldest, gave unreal answers:

"Your parents will soon be back again?"

"Yes; Father comes to-morrow, Mother too."

"I hope they have enjoyed their little change."

"I think so—thank you."

Gradually the Congregation melted away, broughams and victorias drove off sedately down the road, the horses making as little sound as possible with their hoofs. The Choir-boys emerged from a side-door and vanished into a field; a series of Old Ladies and Invalids felt their way down the gravel path with sticks; the "Neighbours," looking clean and dressed-up, went off in various directions—gravely, voices hushed, manners circumspect. Tim, feeling as usual "awfully empty after church," was sure they ran as fast as ever they could the moment they were out of sight. A Congregation was a wonderful thing altogether. It was a puzzle how the little church could hold so many people. They watched the whole familiar business with suppressed excitement, forgetting they were hungry and impatient. It was both real and unreal, something better beckoned beyond all the time; but there was no hurry. It was a deep childhood mystery—wonder filled them to the brim.

"Come on, children; we'll be off now," sounded their uncle's voice, and at the same moment Come-Back Stumper joined them. He had been counting over the money with the clergyman, of course, all this time. He was very slow. They hoped their contributions had been noticed.

"You'll come back with us?" suggested Uncle Felix. And Stumper, growling his acceptance, walked home to lunch with them in the old Mill House. In his short black coat, trousers of shepherd's plaid, and knotted white tie bearing a neat horseshoe pin, he looked smart yet soldierly. Tim apologised for his moist finger and the threepenny bit. "I thought it had got down a hole," he said, "but you found it wonderfully." "It simply flew!" cried Judy. "Clever old thing!" she added with admiration.

"I've found harder things than that," said Stumper. "It hid itself well, though—bang in the open like a lost collar-stud. Thought I'd never look *there!*"

They glanced at one another with a curious, half-expectant air, and Tim suddenly took the soldier's hand. But no one said anything more about it; the sin was forgiven and forgotten. Uncle Felix put in a vague remark concerning Indian life, and Stumper mentioned proudly that a new edition of his scouting book was coming out and he had just finished revising the last sheets. "All yesterday I spent working on it," he informed them with a satisfied air, whereupon Tim said "Fancy that!" and Judy exclaimed "Did you really?" They seemed to have an idea that he was doing something else "all yesterday"; but no one knew exactly what it was. Then Judy planted herself in the road before him, made him stop, and picked something off his shoulder. "A tiny caterpillar!" she explained. "Another minute and you'd have had it down your neck." "It would have come back though," he said with a gruff laugh. "It might'nt have," returned Judy. "But look; it's awfully beautiful!" They examined it for a moment, all five of them, and then Judy set it down carefully in the ditch and watched it march away towards the safer hedge.

It was a pleasant walk home, all together; they took the short cut across the fields; the world was covered with flowers, birds were singing, the air was fresh and sweet and the delicious sunlight not uncomfortably hot. Tim ran everywhere, exploring eagerly like a dog, and, also like a dog, doubling the journey's length. He whistled to himself; from time to time he came back to report results of his discoveries. He was full of energy. Judy behaved in a similar manner, dancing in circles to make her hair and dress fly out; she sang bits of the hymn-tunes that she liked, taking the tune but fitting words of her own upon it. Maria was carried over two fields and a half; the down-hill parts she walked, however. She kept everybody waiting. They could not leave her. She contrived to make herself the centre of the party. Stumper and Uncle Felix brought up the rear, talking together "about things," and whirling their sticks in the air as though it helped them forward somehow.

On the slippery plank-bridge across the mill stream all paused a moment to watch the dragon-flies that set the air on fire with their coloured tails.

"The things that nobody can understand!" cried Judy.

"Nobody else," Tim corrected her. "We do!"

They leaned over the rail and saw their own reflections in the running water.

"Why, Come-Back hasn't got a button-hole!" exclaimed Judy—and flew off to find one for him, Tim fast upon her heels like a collie after a dipping swallow. They raced down the banks where the golden king-cups grew in spendthrift patches and disappeared among the colonies of reeds. Between some hanging willow branches further down they were visible a moment, like dryad figures peering and flitting through the cataract of waving green. They searched as though their lives depended on success. It was absurd that Stumper had no button-hole!

Maria, seated comfortably on the lower rail, watched their efforts and listened to the bursts of laughing voices that came up-stream—then, with a leisurely movement, took the flower from her own button-hole and handed it to Stumper. The eyes rolled upwards with the flower—solemnly. And Come-Back saw the action reflected in the stream below.

"Aw—thank you, my dear," he said, fastening the forget-me-not into his Sunday coat, "but I ought not to take it all. It's yours." The voice had a quiet, almost distant sound in it.

"Ours," Maria murmured to herself, addressing the faces in the water. She took the fragment Stumper handed back to her. All three, forgetting it was time for lunch, forgetting they were hungry, forgetting that there was still half a mile of lane between them and the house, gazed down at their reflections in the stream as though fascinated. Uncle Felix certainly felt the watery-enchantment in his soul. The reflections trembled and quivered, yet did not pass away. The stream flowed hurrying by them, yet still was always there. It gave him a strange, familiar feeling—something he knew, but had forgotten. Everything in life was passing, yet nothing went—there was no hurry. The rippling music, as the water washed the banks and made the grasses swish, was audible, and there was a deeper sound of swirling round the wooden posts that held the bridge secure. Bubbles rose and burst in spray. A lark, hanging like a cross in the blue sky, overhead, dropped suddenly as though it was a stone, but in the reflection it rushed up into their faces. It seemed to rise at them from the pebbly bed of the stream. Both movements seemed one and the same—both were true— the direction depended upon the point of view.

It startled them and broke the water-spell. For the singing stopped abruptly too. At the same moment Judy and Tim arrived, their arms full of flowers, hemlock, ferns, and bulrushes. They were breathless and exhausted; both talked at once; they had quite forgotten, apparently, what they had gone to find. Judy had seen a king-fisher, Tim had discovered tracks of an otter; in the excitement they forgot about the button-hole. But, somehow, the bird, the animal, and the flowers were the same thing really—one big simple thing. Only the point of view was different.

"We've looked simply everywhere!" cried Judy.

"Just look what we found!" Tim echoed.

To Uncle Felix it seemed they said one and the same thing merely—using *one* word in many syllables.

"Beautiful!" agreed Stumper, as they emptied their arms at his feet in wild profusion; "and enough for everybody too!"

Stumper also said the thing they had just said. Uncle Felix watched him move forward, where Maria was already using the heaped-up greenery as a cushion for her back, and pick something off the stem of a giant bulrush.

"But that's what I like best," he exclaimed. "Look at the colour, will you—blue and cream and yellow! You can hear the Ganges in it, if you listen close enough." He held a small, coloured snail-shell between his sinewy fingers, then placed it against his ear, while the others, caught by a strange enveloping sense of wonder, stared and listened, swept for a moment into another world.

"How marvellous!" whispered some one.

"Extrornary!" another murmured.

"Yes," said Maria. Her voice made a sound like a thin stone falling from a height into water. But Maria had said the same thing as the others, only said it shorter. An entire language lay in that mono-syllable. Again, it was the point of view of doing, saying one enormous thing. And Maria's point of view was everywhere at once—the centre.

"Listen!" she added the next minute.

Perhaps the sunlight quivering on the surface of the stream confused them, or perhaps it was the murmur and movement of the leaves upon the banks that brought the sense of sweet, queer bewilderment upon all five. A new sound there certainly was—footsteps, as though some one came dancing—voices, as though some one sang. Figures were seen in the distance among the waving world of green; they moved behind the cataract of falling willow branches; and their distance was as the distance of a half-remembered dream.

"They're coming," gasped Judy below her breath.

"They're coming back," Tim whispered, the tone muffled, underground.

"Eh?" ejaculated Stumper. "Coming back?" His voice, too, had distance in it.

Whether they saw it in the reflections on the running water, or whether the maze of shadow and sunshine in the wooded banks produced it, no one knew exactly. The figures, at any rate, were plainly visible, moving along with singing and dancing through the summery noontide of the brilliant day. No one spoke while they went by, no one except Maria who at intervals murmured "Yes." There was no other audible comment or remark. They afterwards agreed that Weeden was seen clearest, but Thompson and Mrs. Horton were fairly distinct as well, and bringing up the rear was a figure in blue that could only have been the Policeman who lived usually upon the high road to London. They carried flowers in their arms, they moved lightly and quickly—it was uncommonly like dancing—and their voices floated through the woodland spaces with a sound that, if it was not singing, was at least an excellent imitation—an attempt to sing!

"They're not lost," said Tim, as they disappeared from view. "They're just looking—for the way."

"The way home," said Judy. "And they're following some one—who knows it."

"Yes," added Maria. For another figure, more like a tree moving in the wind than anything else, and certainly looking differently to each of them—another figure was seen in advance of the group, seen in flashes, as it were, and only glimpses of it discernible among the world of moving green. This other figure was singing too; snatches of wild sweet music floated through the quiet wood—one said the singing of a bird, another, the wind, a third, the rippling murmur of the stream—but, to one and all, an enchanting and enticing sound. And, to one and all, familiar too, with the familiarity of a half-remembered dream.

And a flood of memory rose about them as they watched and listened, a tide that carried them away with it into the heart of something they knew, yet had forgotten. In the few moments' interval an eternity might have passed. Their hearts opened curiously, they saw wonder growing like a flower inside—the exquisite wonder of common things. There was something they were looking for, but they had found it. The flower of wonder blossomed there before their very eyes, explaining the world, but not explaining it away, explaining simply that it was wonderful beyond all telling. They all knew suddenly what they didn't know they knew; they understood what nobody understands. None knew why it came just at this particular moment, and none knew where it came from either. It was there, so what else mattered. It broke upon them out of the heart of the summer's day, out of this very ordinary Sunday morning, out of the brimming life all about them that was passing but could never pass away. The familiar figures of the gardener, the butler, the policeman and the cook brought back to them the memory of something they had forgotten, yet brought it back in the form of endless and inexhaustible enticement rather than of complete recovery. There had been long preparation somewhere, growth, development; but that was past and they gave no thought to it; Expectancy and Wonder rushed them off their feet. The world hid something. Every one was looking for it. *They* must go on looking, looking, looking too!

What it was they had forgotten—they entirely forgot. Only the marvellous hint remained, and the certainty that it could be found. For, to each of them it seemed, came this fairy reminder, stealing deliciously upon the senses: somewhere, somehow, they had known an experience that had enriched their lives. It had become part of them. It had always been in them, but they had found it now. They felt quite positive about it. They believed. To Tim came messages from the solid earth about him, secrets from creatures that lived in it and knew; Judy, catching a thousand kisses from the air upon her cheeks, divined the mystery of all flying life—that brought the stars within her reach; Maria, possessing all within herself, remained steady and calm at the eternal centre of the circle—a clearing-house for messages from everywhere at once. Asking nothing for herself, she merely wanted to give away, give out. She said "Yes" to all that came her way; and all did come her

Algernon Blackwood

way. To every one of them, to Stumper and Uncle Felix too, came a great conviction that they had passed nearer, somehow, to an everlasting joy. There was no hurry, life had just begun—seemed singing everywhere about them. There was Unity.

"It's a lovely day," remarked Uncle Felix presently. "I want my luncheon."

He picked up Maria and moved on across the bridge.

"It's the Extra Day," Maria whispered in his ear. "It's my adventure, but you all can have it."

The others followed with Come-Back Stumper, and in the lane they saw the figures of Weeden, Thompson and Mrs. Horton in front of them, coming home from church. They were walking quietly enough.

"We're not late, then," Tim remarked. "There's lots of time!"

Crossing the field in the direction of the London road a policeman was moving steadily. They saw him stoop and pick a yellow flower as he went. He was off to take charge of the world upon his Sunday beat. He disappeared behind a hedge. The butler and the cook vanished through a side-door into the old Mill House about the same time.

In due course, they also arrived at the porch, and Uncle Felix set his burden down. As they scraped their muddy boots and rubbed them on the mat, their backs were turned to the outside world; but Maria, whose boots required no scraping, happened to face it still. As usual she faced in all directions like a circle.

"Look," she said. "There's some one coming!"

And they saw the figure of a tramp go past the opening of the drive where the London road was just visible. He paused a moment and looked towards the house. He did not come in. He just looked—and waved his hand at them. The next minute he was gone. But not before Maria had returned his wave.

"He'll come back," suggested Stumper, as they went inside.

"Yes," said Maria. "He's mine—but you can have him too."

Ten minutes later, when they all sat down to lunch, the big blue figure of the policeman passed the opening of the drive. Being occupied with hot roast beef, they did not see him. He paused a moment, looked towards the house, and then went slowly out of sight again along the London road, following the tramp....

Choose from Thousands of 1stWorldLibrary Classics By

A. M. Barnard
Ada Leverson
Adolphus William Ward
Aesop
Agatha Christie
Alexander Aaronsohn
Alexander Kielland
Alexandre Dumas
Alfred Gatty
Alfred Ollivant
Alice Duer Miller
Alice Turner Curtis
Alice Dunbar
Allen Chapman
Alleyne Ireland
Ambrose Bierce
Amelia E. Barr
Amory H. Bradford
Andrew Lang
Andrew McFarland Davis
Andy Adams
Angela Brazil
Anna Alice Chapin
Anna Sewell
Annie Besant
Annie Hamilton Donnell
Annie Payson Call
Annie Roe Carr
Annonaymous
Anton Chekhov
Archibald Lee Fletcher
Arnold Bennett
Arthur C. Benson
Arthur Conan Doyle
Arthur M. Winfield
Arthur Ransome
Arthur Schnitzler
Arthur Train
Atticus
B.H. Baden-Powell
B. M. Bower
B. C. Chatterjee
Baroness Emmuska Orczy
Baroness Orczy
Basil King
Bayard Taylor
Ben Macomber
Bertha Muzzy Bower
Bjornstjerne Bjornson

Booth Tarkington
Boyd Cable
Bram Stoker
C. Collodi
C. E. Orr
C. M. Ingleby
Carolyn Wells
Catherine Parr Traill
Charles A. Eastman
Charles Amory Beach
Charles Dickens
Charles Dudley Warner
Charles Farrar Browne
Charles Ives
Charles Kingsley
Charles Klein
Charles Hanson Towne
Charles Lathrop Pack
Charles Romyn Dake
Charles Whibley
Charles Willing Beale
Charlotte M. Braeme
Charlotte M. Yonge
Charlotte Perkins Stetson
Clair W. Hayes
Clarence Day Jr.
Clarence E. Mulford
Clemence Housman
Confucius
Coningsby Dawson
Cornelis DeWitt Wilcox
Cyril Burleigh
D. H. Lawrence
Daniel Defoe
David Garnett
Dinah Craik
Don Carlos Janes
Donald Keyhoe
Dorothy Kilner
Dougan Clark
Douglas Fairbanks
E. Nesbit
E. P. Roe
E. Phillips Oppenheim
E. S. Brooks
Earl Barnes
Edgar Rice Burroughs
Edith Van Dyne
Edith Wharton

Edward Everett Hale
Edward J. O'Biren
Edward S. Ellis
Edwin L. Arnold
Eleanor Atkins
Eleanor Hallowell Abbott
Eliot Gregory
Elizabeth Gaskell
Elizabeth McCracken
Elizabeth Von Arnim
Ellem Key
Emerson Hough
Emilie F. Carlen
Emily Bronte
Emily Dickinson
Enid Bagnold
Enilor Macartney Lane
Erasmus W. Jones
Ernie Howard Pie
Ethel May Dell
Ethel Turner
Ethel Watts Mumford
Eugene Sue
Eugenie Foa
Eugene Wood
Eustace Hale Ball
Evelyn Everett-green
Everard Cotes
F. H. Cheley
F. J. Cross
F. Marion Crawford
Fannie E. Newberry
Federick Austin Ogg
Ferdinand Ossendowski
Fergus Hume
Florence A. Kilpatrick
Fremont B. Deering
Francis Bacon
Francis Darwin
Frances Hodgson Burnett
Frances Parkinson Keyes
Frank Gee Patchin
Frank Harris
Frank Jewett Mather
Frank L. Packard
Frank V. Webster
Frederic Stewart Isham
Frederick Trevor Hill
Frederick Winslow Taylor

Friedrich Kerst	Hayden Carruth	James Branch Cabell
Friedrich Nietzsche	Helent Hunt Jackson	James DeMille
Fyodor Dostoyevsky	Helen Nicolay	James Joyce
G.A. Henty	Hendrik Conscience	James Lane Allen
G.K. Chesterton	Hendy David Thoreau	James Lane Allen
Gabrielle E. Jackson	Henri Barbusse	James Oliver Curwood
Garrett P. Serviss	Henrik Ibsen	James Oppenheim
Gaston Leroux	Henry Adams	James Otis
George A. Warren	Henry Ford	James R. Driscoll
George Ade	Henry Frost	Jane Abbott
Geroge Bernard Shaw	Henry James	Jane Austen
George Cary Eggleston	Henry Jones Ford	Jane L. Stewart
George Durston	Henry Seton Merriman	Janet Aldridge
George Ebers	Henry W Longfellow	Jens Peter Jacobsen
George Eliot	Herbert A. Giles	Jerome K. Jerome
George Gissing	Herbert Carter	Jessie Graham Flower
George MacDonald	Herbert N. Casson	John Buchan
George Meredith	Herman Hesse	John Burroughs
George Orwell	Hildegard G. Frey	John Cournos
George Sylvester Viereck	Homer	John F. Kennedy
George Tucker	Honore De Balzac	John Gay
George W. Cable	Horace B. Day	John Glasworthy
George Wharton James	Horace Walpole	John Habberton
Gertrude Atherton	Horatio Alger Jr.	John Joy Bell
Gordon Casserly	Howard Pyle	John Kendrick Bangs
Grace E. King	Howard R. Garis	John Milton
Grace Gallatin	Hugh Lofting	John Philip Sousa
Grace Greenwood	Hugh Walpole	John Taintor Foote
Grant Allen	Humphry Ward	Jonas Lauritz Idemil Lie
Guillermo A. Sherwell	Ian Maclaren	Jonathan Swift
Gulielma Zollinger	Inez Haynes Gillmore	Joseph A. Altsheler
Gustav Flaubert	Irving Bacheller	Joseph Carey
H. A. Cody	Isabel Cecilia Williams	Joseph Conrad
H. B. Irving	Isabel Hornibrook	Joseph E. Badger Jr
H.C. Bailey	Israel Abrahams	Joseph Hergesheimer
H. G. Wells	Ivan Turgenev	Joseph Jacobs
H. H. Munro	J.G.Austin	Jules Vernes
H. Irving Hancock	J. Henri Fabre	Julian Hawthrone
H. R. Naylor	J. M. Barrie	Julie A Lippmann
H. Rider Haggard	J. M. Walsh	Justin Huntly McCarthy
H. W. C. Davis	J. Macdonald Oxley	Kakuzo Okakura
Haldeman Julius	J. R. Miller	Karle Wilson Baker
Hall Caine	J. S. Fletcher	Kate Chopin
Hamilton Wright Mabie	J. S. Knowles	Kenneth Grahame
Hans Christian Andersen	J. Storer Clouston	Kenneth McGaffey
Harold Avery	J. W. Duffield	Kate Langley Bosher
Harold McGrath	Jack London	Kate Langley Bosher
Harriet Beecher Stowe	Jacob Abbott	Katherine Cecil Thurston
Harry Castlemon	James Allen	Katherine Stokes
Harry Coghill	James Andrews	L. A. Abbot
Harry Houidini	James Baldwin	L. T. Meade

L. Frank Baum
Latta Griswold
Laura Dent Crane
Laura Lee Hope
Laurence Housman
Lawrence Beasley
Leo Tolstoy
Leonid Andreyev
Lewis Carroll
Lewis Sperry Chafer
Lilian Bell
Lloyd Osbourne
Louis Hughes
Louis Joseph Vance
Louis Tracy
Louisa May Alcott
Lucy Fitch Perkins
Lucy Maud Montgomery
Luther Benson
Lydia Miller Middleton
Lyndon Orr
M. Corvus
M. H. Adams
Margaret E. Sangster
Margret Howth
Margaret Vandercook
Margaret W. Hungerford
Margret Penrose
Maria Edgeworth
Maria Thompson Daviess
Mariano Azuela
Marion Polk Angellotti
Mark Overton
Mark Twain
Mary Austin
Mary Catherine Crowley
Mary Cole
Mary Hastings Bradley
Mary Roberts Rinehart
Mary Rowlandson
M. Wollstonecraft Shelley
Maud Lindsay
Max Beerbohm
Myra Kelly
Nathaniel Hawthrone
Nicolo Machiavelli
O. F. Walton
Oscar Wilde
Owen Johnson
P.G. Wodehouse
Paul and Mabel Thorne

Paul G. Tomlinson
Paul Severing
Percy Brebner
Percy Keese Fitzhugh
Peter B. Kyne
Plato
Quincy Allen
R. Derby Holmes
R. L. Stevenson
R. S. Ball
Rabindranath Tagore
Rahul Alvares
Ralph Bonehill
Ralph Henry Barbour
Ralph Victor
Ralph Waldo Emmerson
Rene Descartes
Ray Cummings
Rex Beach
Rex E. Beach
Richard Harding Davis
Richard Jefferies
Richard Le Gallienne
Robert Barr
Robert Frost
Robert Gordon Anderson
Robert L. Drake
Robert Lansing
Robert Lynd
Robert Michael Ballantyne
Robert W. Chambers
Rosa Nouchette Carey
Rudyard Kipling
Saint Augustine
Samuel B. Allison
Samuel Hopkins Adams
Sarah Bernhardt
Sarah C. Hallowell
Selma Lagerlof
Sherwood Anderson
Sigmund Freud
Standish O'Grady
Stanley Weyman
Stella Benson
Stella M. Francis
Stephen Crane
Stewart Edward White
Stijn Streuvels
Swami Abhedananda
Swami Parmananda
T. S. Ackland

T. S. Arthur
The Princess Der Ling
Thomas A. Janvier
Thomas A Kempis
Thomas Anderton
Thomas Bailey Aldrich
Thomas Bulfinch
Thomas De Quincey
Thomas Dixon
Thomas H. Huxley
Thomas Hardy
Thomas More
Thornton W. Burgess
U. S. Grant
Upton Sinclair
Valentine Williams
Various Authors
Vaughan Kester
Victor Appleton
Victor G. Durham
Victoria Cross
Virginia Woolf
Wadsworth Camp
Walter Camp
Walter Scott
Washington Irving
Wilbur Lawton
Wilkie Collins
Willa Cather
Willard F. Baker
William Dean Howells
William le Queux
W. Makepeace Thackeray
William W. Walter
William Shakespeare
Winston Churchill
Yei Theodora Ozaki
Yogi Ramacharaka
Young E. Allison
Zane Grey